M000220322

ENDORSEMENTS

"*Chasing the Show* aligns with the All-American dream for many young and aspiring student-athletes. The personal plight of Anthony is relatable and consuming. This read is applicable for players, parents, and coaches alike, offering valuable insight throughout the journey: the ups and downs, the ability to adapt and adjust, and the reality that life is going to keep the curveballs coming. The only difference as we age is that the 'spin rate' speeds up, and the lessons we learn are what enable us to handle the increasing challenges life brings our way. A must-read for any and all – I highly recommend this piece."

Brooke Knight, former football player and current baseball coach (Perth, Australia)

"*Chasing the Show* provides an engaging perspective on multiple contributors to a child's ecosystem. Pete illustrates the passion and ferocity of a high school athlete genuinely, while also encapsulating the role that coaches, teachers, and parents play in fostering a positive environment for growth and adaptation in the face of adversity. Each character in this book plays a valuable role, and the variety of perspectives creates a space for conversation among all community members. *Chasing the Show* is an engaging read, while also acting as a strong tool to facilitate collaboration and understanding. This novel successfully provides multiple perspectives, and acknowledges the importance of truly supporting youngsters in their development, providing space for their own exploration, and supporting them when situations sway off-course."

Margie Muñoz, former dancer and current community school coordinator (Grand Rapids, Michigan)

"As an obsessed athlete, I can completely relate to Anthony and his drive and desire to achieve his athletic dreams. From the first chapter, I couldn't put the book down. I needed to know what happened, what Anthony would achieve, and how he would get there. The author, Pete Hall, does a wonderful job of playing up the excitement and anticipation of his successful baseball career and I can totally put myself in the place of Anthony, wanting to make sure I didn't do anything to ruin my chances of continuing on in softball."

Alicia Jager, former softball player and current vice president of digital partnerships at Mastercard (San Diego, California)

"Pursuing a dream is hard and can make you distance yourself from reality, but *Chasing the Show* captures how a young boy does whatever he can to continue doing what he loves. I had an injury in high school preventing me from pursuing my sport, so I was able to relate to Anthony in that way. Young people who read this book will see the struggles and excitement of beginning a career – and will also see how important it truly is."

Jadyn G., former cross-country runner and current college student (Texas)

"In a field desperately needing new literature, Pete Hall has created a must-read with *Chasing the Show*. Hall's work is chock full of truths that will spark discussion at the dinner table and equip parents with tools to help their children navigate the world of competitive athletics. With deeply realized and human characters, this book is a sincere dive into pursuing dreams and, ultimately, having to come face to face with hard realities. As an educator, coach, parent, and administrator, I consider *Chasing the Show* to be a must-read and I have no doubt it will transform the lives of many."

Nick Whitmore, former basketball player and current associate director of athletics (Asheville, North Carolina)

"In *Chasing the Show*, Pete Hall masterfully weaves a story of parenting, hope, resilience, and redemption through the life of a young man who has his dreams deferred. The powerful concepts of mentoring, leadership and service, often forgotten in the stories about our young people, are consistent in this amazing book. I can't wait for the sequel so I can read about Anthony becoming a teacher, coach and leader in his own school! This is a must-read for every student-athlete, parent, teacher, and sports enthusiast."

Salome Thomas-EL, Ed.D, former basketball player and current school principal (Wilmington, DE)

"I loved every sentence in this book. I mean, there are ups and downs, just like in life, and that's frustrating – and real. The story itself is compelling, and I found myself reflecting on my own goals and path along the way. *Chasing the Show* is a page turner, thought-provoking and deeply authentic."

Thomas N., current football player and
high school student (Illinois)

"In *Chasing the Show*, Pete Hall tells a poignant story coalescing the importance of youthful dreams and the life-lessons those dreams frame as we gradually approach adulthood. Whether it's my generation that mimicked Yaz's stance or Mays's basket catch, or today's youngsters seeking Trout's cobra-swing or Kershaw's jaw-dropping curve, the lessons are universal...the timeless journey buoyed by dreams and tempered with the reality that life presents challenges. In a fun and relatable manner, Pete Hall reveals how those challenges often open opportunities for each of us to consider what service we may be to others rather than what entitlements are due us."

Sandy Simpson, former basketball player and
retired basketball coach (Davis, California)

CHASING THE SHOW

BY
PETE HALL

AUTHORS PLACE
—PRESS—

Published by Authors Place Press
9885 Wyecliff Drive, Suite 200
Highlands Ranch, CO 80126
AuthorsPlace.com

Manufactured in the United States of America.

ISBN: 978-1-62865-789-0

TABLE OF CONTENTS

NOTE FROM THE AUTHOR

Dear Reader: Thank you for choosing this book! I am forever grateful for you – after, all, if it weren't for Readers, books would simply be trees falling in an abandoned forest.

It is my sincere hope that you find this book both entertaining and helpful. That's right, helpful. While it clearly has all the elements of a story – characters, theme, plot, dialogue, conflict...you know, the stuff that makes a tale enjoyable – it also contains opportunity. And the opportunity, my Reader, is what I expect you will find helpful.

As you read, you'll have the opportunity to connect with a character (or perhaps more than one), to reflect on a situation, and to consider what this all means to you. And, very importantly, you'll have the opportunity to act – to try something new, to do something special, to engage in a different way. You'll have the opportunity to look at things through a different lens, to use talking-points to express your own emotions, to take a story about a fictional character and use it to strengthen your bonds with those closest to you. My vision for you, my Reader, is that this book is a seed from which a healthier, happier, more productive, and more successful life grows.

To help with that, I've created Discussion Guides for you. One is for the "young adult" Readers, going through life and trying to navigate the many challenges of growing up, of having a dream, of winning and losing, and of viewing the world beyond your own nose. The other is for the "not-so-young adult" Readers, the parents, teachers, coaches, mentors, and other grown-ups in the Young Adults' lives. In the Discussion Guides, I offer reflective prompts, suggestions for introspection, tasks to tackle, story-elements to analyze, and questions that encourage discussion with each other. This journey is far too complicated and challenging to travel alone, so partnership, communication, love, and togetherness are there for you to take. That's your opportunity.

These Discussion Guides, along with additional resources, blog posts, and a link to connect with me if you want, are posted at www. ChasingTheShow.com. You can scan the QR code below to go there immediately:

You may already know that most authors write about what they know. That said, this book is based loosely on actual events. In a way, it's semi-autobiographical. Names, locations, events, interactions, plot twists, dialogue, and just about everything in here is a collage of memories, yarns, and tales, all cut and pasted and rearranged with a healthy dose of creative liberty. Maybe it happened, maybe it didn't. Coulda been fact, coulda been fiction. And in the end, that doesn't really matter.

What's important is that you find it both entertaining and helpful.

This journey, some 30 years in the making, is not something I take lightly; nor are the help and guidance and support I've received in making this dream come true. In that light, I'd like to send a few shout-outs to some of the many folks who have been instrumental in this production.

First, obviously, are my parents: Alice, Cliff, Gay, and Guy. That's right, all four of 'em. They've been 100% behind me as I've traveled this path, always supportive, always curious to see how this story unfolds.

To my wife, Mindy, and my kids: thanks for your patience as I get sucked into the whirlpool of writing – it's a special place to be, and you've always encouraged me as I dart off to the computer to jot an idea or update a chapter. I love you to the right-field bleachers and back.

I owe a gigantic debt of gratitude to B, my editor and advisor and confidante throughout this process. I cannot even begin to express how influential your questions and insights and attention to detail have been. Holy wow, thank you.

Special thanks (in no certain order, and if I've missed you, it's simply because the aforementioned whirlpool has drained my short-term memory, not because I don't appreciate your support) go to: Jack for your willingness to share your knowledge of forestry; Uncle Nelson for being that coach for me; Dan, Kiki, Niner, Ted, Jorja, and Sandman for all the hours and role-modeling of incredible coaching; Lori for calling me "Sweet Pete" and making me feel like something more than an awkward, pimply-faced sixth grader; Danny, BK, Hook, Heifer, AJ, TJ, Ice, and the fellas, you know who you are; Kristin for your feedback in some of the clinical elements; all my in-process pre-readers for your feedback and suggestions; and Tony, Teri, and the team at Authors' Place Press for giving this guy a shot.

Thank you all for being you. I wouldn't be me without you.

Pete Hall, Coeur d'Alene, Idaho June, 2020

SUMMER

10 YEARS AGO

CHAPTER 1

Thwack!

"Nice hit, son! Now try to line one over the shortstop's head."

Anthony's father took another baseball out of the bucket by his feet, looked at his son in the left-handed batter's box, and paused. The sun shone brightly on the field, baking the thirsty grass, and a warm breeze offered little relief. The chain-link backstop behind his son curved slightly skyward where it met the ground, metal shards tattered and unraveling, the result of years of rec-league play and dwindling maintenance resources, like the fraying ends of a favorite childhood blanket.

Anthony shifted his weight onto his front foot, then to the back. He waggled the aluminum bat high, eyes intense and focused, a slight snarl on his upper lip.

"Bring it," he whispered. His father grinned.

With a half-windup, Drew Sumner took aim and hurled the sphere toward the outer part of the plate, intending to make it easier for his eight-year-old son to launch one toward the opposite field. Quick as a snake, Anthony uncoiled and struck.

Thwack!

Drew ducked just in time as the ball whistled by his ear, a missile headed for center field. Defensive arms up and protective legs down, he landed in a heap at the front edge of the pitcher's mound, a mix of dirt and sweat and adrenaline and pride. One foot caught the top lip of the bucket, and baseballs scattered and rolled haphazardly toward third base. He looked up to the sound of laughter.

———

"Whoa, sorry Dad! You okay?"

"I think so."

"You've lost your balls," Anthony snorted.

"Very funny," Drew said, dusting himself off and reaching for the stray baseballs. "What happened to going to the opposite field? You trying to kill me? Then who will pitch to you?"

Anthony had joined the cleanup crew to refill the bucket. He tapped the balls with his bat, knocking them toward the mound, and grinned back at his father. "You know what Ted Williams said: the tougher the situation, the harsher the crowd, the meaner the pitcher, the more you try to hit it back up the box."

Drew stopped and stood up straight for a second. "You calling me mean?"

Anthony laughed, resuming his batting stance, pawing his foot at the dirt.

"And how do you know Ted Williams quotes?"

"Grampa Sumner," Anthony shrugged. "And I know everything about the Boston Red Sox, especially the greatest hitter who ever lived."

Drew should have known better than to ask. He saw himself in the batter's box, Grampa Sumner on the mound, New England heat wringing sweat out of the very baseballs he attacked with his old wooden sword. Between pitches, stories of the good ol' days, the long summers filled with hope and promise and inevitably dashed by the Boston ballclub's self-destruction and demise as the days began to shorten. The smells of leather and grass last cut months ago and dirt, those never changed, never faded.

Drew pitched another, raising his glove instinctively for self-preservation, just in case.

Thwack!

It was a line drive, safely down the right-field line. "Nice hit, Anthony!"

Anthony stood at home plate, admiring his handiwork. "I know."

A voice called out from the shade of a nearby apple tree. "Say 'thank you,' son. That's how we respond to compliments." Amanda Sumner, in her running shorts and tank top, had recently returned from one of her incomprehensibly long runs and was stretching.

"Right," Anthony winced. "Thank you, Dad."

"Time out," called Drew. "Go scoop 'em up."

Groaning, Anthony raced around the field, retrieving the browning balls that dotted the browning field and tossing them back toward the waiting bucket at the mound. The summer days were long in the Willamette Valley of western Oregon, and the uncharacteristic heat that year had dried the grass mercilessly. It crunched under Drew's worn-down tennis shoes as he took advantage of the moment to sneak out of the sunlight, joining his wife under one of the many apple trees lining the elementary school's playfield. Amanda offered her husband a kiss and tossed him his bottle of water.

"How's he hitting today? They sound loud," she asked, returning to a stretching pose.

Twisting off the metal cap, Drew took a mighty swig, exhaled, and admired the sticker on his water bottle. *Old Faithful,* it read, a souvenir from a past summer's trip to Yellowstone. Using his glove, he wiped his brow, freeing a few droplets of sweat to run down his temple. "He's trying to hit me. I'm sure of it," he laughed. "I think it's time we invested in an L-screen. I can pitch and duck for cover. It's either that or take out another life insurance policy."

After tossing the water bottle back to Amanda, Drew reached into the apple tree and grabbed an apple, snapping it off the branch, and examined it. He rubbed it on his shirt and took a bite. Sour but juicy, the apple provided additional hydration. "Why did they plant Granny Smiths on the school playground?" He muttered to himself, grimacing at the fruit's effect on his mouth. "Not exactly a delicious choice." He took another bite nonetheless as he looked out at the field.

His son was kneeling on the ground in the outfield, focused intently on something in a shallow clover patch.

"Anthony, what are you doing?" he yelled.

No response. Anthony was prodding at something, or picking. Another try: "Anthony!"

"Yeah, Dad?" The eight-year-old called back.

"What's going on out there?"

"Bumblebee. They love this clover." He appeared to be petting it as the misshapen bee lumbered from flower to flower.

"You all done for today then?"

At once Anthony leapt up and sprinted back to the mound, re-stocking the bucket and placing it by home plate. "Let me have a drink." He put out his hand as he reached his parents' shady spot. His mom handed *Old Faithful* over.

"How's it going, sweetie?" asked his mother, switching legs to stretch and offering a hand for a high-five. Anthony slapped her hand and looked up at his father. "Great! Dad, will you hit me some grounders?"

Drew rolled his eyes, took another bite of his apple, and threw up his hands in mock dismay. Mouth full, he exclaimed, "This old man? What makes you think I have any energy left?"

"C'mon, Dad." Anthony had already tossed the bat toward home plate, grabbed his glove, and was bounding out to the field before his dad could respond. Over his shoulder, he yelled, "I'll be Rick Burleson! *The Rooster!*"

Amanda was now squatting in a pose that looked thoroughly uncomfortable. Her eyes followed her son for a moment, then she looked up at her husband. "Where did he get that energy? And who is Rick Whatshisname? A new friend from school?"

Drew took a final bite of his apple and tossed the core into the tall grass beyond the trees. To his wife he asked, "How far did you run today?"

"A little over 11 miles. Made the loop on the old dirt roads, over past the Travallions' Farm. Why?"

"There's your answer. He probably inherited your triathlon gene. It's a curse, all that endurance." As he walked backwards toward home plate, he said, "And Rick Burleson was an old Red Sox infielder. From the 1970s, I think. Grampa Sumner would know for sure. For some reason, he's infatuated with those teams, back before they broke the Curse of the Bambino. He even copies some of their batting stances. He can't get enough of that stuff. Of course, those were some darn good players, so they're not bad ones to imitate."

"Well," replied Amanda. "Maybe he'll be a Red Sox infielder himself someday." She returned to her stretches as her husband picked up the bat. Out at the shortstop position, Anthony spat in his glove, rubbed it in with his hand, then punched it for the full effect. Drew could have sworn he heard him whisper, "Bring it," as he assumed his defensive positioning.

Even from a hundred feet away, Drew could see the love in his son's eyes. The love of the sport. The game. The love of baseball.

CHAPTER 2

The setting sun fired its horizontal rays through the Sumners' kitchen windows where the slat-blinds were only partially closed. Truth be told, the strings were beginning to give out, and Drew's jerry-rigging only marginally solved the problem. As Amanda often said in matters of home-improvement, it's the thought that counts.

Blinking away the sunlight, Anthony's sister, Jenna, three years his elder, was putting the finishing touches on her famous turkey-avocado wraps.

"I appreciate you making supper for us tonight; that's very sweet of you," Amanda Sumner said as she poured water into glasses for Anthony to set at the table.

"I wish you had told me it was wraps. We didn't need forks," complained Anthony, who was done with the glasses and was now busy putting the forks back in the utensil drawer.

Jenna let out an audible sigh. "Sorry, little brother. Not everyone was playing all day."

Anthony took the bait. "Not my fault you have to take summer school. Summer's supposed to be fun!"

"It's an extra *clase de Español*," Jenna emphasized. "Then I'll know two more languages than you!" She laughed her special older-sister laugh.

"Spanish and gibberish? Wow," Anthony muttered.

She heard him. "Precisely. So I can talk to you, *loco*-boy."

"Mom!"

"Enough of that nonsense," Amanda declared. "It's supper time, and we should enjoy the fact that we're all able to spend so much time together this summer, with your dad's hours cut back," she took a deep breath. "Anyway, we're lucky. I'm not teaching summer school, and the in-services don't pick up for a couple more weeks, so let's just enjoy. And Anthony, mind your manners. Now, who's got the napkins?"

"Smells great!" announced Drew Sumner, waltzing into the kitchen. "What's for dinner?"

"You can't smell anything," replied Jenna. "Turkey wraps."

"I don't have to smell it to know it's going to be amazing." Drew kissed his daughter on the top of her head. His eyes met his wife's. "Did I miss something?" Amanda shook her head.

Rustling Anthony's short-cropped hair, he took his seat. A buzzing from his pocket prompted an exclamation. Retrieving his phone, he spied an incoming video call.

"Grampa Sumner on the line!" Drew called. He clicked to accept the call, and his father's smiling face came into view. "Grampa! How ya doing, old feller?"

"Hello. How are the kids?" Grampa Sumner smiled into his phone, scanning the room thousands of miles away.

"We're great!" shouted Anthony from the other side of the kitchen, and his dad held up the phone so grandfather and grandchildren could see each other. "Played a lot of baseball today!"

"That's wonderful, Anthony. How are you hitting 'em?"

"Pretty good, I guess," Anthony tried to sound modest.

Drew turned the phone again. "He's hitting well. Tried to take my head off a couple of times. How are things in New Hampshire?"

"Well, it's just about bedtime here. Your mother is out in the garden. Hot as blazes, but she loves it. Me, I prefer the AC." He laughed. "So the kid's hitting well? He's always been a good hitter. I'm glad you've taught him how to switch-hit. Makes him that much more versatile, more of a weapon."

"He's kind of a natural lefty, actually." Drew looked at his father's aging face in the screen. He could see himself in the future, the not-too-distant future. "And Jenna is taking summer classes, she's really becoming bilingual, I think, like her mom."

"That's fantastic," continued Grampa Sumner. "I'd love to see his name in lights someday. We could use a professional baseball player in the family." Across the room, Anthony flushed. Jenna turned to her mom, who simply smiled sympathetically.

"What?" Grampa Sumner yelled as he turned away from his phone. "Okay!" He turned back. "Your mom wants help coiling up the hose. I swear. Those little yellow tomatoes might not be worth all this hassle. Now, I have to go outside. But she loves 'em. Bite-sized. They are good in a fresh salad, though, you know." He was already on the move, the image on the screen jostling in his shaky hand.

"No worries, Dad. Always a pleasure talking to you." Holding the phone toward the table, he called, "Say good-night to your grandfather, everyone!"

After the chorus of "Good night, Grampa," Jenna rumpled her lips and whispered to her brother, "We're still gonna need the forks, all-star." She was setting wraps on plates with fruit salad at everybody's place at the table.

Grampa Sumner looked straight into the camera. "The kid's gonna be there, that's for sure." Smiling, he hung up.

FALL

PRESENT DAY

CHAPTER 3

"One hundred forty-six!"

Anthony Sumner bursts into Mrs. Andrews' government classroom, interrupting the activity and announcing his presence with his usual flair. Arms raised exuberantly, he marches directly to the whiteboard in the front of the room, erases the "149," and scribbles "146" in red ink. "Happy Monday!" He winks at his teacher, high-fiving a classmate at a nearby table as he sits proudly at his seat.

"Thank you, Mr. Sumner, for again gracing us with your presence and your countdown. How in the world would we survive without you?" Mrs. Andrews has paused her discussion about the limits of the executive branch to entertain the daily disruption. "If you must share with us the number of days until baseball season starts, could you at least arrive to class on time, so you don't mess with our mojo? Keep this up, and I'll start keeping track of the number of days until you graduate."

Muffled laughter around the room. Anthony is undeterred. "Don't you already?" he asks, cocking an eyebrow at his teacher.

"Not publicly," she retorts. "Now get caught up. We have learning to do. And stop with the eyebrow."

This time the laughter isn't as muffled as before. Anthony digs into his backpack, extracts his binder, and tries to shift his attention to the presidency. But that date sticks in his head: February 20. The first day of baseball practice. His senior year. The magic. The glory. February 20, 146 days from today.

Anthony leans sideways in an attempt to make eye contact with Nick

Greene, his best friend and the team's center fielder. In stark contrast to Anthony's boisterous entrance, Nick is silently attending to his notes, alternating his focus between his laptop and a printed diagram of governmental checks and balances. They've been friends for years, since the first day of sixth grade. And now they are virtually inseparable, one's Mike to the other's Marcus.

"One forty-six, man! You ready?"

Nick shifts his eyes uneasily toward the front of the room and shuffles his materials at his table. Other students straighten up in their seats, though Anthony seems oblivious to it all. "Nick!" he hisses. "Hey!"

The silence finally catches Anthony's attention, and he calmly settles back into his chair, tongue in his cheek as he attempts to subtly attend to his unopened binder. Mrs. Andrews, as he suspected, is standing directly behind him.

The giggles of his classmates become hoots as the teacher pronounces, "Mr. Sumner, I'll expect to see you for a few minutes after class today," and she swirls back to the front of the class. As she resumes her questioning about presidential power, Anthony steals a glance at Nick. Across the room, his friend looks back. Anthony shrugs a "What's the deal there?" gesture, to which his pal simply nods obediently back toward the teacher. And into the government lesson they go.

As the final bell rings, the cacophony of high school voices serenades Anthony from the hallway. His classmates file past him, some jostling, others whispering "good luck," and the rest simply ignoring him en route to third period. Someone drops a book, and Anthony picks it up, hands it back to its owner, and eyes the empty room. Mrs. Andrews waits, now seated at her desk. Anthony strolls over and pulls up a chair opposite her desk, swinging it around backwards and straddling it. "Thank you," he says.

"Thank you, *ma'am*?" Mrs. Andrews looks at Anthony, then the chair he is perched upon, then back to Anthony. She waits.

Anthony catches the hint like a pop fly in the infield. Gracefully, he stands, twirls the chair around, and sits properly facing his teacher. "Yes. Thank you, ma'am."

"For what, young man?" Mrs. Andrews directs her focus to her laptop, where she is entering grades, checking her email, or updating her notes for a future class.

"For letting me keep the countdown in here. None of the other teachers will let me. You're the only one that gets how important it is."

"Why were you late today?" she asks, still typing. "Walking Meaghan to class?"

"No," Anthony feels himself blush. "We broke up. Too much drama, plus I need to focus on baseball. It's better that way. I was just late, no reason."

"That's honest, thank you. You wouldn't believe the excuses I hear." Mrs. Andrews sighs and looks up at her brash pupil. This is the third year in a row that they have had a class together. Sophomore year was World Cultures, last year U.S. History, and now U.S. Government. He is an intelligent student, keen on how to play the school game, but academically lazy. He seems to do just enough to get by, just enough to keep the wolves at bay. It isn't his scholastic drive that intrigues her, rather it is his personality. He is playful, yet driven. A lovable scamp. She smiles and shakes her head simultaneously.

"Have you decided about basketball?" she asks, returning to her computer. "You know, the college coaches like student-athletes that are well-rounded and involved all across campus. Another sport might..."

"No way, man," his animated response demonstrates his happiness at not being called to the carpet on his tardiness. "I'm a single-sport athlete. A specialist. I can't split my training time, anyway. Plus, you give so much homework, it'd be impossible." He grins, hoping she'll see it.

Her unamused look flattens his smile. "Indeed," she sighs again. "Well, just remember: If you want to talk through any of this, just let me know. I've done that dance before." Glancing at the framed team photo from her own college basketball days, the memories flicker in her mind: the recruiting trips, the scholarship hunts, the joys of camaraderie on and off the court, and the many paths that led absolutely, sadly nowhere. Her slate-gray eyes meet his, and she sees the sparkle that was at once disarming. "Now go. Can't be late anymore."

Leaping up with athleticism and flair, Anthony pushes the chair back to its table and shoulders his pack. "Thank you, Mrs. Andrews," he calls over his shoulder. In a blur, he disappears into the noisy hallway.

CHAPTER 4

After school that day, Anthony beelines to the athletic department. High-fiving the office manager, Ms. Houk, on his way past, he struts directly into the athletic director's office. Coach Shepard is already there, laptop open, and a pile of papers strewn about the giant oak conference table.

Vineyard Mountain High School's head baseball coach, Dwayne Shepard, is preparing for his fourth season at the helm after a successful run of over two decades coaching in Oklahoma. Coaching has been his true love ever since his own playing days came to an end, the result of a blown-out arm. A retired auto-supply store manager according to his résumé, he is a diehard baseball man at the core. When he isn't coaching it, he is thinking about coaching it. Former colleagues joke that his head is probably held together with 108 red stitches, just like a baseball.

"What up, Rooster?" Coach Shepard gives his shortstop a hearty handclasp and a quick bro-hug. "How was learning today?"

"Right," says Anthony, tossing his backpack on one chair and scooting the other one up to the table. "Whatcha got going on here? Got the questionnaires?"

Coach Shepard enjoys the singular focus on baseball that Anthony brings to every conversation. He lives it, breathes it, and it oozes from every pore in his body. *A kindred spirit*, he thinks, *This is probably going to be my final season as a head coach, thanks to my wife's insistence that we enjoy our golden years together, and with kids like Anthony – talented, focused, and in love with the game – it might just be a success.*

He shoves the papers aside and pulls the laptop in front of Anthony. "Each tab has a school loaded already. You'll just have to fill 'em in. Then we need to get that video uploaded. You can thank Coach Schneider when you see him."

Assistant baseball coach Gus Schneider, a former minor-league outfielder, is Coach Shepard's right-hand man and 30 years his junior, and he handles everything related to technology, logistics, scheduling, and inventory. Shepard likes it like that, so he can focus on what he knows best: baseball, strategy, skills, and motivation. He lets Schneider handle calculating the stats and, in this case, setting up the computer for their promising athletes.

Anthony clicks across the tabs on the browser, looking at the recruit questionnaires from the west-coast colleges he and Coach Shepard had discussed a week earlier. Arizona State University. University of Southern California. University of Arizona. Oregon State University. UCLA. Yavapai Community College. That is a new one. "What's Yavapai?" He looks at his coach quizzically.

"Baseball player factory in Arizona. They know their stuff. Look, kid, you have the talent to play anywhere – the big programs will get you on TV, but trust me, the big league scouts know about this place. You'll get noticed. Let's drop all these lines in and see what we get on the hook."

"Oh yeah, I'm game," says Anthony, missing the fishing reference and tabbing through the rest of the colleges. "I appreciate you pulling all this together. And I'll thank Coach Schneider when I see him." He reflects on what his coach has just said. He could play anywhere. Damn straight – this school has never seen a baseball player like him. And this year is going to top 'em all.

He pauses. "Hey Coach," he swallows hard. "What about the pros?"

Coach Shepard has busied himself in his briefcase and looks haphazardly over his shoulder. "What do you mean? Like you going to the Major Leagues?"

Anthony's voice quavers just a tad. "Yeah, you think I could make it?"

"Absolutely, why not? But they don't take applications for *The Show*, so you'd better get the stuff done on that computer."

Anthony's gaze shifts from his coach to the wall, the clock, the table, the door. Silence sneaks in the room. Nodding slightly to himself, he turns back to the laptop.

He starts with Arizona State University, a prodigious baseball program whose alumni include Reggie Jackson, Barry Bonds, and Dustin Pedroia. And maybe Anthony Sumner? He enters his junior year's statistics: .395 batting average, 21 stolen bases, 30 walks against just 9 strikeouts, 27 runs and 18 runs batted in over the 24 games, a season in which the Mountaineers were 12-12. The next box asks for honors and awards. "I hate this part." Anthony shakes his head.

"What's that?" Coach Shepard looks up from a pile of papers he's extracted from a manila file folder labeled "drills."

"Honors. I hate writing 'Second-team all-league,' 'cause I should have been first-team."

"Well, the coaches of the Salem schools thought otherwise," Coach Shepard replies. "Guess they liked the kid from Salem who hit all the homers. It wouldn't hurt you to go yard a few times this year, right?"

"I've been lifting," Anthony replies, almost defiantly.

"You want to change that? Get 'em back on the field. Haunt 'em this year. You can be their worst nightmare."

"Roger that," Anthony exclaims, turning back to the computer. Haunt 'em. They don't know what's coming, but they'll know when they clear the battlefield. *I'm gonna haunt 'em,* he thinks, as he goes back to the questionnaires.

CHAPTER 5

An hour later, Anthony emerges from the AD's office, satisfied with the impression he is sure the college coaches will have as they read his questionnaires. While Coach Shepard had fussed with paperwork, he and Coach Schneider finished editing Anthony's junior year highlight video – a blend of defensive gems, line drives, stolen bases, and a couple of picture-perfect bunt hits – and it was successfully uploaded with the link included in each school's questionnaire. Once they catch a sniff of his promise, there will probably be a feeding frenzy come scholarship time. He'd better prepare.

Stepping outside, he notices it has started raining. Or drizzling, more accurately. He skirts the quadrangle courtyard in favor of the covered walkway and notices the leaves dancing in the gentle breeze. There are reds and yellows and oranges mixed with various shades of green all around the quad, all rather muted, a watercolor scene behind a fuzzy filter. Fall is always a peaceful season – cool breezes, warm drinks, and baseball caps traded for beanies, sweatshirts, and rain. It always rains in Oregon. He takes it all in as he crosses the creek that runs through campus and heads to the locker rooms.

At the school's indoor batting cage off the gym, Anthony connects with his pal, Nick, and Kai Baker, another senior and a baseball star of his own. Kai had transferred to Vineyard Mountain from a school in Houston last year, something to do with his parents splitting up and his dad moving to Corvallis. Anthony, Nick, and Kai are the only three from the baseball roster who aren't playing football, so they have ample time to work on their hitting. Kai has hooked up the pitching machine and is calibrating the settings, and Nick is receiving the practice pitches in a catching stance.

"Glad you could show up after all the work is done," Kai calls. "You wouldn't believe all the crap someone had piled on this arm in the shed."

Anthony had grabbed workout shorts and a tee shirt from his pack and is hastily changing. "Yeah, sorry. I had some work to do with Coach."

"We're good now," declares Nick as he takes a gloveful of balls to dump into the bucket behind the cage's protective L-screen. "And Anthony, I got you something." Digging into his bat bag, he extracts a small plastic baggie and tosses it to his friend.

Anthony catches it with flair. "Gummy worms! Thanks, man." Tearing open the baggie, he stuffs four or five of them into his cheek.

Kai rolls his eyes. "What is that all about? I don't understand all y'all Oregonians."

Anthony points to his protruding cheek. "Looks like I'm chawing, but it's just gummy worms. It's a healthier choice, my Texan friend."

Nick interrupts by announcing, "Okay, let's go. I'll hit first."

"Do y'all always have to go by the batting order? I'd like to hit before I have to go home," asks Kai, who was already penned as the third hitter in the lineup for this season, after Nick and Anthony. He has power and an innate ability to make solid contact – last year, in just half a season after his transfer, he had hit over .400 and clubbed five home runs.

"Deal with it, *y'all*," replies Anthony, laughing and ushering Kai out of the cage as Nick takes his spot in the batter's box.

For the next 90 minutes, the threesome rotates from pitching-machine feeder to hitter to the on-deck circle. Sometimes the third player would offer his teammate some feedback on technique, other times he'd hit off a tee into a net, and occasionally he would stretch. The latter was more likely Kai, who often dove into some stretches that the other two had never seen before.

In that hour and a half, they punish the baseballs. Nick and Anthony, both switch-hitters, drill one after another off the L-screen – drawing exclamatory cheers from everyone involved – and pepper the back netting with line drives. Kai, meanwhile, hits lightning bolts. The echoes explode off the walls of the hitting space, like firecrackers in a tight garage. They share the duties of cleanup: Kai unplugs and whisks the pitching machine back to its roost in the shed, Nick collects all the balls, and Anthony takes the various tees and plates and resistance bands back to their spot in the closet.

As they walk out to their cars, the temperature has dropped, but the rain has diminished. "Nice hitting, boys!" calls Anthony as he quickens his pace toward his car.

Kai peels off. "You too, fellas. See y'all tomorrow!"

Nick begins jogging to keep up with Anthony. "How ya feeling?" he asks.

"Never better," breathes Anthony. "Physically, I feel amazing. Mentally, I'm ready. Spiritually, I'm solid. Mind-body-spirit. The next 146 days had better go by quickly. I can't wait!"

"Me neither," says Nick. "Except I have open gym starting next week for basketball, then I'll pretty much be in hoops mode until baseball starts. You and Kai will have to hit on your own."

They have reached their cars, parked next to each other underneath one of the dozens of bitter cherry trees lining the massive high school parking lot. The two friends pause, standing in the doorways of their respective vehicles, Nick's a newer, white Honda Accord and Anthony's a rusty, powder-blue Ford Ranger pickup. Anthony turns the key, and the truck comes roaring to life, followed by a familiar, peculiar knocking sound emanating from somewhere under the hood. He ignores it.

"You have a lot of homework tonight?" asks Anthony.

"Nothing," says Nick. "Wanna hang?"

"How about tennis? I think I owe you a whooping."

"Oh, you're hungry? Sure, I can feed you a couple of bagels. Meet you at the Center around 7:30, after dinner. And seriously, good job hitting today. You were on fire!"

Anthony smirks to himself as he settles in his truck. "Of course I was. 7:30 pal, bring your A-game. You're gonna need it!"

They drive their separate ways as the clouds reopen and the rain resumes its work.

CHAPTER 6

As Anthony's pickup's taillights disappear down their driveway after dinner, Drew and Amanda Sumner exchange looks. Drew looks pensive for a moment, feigning a serious pose with his finger crooked under his chin as he gazes into the distance. "Well, he seems to be quite focused, doesn't he?"

"Understatement of the year." Amanda has busied herself with clearing the table while Drew moves to the sink to work on the dishes.

The running water and clanging pans fill the kitchen's emptiness, now that it is just the two of them and the remnants of their conversation with Anthony.

"It's all baseball, all the time," she resumes, handing Drew a couple plates and forks. "I love that he's into sports – he always has been. He seems to be pretty sure he's going pro, is that what you got from that?"

Drew pauses, shutting off the faucet and turns to look at her. "It's never been anything but that, since he was a little kid bopping his sister with that wiffle bat. Always wearing that dirty old Red Sox hat my dad gave him, reading the stats on baseball cards. And sometimes I think the only reason he's still in school is that it's his vehicle for playing baseball."

"I think we should have let him play football. He did ask about that a while back." Amanda gathers some crumbs in a napkin.

"Heck, no. That boy? He's all arms and legs. They'd crack him in half the first time he's tackled. Or he'll get a dozen concussions. No way, we talked about that. Football is too rough, too dangerous. Have you seen his neck? It's a pencil connecting his head to his body. I think we made a good parenting decision on that one."

"What about basketball?" Amanda asks, standing at the sink. "This is the first year he didn't play. I'd sure like him to stay busy. And those games are always fun to watch."

"I know, that drives me crazy. Remember, though, that was his choice, and I think he'll be fine. He stayed after school hitting for almost two hours today, right? It's better that he stick with baseball, and then go play tennis or bowling or Pictionary. He's not partying or getting girls pregnant or smoking anything, at least that we're aware of. The kid is pretty safe. He chooses well."

Amanda dumps the crumbs in the sink and sets the napkin down. She leans against the kitchen counter and frowns at her husband. "Is he good enough to go pro? I mean, really. Is he? I'm worried that he doesn't have a backup plan. He doesn't seem to care about anything but baseball."

"We'll see, won't we," he says. "He is darn good, and Coach Shepard told him the sky's the limit."

"Is that just a line, though?" asks Amanda. "Don't coaches feed their players' egos to keep their attention? I mean, maybe it's working – Anthony's all baseball. And he hardly responds when we talk about college, except about the school's baseball program."

"I don't know," shrugs Drew. "Let's see how this senior year goes."

Amanda furrows her brow. "I'm not sure sitting back and letting things develop is the best way to do this. It's his senior year – next year he's out of the nest and on his own, either to college or to work or to play baseball or, heaven help us, out on the street. Don't you think we should be a bit more involved, at least in the conversations?"

"He's a big boy," Drew answers, turning back to the dishes. "We can't do everything for him."

"But we're expected to pay for it. We have some money saved for college, and you and I both know it's not enough to fully support him. We have to build a plan for him – *with* him – don't you think?"

Drew stops his work in the sink, tossing the scrubber aside. "I know, your parents were super-involved with you, and that's great. My folks didn't do a damn thing for me, and I figured it out. I mean, look, I'm a college professor! Anthony's a smart kid, he's a bit goofy, but he loves baseball. He'll make it work."

———

Amanda sighs. She watches silently as her husband finishes cleaning up. It is already dark outside, though she can see the wind blowing through the kitchen window, the branches of the evergreens swaying gently, awaiting the night's rainfall.

Tasks complete, Drew adjourns to the living room. Amanda hears him turn on the TV. Eyes still out the window, she listens to the animated voices exchanging thoughts about the upcoming weekend's college football matchups, the injury report, and the importance of winning the home games. It is several minutes before she leaves the kitchen to join him on the sofa.

CHAPTER 7

Anthony pulls into the parking lot of the Tennis Center at 7:30 on the nose. Nick is already there, hitting balls against the practice wall adjacent to the office building.

"Tell me you got an indoor court," Anthony pleads, grabbing his racket and bag from the passenger seat and flicking the hood of his sweatshirt over his head. He looks up at the clouds, which have taken a short break from their drizzle, but are still gathered tightly in the dusk sky. The dark, gray billows droop heavily, menacing.

"Yup, number three," cheers Nick, and the teenagers dash into one of the large, warehouse-style buildings. Inside are two tennis courts, divided by a net, with exposed studs and exterior plywood lining the walls. It isn't much warmer inside than out, but there is no wind, and it won't rain on them in here. Nick had flicked the switch several minutes earlier, and the high lights hum as they slowly begin to chase away the many shadows.

The boys tie their shoes, paw their rackets, and toss a couple of volleys back and forth as they warm up. Anthony smiles to himself as he and his best friend began to hit with a little more force, an urgency that belies their competitive nature. Though Anthony is 13 months Nick's senior, they are remarkably close in physical ability, strength, and grit. Both are superb all-around athletes, and they scrap and fight like wolverines in any contest. "If you keep score, you play to win," is Anthony's rationale. "I hate losing more than anything," Nick would say. And so they battle, on the basketball court, around the billiards table, in front of video-game screens, with a deck of cards and Egyptian Rocular set up, or throwing rocks at one of the many oak trees behind the baseball field.

Tennis, as with so many of the other competitions, could go either way. Over the years, they have traded games, sets, and matches, each trying to win as gracefully as he hopes his opponent will lose, and both failing miserably as they alternately talk trash and snarl in bitter response.

The match begins with the two trading sets on serve, and Nick wins the tiebreaker to take the first, 7-6. While they sit on the bench drinking water between sets, Anthony mentions his earlier visit with Coach Shepard, the questionnaires, and his motto for the season.

"'Haunt 'em,' he said. Said I can play anywhere. These next five months are just a lead-in to the main event. Every path has pointed me to this place, right here, right now. I'm going to apply to all the big baseball schools: ASU, UCLA, Georgia Tech, LSU, you name it. Even some place in Arizona called Yavapai."

"I think I'm going to go to California. Maybe one of the UC schools," Nick answers. "Maybe I'll play baseball there, maybe not."

"Well, I'll get you tickets, so you can come see me play any time. I've never felt physically stronger or more ready. You probably can't tell, but I've got 10 extra pounds of muscle since last year."

"It's all between your ears, man," laughs Nick.

"Right. You saw me hit today. Lasers. Baseball is 90% mental, yes? Is anyone more confident than me?"

"Than I, you mean?"

"Don't grammartize me, buddy. Seriously, I'm ready for the season to start today. Bring it! I'll put our team on my back. And with you hitting first, the 1-2 combination will be in full effect. Then Kai hitting third? Mercy. It'll be 3-0 before they even get an out!"

"You're just stalling now. Are you ready?" Nick says, as he stands up and crosses to the other side of the net for the next set.

Smiling and dripping confidence, Anthony sets down his water bottle, grasps his racket, and says, "Whether I am or not, you've been more than fair."

Nick laughs. "You can never go wrong quoting *The Princess Bride*."

"There's a movie line for every situation. Ten bucks says I take this set."

Nick laughs again. "You can take a picture of it. And you'll take a beating. That's all the taking you get."

For the next half-hour, the sounds of tennis carom off the spacious walls surrounding their battle. Squeaking shoes, the hollow bounce, the vicious threads of the rackets. And some grunting. Occasional swearing. The scores called out before every serve.

It is 4-4 in the second set when Nick hits a ferocious forehand deep into the backhand corner that Anthony will never reach. Refusing to allow the shot to pass him by, Anthony strides mightily, slides on his plant foot, and reaches far, farther than he thought he could. Farther than his body will allow. He flicks his wrist to try to generate enough oomph to send the ball back.

Whether the racket and the ball connected, no one remembers. The only sound is the hollow, dreadful pop as his shoulder violently removes itself from the socket. The pain of the dislocation sears Anthony's shoulder like nothing he's ever felt before. He roars, his racket clattering on the ground as he grabs his raw, burning arm.

As it dangles helplessly in front of him, Anthony instinctively runs. He runs in indiscriminate circles, ending up on the unoccupied court beside them. Nick trails behind, unable to fully process what has just happened to his best friend. Anthony roars again, this time a result of swinging his arm madly above his head, and then again, unsuccessful in trying to knock it back into place.

"Stop!" Yells Nick. "Let me help you. Jeeez…" he trails off, noting the crimson of his friend's face. Anthony's eyebrows meet at a furious angle as he swings his arm again, and this time a scratching sound followed by a sort of relief.

"I think I got it," gasps Anthony. Then he rolls his head back and looks up at the tennis court lights, a spinning array of whites and blacks and brights and darks. "Shit. Shit, shit, shit. Oh, shit." The color drains from his face as quickly as it had arrived. Nick sprints to get his keys, and leaving Anthony's truck in the parking lot, drives him directly to the ER. It rains mercilessly the entire way.

CHAPTER 8

Two days later, a Wednesday, marks Anthony's return to school. The campus is abuzz with chatter about his injury and how he sustained it. "Would've been safer at football practice," is the social media consensus. Scottie Johnson, the baseball team's third baseman and starting quarterback during the off-season, had long tried to talk Anthony into playing football. He would love to have another speedy target with great hands running post routes to the end zone.

Instead, Anthony is a one-sport specialist, and one of the first people he runs into that morning is Coach Shepard, who gestures to the sling, rolls his eyes, and waves his arms to the heavens. "What the heck, Rooster? How long are you in that thing?"

Anthony tries to smile, but ends up wincing instead. "Doc says three weeks. I'm not buying that, and I've got better things to do, so I'll shuck it this weekend."

"How's the pain?" Coach Shepard asks, resuming his initial path toward the office.

"Brutal," says Anthony, wincing again. "I go back early next week when the swelling decreases, so they can determine if there's any damage to the ligaments. If I'm lucky, they'll be fine. If not, I'm screwed."

Coach Shepard stops and turns around. "What's the time frame? When can you get back to baseball activities?"

Anthony looks down. "Maybe six weeks if everything's golden. If the ligaments are jacked and they have to operate, six months."

"Aw, Rooster," Coach Shepard calls over his shoulder. "Don't make me go out looking for a new shortstop. Get that thing healed fast!" He disappears behind the door into the athletics office. Anthony thinks he hears him swear in his greeting to Ms. Houk before the door swings shut.

Anthony finds maneuvering the busy high school hallways to be quite a chore with one arm in a sling. Even though his classmates know about the dislocation, it appears they all forget when it is time to get to class, pushing and shoving each other, sometimes accidentally, sometimes intentionally. With a wounded wing, Anthony seems drawn to the receiving end of such punishment.

"The best defense is a good offense," he mutters as he throws his left arm forward, elbow crooked at 90 degrees, shielding his body as he walks and offers pre-emptive shoves to create a bubble. As he rounds the corner to enter the social studies wing, his screen deflects a young lady merging into his lane.

"Watch out, wide load coming through!" he calls.

Two bright blue eyes meet his gaze, and the smile they belong to serve as a peace treaty. "Wide and driving erratically," she laughs.

"Oh, hey Elena," Anthony groans, making sure they both have room to settle into the traffic.

"That's inconvenient, huh?" she motions toward the sling.

"Tell me about it."

"You doing okay?"

"I've been better." Navigating a crowded hallway is a new challenge, and it is all Anthony can do to prevent getting body-slammed into a bank of lockers. Evidently, he is heading to class without his books, backpack, or any other materials. Great.

"Well," Elena states as she prepares to veer into her class. "When you're ready for physical therapy, just give me a call. I know some moves that'll help your shoulder." The innuendo is lost on Anthony, who instead is now running some numbers in his head. The same calculations that have consumed him over the past 24 hours. Six months rehabbing will cost him half his senior season.

Just like that, Elena is gone, and Anthony sleepwalks into Mrs. Andrews' room. He is on time, but that is little consolation.

Mrs. Andrews is still at her desk when she notices Anthony's presence. "Come up here, Mr. Sumner, let's have a look at you." He obliges, standing in front of her desk, unsure if even the great Mrs. Andrews can cheer him up today. He's heard enough about how sorry everyone is that he's been injured.

"So…that doesn't look promising. What's the countdown?" Up on the board, the red "146" from Monday remains. Anthony sighs.

Leaning closer to him, Mrs. Andrews lowers her voice. "And if this causes you extreme pain for an extended period of time or if there's damage that limits your range of motion, what's next?" She has a way of being rather forthright. Anthony senses a conversation heading down a path he doesn't want to follow.

"What do you mean? For baseball?"

"Well, what if this is a sign that baseball isn't the one and only future for you. What's your backup plan for life? Do you have a Plan B?"

Silence descends upon the entire room. The other students have filed in and begun addressing a scenario Mrs. Andrews has projected onto the screen as an entry task. Or maybe they are just pretending to work, eavesdropping on the unfolding drama. Perhaps the bell has already rung. Anthony didn't hear it, didn't hear them, didn't hear her. Plan A is the only option. He turns on his heel and walks directly out of the room.

WINTER

CHAPTER 9

The days turn to weeks and the weeks to months. Outside, the leaves of the beautiful and mighty oak trees have long fallen, their galls split open and littered across the countryside. Without cover, the twisting, writhing limbs, and gnarled, ridged bark become hundreds of giant, ancient snakes reaching outward, petrified by the bitter cold. In the winter breeze they come to life, grossly stretching toward the heavens, the hills, the fields. Every morning, a blanket of frost descends upon the surrounding ground, giving an impression of majesty, a stately, delicately prepared surface over which the snake-tree reigns.

Anthony feels less than regal. His frustration at his shoulder injury grows to irritation that it isn't healing on schedule, and that combined with his stubbornness creates a staunch refusal to follow the doctor's orders. "His timeline doesn't mesh with the start of the baseball season," he told Nick one afternoon. And now he is worried. First practice is in 31 days, and he still hasn't even thrown a baseball. Or an acorn, for that matter. His arm isn't ready.

Instead of the medical professional's prescribed physical therapy regimen, Anthony opts to accept Elena's offers to nurse the shoulder back to health. True to her word, she provides a variety of treatments, and Anthony can't help but notice the maneuvers address the muscles *around* his shoulder much more than the shoulder itself; in fact, many include snuggling up close and an intermittent foot massage. Having already sworn off formal relationships until this ultra-important baseball season is over, Anthony tries in vain to politely excuse himself from many of these sessions with her. Truth be told, her company is exquisite, so they end up spending quite a bit of time together, talking or watching videos or pretending to do homework. It is almost enough to make him forget his injury.

She is all for it. "Is there anything I can get you?" she asks one evening as they sit on his living room sofa, watching a movie half-heartedly.

"I'm not incapacitated, you know. I just would swim in circles if you were to drop me in the lake."

Elena sits up, aiming her eyes directly at his. "Isn't that what your doctor suggested you do? Swim? Have you been to the pool?"

Anthony frowns. "No. I hate swimming. Always have. Can't seem to get myself to stick my head under water. So no pools, no lane lines, no chlorine for me. I've been working with resistance bands and trying to activate my parascapular muscles. It's just taking forever."

Elena moves a little closer, angling herself so she is facing him. Her hand seeks his back, touching his spine ever so lightly. "Is this where those muscles are?"

"A bit further to the outside," Anthony responds, turning his head to her.

She moves her hand. "Here?" Now she is whispering. Her other hand has somehow made its way to his chest. Her hands are a spring breeze on his body. Anthony feels all at once enthralled and agitated. *Maybe this would be a good thing, but it's just a distraction.* Elena shifts even closer, and her breath is warm on his neck. She smells of sweet lavender.

In an awkward, quick moment, Anthony takes her hand from his chest and launches himself off the sofa. "Hey!" He tries to sound light-hearted. "Let me show you some of the exercises I was *told* to do. The doc says I've got to work on flexion and abduction and whatnot, so I can build up strength for the full range of motion needed for baseball. The shoulder's really important," he says, now fully into an introductory lesson on the rehab plan for his dislocated shoulder. "Any limitation will hinder my ability to swing the bat, throw, and even run properly. And I like to dive when I steal bases, so I've got to get this thing ready."

"Really."

"Yeah!" Anthony grabs a resistance band and loops one end around his foot. The movie on the TV plays on, and Anthony proceeds to lift the band gently, arm straight in front of him. At about parallel to shoulder height, he descends. Elena can see the pain in his face, though he tries to smile through it. "Want to try?" he asks her.

She shrugs, coordinated eyebrows exposing her bemusement. Eyeing the now vacant spot on the sofa next to her, she turns to him. "If you'd rather work out than enjoy this moment, be my guest. And sure, I'll take a turn. Why not?"

Before she leaves later that evening, he has shown her three more exercises, and his shoulder is killing him.

CHAPTER 10

Anthony has never been so grateful for a Saturday morning. He stays in bed until almost noon. His shoulder is throbbing. He reaches for his phone, plugged in on the shelf just above his bed, and is met by a stabbing pain. Wincing, he retreats under the covers. He can hear the rain knocking at his window, angrily reminding him that the world is proceeding without him. 30 days. He knows the countdown. And the pain is constant, some days worse than others.

More knocking. This time it is his mom at the bedroom door. "You getting up, sleepyhead?" she calls.

"Not interested," he groans from under the covers.

"How's the shoulder today?"

"How do you think?" he grumbles. "Worse than ever. I need a new doctor. Isn't there something that'll speed this up? This is ridiculous."

"Well, you've been taking ibuprofen, right? That should keep the swelling down and ease the pain. How's your PT? I haven't seen you with your swim bag recently."

Anthony rips the covers off his head and shoots a look across the room. "You try swimming with this thing. Hurts like a mother."

"Not my favorite expression," Amanda replies with a look of her own.

"Well, I'm sorry. It hurts. It hurts all the time. I can't hit, I can't throw, I can't even brush my teeth without nagging pain. And I don't need you nagging me about swimming. I need a doctor that's not a quack." The covers go back over his head. "Have a nice day."

Amanda looks at her son, crumpled and curled up. "Let me know when you want something to eat. The rest of us have already moved on to lunch. And your sister called this morning from college. She said to tell you hi."

Nothing. She closes the door behind her.

Downstairs, Drew is standing over the kitchen table, working on a pesto chicken sandwich. "Want one?" he asks.

"Sure," she responds, taking a seat and resting her chin in her palm.

Drew puts the finishing touches on their sandwiches, and they begin to eat. After a couple of bites, Amanda brings up the obvious. "Anthony's sure cranky. He won't eat, I haven't seen much homework, and he sure isn't doing his exercises, at least not where we can see him."

"He's fine," replies Drew immediately. He is still standing while he eats. "A little pain never hurt nobody," he chuckles.

"He's not fine." Amanda puts down her sandwich. "This isn't the happy-go-lucky kid we've raised. We've fed the baseball beast, and now it's consumed him. He's hollow and angry and hurting and rather anti-social."

"Anti-social? He's doing stuff all the time. He just doesn't talk to us much."

"Exactly. And because he doesn't want to talk to us, we avoid talking to him. When was the last time either of us sat and talked with him about school? Or college? Or how serious this thing with Elena is? Or anything to do with that 'stuff' he's out doing, or anything other than him being all sourpuss about his shoulder? He hasn't even been going to the basketball games, has he? And Nick hasn't been over much lately. We don't know anything that's going on in that head of his."

Drew gazes out the kitchen window, past the wonky blinds, and takes a deep breath. "Nick's busy with basketball every day. Anthony just needs to get baseball started, and his attitude will shift. Just wait. And I don't think there's anything going on with Elena. She's sweet, but he said he and Meaghan broke up so he could concentrate on baseball, which is exactly what he should do."

"Is that him talking or you talking?" Amanda asks, eyes fixed and head tilted.

"I know my kid, that's all. He won't do anything that jeopardizes his baseball season."

"*You* know? *Your* kid? Wow. I think I've actually lost my appetite."

"That's not what I meant," Drew starts, but Amanda has already dropped her plate and half-eaten meal in the sink.

Drew takes the final bite of his sandwich as his wife stalks silently toward the stairs. "I'll talk with him about his stretching. Maybe we'll stretch together. I could use a couple extra workout sessions, anyway. And swimming is over-rated," he says, patting his tummy. "I go to the pool three times a week, and I'm still packing a spare tire."

Over her shoulder, Amanda yells, "Just promise you'll chat with *your son* before he implodes and takes us all with him."

"Promise," Drew says. He is already doing his dishes.

CHAPTER 11

The weekend wears on without much change in Anthony's status. While he sits in his bedroom, darker than normal due to the thunderclouds blanketing the valley, he looks angrily at the multiple resistance bands and the five-pound kettlebell on the floor in front of his closet. He hasn't even bothered to turn a light on, yet his exercise tools seem to glimmer, inviting him to their torturesome rendezvous. Defiantly, he turns back to the window, his thoughts wrangling him back to baseball.

Across town, the guys are probably hitting in the cage at the school. Anthony envisions Kai swinging mightily and destroying baseballs while Scottie feeds the pitching machine. Reggie Robinson is probably there, too, getting his hacks in. Reggie is the team's catcher and an incorrigible practical joker off the field, but a true gamer between the lines. He's probably hooting and hollering every time Kai ropes one, then takes his turn and digs in, all business in the batter's box, eyes locked in and every muscle in his body ready to uncoil. They are getting their hacks in.

Anthony, usually leading the charge, is falling behind.

That afternoon, Nick leads the basketball team to a road victory over one of the Eugene schools in a non-league game. Anthony's phone buzzes, and he checks in. Elena, who has gone to the game with Nick's longtime boyfriend Simon, offers a score update, then a video, then a simple "How ya doing?" Anthony flips the phone over and ignores it. The span between buzzes lengthens, and it eventually sits quietly on the bedside table.

The silence continues through the day Sunday, with Anthony prone on his back, eyes closed, unable to sleep, mind whirring. Scenarios of his senior baseball season play out in his head, each a darker version of the one prior. In one vision, his weak relay throw allows the winning run to score in the league championship game. In the next, his feeble strikeout with the bases loaded costs his team the season. When he sees himself in the stands, wearing a sling, watching his teammates walk off the field in defeat, he notices the rain. In each of his visions, it is pouring. The players are muddy. The fans are drenched. Heavy, thick clouds angrily dump their payload, slogging the entire ballpark. His face, his hair, his clothes, all soaked.

Opening his eyes, he turns his head to the window. It is raining indeed. Droplets pepper the sill, drumming a pestering beat. And inside, beads of sweat drip off his head and onto his pillow. Anthony punches his fists into the mattress, wincing at the pain. He has to do something about this damaged shoulder. But what?

On Monday, he begrudgingly drags himself out of his dungeon and off to school, running the gauntlet of bodies in the hallways, past the classmates and teammates asking how he's doing, through the classes that fail to keep his attention, and trying to avoid any real conversations. Though he had weeks ago abandoned the sling, his shoulder provides very little help to his right arm, which he safely protects by keeping his hand in the pocket of his letter jacket. He had begun taking notes left-handed, which barely meets the definition of "legible," but it distracts his mind from the pain.

In government class, Mrs. Andrews stops by his table while the class is completing a review packet for an upcoming quiz. Kneeling next to his seat, she gets his attention away from his group.

"Anthony, how's it going?

"Not great."

She waits.

"Sorry," he blinks. "Not great, ma'am."

"I've been thinking. How serious are you about playing baseball in your future?"

"Dead. That is, if I can throw again," he self-consciously half-laughs.

"If you're that serious and if you're willing to commit to that goal, I'd be happy to help you."

"How?"

"Stop by at lunchtime, and we'll chat."

Anthony nods as Mrs. Andrews resumes her circuit of the classroom, answering questions and providing suggestions for ways to remember important details and position critical laws in the context of social and cultural history. She has a way of making the content seem important. Heck, she has a way of making each and every student in her classes feel important. Anthony wonders how many of his classmates think she feels they are special. He sure does.

As he goes back to writing left-handed, Nick enters the room. Handing their teacher a note, he sits down and takes out his notebook.

"Hey, man. Where've you been?" Anthony asks.

"Counselor. They wanted to go through my transcripts, talk about college and post-graduation stuff. You know, like they do with everyone."

"Right," Anthony responds as his friend turns to work. *Good thing I already have a plan.*

At the beginning of their lunch period, Anthony passes Nick and Simon in the hallway.

"Anthony," Nick calls. "We're sneaking off to grab some tacos. You coming?"

Anthony stops, looking down the hallway toward Mrs. Andrews's classroom. "Nah, you go ahead. I have to check in with Mrs. A real quick."

Simon laughs aloud. "In trouble again? Lunch detention, I bet."

Anthony sighs. "Yeah, something like that."

Nick grabs Simon's hand and takes a step to leave. "Okay, you want us to get you anything?"

"No thanks, I'm good."

As they set off, Anthony could have sworn he heard Simon whisper, "That dude's gotta learn to keep his big trap shut!" Their laughter joins the other clamor in the busy hallway as Anthony makes his way to the government classroom.

Inside, Mrs. Andrews is seated at her desk. Seeing Anthony, she motions for him to sit at a chair near her desk. He complies, this time using the chair as it is intended.

"What's up, Mrs. A?"

"Well, as you know I have playing and coaching experience. I've helped kids navigate these waters before, and I see talent and drive in you." Straight to business, as usual, Anthony notes. "Plus you're a nice kid, and you deserve great things in your life."

"Agreed," he blushes a little. "So what do I have to do?"

"I'm glad you asked. I've got a couple of quick forms for you to fill out. I want you to really think about them – they're designed to help you focus your thinking and your energy and to make sure you're doing the right work to move you in the direction of your dreams. You can't half-ass it, though, if you're serious about this."

"I'm game," says Anthony. "But don't give me any extra homework."

"It's homework, all right. But it's the good kind. It's all about you, about baseball, and your future. If you're truly committed to that goal, you won't mind."

"Right," he says. "Have you met me?"

Ignoring his comment, Mrs. Andrews stands up and walks over to a giant file cabinet. Anthony takes the moment to examine the photos behind her desk – family snapshots, mostly. Some on a beach, one in front of the Eiffel Tower, and one he has seen many times before catches his attention, and his eyes linger on it: her college basketball team, celebrating a championship with giant smiles, fingers waving, hugging, and a cut-down net around the coach's neck. *How cool is that? And how did she go from being a superstar basketball player to a history teacher?*

The slap of a manila envelope landing on the desk in front of him jars Anthony back to the moment. He looks up at his teacher.

"Get 'em back to me whenever you're ready," she says. "When you're serious. And focused."

"For sure, Mrs. A," Anthony smiles. "I'm always serious about baseball! I'll get this back to you before you know it."

Stealing another glance at the framed team photo, he grabs the envelope with his good arm, says, "Thank you, ma'am," and heads back to his locker.

Curious, Anthony plops down on the floor of the quiet lunchtime hallway and opens the envelope to see what mysterious forms his teacher has given him. The first page appears to be some sort of poem. Figuring he'll save the poetry for later, he flips to the next page. On it, one question: What is your goal? That's easy, he thinks, so he writes in his messy left-handed scrawl: *Become the shortstop for the Boston Red Sox.*

On the next page, another single question: Why is that important to you? *'Cause that'd be sweet. Plus it's destiny.*

Then comes a series of boxes with simple directions: What are you prepared to do to reach your goal? Write the very specific action steps, the timelines, the support you think you'll need from others, and the way you'll measure your success, in the space below. Mrs. Andrews has hand-written an additional note: *Remember, be very specific!*

Anthony closes his eyes, imagining a future spent in uniform, doing what he loves. When he opens his eyes again, he writes simply: *Kick butt and play baseball.*

He folds the paper and stuffs it back in the envelope, hopping up to grab something to eat before the lunch period ends.

CHAPTER 12

After school, Anthony goes straight to his truck. His phone rings as soon as he sits down. Dad.

"Hello?"

"Hi, son, how was school?"

"Lame, as usual. What's up?" Anthony clenches his teeth as he turns the key in the ignition. Even the routine actions cause extreme pain. He adds to it by cranking the heat. It is freezing.

"Well, sunshine, I made you an appointment with a sports medicine specialist. Probably should have done so a while ago, but you know, when's the best time to plant a tree?"

"20 years ago. The second best time is right now. I know," Anthony rolls his eyes at his dad's favorite expression. "So when's the appointment? March something or other?"

"Right now, smart aleck. I'll text you the address. I can't meet you there, so you're on your own. It's Dr. McGregor. You've met him before. His daughter Cindy is graduating with you guys this year too. Dr. McGregor consults with the OSU athletics department and used to do some work with the Portland Trailblazers back in the day. I called in a favor for this, so you've got to go."

Anthony smiles for the first time in a long time. Finally, a hint of light at the end of the tunnel. "Thanks, Dad," he calls as he tosses his phone on the passenger seat and connects it to Bluetooth.

"I love you. Good luck," answers Drew.

"Love you too." Anthony hangs up, shivering with excitement and cold. Why doesn't this heater work any faster? It isn't long before his dad's text arrives with an address. He clicks on it, so his phone will provide him with directions, though he recognizes it as the medical center on Circle Boulevard.

He drives in silence, ignoring the texts from friends and teammates, and thinking about seeing Dr. McGregor. He doesn't remember ever meeting him before. He's known Cindy for a long time. She had been in one of his classes last year and was an amazing artist, as he remembers. She could draw blindfolded. He seems to recall that she had done that at the school talent show in the spring. Her dad is probably pretty gifted too. That's a good sign. He needs someone in his corner who knows what he's doing right about now.

Mrs. Andrews stops by her mailbox in the main office on her way out the door. In it, she is surprised to see the manila envelope with Anthony's name on it. *Could he have already filled this out?* Digging in, she reads his brief, incomplete responses, and sighs. *The kid's got a ways to go.* As much promise as she sees in him, he can be excruciating. She tosses the envelope and the rest of her mail in her bag, already overflowing with papers to grade and lesson plans to write. *Why do I keep doing this to myself? I have enough on my plate without fussing with the Anthony Sumners of the world.* She stares at the bag sitting urgently at her feet. Other teachers come and go, the busyness of the school day never seeming to slow down, even after the final bell.

Her thoughts catch a draft and float to her past. She is in a dusty middle-school gym, shooting baskets alone on a side hoop while the boys play on the main court, just like every day. It is lunchtime. Mr. Goodwin, the school's basketball coach and a math teacher, stands nearby, arms crossed, analyzing their play. That was the day Jacob sprained his ankle and had to go to the nurse. "Andrews, get in there!" Mr. Goodwin is waving to her. "We need a tenth player. Go!" Tentatively at first, she joins the game. Before the recess period ends, she has scored a couple buckets, blocked a shot, and more than held her own. Mr. Goodwin's high-five turned her hand red. Lost in the memory, Mrs. Andrews smiles. Maybe it was Jacob's ankle's doing. *Nah, it was Mr. Goodwin.* His relentless encouragement lands her the only girl on the boys' team in 7th and 8th grade. That was a game-changer for her. He'd been a game-changer for her. Taking a deep breath, she hoists the bag to her shoulder and sets off for home.

CHAPTER 13

Dr. Ethan McGregor fills the room with his presence and his personality. Not terribly tall but wide and stocky, his forearms are the size of Anthony's legs. And hairier, Anthony notices. Balding with glasses, he seems to have hair everywhere but the top of his head. As he reaches to shake hands, Anthony notices even his knuckles are hairy. And the eyebrows are like caterpillars. "Good to finally meet you, young man! I've watched you play ball a couple times over the years. Cindy's mentioned you here and again."

Anthony smiles.

"Your dad tells me your shoulder's not getting much better," he launches right into it.

"Not getting *any* better, actually," Anthony replies. He is standing, awaiting instructions.

"Have a seat. Take off your shirt. Let's see what we're dealing with." Washing his hands in the examination room sink, Dr. McGregor asks over his shoulder, "How long 'til baseball season starts? This is going to be a big year for you guys, right? That whole group of you are seniors."

Anthony tosses his shirt on the chair next to his keys and phone and shuffles back onto the exam table. "28 days. Four weeks from today. And I can't throw or hit yet. My GP said it was a typical dislocation, but if that were true, I'd be back at full strength by now, right? It's been almost four months."

Dr. McGregor is drying his hands and rubbing them together. On Anthony's shoulder they are warm as he pokes and prods.

"So you don't trust Dr. Burgess? I wonder if we should operate."

"What? What's wrong with it? I can't have an operation now!" A surge of panic runs from Anthony's shoulder throughout every cell in his body. That would mean months and cost him his entire senior season.

"Relax, you don't need an operation," Dr. McGregor chuckles, as he moves back to Anthony's file and is flipping pages, nodding, and murmuring to himself. "What position do you play?"

"Shortstop. What can you do to speed up the recovery?"

Dr. McGregor turns and looks Anthony in the eyes. "Well, we have a couple of options. First, tell me about the PT regimen Dr. Burgess suggested. How's the swimming?"

Anthony shifts. "I haven't swam. I hate swimming."

"Okay, resistance bands? The exercises? How often do you do those?" The doctor goes back to thumbing through the chart as he asks.

"Sometimes," Anthony answers honestly. "They hurt like crazy. I know there's something damaged in there," he says, motioning toward his shoulder, even though Dr. McGregor isn't looking at him. "I've heard there are some medicines that speed up the healing process. Strengthen the ligaments and muscles and whatnot." He gathers his courage. "Can't you prescribe me some anabolic steroids for this? Won't that help? I don't have time to wait." He knows a couple of the football players at his school claim to have taken them to recover from knee injuries. They were back on the field in less than two weeks.

Dr. McGregor looks up from the chart, but not at Anthony. He gazes out the window into the parking lot, watches the branches of the old Douglas fir tree wave in the winter breeze. A few browning needles dislodge and flit toward the earth, tumbling onto windshields and dancing on the grasses below.

He turns back to Anthony with a serious expression. "That's quite a request, young man," he says, looking over his glasses.

Anthony swallows hard. "I'm not looking to cheat," he says, trying to act confident. "I don't need an unfair advantage. I just need to heal."

Dr. McGregor maintains eye contact longer than Anthony feels comfortable. His eyes shift to his right shoulder. "You could mask it in case they tested me, right?" he asks, still gazing at his wounded wing. "It wouldn't be that big of a deal. Just enough to get me back on the field."

"Stay put," replies the doctor. "I'll get what you're looking for." He steps out of the examination room, closing the door behind him as he whisks down the hallway.

Finally, thinks Anthony. A feeling of joy and nervousness fills him. His skin tingles. Could this be the answer he is looking for? This Dr. McGregor is all right.

The two minutes before the doctor's return seem like an eternity. When he comes back in, Dr. McGregor bellows, "Stand up. Turn toward the mirror." Anthony follows orders, noticing the small packet of pills the doctor places on the counter beside him.

They are standing side-by-side looking in the mirror. For the first time in a while, Anthony feels a little self-conscious about his body. Since he hasn't been working out, he is even skinnier than usual.

"Anabolic steroids can indeed help your muscles heal after a traumatic physical event like a dislocation," says Dr. McGregor, eyes meeting Anthony's through the mirror. "They can also help you gain muscle mass and strength, paired with a smart weight-training regimen." His hands poke at Anthony's chest. "You see, it's difficult to see where your pectoral muscles are. You're a rail. I can get you the medicine to bulk you up a bit. Might even get you to put one or two over the fence this year," he says as he raises a furry eyebrow.

Anthony stands taller, trying to flex his chest muscles. Dr. McGregor is right. He is a beanpole.

"I can also get you some HGH. Human growth hormone. We can stack it with the steroids to give you all sorts of additional testosterone, which will help with strength and size. Not only will you heal your shoulder faster, you'll become a beast. Stronger, bigger, faster, more powerful. You're already quite talented; this ought to put you over the top. Sound good?"

Anthony is in semi-shock. All he could muster was, "Really? How?"

"Your body produces testosterone naturally. We'll just add to that. In incremental doses, coupled with the steroid to help you – like a boost to a growth spurt. What are you, 5-11, 150 pounds?"

"Exactly."

"How does 6-1, 180 sound?" Dr. McGregor's eyes haven't left Anthony's.

"Amazing. Can you mask it? You know, for testing. Just to be safe."

"Sure, that's easy. I have a product that neutralizes the chemical appearance of your urine. Makes the steroid invisible and shows a reduction in your natural testosterone. It won't work for a blood test, though. And I can write the HGH prescription for your father, a kind of anti-aging treatment, so it won't be traced to you. If anyone asks, it's for his hair loss, and so he can keep pitching you batting practice without falling apart, like we all do."

"So how do we do this?" Anthony asks, his excitement building.

"Well, that's not all," said Dr. McGregor. Catching him off-guard, the doctor grabs at Anthony's crotch, squeezing his testicles through his pants.

"What the..." Anthony exclaims.

Dr. McGregor is now looking directly at Anthony, away from the mirror. "These will be gone, though. They'll shrivel up to nothing. You like these?" he says sternly. "And how do you like acne? You're a good-looking kid," he says, removing his hand and grabbing Anthony's jaw with it. "Perpetual acne, terrible scarring, all over your face and neck and back and chest. Maybe even on your legs and cock. How does that sound?"

Anthony, wide-eyed, feels his pulse quicken. *What the heck is going on?*

"Ever heard of '*roid rage*?" the doctor's voice is louder now. "You like losing control of your emotions? Crying, screaming, angry, sad, confused all the time? Unable to maintain normal human relationships? We can make sure that happens, no doubt about it."

"Wait," Anthony stammers. "You said..."

"Right," answers Dr. McGregor, releasing Anthony's jaw and putting his clipboard on the counter. His hands relax in his white doctor's coat. "There are no shortcuts, son. Not without terrible, terrible consequences."

Anthony breathes audibly, his lower lip quivering. This is unexpected and quite uncomfortable. He can't speak.

"You want bigger muscles? You want to heal that shoulder? You want to be the shortstop for the Boston Red Sox? I have a prescription for you. It's simple." He takes a stylus out of his chest pocket and picks up the tablet from beside Anthony's chart. Scribbling a bit in the silence, he then turns the tablet toward Anthony.

On it, Anthony reads: *Do your exercises. Go swimming. 200 pushups a day. Pain is temporary.*

Anthony looks up at his doctor, tears threatening his eyes. This appointment has taken a turn for the worse.

"Look, son," says Dr. McGregor, removing his glasses and meeting the teenager's gaze. "Rehabbing a dislocated shoulder isn't easy, I know. I can write you a prescription for a stronger NSAID – it'll help with the pain, but it won't make it go away. You're going to have to tough it out a bit if you want to play baseball next month. I have a feeling you've avoided the exercises long enough. It's time to soldier forth."

The doctor sighs. "If your arm hurts, lift legs. Work on your core strength, endurance, flexibility, agility. There's a ton you *can* do if you can see your way past what you *can't* do. You're young, and the sky is the limit. No shortcuts."

Anthony blinks hard, shifting his focus to the window, the framed painting of two sumo wrestlers locked in combat, his phone buzzing with incoming texts on the chair, the countertop, anything and everything but Dr. McGregor's scrutiny. "What are those pills?" he asks, nodding to the pills Dr. McGregor had brought into the room.

"Expired samples of an anti-nausea medication," he says, picking them up and smiling. "They're a prop. You're not the first kid who got confused about what's important."

"I can't even do one pushup right now. My shoulder is killing me."

"Hey, look here," Dr. McGregor says. Their eyes meet one final time. "You can, and you must. Pain doesn't stop us. It's just a message. Once you strengthen all those muscles in and around your shoulder, you'll feel a ton better. Tell your mom and dad hello for me. And good luck this season. I hope to get out there to watch you play once or twice."

With that, the doctor picks up the useless pill packet, grabs the chart, puts it under his arm with the tablet, and disappears out the door. Anthony collapses into a chair and lets the tears loose.

CHAPTER 14

It takes a couple days for the aftershocks of his doctor's visit to dissipate. During that time, he mostly avoids talking with his parents about the awkward and emotional appointment with Dr. McGregor. Besides, he has a feeling they already know. They always seem to know everything about what is going on in his life, even as he tries to maintain a tiny bit of privacy.

The simple answer he's given them when asked what Dr. McGregor had said is, "Go swimming and fight through the pain. Pain is just weakness leaving the body, all that crap. All those docs are hacks, but thanks anyway. They probably own stock in the aquatic center."

Amanda and Drew simply exchange a bewildered look as Anthony busies himself with whatever it is he's started doing.

The long winter promised by the Old Farmer's Almanac and reiterated by the meteorologists is verified by Mother Nature. Over the first two weeks of February, the constant Oregon drizzle meets with a cold front, causing sleet, black ice, and a handful of overnight snowfalls.

As a result, Anthony has to drive a bit more cautiously than usual. Even with four-wheel drive, the roads are treacherous, and with the sun rising late and setting early, there isn't much daylight to work with. On ordinary school days, he heads out before sunrise, and by the time he leaves the batting cage in the evening, the sun has long since abandoned its post.

Several of his teammates begin to converge upon the indoor facilities after school, readying themselves for the upcoming season. No one likes practicing baseball inside, but with frost on the field, ice in the air, and aluminum bats, they really don't have an option.

Kai, Scottie, and Reggie, all of whom don't play basketball, swim, or wrestle, are regulars, just as Anthony suspected. Fellow senior teammates José, Johnny, and Adam, all better known for their pitching than their hitting, throw bullpen sessions off a rigged-up pitcher's mound in a portion of an old, deserted weight room. On occasion, teammates drop-in for an hour or so to connect and work off the rust. A few younger kids gather around the cages, but end up getting their hacks off the tees, since the senior boys dominate the pitching machine.

Back in his element and surrounded by all things baseball, Anthony summons his nerve and steels himself back toward his mission, finally taking advantage of the rehab regimen prescribed by Dr. Burgess. This includes two swimming-pool workouts a week, which Anthony completes before school on Tuesdays and Thursdays, intentionally selected because his dad's lap swims are routinely scheduled on Mondays, Wednesdays, and Fridays. Though they, and the weight and resistance work, are painful, he is gaining strength and mobility. The pushups are excruciating, but with each one he envisions hitting a fly ball deep over the right-field fence, and he battles through it.

Flexing in the locker-room mirror, he agrees with Dr. McGregor's assertion that he is, indeed, a rail. *Nothing a few hundred pushups can't fix,* he tells himself. Plus, pushups had been Ted Williams' workout of choice – and that beanpole was the greatest hitter who ever lived. He drops and gives himself five. Yesterday was four, so it's progress.

In the cages, his is a different story. While his teammates work on making solid contact and lining the ball back up the middle, Anthony's limited shoulder mobility allows him only to work on his bunting. From the right side and the left, he squares, trying to *catch* the ball on the bat, dropping it gently on the cage's artificial-turf floor. Then, imagining game speed, he practices dropping bunts down both baselines, finishing with 10 attempts at *dragging* from the left side or *pushing* from the right, imagining his speed gaining him some timely base hits.

When the basketball teams aren't in the gym, the boys create a makeshift infield and fungo each other hundreds of grounders. Surprisingly, the smooth wood floor doesn't provide simple, predictable bounces, as the raised laces of the baseballs force the fielders to adapt with quick hands, full concentration, and proper footwork. Although Coach Shepard isn't officially allowed to have contact with his players until the season begins on February 20, he is often spotted in the gym, yelling feedback from the bleachers and pretending to be screaming at whatever videos Coach Schneider has set up on his tablet, just in case league officials are watching.

Anthony works tirelessly on getting his feet in proper position to field each ground ball and make a quick throw. On every grounder, he imagines the situation, the baserunners, the score, and the number of outs. He always has a plan for what he'll do on each play, depending on the speed and location of the ball when he gets it. The new glove he'd gotten from his parents for his last birthday, his first-ever true infielder's glove, is getting broken in nicely. His arm, however, is not yet ready to be tested, so after each grounder, he gently tosses the ball behind him, underhanded, to a sophomore named Dave, who in turn fires them to whichever base Anthony orders him to.

Kai, who takes the liberty of hitting the majority of the grounders, calls across the gym, "Anthony, man. When y'all gonna start throwing? Will I have to strike everybody out this year, so they don't hit 'em to you?"

"If you were capable, that'd be great! But I'll be fine," Anthony yells back, making a slick stop on a backhand. He tosses the ball to Dave and watches his throw short-hop Stephen, the big brute of a first baseman, who scoops it up nicely.

"Should we get a DF for you? A designated fielder? Maybe you can DH this year," teases Scottie, who gloves another grounder from his spot at third base. "Has anyone ever bunted his way through an entire season?" He tosses a laser beam to first, where Stephen takes the throw on the fly.

That is enough. He'll show them.

It is time.

"Watch what I've got. Bring it, Texas!"

Kai hits a rocket two-hopper at him, and despite a funny lace-aided hop, Anthony fields it cleanly. He takes two steps toward first, clenches his jaw, and rears back to throw. This is a motion he hasn't used in months, so the result is a half-underhand, half-sidearm, exaggerated wrist-flick as he flings the ball at Stephen. More accurately, he lobs it. Two bounces later, it reaches its target.

The entire gym is silent. Anthony grits his teeth and gently shakes his arm. Maybe they'd thought he'd been exaggerating his pain, that he was milking it. That settles that theory. At least half the eyes in the infield turn to Coach Shepard in the stands. His eyes are wide, mouth slightly open. Less than two weeks to go, and his star shortstop can't throw.

CHAPTER 15

"We're having dinner with Jay Young and his wife on Sunday," Amanda Sumner announces from her seat on the bike trainer set up in the utility room as her husband carries a load of dirty clothes to the laundry. Amanda is concurrently engaged in a simulated ride up one of the French Alps on her training program and tinkering with lesson plans on a second tablet, both set up over her handlebars to create a sort of tech station for workouts. This is how she spends her weekend mornings.

"That's tomorrow," Drew says, dropping the basket on the floor and picking up Peaches, their speckled cat. She purrs in appreciation. "What's the occasion? And when are we having our Valentine's Day dinner?"

"Tuesday, dear," smiles Amanda, breathing heavy through a treacherous climb. She rises from her seat and pedals upright, legs straining against the computer-generated incline.

Drew pets Peaches while he waits for the rationale for this dinner. They rarely go out to eat, especially with other couples. Whether it was a budgetary decision or a byproduct of being engulfed by the busyness of day-to-day life or the natural evolution of marriage, he couldn't say. Alternating his focus between the bike's spinning wheels and his own midsection, he frowns. "Maybe I'll catch the next ride," he whispers to the cat. Then, to Amanda, "Hey, is there a downhill program for that thing?"

"Jay is our school psychologist," she says as she retreats to the saddle, ignoring his comment. "He's there twice a week, and he's been a major proponent of our school's social-emotional learning efforts – and last week he led a workshop on trauma-informed practice during our faculty-meeting time. Brilliant guy." She takes a towel off the handlebars and wipes it across her brow. Even her orange headband is taking a beating. *Tough Mudder*, it reads, from one of her many physical adventures. *Yeah, no kidding she's a tough mother.*

"And we're having dinner with them why, because I need therapy?"

"Well," breathes Amanda, now increasing her cadence with a lower resistance, indicating a lesser grade on the biking program. "I think he might offer us some insight into how to best support Anthony."

"You mean *deal* with him? Grumpy monkey." Drew says, placing Peaches gently on the sofa. At twelve years old, her paws have really started getting sensitive.

Amanda watches her husband with the cat and sighs. Or maybe she just breathes heavily as part of her workout.

"He's had a clinical practice for years; he works with kids every day at my school and the high schools. I just think it might be worth bending his ear a bit. I already prepped him a little, and he said he'd think about some questions to ask us."

"Oh, he'll ask *us* the questions? Great." *Isn't that the opposite of how advice is doled out?* He returns to the laundry.

CHAPTER 16

The following night, Drew and Amanda meet Jay and Sandy Young at Mazzi's, a nearby Italian place. Known for its thick rock interior walls, red tablecloths, and open fire oven, the restaurant is a local institution. The four have a seat in the corner of the back dining room, two candles lighting their discussion. The conversation covers many topics as the couples get to know each other.

The Sumners cheer after hearing that Sandy is an elementary school counselor, just beginning her first year in the school district after working for a dozen years as a doula. Her hair is cropped short, and she displays a mischievous smile on several occasions, giving the impression that she can handle unruly youngsters just fine. Jay, graying at the temples, has a kind face and the disposition one might expect from a therapist. Calmly and deliberately, he sips his water and asks, "So tell me how I can help you with Anthony."

"We are hoping you'll be able to answer that question," Drew laughs.

Amanda smiles and put her palms together. "Before we dig too deeply into his – and our – psyche, I want to make sure you're comfortable with this, Jay. I mean, we work together, and we're friends. If this conversation puts you at all in an awkward position, professionally, just let us know, and we'll either change course or make an appointment to meet in your office."

Jay's gentle smile assuages her concerns. "That's a fair disclaimer, Amanda, thank you. Yes, I consider this a conversation between friends. I'm happy to help." Sandy elbows him gently. "*We're* happy to help, however we can. We know raising kids is hard work, and if we can help you feel more confident, great!"

Amanda and Drew both exhale their "Thank you" at the same moment.

"So," Jay says, putting his glass down and holding both hands around it. "What do you want? For him and for your family. What are your goals?"

Drew and Amanda share a sideways glance at each other. Goals. Isn't that where everything begins? "Well," Drew starts. "We want him to be happy. Productive. Successful. You know, so he can take care of us when we're old and demented."

"Try to stay serious for a bit," Amanda playfully scolds her husband. "Yes, happy, productive, successful. We want him to enjoy life, to be healthy, and to spend his life doing what he wants to do. Like we do, right?" Drew nods.

Jay hums pensively, the candlelight flickering in his deep eyes. Sandy sits quietly next to him, listening intently. "And what does that look like, with just a couple months 'til graduation?" he asks.

The waitress comes to take their order, which buys the Sumners a couple extra minutes to corral their thoughts. After the meals are requested, all eyes are on Drew.

"Well," he says again. "He's all about baseball. Wants to go pro. He's looking at colleges that have strong baseball programs, so he can get drafted."

"And how do you feel about that goal?" asks Jay thoughtfully. "Is that his goal or yours?"

Drew goes to speak but stops. He frowns a bit and turns to Amanda. Best for her to answer this.

Amanda took the cue. "Here's the deal, Jay. Like I was telling you this week, Anthony believes he's going to be a professional baseball player. He believes this with all of his soul. Or at least that's how he presents himself. He hurt his shoulder a couple of months ago, and it's tormented him all winter. Now, baseball season is right around the corner, and he might not be ready. I guess the real question that we have to ask is this: even if he's healthy, is he good enough to go pro? I mean," she pauses, looking at Drew, who is nodding in agreement so far. "He's not a big, strong kid. He's fast, and he's talented. What if he's not good enough? Then what? He puts every waking thought into being a professional shortstop. How do we do this? How do we support him in his dream, be realistic, and help him to have something to fall back on if – shoot, *when* – it doesn't work out with baseball?"

It is good to say it aloud. Amanda and Drew both feel a giant burden release from their shoulders, and they simultaneously look across the table at their guests. The experts.

"Ah, yes, the million-dollar questions. How do we help our kids prepare for the *other* path? The backup plan."

Sandy responds by raising her eyebrows and nodding once. "Plan B."

Their starter salads arrive just then, house greens in carved wooden bowls, piled high with radishes, sliced red onions, cherry tomatoes, baby carrots, and sunflower seeds. For the next few moments it is just forks, subtle crunching, and intermittent nods of approval.

Jay returns to the conversation as he swallows a mouthful of salad. "Interesting statistic: Across the nation, a little over 5% of high school ballplayers will play in college. Of those, about 10% will be drafted. In that lot, only about 10% ever make it to *The Show*."

Drew is doing the math in his head. "So about one out of every 2,000 high school kids will make it? That's not so bad, right?" he turns to Amanda, whose brow has furrowed.

Jay continues, "That's zero-point-zero-zero-zero-five percent. So 99.9995 percent of high school players never crack a major league roster. Those are just the stats."

After staring at his salad for a minute, Drew looks curiously at Jay, who simply shrugs. "I'm a huge baseball fan. Always have been. And this isn't the first time this scenario has come up in conversation."

"Okay," Drew says, pawing absentmindedly at his bowl. "There are about 20 kids on a team. We have 10 teams in our league. That's 200 kids. So, statistically speaking, it'd take 10 of our leagues to find one pro-bound player? That's incredible. There aren't 10 leagues in this state. Good lord."

Sandy smiles and waves her fork gently. "You both agreed you wanted your son to be happy, productive, and successful. Sounds like you value a life of joy, contribution to society, and self-sufficiency. You're both teachers, right? So that's not surprising. What else do you value, as a family?"

Amanda and Drew exchange looks again, and when Amanda nods, Drew responds. "Well, you're right, Sandy. We're both teachers, so we value education. That doesn't mean we want Anthony to be a teacher like us. In fact, he often says he's unhappy with his teachers. Not all of them, but some. I personally think he's just disappointed in them, that he expects more from them. You know, because he has such great role modeling at home."

When no one laughs, he continues, "We want him to get a good education, learn to think critically, know enough about the world to help make his life better, to make the world a better place – leave it better than he found it."

"So what does that mean for you and your son?" presses Jay.

"We want him to go to college. Baseball or not," Drew responds. "Right, hon?"

Amanda nods. "If he can be in that top 5% that play in college, great. But what if he's not good enough for college ball? What if he doesn't get a scholarship? We have some money socked away, just like we did for Jenna, but it's not enough for four years. In fact, Jenna's accounts are just about gone, and she wants to go abroad next semester to Barcelona. We'll be scratching as it is."

"There are plenty of smaller grants, and we can always take out loans. Going to college has always been an expectation in our household," states Drew. "The money part we can figure out. I think we're worried about how to handle him these last couple of months of high school."

"Especially if he's part of the 95%," Amanda shrugs. "And Plan B is most likely his reality."

Jay smiles. "Well, parenting is no picnic, that's for sure," he said. "Like Sandy was saying, emphasize your values. Talk with him about what's important to you as parents, about what your family stands for. What's non-negotiable, and what's up for debate. Ensure equal air-time for discussions about baseball, his schooling, politics, astronomy, saving for retirement, connecting with family members that live elsewhere, doing chores, maybe even volunteering at a shelter or your local church."

"So it's not so hyper-focused on baseball, huh?" nods Drew. Amanda nods too.

___

"And one more thing. Really important," says Sandy, as the waitress arrives with a giant tray. Manicotti for Sandy, a steaming heap of spaghetti with meatballs for Drew and Amanda, and Jay raises his eyebrows in anticipation of his ravioli in vodka sauce. "Tell him you believe in him and that you love him. Often. Unconditionally, and frequently without context. Not just when he hits a game-winning hit or makes a super play. Just because."

"Like in that workshop you led last week, Jay. In the book we read, the authors were talking about praising effort and attitude more than results. And everyone appreciates unconditional love," Amanda says, putting a hand on her husband's shoulder.

Eyes on his spaghetti, Drew responds, "Yup. Love you, honey."

SPRING

CHAPTER 17

On Monday morning, February 20, a rare snowstorm blankets the entire Willamette Valley, canceling school throughout the district and, by association, the first official day of baseball practice. Anthony and his teammates are infuriated. Blowing up each other's phones, they conspire to meet at the batting cage in the gym at 2:00 anyway, and Anthony volunteers to call Coach Shepard to be sure he can meet them there.

"Can't do it, Sumner," says his coach over the phone. "No four-wheel drive. And I live way the heck south of town. Forecast calls for higher temps tomorrow. One day won't be the end of the world. How's your arm?"

"Better," Anthony answers honestly. "Saw the doc last week, and he said I could start some light swings this week. Maybe play catch up to 10 feet with a wiffle ball. I'll be ready come game-day, Coach, not to worry. I'll still dominate!"

"Circle March 14 on your calendar, Sumner. That's opening day at Sheldon High School. Just got confirmation of a home-and-home with them. Don't know why they waited this long. We'll play 'em again at Vineyard Mountain on the 20th. You're going to need both arms by then. Got it?"

"Yes, sir!" Anthony looks at the calendar on his phone. In all his excitement to count down to the first practice, he hadn't even thought about the first game. *22 days. It's happening. It's finally here.* His mind pictures the red "3" scribbled on the whiteboard in Mrs. A's classroom. He's going to have to start a new log.

"Oh, and Rooster, one more thing. Since I'm not gonna be there today, someone's gotta talk 'em up. You up for the challenge?"

Anthony imagines Coach Shepard's pep talks to the team. Often energetic, sometimes profane, always inspirational. "Roger that, Coach." He clicks off his phone, grabs his bag and a granola bar, and runs out to the truck.

At the cage, Scottie, the third baseman and *de facto* team captain, has organized the varsity players into groups and set up a series of rotations. Like a mother hen, or a future head coach, he clucks orders and assigns duties to all the boys. Together, they prep all the gear, inventory the balls, bats, helmets, and uniforms, and practice their intricate high-five routines in between.

Anthony issues a sharp two-fingered whistle and gets their attention. The teammates assemble in a huddle just outside the cages, eyes and ears perked. Anthony takes them in. They have arrived on time, in shape, attitudes in check, ready to work. He clears his throat.

"I'm not one for public speaking," he starts.

"Since when?" Someone chirps, followed by guffaws and more high-fives.

Like Mrs. A, Anthony waits until the silence falls.

"This is it, boys," he announces. "Senior season for most of us. All the hard work we've put in for the last however many years, all the practices, the drills, the monotonous day-by-day routines, all the long spring days at the ballpark, all of it. It all comes down to this."

Silent fist-bumps; 13 of the 17 varsity players are seniors, though just two – Anthony and José, the talented, hulking pitcher – have endured both the dismal varsity seasons prior to last year's .500 campaign. Anthony is going to leave nothing to chance. He will lead them into battle, even if he has to bunt every time and learn to throw left-handed.

Channeling his best Coach Shepard, he continues, now just a tad louder and surer of himself. "Nothing is more important than how we approach this season. This team is special, guys, just look around. We've got talent up the wazoo, we can hit, we can field, we can pitch, and there ain't nobody that can run like us, and you know what'll make the difference between us winning and us losing?"

Eyes dart about.

"Obviously, the starting catcher." Reggie's voice is unmistakable, and the boys burst into raucous laughter as he flexes his muscles and nods emphatically at them.

"Right," Anthony regroups. "And there's even more than that, if you can believe it."

As the laughter subsides, he continues. "We are a team. If we stay together, if we work together, if we press each other, if we support each other, then…" He pauses again, this time for effect. "There's no limit to what we can do."

A rumble begins to shake the floor of the gym.

"This year," Anthony says as the rumble grew.

"This team!" he yells.

Thunder.

"This moment!" he screams. "On three. One, two, three:"

"KATN!" Comes the call they'd learned from Coach Shepard, and the gym bursts into a cascade of hopping, bear hugs, and another round of choreographed high-fives. Moments later, the players break into groups for hitting, infield scenarios, bullpen sessions, and footwork and fitness.

It is good to see Nick again, besides their daily connection in government class and lunch once a week or so. He's just finished setting the school's record for assists on the basketball court, and because they had lost in the league playoffs that weekend, he and a couple others are now free to focus on baseball. And, hopefully, some brutal battles on their video game systems on the weekends.

For now, it is all business.

Nick and Anthony are paired in a footwork drill with José and Johnny, who are equally inseparable, buddies on and off the baseball field. Alternating between the rope ladder, a series of step boxes, and a jump rope, the young student-athletes work like it means something. In years past, Anthony had been disappointed with the work ethic and the lack of preparation his teammates had shown. The older players hadn't set a very good example – playing mostly for kicks, not to win. This crew has established a different tone. They are sweating.

Between stations, the two best friends chat a bit.

Then Nick drops a bomb. "This weekend, my folks and I decided that I'll be going to UC-Davis this fall. I accepted online yesterday."

"Whoa, seriously?" asks Anthony. That was one of the dozen or so schools he had applied to also. "Congrats, man. That's awesome. What about baseball?"

"Not sure yet," Nick confides. "Their coach says I could play there, and I left a message with him yesterday too. That's not what drove the decision, though."

"How come you didn't tell me?"

"I'm telling you. Just made the call yesterday. It's got a great academic reputation, it's in the California sun, and if I can play baseball, great. If not, no hair off my back." Nick grabs a Gatorade out of his bag.

"Why do you use that expression? It's gross," laughs Anthony. "Well I'm happy for you. Davis will be great. I haven't heard from their coach yet myself, and I'm not even sure if I've been accepted there, so I'm probably heading elsewhere to play ball. And like I said, I'll get you tickets no matter where it is."

They high-five and return to their drills. Outside, the snow has stopped.

CHAPTER 18

With the gift of school being canceled, Amanda Sumner spends the majority of her snow-day, as most teachers do, with papers and folders and books spread across the dining-room table, her laptop open with tabs set for her electronic gradebook, lesson-plan template, and a half-dozen websites feeding her information about upcoming topics and resources to enhance her lessons. She takes it in stride and actually relishes the opportunity to get *ahead* of her endless to-do list for a bit. At this time of the school year, with her evaluation and the ever-present standardized tests looming, the pace of things in the schoolhouse tends to accelerate.

In between analyzing the plans for a week of full-immersion activities set in a makeshift market and reaching for a pile of quizzes to grade, her phone buzzes. She recognizes the prefix as a school district number, so she picks up.

"Hi, Mrs. Sumner?"

"Speaking."

"It's Lynette Jamison over at Vineyard Mountain. How are you?"

Amanda recognizes the voice and name that belong to one of the high school's guidance counselors. "I'm good, thanks Lynette. What in the world are you doing at work today? Isn't the district policy that only essential personnel report on snow days? How'd they rope you into that?"

Lynette laughs across the line. "I bet I'm doing exactly what you're doing, except from my office."

Amanda looked at her piles of work and sighs.

"I actually was almost here when they made the decision to cancel today, so I just stayed. I've gotten a ton done, too. It's amazing how much easier it is to check all these boxes when there's no one around!"

Amanda returns the laughter. "It's not as much fun, though. So what box can I help you check today?"

"Well," started Lynette. "I'm following up with all our seniors, going through transcripts, checking on graduation requirements, making sure they're all on target, and I've come to Anthony's name."

"Just tell me he's going to graduate," Amanda sits back in her chair and gazes out the kitchen windows. They need cleaning.

"Yup, on track to graduate. He's done just fine." There's a pause. "I just don't have his post-graduation plan yet. We need to update the database with the schools he's applied to, where he's going, what kind of scholarships he's gotten, what he thinks he might want to study, that sort of thing."

"Oh, okay, is that something he should have already done by now?" Amanda asks.

"Most kids meet with me for 10-15 minutes at some point in the fall or winter, others just turn in the form. Either way, as long as we have an idea of what his plans are."

"Want me to send him to you tomorrow morning, then?"

"That would be great. Thanks a lot, that'll really help."

"You bet. Go home at a reasonable time today, enjoy this rare treasure!"

After they hang up, Amanda closes her laptop, leans forward, and rests her chin on her hands. They've just been dancing around Anthony's plans for his future, and with graduation just a couple of months away, that *future is* quickly becoming the *present.*

Drew Sumner arrives home a little earlier than normal. He's canceled his office hours and told the department secretary he wants to get home while it is still light, for his own driving safety, when in reality he and Amanda had traded texts all afternoon about Anthony's post-graduation plan. Or lack thereof. The urgency of Jay and Sandy Young's *Plan B* conversation has just ticked up. They have to talk.

"Hi honey," he sings as he enters the front door.

"I'm in here," Amanda calls from the dining room.

Drew finds her seated, the table cleared except for her laptop. They kiss, he drapes his coat over a chair at the table, and steps into the kitchen. "I'm gonna grab a beer. You want anything?"

"No, thanks. I'll have wine with dinner." She is clicking on her laptop.

Drew takes a beer out of the fridge, screws off the top, takes a swig, and sits down at the table. "You've got that look in your eye," he says, smiling. "What are we gonna do with Anthony?"

Amanda laughs gently without removing her eyes from the computer. "Well," she starts. "The call from Lynette, who is Anthony's counselor, got me thinking. So I've been looking at our finances, our FAFSA application, and Anthony's 529 account to see what this is going to look like for us."

"You mean how it's going to sap us dry?" Drew says, taking another gulp. He grabs a napkin off the hutch behind him and places the bottle on it on the table.

"I'd love it if you took this seriously," Amanda says, looking up for the first time.

"Okay, I am taking it seriously."

"Right. I know how you like to joke about things that are hard to deal with. I think this deserves our undivided, uncomedic attention."

"Sorry," Drew says. "So what have you found out, detective?"

"Scoot over here," Amanda says, and Drew shuffles his chair next to hers. "We've socked away some money for college in his 529 account, and that'll help. If he goes out of state, it's not going to last two years. He hasn't applied for any scholarships, and no one's banging on the door offering him anything, which means we're going to be on the hook for quite a bit of money over the next few years."

"Right," Drew says. "Just like with Jenna. That comes with the territory. He'll have to apply for loans or get some scholarships."

Amanda sighs. "Jenna's got her two scholarships and she's going to graduate early, remember? Her loans aren't even going to be $5000. With Anthony, we could be looking at ten times that amount. Do you want him to graduate with huge college loans to pay off?"

"Well, no, of course not," Drew says, reaching across the table to reclaim his beverage. "But loans are part of the experience, right? It's kind of expected. I wish you and I made more money, so we could just pay for it, but we decided to be educators instead."

"Agreed," Amanda sighs again, glancing at the bag of homework at her feet.

"Anyway, what do you want me to do about it?" Drew asks.

"This is an *us* situation, dear," Amanda says, exasperated. She clasps his hand in hers. "Like Jay and Sandy said the other night, *we* need to have a conversation with Anthony about his future. What is his realistic plan for baseball? Where does he want to go to college? Can we talk him into an in-state university? OSU offers amazing deals for children of faculty, maybe he'd consider staying home. And for heaven's sake let's get back online and look at scholarships that are out there. He's been a good student, he must qualify for something, right?"

"And tell him we love him, he's capable of doing anything he wants, and how important it is to have options. There's no sense in closing doors before they're even opened. Gotcha." Drew leans over, so they are shoulder-to-shoulder. "Curious, though. There's all Anthony's talk about going pro, but we haven't heard one word about a college scholarship for baseball."

"Mmm-hmmm. I think it's worth asking him about it."

"Absolutely. Sounds like a dinner chat." Drew stands up. "Better finish this beer, then," he laughs, grabbing the bottle and swigging it down on his way to the kitchen.

CHAPTER 19

When Anthony returns home from the makeshift practice, supper is already on the table, and his parents are seated. His spirits are high, and he coasts into the dining room whistling. "So," he says. "This is what happens when we all get snowed out, huh? I still go to work, and you two have time to make a nice dinner and sit all cheerfully and worry-free at the table? What is this, chicken pot pie? My favorite!" He kisses his mom on the cheek as he dashes by to wash his hands.

Amanda Sumner looks across the table at her husband. He shrugs, "Good practice, I guess. How were the roads?" he calls out.

Anthony shuts off the faucet. Drying his hands, he responds, "Not bad. Most of the snow is melted by now. I'm sure we'll be back in school tomorrow. And we should have a real practice, though today's was pretty good. Longer than it would have been, since we were in charge."

Sitting down, Anthony surveys the scene. "Wait a minute. This is the sort of creepy dinner we have when you have bad news. What happened? Is Peaches okay?"

His parents share a glance, smiles escaping their lips. "Nothing," answers Drew. "The cat is fine, and like you said, we sat around all day doing nothing, so we cooked. I mean, besides me going to the office and your mom doing a ton of planning and grading. Everything's fine, sunshine. Dig in."

Anthony looks warily at his folks and begins eating. After regaling them with tales from the player-led workout, he shares, "Oh, and Nick said he's decided on UC-Davis. No scholarship or anything, not even a promise of playing baseball. That's crazy, isn't it? He's good enough. He should have waited."

"Why do you say that?" asks his mom.

"Cause I'm waiting. I was hoping we'd go somewhere together. You know, keep the 1-2 combination alive and rolling. We work well together, and we're unstoppable back-to-back. This is really good, by the way," he says, stuffing more food into his mouth.

Amanda smiles faintly. "Glad you like it."

Drew returns the conversation to Anthony's best friend. "Aren't you happy for Nick? He's going to attend a really good school. He'll get a good education, be prepared for whatever life has to offer. We're proud of him for making that choice."

Anthony stops chewing. He cocks his head toward his father. "It was too quick," he says. "If I did that, it'd be a lame decision. Would you be proud of me for that? For giving up on my dream?"

Drew exhales. "That's not what I'm saying. For Nick, that's great. We don't know what your future holds yet. And no matter what you decide, we'll be proud of you. We love you, son."

Anthony still hasn't resumed chewing. Now he does so, shaking his head. "What does that mean, 'whatever you decide'?"

"Well," Drew continues. "Wherever you go to college. What you study. Whether you play baseball there or not, you know. You have a lot of options."

Anthony's head spins. "Whether or not I play baseball? Is there a question about that?"

Amanda interjects, starting, "What your father's trying to say is, you have a lot to offer the world. You're smart, funny, talented at a lot of things. You can make the world a better place. Like your dad always says…"

Anthony finishes the line: "Leave the world better than you found it. Right. Don't you think the world would be a better place with me at shortstop in Beantown?" He bobs his eyebrows, taking a gulp of water.

"You don't even have an offer for a scholarship to college, son," Drew says, exasperated.

Anthony's eyes say everything for him. The table is silent.

Amanda watches Anthony carefully, spotting a crack in his uber-confident protective shield. He's not the little boy he once was, and he's not a man yet, either. He's somewhere in the middle, straddling the line, pushing away with one arm and reaching back with the other, craving independence while yearning for security.

Her gaze then shifts to Drew, who is breathing a little heavier than usual. "If a life of baseball brings you joy and success, that's wonderful," he says. "If you end up as a teacher, that's wonderful too. You can…"

"I didn't know you'd lowered your expectations for me that much," Anthony simmers.

Drew considers that comment for a moment, then resumes. "You can do whatever you want to do, if you put your mind to it and dedicate yourself. Marine biologist, systems analyst for a software firm, actuary, airline pilot. You name it."

Anthony rolls his eyes. "Well, all that is bullcrap, and you know it. I've already named it."

Looking around the table, he states, "I'll clear the table. That'll make the world a better place."

The doorbell rings. Since he was already getting up, Anthony pivots to the front door. It opens before he reaches it.

Barging in come Nick and his boyfriend Simon. Holding up a box, Nick announces, "No homework, it's game night! We brought *Imaginiff*, who's in?"

Simon grabs Nick's arm, halting him in the foyer.

"What?" Nick asks. He notices Anthony's reddened face and stiff demeanor. In the dining room, the Sumners are seated quietly, looking at each other without yet acknowledging their guests.

Simon speaks first. "Okay, so we've interrupted something tense, yes? Do you need a few minutes to pull all this back together, or should we go? Maybe we should go."

Anthony nods over his shoulder. "Ask them. I'm fine to play."

Standing at the table, Drew motions for the boys to join them in the dining room. "Welcome, boys. If you'd like to help clear the table, we can set up shop right here."

Amanda turns and shares a muted smile. "Yes, indeed. And we've got cobbler that just needs to be eaten."

Nick immediately begins clearing the table while Simon coordinates the game setup. Drew and Amanda reposition themselves at the sink, one washing and the other drying the dishes, pots, and pans.

Drew calls over his shoulder to Nick, "So you two braved the roads just to hang out with this bum and his folks, huh? Everything going well at school? Saw your basketball season was pretty good."

"The roads were clear, and yes, thank you. It ended a little too soon, but that's life."

Drew nods. "You in baseball shape?"

"Always. Basketball's a good warm-up."

"It'll be good to have you back in the cages with us," Anthony chimes in. "The 1-2 combo kind of loses its luster when it's only me."

"We coulda used you on the basketball court, buddy."

"Yeah, well, I gotta focus. I've got one shot at this, and I want to get it right."

Simon has opened the game box and is busy setting up the board on the dining room table. "There are five of us, and this game requires eight names. So we need to add three people that we all know."

Amanda has a cupboard open and her mind immediately goes to her daughter, hopefully in the midst of a good night's sleep in Spain. She wonders if her eldest dreams in Spanish yet. "How about Jenna? I think it'd be nice to include her."

Anthony shrugs. "Sure. And since we don't want you to be the only old folks in the game, let's put Nick's parents in there." With setup complete, their game-night commences.

A couple of rounds of the game in, Drew divvies up the cobbler and the rapid clanking of silverware replaces conversation for a while.

"Amazing," compliments Simon. Nods and grunts around the table echo the sentiment.

"Family recipe," Drew says plainly.

"I knew there was something I liked about our family," Anthony laughs to himself, picking up his bowl and licking around the edges. Noticing the looks from around the table, he sheepishly puts the bowl down.

Collecting the bowls and reaching back to set them on the counter, Amanda turns to Nick. "Anthony tells us you've decided on UC-Davis. Congratulations! What made you choose that school?"

"Thank you! And I wanted to go to California. I've had enough of this constant rain, and they've got a good mathematics program. I think I'm going to look at being an accountant or financial planner or do something with investments. I love numbers, and if I can learn in the sunshine, it's a 2-for-1."

"That sounds like a very rational decision," Drew smiles. "And baseball? Is that an option?"

"Not sure," Nick says, looking at Anthony. "They have a decent program, it's Division 1, but there are tryouts in the fall. We'll see."

"And how about you, Simon? What are your plans for next year?" Amanda asks.

"I've got a partial golf scholarship at Sac State," he says. "And that'll be nice, only being about 15 minutes away from this guy," he waves a thumb toward Nick. "What I really want to do is study medicine. Ever since my cousin was diagnosed with leukemia, I've really been interested in pediatric oncology. I'm not going to be a professional golfer, but the scholarship was too much to pass up. And I like sunshine too!"

"Congratulations to you," Drew and Amanda say in unison, and Drew adds, "I'm so sorry to hear about your cousin. Is everything going okay now?"

"She's had some radiation therapy, which they're optimistic about. Too soon to tell. She posts a lot of videos about how she's doing, and my uncle got her an emotional support dog. An Aussie-doodle. The dog's pretty needy, though," he laughs. "I'm not sure which one is supporting the other!"

"She sounds awfully tough. Give her our best when you talk to her, please," Drew offers.

"Thank you, I will. Her strength and experience will give me a little more inspiration to study hard, I think."

The board is cleared and the next round begins.

After Nick and Simon thank their hosts for a fun evening and bid farewell to Anthony, it is just the Sumners in the kitchen.

"That Simon is sure a sweetheart," Amanda smiles. "And a good head on his shoulders. He'll be a great doctor."

"And Nick has always been a stats nut, just like you," Drew nods at Anthony. "Sounds like they both have made some wise decisions for their futures."

Anthony sets his empty glass in the dishwasher. "I get what you're trying to do, and you don't need to worry about me. I've got this under control. And yes, Nick and Simon are smart, and they'll do fine. I just wish Nick had waited for me, so we could go play baseball somewhere together. I think he's good enough, too."

Amanda looks warily at her husband, then ventures forth. "I think it was healthy that they both realize that sports aren't the only path." She pauses, waiting for a reaction. Not getting one, she continues. "All three of you have a ton of potential. It's good to keep an open mind."

"Mom, I've only ever wanted to do one thing. Play baseball. It's not a path, it's destiny."

"Destiny, huh?" Drew raises an eyebrow.

"Of course it is. What, you doubt that?"

"Of course not. Your mom and I were looking at our finances this afternoon, and we have some money saved for your college. We're wondering if you've looked at applying for any scholarships. And do you have some idea of where you want to go? It'll be here before you know it."

"Yeah, I know, but you won't need to worry about all that. Destiny."

"We just don't want you to be disappointed…"

Anthony cuts him off. "Wait, Dad. Seriously, you guys don't get it.

CHASING THE SHOW

Well, I'm out. Thanks for dinner and the game. I guess the fun is over."
Avoiding eye contact, he heads upstairs.

"Why don't you come back and sit down?" calls Amanda.

Anthony changes directions halfway up the stairs.

"Thank you," his mom says.

Pulling his keys out of his pocket, he bounds toward the front door.
"No, you can't just tell me what to do. I have a plan. See you later."

"Where do you think you're going, young man?" Drew demands.

"Out. Just out. Away from this." In a second, the door slams behind
him.

Drew and Amanda look at each other, incredulous. Anthony's truck
rumbles in the driveway, and they hear it back up, turn, and drive away.
"Isn't that what your pal Jay told us to say?" asks Drew, shaking his head.

"Yeah, I think so," says Amanda, quietly. "He might not have been
listening, but I'm sure he heard us. Where do you think he's going?"

"Probably Nick's," Drew says. "I'll call his parents and warn them."

CHAPTER 20

Anthony doesn't go to Nick's. He doesn't really know where to go.
Things had looked so good an hour ago. School had been canceled, which
is always nice. He had spent the day with the guys, they were playing
baseball, the season had begun. Then Nick and Simon drop by for game-
night, but all his parents want to do is talk about college, their plans, and

97

everything except baseball. The only thing that really matters. *They are on something if they think I'm going to sacrifice baseball for college. Man, I don't even like school. And I could be a great teacher? In what world? And gushing about how proud they are of Nick, and Simon for that matter. Where did that come from?*

Absent-mindedly, he drives. A couple of months ago, this would have been a time he'd have sought out Meaghan. While they had been dating, things had been good. And her family was nice. They really liked him and made him feel like a part of their family. But after a little over a year, they'd gotten into a couple of arguments about how they spent their time. Meaghan had wanted to spend it together, and he'd wanted to spend his at the ballfield. It went downhill from there.

Without thinking, he takes a couple of turns. Before he realizes what is happening, he is parking his truck in Elena's driveway.

What snow had accumulated had turned to slush, and his shoes are immediately soaked when he hops out of the truck. Elena must have had her sixth sense operating, for she is running down the walk and gives Anthony a full-speed, two-alarm hug before he even closes the door behind him. Only when he looks down at her beaming smile does he realize she is barefoot.

"What the heck? Aren't you freezing?"

"No way, I'm warmer than I've ever been." The smile on her face provides ample evidence of this truth. He feels her body pressed against his.

Then he looks toward the house. Elena's father is standing in the doorway, scowling. A giant of a man, he fills almost the entire span, north-south and east-west. His downturned mouth stands in stark contrast to

Elena's ecstatic smile. "Um," says Anthony, nodding toward the house.

"Oh, don't worry about him," says Elena. "C'mon, I'll introduce you."

Anthony isn't convinced not to worry, not even after making solid eye contact and engaging in a firm handshake with Mr. Jim Martin – almost too firm, Anthony thinks, as her dad seems to tug to pull him off balance. He grimaces, wondering if the gesture is aimed at his shoulder.

"Hello, young man," says Mr. Martin sternly.

"Good to meet you," Anthony returns, standing tall.

"You planning to take my daughter out? On a school night? You'll have her home by 9."

Anthony swallows hard, and Elena rescues him. "Dad, we're not going anywhere, just a little studying." Then, to Anthony, she calls, "C'mon, let's go."

Nodding to her still-scowling dad, Anthony follows Elena's wet footprints downstairs, where she towels off her feet and sits next to him on the couch. "So what are you doing here?" She smiles, clearly excited about his impromptu visit.

"I'm not really sure."

"Well, talk to me," Elena says sweetly, and curls up next to him. "Want some hot cocoa?"

For the next hour and a half, he spills his guts. She seems so interested, so caring, and so open to hearing everything in his life, he shares it all. The facts all come out of order, the chronology of events in his life disrupted like a shuffled deck of cards, a blur of dates and goals and fears, an emotional tornado of bravado mixed with insecurity and detachment battling with intimacy. He knows what he wants his life to look like, but what if it doesn't materialize? And what if the people in his life don't believe in him as much as he believes in himself? Before he knows what hit him, he is sitting back, tears streaming down his face, and Elena is there, empty cocoa mug still held between her hands as she lets him talk.

CHAPTER 21

The next day it rains like the dickens. That serves two purposes: it washes what was left of the slush and snow away, and it creates massive, muddy puddles all over the baseball field and the practice field just across the creek. So, for the first hour of the initial, official practice of the season, Coach Shepard sits his players down in the locker room, and they talk.

Like most great coaches do, he finds what they all have in common and begins the very deliberate practice of rallying them all toward it. For this group of kids, that goal is simple: win the league championship, then take state. Four years ago, when Coach Shepard first arrived at Vineyard Mountain High School, that goal would have seemed absurd. His first year the team finished 1-23. Then 7-18. Last year was another step up at 12-12, and this year? Coach Shepard looks around the room and takes stock.

Kai Baker, last year's surprise newcomer, had shifted the baseball landscape at the school and single-handedly made the turnaround believable. What the team had needed was a bona fide star, and he was it. Tall, strong, athletic, he looked the part, too. In the last few weeks of the season last year, he'd belted those five homers and helped the team win 8 of its last 10 games. And he could pitch. Boy could he pitch.

The other stud pitcher is José Vazquez, whose giant body and equally large social appetite often overshadow his rocket right arm. From what Coach Shepard hears, it is almost as strong as his desire to go out partying, which is a little bit of a concern. Hopefully he'll maintain his focus during the season. He's touched the low-90s with his fastball, and they'd need that to bring home the crown.

Reggie Robinson, the team's playful catcher, is a stocky, crafty game-caller behind the plate with a wickedly powerful left-handed swing beside it. He keeps the boys loose, as was evidenced by his showing up to the team meeting wearing only his jockstrap. Some of his dance moves had made a few of his teammates uncomfortable, and when Coach Shepard arrived, he'd ordered the young man to don his uniform pants.

At first base is the monstrous Stephen Scott, who would be on varsity for the first time this year. He has a mighty bat when he makes contact, though he struck out a lot in JV last year, and he provides a big target over at first base but has slow feet and tends to let his attention wander. Sometimes it is hard to get him to show any emotion or excitement. But if anyone can put some spring in his step, it's Coach Shepard.

Second base is up for grabs, as sophomores Dave Jorgensen and Marlon Mavis will battle it out. Dave is fast and tactical, while Marlon hits with power and can be erratic on the field. It will be an interesting battle, and Coach Shepard will probably consult with Anthony to determine who will end up as his infield-mate.

Anthony is at shortstop, arm or no arm. Well, that isn't entirely true. If his throwing doesn't take a dramatic turn quickly, perhaps he can survive by hiding Anthony at second base, and moving either Dave or Marlon to short. Anthony is going to be a four-time varsity letterman and a leader on and off the field, and he has a future in this game. His healthy shoulder might be the deciding factor.

Scottie Johnson, the captain and heart and soul of the team, is another no-brainer in the lineup every day. He takes charge whenever necessary, like in yesterday's players-only practice. Coach Shepard appreciates having a player-coach on the roster, and as a football quarterback, Scottie shies away from nothing. His gun of an arm and potent right-handed bat are a deadly combination.

In the outfield, Nick Greene, Anthony's bosom buddy, mans center. He is rabbit-fast and has instincts like no outfielder Coach Shepard has ever seen. Last year he set an Oregon high school mark by recording 12 putouts in center field during a single 7-inning game. A switch-hitter with legitimate baserunning speed and an uncanny eye, he'll bat leadoff.

Corner outfielders are a rotating door. When Kai isn't pitching, he will take one spot. José will take the other if either Johnny, Adam, or Marquis take the hill. After that, it is anyone's guess. Maybe Adam will lead the depth chart, though he is better known for wearing his hat backwards, rapping incessantly, and leading the dugout chants. The roster has it all: hitting, speed, power, pitching, defense…and attitude. Boy, Coach Shepard has never met a group of guys that are as cocky as this bunch. They talk more smack than any team he's ever coached. And this year they'll find out if they can back it up.

What a swan song this will be for him. After 27 years of high school coaching, he'll be hanging up his spikes. He can't wait to get started.

In his wrap-up speech, he tells the boys how excited he is, how thrilled he is to be surrounded by that much talent. Then, conjuring a quote from The Greatest of All Time, Muhammad Ali, he bellows, "Hard work beats talent every time, if talent doesn't work hard." On the white board in the locker room, he writes their goals: *Win league, take state.*

One last look around the room at their faces. So young, so eager. So ready. "Everything *we* do has to lead us toward those goals. Everything." He pauses for emphasis, scanning the room again. In one of the lockers behind them, a cell phone buzzes. "That's a good reminder," Coach Shepard says, motioning in the general direction of the noise. "No phones during baseball. None. No distractions." They all nod.

"Our goals will drive us, and we will drive our goals. And each and every one of you has unique and distinct strengths, a special and important role in helping *us* reach our goals. Think of your own behaviors, your own actions, your own work ethic, and your own attitude. They, too, must lead us directly toward *our* goals. Each of you is critical for *our* survival, *our* success. We are not 17 individuals, we are *one team.* We will win together, or we will lose together."

Anthony feels the eyes of his teammates on him, as Coach Shepard's speech had echoes of Anthony's snow-day practice message woven in. He blushes inwardly.

Coach Shepard simply whispers his permission for the release of testosterone. "Let's go."

The boys bellow, holler, scream, and hoot. The exuberance of promise, the undeniable excitement of the game, the anticipation of competition, the expectation of victory carry them together into the center of the locker room, leaning on one another, punching, hitting, shoving, and hopping noisily on the concrete floor.

"All right!" Screams Coach Shepard. "On three. One, two, three:"

In unison, "KATN!" Their screaming echoes through the hallways as the team stomps and parades upstairs to the gym. The chant has become synonymous with Coach Shepard's pursuit of greatness and his ability to keep an eye on right and wrong on and off the field. It was an acronym: *Kickin' Ass and Takin' Names.*

CHAPTER 22

To the players' dismay, the first several practices are conducted indoors. Yes, baseball is an outdoor game, but in the Willamette Valley of western Oregon in late February, rain dominates the weather pattern. So when the sky clears on a Sunday morning, Nick's phone rings over and over until he finally picks up.

"Yeah?"

"C'mon, man, let's go hit. It's sunny and supposed to get up to 50 degrees today." Anthony's enthusiasm is clearly confused about what time it is.

Groggily, Nick asks, "Can you pitch?"

"Sure," says Anthony. "My arm's doing better, and there's an L-screen at the park so I can move it up a little closer. Should be fine."

Nick grunts an assent, and an hour later they meet at Cottonwood Park, so named for the massive black cottonwoods that line the riverbanks along a two-mile stretch of rose gardens, running paths, and open fields. At over 120 feet tall, these beasts, with their thick trunks, will provide ample shade later in the year, once their triangular leaves come in. For now, they stand proudly over the park, indicating to passers-by where the river might be found.

The frost has mostly burned off by the time Anthony and Nick arrive, leaving just enough dew on the grass to show their footprints as they walk. At the north end of the park is a softball field, a common meeting ground for these two boys over the years, as they honed their batting skills and emptied bucket after bucket of baseballs. Oh, the blisters and calluses they'd collected from these batting-practice sessions. But they don't remember that, only the joy of hitting, the challenge of attacking the outfield wall, some 300 feet away.

"Home run derby?" asks Anthony, as he moves the L-screen into position, well in front of the pitcher's rubber, and puts on his glove to warm up.

"Yeah, sure. Just gimme a minute," answers Nick, still rubbing the sleep from his eyes. They both love the game, but Anthony's energy this morning is a bit over the top. It isn't even nine o'clock.

After playing catch – Anthony's throws are markedly ginger at first, testing the reliability of his arm strength – Nick grabs his bat and steps into the box. They have dragged a thick rubber mat from Anthony's pickup bed to serve as a stable base and to protect the field's batter's boxes. So many softball players have dug deep trenches that the footing is sometimes suspect without it. And Nick, as the team's leadoff hitter, bats first, as is customary with the 1-2 combination. Anthony is okay with that tradition.

As per routine, the boys hit left-handed first, then righty, then lefty again, peppering balls all over the field. What years ago appeared as a massive outfield to the youngsters became more and more conquerable as they grew and matured. Just two short years ago, neither had been able to clear the fence on a fly. On this day, Nick takes Anthony's soft pitches and pummels them, winning the home run derby 11-2. Three of the balls are lost over the left field fence, somewhere in the thick brush toward the river. *The casualties of greatness*, thinks Anthony. The fact that the dimensions are quite a bit smaller than a true baseball field never enters the discussion.

During the rounds, it is all business. Neither speaks, except to offer compliments on a solid hit or to update the score of the contest. Anthony isn't too concerned about winning today, as his focus is solely on the status of his shoulder, which seems to be strengthening with each new pitch. Right-handed swings feel better, and both of his homers are hit from that side. As a lefty, where his shoulder completes a full rotation with a lengthy follow-through, he is more cautious.

Between rounds, they talk and laugh like kids playing a game. They share competitive barbs, joke about school, discuss the upcoming season, and chat about college. It is all lighthearted, free, and joyous. The future is now. By the time they leave, they don't even feel the blisters, just the euphoria of baseball.

CHAPTER 23

On the morning of March 13, Anthony parades into Mrs. Andrews' class with his typical swagger, erases the red "2" on the whiteboard, and replaces it with a "1."

"Tomorrow's the day," he announces, and several classmates cheer. "Opening day." High-fiving Nick and a couple other classmates, he makes his way to his table and sits down.

"Thank you," says Mrs. Andrews, patiently. "Now, if you don't mind, Mr. Babe Ruth, we have some work to do in here still."

"Call me Rooster," caws Anthony from his seat, smiling broadly.

Mrs. Andrews looks at him, expressionless. "No," she says simply, and proceeds to explain the project for the class. They are to investigate and role-play the steps it takes for an idea to become a proposal, then a bill, then a law, and how it can be challenged, enforced, and interpreted in the court system. They break into teams to start brainstorming, when Mr. Sanders, the school's athletic director, enters the room. He bypasses Mrs. Andrews and goes straight to Nick, motioning Anthony over.

The entire class shifts its focus to this unexpected interruption and responds with a gasp as Anthony shrieks in excitement. "We're playing today!" he repeats aloud, so his whole class, and perhaps the entire wing, can hear. "Whoo-hoo!" He and Nick high-five again. "Can't wait to wear that beautiful #6 on my back again! Can I go get my uni? It's at home."

"At lunchtime, you all have permission to go off-campus if necessary to get your uniforms. Not that you seem to need permission." He nods at Anthony, who is famous for leading a brigade through the closed-campus parking lot once a week. "Good luck," he adds, as he departs to inform the rest of the team.

Anthony's grin widens, and he nods as his classmates echo the well-wishes. Mrs. Andrews is able to bring them back, for the most part. "Okay, the game's not until after school. That means *after* we get started on our projects. Back to work, gang." With another nod to Anthony, she mouths, "Good luck." His smile might extend beyond his ears.

CHAPTER 24

Frequently during early-season spring sports in Oregon, as the boys have already learned, weather wreaks havoc on the schedule. More often than not, heavy rains – or even the light, relentless drizzle – prompt postponements or cancellations of games, matches, and other outdoor events. And in this case, it is indeed the forecast of heavy rains overnight that causes the adaptation to the schedule. In order to get the game in, the athletic directors at Vineyard Mountain and Sheldon high schools agree to move the game up 24 hours, before the skies open and drench the fields.

Immediately after school, the entire squad meets in the locker room, dressing in their Mountaineer best for the first time all year. The energy is palpable, the buzz electrifying, and Reggie methodically makes his way from locker to locker, engaging each of his teammates in their special handshake routines. It's contagious – soon they're all high-fiving and laughing and chattering and flexing as they make their way toward the waiting bus.

Once aboard, each of the varsity players has his own seat. Because of the scheduling switch, there is no junior varsity game, leaving plenty of space for each of the ballplayers to slide into his own personal vortex. Headphones help to focus them on the task at hand as they stare out the foggy school-bus windows during the bumpy drive. Occasionally there is chatter, a fist-bump, or the crackling of a protein bar wrapper; otherwise, the diesel engine's grumbling is the only sound.

That is, until Reggie strikes again. Standing up from his seat near the front of the bus, he commands his teammates to remove their headphones, holster their phones, and pay attention. Anthony and Scottie, usually the vocal leaders, exchange a look across the aisle, and shrug. The bus turns clumsily into the Sheldon High School parking lot. The ballfield awaits on the back forty. The boys look at Reggie, expecting some profound words or a hilarious joke – they aren't sure which.

Instead, he lofts a boombox to his shoulder. The sparkle in his eyes joins a playful snarl. "That's right. Old school."

He pushes a button and a drumbeat pulses. He turns it up. The boys recognize the tune and start singing along, quietly at first and then energetically. Reggie stands near the driver's seat, dancing as if he were on stage at a major concert venue. The fact that Foreigner originally recorded "Juke Box Hero" becomes an afterthought as the Mountaineer boys take over.

"So he started rocking. Ain't never gonna stop. Gotta keep on rocking. Someday gonna make it to the top. And be a juke box hero – stars in his eyes!"

In Anthony's head, the Sheldon High School ballfield becomes Boston's Fenway Park, and his Mountaineer uniform now has "Red Sox" emblazoned across it. The song, an echo in his star-crossed eyes, offers a soundtrack as he strides toward home plate, ready to tackle the challenges of professional baseball. He stops and takes it all in – the roar of the crowd, the smell of the Polish sausage sandwiches, the shadow of the midday sun. He smiles.

And then he is back. Still singing.

By the time the song ends, the boys are whipped into a complete frenzy. Outside, early-arriving fans stare and wonder at the shaking bus. It has been parked for nearly three minutes, but it hasn't stopped moving.

Right before first pitch, Coach Shepard pulls the team together. "This is what we've all been waiting for," he says, quietly and intensely. "All the years of struggle our school has had, all the losing seasons, they end today. All the hard work we've put in, all the extra hitting, lifting, running, video. This is what it's led to. We're ready. What's our goal?"

"Win league, take state," is the choral response.

"Now remember," he continues. "This is a game. Play it like a game. Have fun. Trust in yourself and your teammates. Trust in your ability and your preparation. Stay positive, stay upbeat, stay supportive. We win together, or we lose together. I'd rather win."

He looks around the huddle at the eyes of his boys, intense and bright, full of promise, eager to do battle. "On three. One, two, three:"

"KATN!" comes the explosion, and the boys disperse, cheering and hopping, to their dugout. Coach Shepard and his assistant, Coach Schneider, then engage in their final standard pre-game ritual, walking through the dugout, offering each player a high-five, a fist-bump, or an encouraging word. With some players, Coach Shepard takes their heads in his hands, closing off the rest of the world while he shares his expectations, his pride, or some words of motivation. Anthony always appreciates those moments and considers it a valuable part of Coach Shepard's leadership. In fact, he has copied such practice on many occasions during the last 12 months, helping to bring each individual teammate closer to the collective goal.

The game itself is a coronation of all the off-season chatter around the region. This VMHS team is for real. 13 seniors, several all-star caliber players wielding mighty bats at the plate, fast and annoying on the basepaths, and a stream of powerful arms on the mound.

Kai pitches a complete game, striking out 8, and has three hits as the Mountaineers avenge two pre-season losses to Sheldon High School from a year ago, 5-1. Anthony, Scottie, and Nick each add a pair of hits, all singles, and the team takes advantage of a poor Sheldon catcher to amass five stolen bases.

Anthony takes grounders at shortstop before the game, and when Coach Shepard sees his throws, it's an easy decision to move him to second base. "Shorter throws, less risk, no worries," he tells Anthony. "At least early in the season." Secretly he is worried, but Anthony turns in two stellar plays in the late innings to help preserve the win, and Dave Jorgensen plays a solid shortstop in Anthony's stead. *This might work.*

After the game, Anthony's parents, who have made the hour-long trip for the contest, offer to drive him home, but their son opts instead to ride the bus. He somehow convinces all his teammates to do the same, so they can relish the win and bask in the first high of the year. Together. It may be sweaty and wet on the plastic school bus seats, with half the windows open and the rain sneaking in, but the bragging and laughing and singing – Reggie blasts *Juke Box Hero* at least four more times – more than make up for it.

CHAPTER 25

Strolling into the main hallway the next morning, Anthony and Nick cross paths with Mrs. Andrews. "Gentlemen, congratulations on the big win yesterday. I read about it in the paper."

Nick politely says, "Thank you," and Anthony laughs. "The paper? Seriously, our generation doesn't know what the paper is. What is this 'paper' you're referring to? Is it something you have on your horse-drawn carriage? Can you call a paper with your rotary phone?"

Mrs. Andrews has come to expect such nonsense, and she brushes it off. "First of all, remember: call me 'Mrs. Andrews' or 'Ma'am.' And, I'll have you know, I read the paper online. In fact, I clicked on your article first thing, just so I'd know what sort of mood you'd be in today."

Anthony smiles and bows. "Color me impressed, ma'am," he says. "I'm in a fabulous mood, by the way. 2-for-3 yesterday, stole two bases, and I'm sure the scouts will be flocking soon. Shoulder feels good, the guns are loaded." He flexes his biceps and squeezes with his other hand. "Ooh, mercy. Massive. Majestic!" The bravado elicits groans from around the hallway.

"Well, your self-selected nickname is appropriate," Mrs. Andrews laughs. "Have a great morning, gentlemen. See you second period."

"Hey," retorts Anthony. "Rooster was Rick Burleson's nickname, the Red Sox shortstop from 1974 to 1980. He was dynamic. An all-star four times. Brilliant on defense, just like me."

Mrs. Andrews has turned toward the main office, then changes her mind. "Let's keep everything in perspective," she says calmly. "That's one game. One great game, sure. Don't get too high when it's going well, and don't get too low when it's not. Great athletes have to maintain balance. They develop selective amnesia – forget the good and the bad, because each day is a new day. Each game is a new game, wiped clean from the day before."

"Sure, I understand," rolls Anthony. "And if there's only good, and no bad? I don't have to forget anything. I just can't wait for the next game!"

"Okay, then," Mrs. Andrews nods. "Your enthusiasm is admirable. Just remember: Even Rick Burleson went 0-for-4 some days." With that, she leaves the boys and heads down the bustling hallway.

Later that day, as Anthony sits at a table in the school library, splitting his attention between a writing project for his English class and YouTube videos on the physics of hitting a curveball, he feels a tap on his shoulder. Thinking he's been caught off-task, he quickly minimizes his browser and spins around. "I was just…" he starts.

It is Mrs. Andrews. He exhales loudly. "Why you gotta sneak up on me like that?"

Mrs. Andrews waits.

"Sorry," he quickly regroups. "How are you, Mrs. A? And what are you doing in here? Looking for a newspaper?"

"It's 6th period, my prep. I sent some things to the big printer in here, and I saw you, dedicatedly working on school projects, so I thought I'd check in."

Anthony returns a sheepish look and motions to his library desktop, but doesn't say anything.

"Also," continues his teacher, placing a small pile of folders on the table, extracting a manila envelope, and setting it next to him. "This won't get you very far, will it?"

Anthony looks at the envelope, remembers what is inside, and smiles nonchalantly. "Mrs. Andrews, I have a plan. I'm going to play the best baseball this school has ever seen. We're going to win, win, win, and everything will work out. You'll see. I don't need to write it out, do I?"

Mrs. Andrews, nodding slightly, sees the work she has cut out for her. "Have you ever noticed this building?" she asks. "This school?"

"Ugh. Yes," he says with another generous exhale, catching a snicker from a neighboring table.

"Do you think the architects and builders and contractors and school district officials just kind of said, 'Oh, let's just build this big ol' school, and it'll be great,' and then it just *worked out* this way?"

"No, but we're not talking about school," he says. "We're talking about me. And baseball. We were made for each other."

"Right. This is your goal, you say. It's your future. What if the school builders had just winged it, kind of like you're doing? Do you think the end product would have been a fully functional, 1,500-student, comprehensive high school?"

"Maybe not," he says. "That would actually be awesome." This elicits another snuffled laugh from nearby.

"And who would you be playing baseball for, if there weren't a school, and there weren't a school team?"

"Maybe I'd go straight to the BoSox."

Mrs. Andrews stands up. "Like I told you before, when you're serious about this, and when you're willing to commit to the goal, I'll be happy to help. In the meantime, hang onto these," she adds, pushing the envelope toward her student and picking up her folders.

"Gotcha," says Anthony, looking back at the envelope. "Thank you, Mrs. Andrews."

She is already walking away, around the counter and into the librarian's office where the school's best printer sits. Anthony sticks the envelope in his backpack, reopens his browser, and gets back to work.

———

CHAPTER 26

As the non-league early-season games progress, the team starts to jell even more. Kai, José, and Johnny are pitching in mid-season form, the bats are alive up and down the lineup, and the defense has only committed two errors in their first five games. In game six, shaky pitching from Adam, a couple big defensive miscues, and an unusually poor hitting performance leads to their first loss, a 6-1 defeat to the team from Milwaukie. In their post-game meeting, Coach Shepard rips their lack of focus, questions their collective willingness to work 24/7 to achieve their goals, and sends them running 17 circuits around the bases – one for each walk, error, poor at-bat, and five for the run differential.

As the boys alternate their sprints and jogs, taking left turns every 90 feet, they run together. Though some could run faster than others, they regroup behind home plate after each circuit. This allows them to talk, to encourage one another, and to emphasize their common goals. This isn't lost on Coach Shepard and Coach Schneider, who watch from the home dugout. "They'll be okay," notes Coach Schneider. "I've seen teams turn on each other after games like this. There's none of that going on. This here's a team, pure and simple."

Coach Shepard nods, unwilling to accept anything less than perfection. His final season will not be jeopardized, not if he has anything to say about it. "Yup, but we can't have any more games like this. We were better than them, and they kicked our tails. There's no excuse."

CHAPTER 27

Anthony has a couple dates identified by alerts on his phone calendar. One is March 27, the first league game, and the others are the six games against the three Salem schools that hadn't voted for him for all-league honors last year. *Haunt 'em,* Coach Shepard had told him, and that's what he plans to do.

By the time the first *haunt-worthy* game arrives on the schedule, VMHS is 5-0 in league, 11-1 overall, and tied for first place with that day's opponent, North Salem High School.

"Welcome to Sunset Oaks Park, home of the Vineyard Mountain Mountaineers," bellows the public-address announcer, Paul Berg. Mr. Berg teaches a finance class and coaches volleyball at the high school, and seems to live for his PA duties at baseball and football games. He is always making up nicknames for the kids, identifying where their parents are sitting, and switching the walk-up songs he plays when the home players come to bat.

Spring has fully settled into the Willamette Valley by that day, and the sun shines brightly over the ballpark. The field's name, Sunset Oaks, is a Mr. Berg invention. In reality, the ballpark has no official name, but the orientation of the field is such that the spring sun descends beyond the mighty grove of oak trees that envelop the backstop behind home plate. And by then, the Oregon white oaks, which indeed are prevalent throughout the entire valley, a symbolic, natural mascot of sorts, have begun to bud, and their infant leaves provide a glimpse of bright and powerful life.

Surrounding the oaks are thickets of blackberries, leafy but far from fruit-bearing just yet, and a host of mixed evergreens. Their full branches offer a respite from whatever northern wind can come crashing through the valley across the field. On this day, that wind meets with Anthony's approval, for it blows out toward the right field fence. In batting practice on such blustery days, that gives him a distinct advantage in home run derbies, if he can launch the ball high enough in the air to be caught and guided by the breeze over the wall.

For the first few innings, it seems that the game will be a repeat of last year's, as the defending league champs storm to a 4-1 lead against an uncharacteristically wild pitching start from Kai. Entering the bottom of the seventh and final inning, VMHS has cut the gap to 6-4. After Scottie, the cleanup hitter, made the final out in the sixth, the prospects of winning look bleak. The tail third of the order is coming up against North Salem's hard-throwing right hander, Larss Kircher, who had just cleaned up the mess their starting pitcher had gotten into in the sixth. It is a mountain to climb, to be sure.

Compounding matters, Anthony isn't due to hit again. He will be the seventh batter of the inning, and by the time his spot in the order rolls around, they'll either already have won or lost. He joins his teammates in the dugout, sporting backwards hats – rally caps – shaking the dugout fence and hollering encouragement to their boys, mixed with taunts at their opponent.

Before anyone at the park realizes what has happened, the Mountaineers have two on with two out, shortstop Dave Jorgensen, the number nine hitter, is batting, and Nick is on deck. Anthony is in the hole. Grabbing his batting gloves and throwing on a helmet, he watches eagerly from the dugout as Dave fouls off a couple pitches, watches a few more, and eventually works a walk. Bases loaded.

The butterflies, once reserved for first dates, unscheduled summons to the principal's office, and oral presentations in class, attack Anthony from the inside. Normally he prides himself on remaining cool and controlled, especially in times of stress, an image he likes to portray even when he doesn't feel it. This is different. If Nick can somehow prolong the game, he'll get his chance. He will have an opportunity to *haunt* these guys after all.

"Go get 'em, brother," he calls encouragingly to his best friend, who takes his spot in the left-handed batter's box.

Anthony can't bear it. He digs into his bat bag and extracts a handful of gummy worms. He shoves more than necessary into his cheek, spits on the ground, and claps his hands together. As he steps toward the on-deck circle, he hardly feels Kai slap his helmet, and he sure doesn't register his teammates' words of encouragement.

Standing outside the dugout, his gaze wanders to the stands, where he spots his parents watching intently. Nick's parents are nearby, his mother's phone recording every step her son takes. The mighty oaks behind the bleachers sway in the breeze, the setting sun giving enough light to continue the game but not offering any more warmth. He shivers, part cold, part nervous. Anxious. Impatient. *C'mon, Nick.*

Up at the plate, Nick has the count 2-2. The bases are loaded. In the dugout, his teammates scream and chatter and stomp. Along the fenceline beyond, many students clamor, wrapped in jackets and blankets. He spies Elena among them, who is watching him back. He pretends not to notice, and instead looks at the bat in his hands. Flicking it back and forth, he readies his body, takes a deep breath. By his feet, a bumblebee buzzes, hopping from clover to clover. Anthony, soothed by this sight, smiles and thinks how glad he is the groundskeepers haven't yet solved the clover mystery.

3-2, and Nick fouls one, barely, back to the backstop. He is a pesky little feller, that Nick. Competitive as anyone. The next pitch comes, landing wide in the catcher's glove. Ball four. A run scores. Anthony will get his chance. It is 6-5. Bases still loaded.

Mr. Berg, at the PA system, has evidently caught wind of Anthony's goal to exact his revenge on the Salem schools, as he makes the impromptu decision to broadcast Johnny Cash's "The Man Comes Around" when he announces Anthony's name.

The hairs on your arm will stand up.

Anthony knocks the weighted sheath off his bat and leaves it in the on-deck circle.

At the terror in each sip and in each sup.

As José crosses home plate to score, Anthony is there to give him a high-five. His teammates cheer wildly behind him.

Will you partake of that last offered cup?

He takes a couple practice swings, looking out at the field, noting his three teammates on base.

Or disappear into the potter's ground?

His eyes meet Kircher's, both squinting in challenge and determination.

When the man comes around.

One last look at Coach Shepard, in the third-base box, flashing signals. Anthony notices the indicator and reads the *take* sign. Obviously, Coach Shepard doesn't trust Kircher's ability to throw strikes, as he's just walked two batters back-to-back. Or maybe he doesn't trust Anthony's hitting, as he is 0-for-3 so far in the game. Anthony frowns. *We'll see about that*, he thinks. *I have some haunting to do.*

Into the batter's box he steps, first his left foot, then his right. He digs a little to get a firm foothold in the dirt, shaking his upper body enough to get loose, and looks at the mound. In his stance, he holds the bat high, copying Carl Yastrzemski, the great Red Sox outfielder and the first American League player to have amassed 3,000 hits and 400 homers in his Hall of Fame career. *Not a bad guy to emulate*, he figures, as he keeps his back elbow out and focuses on the pitcher's right shoulder, identifying his release point. *What would Yaz do?*

Kircher, a lanky senior and last year's league pitcher of the year, is back into a full windup, so he can generate more power. Anthony predicts a first-pitch fastball, probably right down the middle, because Kircher would know that any good coach will order his player to take a strike in this situation.

"Bring it," says Anthony to himself as the sphere heads his way. A little low, but hard and straight. Anthony lets loose with a tremendous swing.

Thwack!

When bat meets ball, the collision sounds like a shotgun blast. And in that instant, everyone in the ballpark knows what has happened. As Anthony stands and watches the ball fly up into the wind and sail farther, farther away and well beyond the right-field fence, Kircher is already walking off the mound. By the time the sockdolager finds its final resting place, the pitcher is almost off the field. Anthony, meanwhile, has taken but two steps out of the batter's box. He feels a thousand feet tall.

Dropping the bat, he turns to look at his teammates. In sheer jubilation, they have poured from the dugout, arms raised and cheering madly. The baserunners ahead of him are making their way around the diamond, a celebratory counterclockwise romp. Reggie has already crossed the plate with the tying run, and Dave is right behind him to officially win it.

In his joy, Anthony starts hopping. With a succession of fist-pumps, air-punches, and claps, he makes his way exuberantly around the bases. He points to Elena. He points to Coach Shepard, who slaps him one of the hardest high-fives ever as he rounds third base. He points to his parents, his teammates waiting at home plate, to the sky.

Spotting Nick waiting for him at home plate, Anthony's smile widens "Blink twice, baby, did you see that?"

"That was nails, man!"

With an emphatic stomp on the plate, the victory celebration commences. The entire team hops wildly, chanting, screaming, and punching one another in an expression of testosterone-infused exaltation. In the melee, Anthony's jersey is tugged and untucked, all the buttons ripped off, a riotous coronation of the day's hero. It will be several minutes before they can compose themselves enough to get in line and shake their opponents' hands. Anthony rides this high all the way back to the dugout, where Coach Shepard is waiting for him.

Taking Anthony's head in his hands, Coach Shepard gets close. Smiling broadly, he says, "Great hit, Rooster! You finally got a hold of one! What did I tell you? Haunt those guys! Yes!"

"You know it, Coach! I got 'em!"

"Did I give you the *take* sign?" Coach Shepard asks next, eyes intense.

Nonplussed, Anthony nearly chokes on the last of his gummy worms. "Uh. Yeah, I think so."

"Why didn't you take? The kid just walked two guys in a row. I told you to take."

Anthony's mood descends rapidly. "What?"

"Look, son, if you're going to make it, you've gotta be coachable, too. You might be a great hitter, but we've all got to trust the system. Everyone on that bench saw the take sign, believe me. And you ignored it. They know it. You got lucky, kid. Don't make a habit of it. You're better than that."

With that, Coach Shepard releases the day's star, who is immediately ushered to give an interview for the local reporters and one of the TV stations. It takes a while for Anthony to register what his coach has told him, and he is instantly resentful. *I hit a game-winning grand slam, and he's upset with me? That's bull. No one seemed to mind during the home-plate celebration.*

His frustrations are short-lived. As the cameras roll and the interviews begin, he slides comfortably into the role of hero, displaying plenty enough bravado for the whole team.

CHAPTER 28

Over the course of the next few weeks, as the weather heats up, so does the Vineyard Mountain baseball team. Besides the consistency of Kai's all-around greatness, each game showcases a couple different players' abilities. With such a deep, diverse squad, there are many ways the Mountaineers can win. And win they do. Heading into the final two games, they sit alone in first place, 16-0 in league and 22-1 overall.

On the Sunday before that last week, after hitting with Nick for over two hours at Cottonwood Park, Anthony meets Elena at the local grocery store, Richey's Market. Elena orders a hot chai tea latte from the barista at the coffee shop inside Richey's, and Anthony opts for his staple: a bottle of water.

"Mind, body, and spirit," he says, as if he has to explain himself to her. "The body's a temple. I can't put weird stuff in the engine and expect it to hum and rumble." Elena responds with a poke in the ribs and says, "Yeah, well I'm cold, and if you really had your act together you'd stop polluting the environment with plastic bottles. Anyway, I love this stuff. Just like you."

"Easy, there," Anthony says over his shoulder. Despite the extensive amount of time they spend together, he's determined to keep it casual. In his mind, they're just enjoying life.

He leans back toward the counter. "Could we put that in a reusable cup please?"

Without looking up, the barista nods his head toward the shelves. "Pick one. It'll cost more, cool?"

Looking at Elena, Anthony whispers, "It's worth it," and grabs a metal water bottle off the shelf and sets it on the counter. Just then, a small boy peeks around a display stand and their eyes meet. The boy, probably 7 or 8 years old, has a Red Sox cap on, which catches Anthony's attention. "Nice hat, bud," he smiles and nods. The child disappears down the next aisle.

As they wait for Elena's drink, Anthony pretends to study the pastries for sale. A tug on his sweatshirt brings him back. The youngster has returned, this time accompanied by his mother. "I'm sorry," she says apologetically. "Are you Anthony Sumner? My son thinks you're a great baseball player."

Anthony's eyes widen, and he instinctively stands up a little taller, his chest and chin instantly stout. "Yes, I am. Anthony, I mean. Not that I'm great. And," he says, looked down at the young Sox fan, "I'll bet you're a great baseball player too. How 'bout a high-five?" The boy winds up and gives Anthony a solid slap on the palm. Anthony pretends it hurts and rubs his hand as the boy retreats. "Man, that's strength. Good to meet you guys."

"Thank you," says the boy's mother. "Tell him thanks, Derek."

Derek flushes. "Thank you."

"You're welcome, Derek," Anthony says politely. "Go get 'em, slugger!" he calls, as the kid joins his mother in their shopping.

Anthony looks at Elena. She just rolls her eyes.

Like most days, the two of them find a spot in town and just chill. Often it is Central Park, a sprawling two square block expanse of flower gardens, fountains, a playground, and a veritable who's who list of native northwest trees, all marked with engraved labels at their base.

On their walks around the park, often arm-in-arm, the two read the labels, sip their drinks, and simply enjoy each other's company. This day, Anthony has challenged Elena to a test of their knowledge of the tree garden. Running to cover the label of the nearest tree, he calls, "Okay, what's this one called?"

"That's easy," she says. "The white, peeling bark, the droopy branches. White Birch!"

"Correct," nods Anthony, checking the label. "And for a bonus point, what's the scientific name?"

"Um," Elena says, stepping closer to try to see around Anthony's protective hand. "Birchus blanca?"

"Good lord, not even close. It's *Betula pendula*, of course. We've seen this guy before." He flicks a catkin that dangles off the branch, watching it disintegrate and waft toward the ground, a million spores parachuting softly around them.

"How am I supposed to know that? Okay, your turn," she laughs, running past the park gazebo, dodging a young mother pushing a baby stroller. She leaps off the path to cover the next label, ducking underneath the low-hanging branches.

"Let's see," ponders Anthony aloud. "This is a beautiful tree, look at all those pretty white blossoms. It's gotta be an apple tree, yes?"

"What kind, specifically?" Elena pushes, checking and covering the label.

Anthony wanders around the tree, as if to examine it from different angles. "*Malus cultivar*," he proclaims. "It's a flowering crabapple, right?"

Elena looks up and catches him reading from an adjacent tree. "You can't read the signs on another tree, that's cheating!" She stands and grabs his arms, spinning him around to face her. She's put her latte down somewhere, but he still clutches his new water bottle. Her eyes gaze intently at his. *They are so blue, so beautiful*, he thinks. *Man, she's making this rough.*

"Quit cheating or I win," she says softly. She wraps her arms around him tightly, squeezing her head against his chest. "Or do you want me to win?"

Anthony takes a deep breath, steeling himself. "No, no," he says, peeling her arms away gently. "And that sounds like a challenge. Very well, I accept. Your turn!" he calls, running to the next tree. She eventually follows.

CHAPTER 29

On the eve of the last regular-season game, Anthony stays home to get caught up on his homework, analyze video of the last game they played against the next day's opponent, and to enjoy a special-ordered pot pie for dinner. He has already verified that his folks are not planning a serious heart-to-heart, so he sticks around willingly.

After dinner, Grampa Sumner video-calls Anthony's phone. Rather quickly, the topic of focus becomes baseball. "So how's the senior season?" asks his grandfather. "I hear you're lighting it up!"

"It's going really well," answers Anthony. And with Grampa Sumner, his biggest fan, he doesn't have to feel shy about sharing the details. "We're 17-0 in league, ranked #3 in the state. So far I'm hitting .418 with 21 stolen bases in 24 games, only thrown out twice. I think I lead the league in steals and runs. Top five in hits, triples, and RBI. Also hit my first three homers this year!"

Grampa whistles his approval. "Still batting like Yaz lefty and Jim Ed righty?" Another Red Sox Hall-of-Famer, James Edward Rice's MVP season of 1978 had included 46 homers and 406 total bases, not to mention a .315 average, 139 RBIs, and 15 triples. Who wouldn't want to imitate that?

"Darn right, Grampa!" Anthony smiles.

"When's the draft?" Grampa Sumner asks.

Anthony stops and looks up. Then looks back at his phone, "I don't know," he replies.

"Huh. You'd better check that out. It'd be a shame if they drafted you and you missed it," Grampa says gravely. "Well, good luck tomorrow, kid. I'll be rooting for you."

"Roger that, thank you, Grampa," calls Anthony as the phone goes dark.

The draft. He's been so keen on this senior season and his college applications that he's totally forgotten about the Major League Baseball first-year players draft. *Ooooh*, he thinks, and the idea gives him goosebumps. *That'd be sweet.* He looks it up online and sets an alert in his phone for June 10.

That night, he even does his homework smiling.

CHAPTER 30

Steady rain delays the season's final game a day, and Coach Shepard rewards his team by shortening their practice and hosting it in the cage inside. A few rounds of live hitting as his pitchers get their throws in gets them a two-for-one bonus, speeding up the day.

After practice, as Anthony and the boys are changing in the locker room, he catches wind of a couple of his teammates making plans to stop by a classmate's party later that evening. They don't invite him, but he joins their conversation anyway.

"Are you guys nuts? We have a huge game tomorrow. Go home instead, get some sleep."

It's Johnny who responds. "Look, man. We can handle ourselves. We'll be fine. This party's been scheduled for weeks. The rain ain't gonna stop it."

Anthony looks to José next. "One party can't be as important as our whole season, right?"

José laughs. "Maybe not, but Marquis is on the bump tomorrow anyway, and we're not idiots. You go home. Unless you wanna come with us?"

Anthony's expression shows his displeasure. "Just keep in mind *our* goals, fellas."

José addresses that. "Right, it's team-first, right?"

"That's right."

"Even for you, Rooster?"

Anthony jolts. "What's that supposed to mean?"

José strips his practice jersey off, tosses it in his bag, and pulls a shirt over his muscular frame. Tilting his head at Anthony, he says, "There's a lot of *I* in your concept of *team*, that's all."

Anthony turns back to Johnny for support. Getting nothing, he turns back to José. "Meaning what?"

José has sat down and is slipping on his shoes. "Meaning everyone knows you swung when you were told to take. Meaning you put yourself above the team. Meaning you're Mr. finger-wagging home run guy. I don't see you acting like that when I hit one out of the park. You're all about yourself."

"I'm all about the team," he counters angrily. "And I hit a damn game-winning home run, I can celebrate that. For us! For all of us. And I'm not going to go do something stupid tonight to jeopardize what we've got going here. Just be smart."

"Smart?" Johnny laughs and looks at José. "This isn't about smart. It's about being real. We're gonna go blow off some steam. You should too, unless your gummy worms do it for you."

Anthony stares at his teammates, his friends. Confrontation isn't his strong suit. "Whatever," he says, turning away.

He doesn't bother fist-bumping those two, and ignores whatever they say under their breath as he exits the locker room. They are important to the team's success, that is certain, but they also can't be talked out of being numbskulls. *They've obviously misread me if they think I put myself before the team. We have goals: win league, take state. Everyone agrees to that. And, truth be told,* he thinks as he heads toward his pickup, *we can win tomorrow without them.*

CHAPTER 31

Frustrated but not too worried, he makes plans to pick up Chinese take-out and bring it to Elena's house. By the time he gets there, the rain has pretty much subsided, the high clouds parting and showing promise for the following day's game.

Elena meets him at the door with a hug, and he follows her inside with Szechuan beef, lemon chicken, and fried rice. "Let's go for a quick walk before we eat," he suggests.

She puts their take-out boxes on a cookie sheet in the oven warmer, throws on her coat and a beanie, and they cross the street into the paths that wind through the National Forest lands. One is a particularly well-trodden, two-mile loop that they like to explore together. The sunless evening light fades as light flickers between the branches of the giant evergreens that dominate the forest. The path is all needles, bordered on both sides by thick ferns. While there are some inclines and declines, the walkway is mostly flat, which makes for an easy journey.

They walk in silence, the only sounds their footsteps crackling twigs and pine cones. And when Elena reaches to hold Anthony's hand, he clasps it and stops, looking around intently, whispering, "Do you ever feel like you're being followed?"

At that, Elena swats his good shoulder and scolds him.

As they continue, he suddenly points and exclaims, "Watch out, a snake!" Not fooled by the broken branch, Elena administers more swatting. He just laughs, and she eventually joins.

Twilight fades to dusk. In the retreating light, Elena misjudges a step and stumbles on a protruding root. Landing catty-wompus and tumbling forward, she reaches out to Anthony, who catches her just before she hits the deck. "Whoa, are you all right? What happened?"

"I'm fine," she grimaces. "I'll need a minute, though." Rubbing her ankle, she grimaces again.

Anthony kneels next to her. "Let me have a look."

Peeling back her sock, he can see the swelling has already begun. "Looks like you rolled your ankle. I've done that before. Does it hurt?"

Elena shoots him a look.

"Okay, yeah, of course it hurts. Think you can walk?"

Standing up, he extends his hands. Elena takes them, and as he lifts her, she put some weight on her foot, gingerly, and inhales sharply as she stumbles forward. Again, he is there to catch her.

"Well, that's not gonna get us back to our Chinese food, is it? Come here." In one motion, he scoops her up, one arm under her back and the other in the crook of her knees.

"Will this work?"

Their faces inches away, she smiles through the pain. "Yes, it will. Absolutely."

For the last quarter mile, he carries her to her house, her arms draped around his neck, silence once again filling the space between them. His shoulder throbs.

Despite his exhaustion, Anthony is pleased to not find Mr. Martin waiting and scowling at the door. Inside, he sets her down gently at the kitchen table, and as she repositions herself with her leg propped on a second chair, he pours a couple glasses of water. He refills his own twice, as his breathing returns to normal, washing down the shot of adrenaline his body just doled out.

"Ready for an ice pack?"

As he opens the freezer, she points to the drawer with plastic bags, and he stuffs it full. Once her shoe comes off, the swelling accelerates, she clenches her teeth, and Anthony carefully places the ice over her ankle. "That ought to do," he says. "I can't wait to see what color that thing is in a few days!"

"Very funny, thank you."

"Let's eat. I'm starved."

Anthony removes their meal from the oven and divvies the food, they crack their chopsticks and laugh at each other's attempts to capture their quarry, quite a bit of it landing on their plates or the floor around them. Rice escapes hither and yon, and it's not long before Anthony surrenders, extracting two forks from the drawer and rescuing the remainder of the meal.

"That was delicious. How's the ankle?"

Elena shifts cautiously in her seat. "It's okay. I'll survive. Ready for my fortune."

Anthony reaches into the take-out bag and slides a fortune cookie to her. He takes his own and nods for Elena to read hers first. She cracks it open. "'You are the master of every situation.' Oooh, I like it."

"That should have been mine," Anthony scowls.

"Really? I'd like to be the master of this situation," Elena purrs.

"Yeah, this is a big season, and we're gonna win it all. I've got my eyes on the prize – all league, all state. I got this! There ain't nothin' that can stop me!" His braggadocio reaches a faux crescendo as he spreads his arms wide to the heavens, or perhaps to his adoring fans. "I am the master of every situation!"

"Oh, wow," she answers, feigning admiration. "Well, I'm keeping it. And what does yours say?"

"Let's see," he starts, breaking his cookie and revealing the note. "'Beware the creatures that lurk beyond the wooded path,'" he says, ominously.

"Liar!" she shrieks, leaning forward and snatching the fortune. "It says, 'Good things come to those who wait.' Yeah, right. Who writes this crap?"

Laughing, Anthony sweeps what remains of the containers, napkins, and spilled food into the take-out bag and tosses it onto the kitchen counter.

"Need new ice?"

"Nope, this is fine." Her eyebrows dance as she asks, "And hey, you don't have to go rushing off, do you?"

"No, why?"

"My dad's working tonight, so he's not home. Just us," she says.

He cranes over his shoulder, as if expecting to see Mr. Martin standing guard anyway.

She leans closer. "Movie night?"

Anthony agrees, and they adjourn to the downstairs sofa, Elena hopping on one foot and using Anthony as a crutch. She scans her apps and selects a romantic comedy, or perhaps it is a drama, or a science fiction thriller with robots and guns. Those details are lost. Anthony's mind has bypassed his worry about Elena's ankle. Now it is on his teammates, likely getting drunk or high at a party somewhere, with a big game tomorrow. Then he thinks about the draft coming up and Nick going off to California to college without him. He smiles as he considers his Grampa's excitement about him becoming a big-league shortstop someday, an expression that reverses with images of his parents throwing shade on his dreams. He hardly notices that Elena has thrown a blanket over them and snuggles up close, closer than usual. He feels her kiss his neck.

Quickly, almost aggressively, he pulls away and turns his head. "Hey now," he says. "What's going on?"

Elena smiles a generous smile. "I told you. My dad's not home. We've been together a while now, and I'd like to formalize our relationship."

Anthony quivers. "Wait, there's no relationship. This is a friendship. A good one. An important one. I have to focus on baseball. In fact, I can't have a relationship at all until baseball's over. I just can't. We've talked about this."

Her eyes plead with him. "Come on. Don't be scared of me. It's just me."

"I'm not scared," he states, defiantly. "I just can't. Let's just be cool. I like it like that."

"Fine," she dismisses him by yanking the blanket off him and wrapping it tightly around her. "We'll be cool. Let's just watch the movie, then." Her eyes, once wide and sparkling, are now narrow and dull as she focuses her gaze on the TV.

"Okay," Anthony says, glancing quickly at her across his shoulder, at first relieved to avoid her romantic advances and now thrown by her abrupt about-face. He notices the growing expanse between them on the sofa.

As the movie continues, silence descends upon them, heavy, thick, complete. A clock ticks on the far wall, and Anthony becomes acutely aware of it during the silent moments of the film. The screen flickers with images of a car chase, a rooftop meal, a passionate kiss, a gunfight, but Anthony hardly notices. All he can feel is the distance between them, inches to miles. A couple of times he looks over at her, trying to capture some eye contact, unsuccessfully.

While the movie plays on, Anthony frets. *I don't need this stress. She's a really nice girl, and we get along great. Why not leave it at that? Why ruin it by getting involved? I can't deal with this. I have enough on my plate, and I've got to focus. It's baseball first. I just gotta get out of here.*

With the decision to depart solidly made, he looks over to tell her. Only she's no longer on the sofa. At some point, Elena must have unwrapped herself, dropped the blanket beside him, and silently limped out of the living room, leaving her ice pack behind. *Where has she gone?*

Anthony gets up and walks cautiously over to the bathroom. The door is open and the light is off. *Maybe she's headed into her bedroom?* "Hey, Elena," he calls, trying to sound caring and determined at the same time. "I'm gonna go. I gotta get my sleep tonight."

No response.

"Elena," he calls, this time louder.

Still nothing.

He knocks on her bedroom door, even though it is cracked open. Twice. "Elena? I'm gonna head home. You in there?"

Silence.

"Okay, I'll talk to you tomorrow then?" he asks, tentatively.

From inside the bedroom comes her muffled response: "Just leave."

Anthony shrugs his shoulders outside her door, though she can't see it. "That's what I was telling you. I think I'm going to head out."

Sniffles. *Or is that from the movie in the other room? It is hard to tell. Is she crying?*

"You okay?"

"Just leave," she repeats, a snarl in her voice. "That's what you want to do anyway, so hurry up and go. Just get out. Get it over with."

Anthony is taken aback. *First neck-kissing, now this?*

"What's wrong?" he asks, this time in a softer voice, nudging the door open and taking a half-step into Elena's bedroom. She is curled up on her bed, hugging a giant pillow. More sniffles. It isn't the movie.

Her cheerful, seductive demeanor has disappeared. She points to the door. "Out! Get out!" Wiping her face with her other hand, she looks away. "Just go, okay? I'm tired, I'm through. Go away!"

Anthony backs up. "Okay, okay. I'll call you tomorrow?"

"Don't bother. You don't need this. You have bigger things to worry about."

In a stupor, Anthony leaves. The movie plays on, the blanket askew on the sofa.

CHAPTER 32

In his truck on the way home, Anthony pulls over and turns off the engine. *What the heck? Why does she have to make things so complicated?*

I know what'll fix this, he thinks. Revving the truck back up, he shifts his route to Nick's house. Simon's little car is in the driveway, so he parks on the street. Running around back to avoid having to talk to Nick's parents, he knocks on the basement slider. Inside, he can see Nick and Simon on the sofa, playing a video game.

Nick pushes pause and opens the door. "Hey man, what are you doing here? I thought you were over at Elena's. You get kicked out?"

Simon looks up from the sofa, sensing something amiss. "What's wrong?"

Anthony parks on a chair adjacent to the sofa while Nick plops back on the sofa.

"Nothing," Anthony lies. "What are you playing?"

"Some old game my dad had in the closet," Nick responds. "It's called *Baseball Stars*. Pretty primitive, but it's fun."

Simon isn't distracted. "Yes, there's something wrong. What's going on?"

Anthony feels both boys' eyes burning through him, seeing a truth invisible to him.

After an uncomfortable moment of looking about the room and shifting in his seat, Anthony shares the abridged version of his evening. A nice walk, a little food, a movie on a quiet sofa, then an explosion.

"I don't get it," Anthony sighs. "Girls are crazy. Why can't she just be chill?"

Simon also sighs. "You're such a dumbass."

Anthony recoils. "Wait, what?"

Simon sets his controller down, props an elbow on the back of the sofa, and says, "I know this is your business and all, but Elena's a friend of mine, too. And for heaven's sake. You have to pull your head out."

Anthony, stunned, tries to process this. Recapping his evening in his head, he can feel anger bubbling up. All that other stuff is one thing, but now these two are giving him the business. *They were supposed to make this better. Is everyone going mad?*

"Elena's got a lot of stuff going on in her life. Do you ever talk to her about her things? She's going through a rough time," Simon says. "She and her dad fight all the time, and has she told you about her mom? And are you even aware of the mixed signals you send her? You flirt and flirt and then shove her away. That's not cool."

"But we are cool. Most of the time." Anthony shifts uneasily in his seat.

"Seriously. Don't you guys talk at all?"

"Of course we do." Another lie.

"About her? Or anything other than baseball?" This time it's Nick.

"Well, yeah, um, no, not always," Anthony thinks, as the exasperation sets in. Most of their conversations are light, carefree, playful exchanges about baseball. She loves the game, too, and it is an easy topic to focus on. Something Simon just said, though, jabs at his chest.

"Wait. What about her mom? I've never met her."

"There you go. Now you have something to ask her. Don't ask me. Just saying. She might not be the crazy one." Simon pivots back toward the TV and picks up his controller.

"Man, this is why I don't want… I mean, this is just messing with me. Elena's a junior, anyway, and I'm a senior. It wouldn't last. Every minute I spend with all this drama is a minute I can't focus on baseball. I don't need distractions, and you're not helping."

Anthony looks around the room. Nick's eyes are still upon him. He feels hot, uncomfortable, endangered. "I didn't come over for this," he states, standing up. "Enjoy the game. I'm outta here."

Simon calls after him, "Just talk to her, Anthony. And listen to her."

Nick may have called, "See you tomorrow," but Anthony has already slid the door shut behind him. He jogs to his truck, the breeze offering a nice respite from the grilling he'd just taken.

Seated behind the wheel, Anthony stares through the blurry windshield, and thinks of Elena. He smacks the steering wheel with two hands. *What a jacked-up night. Johnny and José are getting wasted at some dumb party, Elena's pissed, Nick and Simon know more about her life than I do, and this is supposed to be my time to shine.*

He yells, the sound echoing in his pickup, as the windshield speckles with raindrops.

His eyes glaze right through them, over them, missing them, oblivious.

Finally, he flicks on the wipers and resumes his drive home.

CHAPTER 33

As it turns out, Johnny and José are just fine after the party. Whatever they did the night before, the next morning, they arrive at school on time, energetic, and in a fantastic mood. The same can't be said for Anthony. All night he stayed up, twice texting Elena – and not getting a response – and worrying. He plays and replays the evening's events in his mind a hundred times.

The more he thinks about it, and the more he thinks about her, the more Nick and Simon's admonitions echo in his mind. And the more frustrated he becomes. *What's the harm in flirting with her? And talking about baseball together, well, we have that in common.* He creates all sorts of scenarios and explanations in his mind, none of which can be verified or dismissed just yet. He hasn't slept, and it shows.

Groggy and emotionally confused, he walks the hallways in a daze. Even Mrs. Andrews can't get him to engage in anything more than simple grunting and one-syllable words, and still that is a stretch. Elena isn't at school, fueling his anxiety. Nobody has heard from her, and she still isn't answering his texts. As a last resort, he gets an office pass from Mrs. Andrews and runs into the athletic department. Spying the office manager, Ms. Houk, he asks for a desperate favor. She logs into the school's attendance database and confirms that yes, Elena Martin is absent today, called in sick by her father this morning.

He exhales, realizing that he'd been holding his breath since he got to

Ms. Houk's desk.

"You okay, Anthony? Can I get you some water?"

Hands in his pockets, he turns and shuffles toward the door. "Nah, thanks." He worries all day. And it is game day.

That afternoon, the team takes the short bus ride to West Albany, a pushover of a team that really has no chance of interfering with the Mountaineers' dream of a perfect league season. That is, of course, the conventional wisdom before Coach Shepard addresses the team in the right-field corner after their warm-ups.

"This is a big game, gentlemen. We walk in here undefeated in league, a chance to make some history, to do something special." The boys nod. He scans the crew, an assortment of youngsters, each with bright and promising futures, their faces intent and alert, a donut-shop display of facial hair, pimples, smudged eye-black, and determination. Each plays a role, each has a set of skills, each brings some personality to the dugout.

"Why are we here?" he whispers. The boys stare back, eyes on tiptoes.

"One goal. One common goal!" he bellows.

"Win league, take state!" They cheered in unison.

A moment of silence follows. "So…Can someone explain to me why, why on heaven's green earth, any of you would have gone out partying last night?" He clasps his hands together in front of him and looks to the sky, dramatically pausing and sighing. The boys nervously look back and forth. How has Coach Shepard heard about that? Anthony intentionally avoids making eye contact with Johnny and José, though his thoughts bounce back to the stressful evening he'd spent with Elena. He still hasn't heard a word.

"One goal. And a couple of you bozos jeopardize it for a couple moments thinking you're big shots, acting a fool. And for what? A couple beers? Getting with some girl? Is that the memory you want to make? Does that take priority over all the work we've done here?" The half-snorts recalling the stories from last night's gathering give way to the worry about what is next. The boys steel their eyebrows and their guts.

Coach Shepard doles it out clearly: "Anyone who went to that party last night, you owe your teammates penance. If you were there, man up. On the line. You owe 10 poles."

Running from the right-field foul pole, along the outfield fence, to the left-field foul pole, and then back again, is a good warm-up. Occasionally, after a game in which they missed signs or were excessively cocky or showed poor sportsmanship, Coach Shepard would line his boys up and run three or four poles as a punishment. But 10? Before a game? Unheard of.

The only thing moving are the boys' eyes, wondering if Johnny and José will take responsibility for their transgressions. Everyone knows where they'd gone last night. High school kids aren't famous for their restraint in posting compromising photos and videos on social media. It's no surprise Coach Shepard knows, too. Neither of those two boys is scheduled to pitch today, so it probably won't affect the game at all, but it will be embarrassing. Anthony looks up at the bleachers, their parents and friends beginning to arrive and fill the stands.

Johnny nudges José ever so gently in the ribs, and they make eye contact. With deep breaths, the two boys stand up and walk over to the foul line. Their teammates watch them in their silent march, slouched and shamed.

"Anyone else?" Coach Shepard demands, turning from the two transgressors to the remaining ballplayers huddled on one knee in the grass. No one budges. It is silent.

Back to Johnny and José, he barks, "Okay, then, boys. 10 poles. Get to running."

As the two began their trek along the outfield's warning track, Anthony slips out of his stupor. *This isn't good for the team, calling out those two and splitting us up like this. And everyone is watching,* he thinks, keenly aware of the bleachers again. He recalls the dressing-down Coach Shepard had given him for ignoring the *take* sign, knowing everyone had seen it. Game-winning homers don't supersede his obligations to the team, his responsibilities as a leader.

He stands up.

In a flicker, Anthony sprints to catch up to Johnny and José, now almost halfway to centerfield, and jogs with them.

Reggie is next. He knows darn well that Anthony hadn't been at the party – in fact, he's the last guy they'd ever invite unless they needed a designated driver – but he knows that the team needs to stick together. Scottie is next, then the floodgates open. Every single one of the players is soon running, like a swarm of bees, their cadence nearly military-like in its precision, flanking Johnny and José along the warning track. Coach Shepard turns on his heel and walks directly back to the dugout. There may have even been a little grin on his face.

CHAPTER 34

Evidently, the extreme pre-game team-first chew-out exercise session works. It is 5-0 before the home team even gets to bat, with Kai and Reggie homering to power the early lead. Entering the fifth inning, Marquis and Adam are carving up the West Albany hitters, and everybody enjoys some raking as the Mountaineers coast to a 15-2 lead. Everybody, that is, except Anthony.

Coach Shepard empties the bench to get his starters some rest, but he leaves Anthony in the game, even though he is hitless – 0-for-4 – after striking out in the fifth. Ordinarily, sitting Anthony at that point, up 13 runs, would have been a foregone conclusion. Anthony might know why he is still in there, too, if his head were in the game at all. He's had at least one hit in every game this year, a 24-game stretch, and Coach Schneider, who pays attention to details like this, convinces Coach Shepard to let him have all the chances he needs to extend the hitting streak throughout the entire regular season.

Hitting streaks are a funny thing within the baseball community. Everybody's aware of them, and everyone knows that everybody's aware of them, but it's an unwritten rule not to mention them for fear of jinxing the outcomes. Pitchers throwing no-hitters are often found sitting alone in the dugout, and batters with hitting streaks on the line are likewise left to their own devices. Baseball superstitions are often revered as much as the accomplishments of fabled players.

In this case, however, it appears that only the coaches know of the streak. Anthony is churning with worry, replaying the previous night's events in his head over and over again, even while standing in the batter's box. So far he'd struck out twice and hit two weak grounders, after one of which he stole a glance at his cell phone in his gear bag to see if there was a reply from Elena. Nothing.

Scottie, the hard-charging captain of the team, saw this offense, and despite the 13-run lead, laid into his second baseman. "What the hell, man? No phones during baseball. No noise, no distractions! You ran poles, right? Get your head right! Maybe if you put your focus here, where *we* need you, you wouldn't be 0-fer, and you wouldn't be playing like crap!" Anthony had dropped his phone back into the bag, and didn't even have the energy to respond to Scottie, who had caused quite a commotion – so much so, in fact, that the big first-baseman Stephen had to step between them to cool him off.

Inevitably, Anthony's last at-bat, in the top of the 7th and final inning, sees the end of his hitting streak. Without even lifting the bat, he is called out on strikes, ending his day 0-for-5. Scottie curses loudly from the dugout, further embarrassing him. Coach Shepard finally orders KJ Evert, a junior who has patiently waited his turn on the bench, to play second base for the last half-inning, then meets Anthony at the dugout entrance.

"You okay, man?" he asks.

"Nothing," murmurs Anthony.

"That don't even make sense, son. What's up with you?" Coach Shepard steps in front of Anthony to look him in the eyes. "We need you, man. We need better than this."

Anthony nods, avoiding eye contact. "I know. Rough day."

"I'll say," says his coach, stepping aside. "Better pull it together before the tourney next week."

On the bus ride home, while the rest of his teammates celebrate a win and an undefeated league season with whooping and cheering and a couple outrageous dance moves from Reggie, Anthony sits, stoic, staring at his phone.

It isn't until he steps into his truck back at school, after largely being ignored by the boys, that the screen lights up. A message from Elena, simple and not terribly relieving, but at least it is something: *Heard you won the game. Good job!*

Immediately, he texts back: *Can you talk?*

Her response: *Tomorrow. Sleep well. See you at school.*

He doesn't sleep well, but he sleeps.

CHAPTER 35

The whole town is abuzz with the amazing success of the baseball team at Vineyard Mountain High School. At her faculty meeting the day after the regular season finale, Amanda Sumner spots Jay Young, and she approaches him. "Hi Jay, good to see you. Do you have a minute or two to chat after the meeting?"

"Sure," he says, smiling broadly. "You must be very proud of Anthony. Great season!"

"That's what I want to talk to you about," she says, nodding nervously.

"Okay, catch you in an hour, then?"

"Great, thanks."

After the meeting, Amanda goes straight to Jay's table and sits down next to him. The rest of her colleagues are gathering their notebooks, tablets, and cell phones and are gladly heading out the school library's door.

"So what's up?" Jay asks, when most of the room has cleared.

"Well, it's Anthony. I know I should be proud, and I am. He's had a good year. He and his dad talk about the statistics all the time, and the team won their league without losing a game. That's all fine and dandy. It's just, I don't know. There's something missing."

"What makes you think something's missing?"

Amanda shifts. "I feel like I'm talking to my shrink. Telling you my deep, dark secrets."

When Jay's response is a kind, silent smile, she continues. "Well, like I said, I'm proud of Anthony. But, you know, everyone knows, he's not even the best player on his team. But he acts like he is. He's flashy, a showman. Cocky, I guess you'd say. And it all runs through his mouth. When he gets a big hit, or steals a base, or whatever he does, he seems to tell everyone about it."

Jay nods. "And this isn't how you'd expect him to act?"

"No, not at all. We're modest people, his dad and I. We don't brag about anything. Not that we have much to brag about, but still. His sister wasn't like this, either, and she's doing great at college and has always done well at everything she tries. He's different. I'm not sure where he picked this up."

"Is it important to find the cause of his cockiness?"

Amanda pauses. "I guess not."

"What's the real issue you're facing right now?"

"It's the same thing we talked to you about before. He's convinced that he's going to be a professional baseball player, and you told us the probability of that. Pretty disheartening."

"Have you shared those numbers with him?"

"Are you kidding?" Amanda exclaims, surprising herself at her volume. With a quick look around the vacant school library, she quietly explains, "He's moody and cranky enough. Imagine if we told him he had a five ten-thousandths chance of making the big leagues. He'd either tell us he's the one in 2,000 or tell us to screw off, or both. I'm not going there."

"Okay, is he being actively scouted?"

"What does that mean?" Amanda's eyes widen.

"Are scouts coming to his games, watching him? Are they emailing, texting, calling? Have any contacted you? These could be scouts from the big leagues or even college coaches. Who's pursuing him right now?"

Amanda thinks for a moment, then responds honestly, "I don't know. No one has called us, but I don't know what's going on with him or even the coaches."

They sit in silence for a moment, then Jay speaks.

"Amanda, remember this. Your son is competitive, probably a little unsure of himself, and he's using that braggadocio to cover his insecurities. His body is still producing mass quantities of testosterone, which puts him in a sort of caveman-mode. He's also hyper-focused on baseball, as you know, and he's been pretty successful at it. The caveman in him helps with that. As far as his attitude is concerned, you and I both know that his frontal lobe hasn't fully developed, and it won't until his mid-20s. Part of the curse of being male," he smiles ruefully. "And that's the part of his brain that allows him to think and reason and perceive his world in a comprehensible way."

"Right, I remember this from your presentation to the staff a while back. So in the meantime, he's ruled by his limbic system, often responding emotionally for no apparent reason."

"That's correct. And what does that mean for you as parents?"

"As I recall from our workshop on this, we have to remember his attitude and outbursts aren't about us, so we shouldn't take them personally. We should remain calm, especially when he isn't. And if we want to talk with him about serious stuff, it has to happen when he's regular."

Jay laughs. "The precise term is 'regulated,' which means he's operating free of emotion and fear. Right. And tell him you love him."

"Unconditionally. Of course."

As they stand to say goodbye, Amanda smirks and adds, "And I hope he's regular, too! Thanks, Jay, I appreciate the time."

"You bet. Good luck," he responds, and they collect their belongings to go.

CHAPTER 36

First thing in the morning, Anthony is determined to find Elena. Turns out that is easier than he expects; she is waiting for him at his locker. When she reaches out to him, he engulfs her with a full bear hug. Neither appears to want to let go. Finally, they break from each other and Anthony holds her at arm's length.

"Man, I'm glad to see you again," he says, smiling broadly.

She returns the smile. "I'm sorry I was a jerk the other night."

"No, I'm sorry. I'm pretty sure I was the jerk."

For a moment, it is silent again. Anthony steels himself and speaks. "I've been so consumed with baseball that I don't even realize how wonderful it is to be around you. And I guess I haven't really asked you about how you're doing. So how are you doing, anyway?"

Elena looks down the hallway as it fills with students, so many eyes and ears seemingly upon them, and gives a half-hearted laugh. "I know Simon reamed you out, he told me. And I appreciate that you asked. But this really isn't the time or place to have a legit conversation, Anthony," she says. "We can talk about stuff later."

Anthony smiles uneasily. Deep conversations, to be honest, are not his forte. "Tonight after practice, then? I'll pick you up and we can go to the park, grab some grub, and you can tell me everything, share with me all the ills of the world…"

She holds up her hand toward him, damming up his babble. "Can you stop just for a moment, Anthony?" Her eyes plead intensely. "Be serious. Look. I really like you. I care about you. I want to talk about what our relationship is. Can we talk about that tonight?"

Though the hallway is crowded and bustling, in that moment, Anthony feels they are all alone. The surroundings melt away, leaving just the two of them. Talk about their relationship, she said. Those words echo in his head. Those eyes, that smile. Too nervous to know how to respond, he clutches her and pulls her into a second embrace. "Sure, we can talk about anything you want."

The bell rings to start class, but it is another three minutes before they go their separate ways.

CHAPTER 37

That night, Anthony stops at a local sub shop and picks up hoagies directly after practice. When he pulls into Elena's driveway, she is sitting on the front porch, idly scrolling through her phone. Only when she hops on one leg across the driveway and into the pickup does he register her injured ankle.

"Wait, how's your wheel? Do you need some help?"

"Um, I'm already in, thank you very much. And it's better, just swollen and kinda gross looking."

"I'm sorry, I forgot all about that." Anthony's sheepish look reinforces the sentiment.

"Don't worry about it. I'll remember enough for both of us. Shall we?" Elena smiles and they head over to Central Park. On the way, Anthony attempts three times to silence the engine's mysterious clicking by accelerating over the railroad tracks. "Speed bumps have worked in the past," he says.

"What's making that noise?"

"Honestly, I have no clue."

"Have you ever looked under the hood?"

"No, but it's not always doing it. Sometimes it's quiet. Weird."

Upon hearing the monotonous sound resume, he shrugs and parks.

For the next couple of hours, they walk and talk, sit and talk when Elena's ankle demands it, and walk and talk some more. Anthony does his best to stay serious, though his default setting is to make jokes to lighten the mood. A habit he's picked up from his father, he realizes, and he struggles to keep it at bay.

"You know how my dad is kind of intimidating?" Elena asks as they make their way along the walking path.

"Um, that's an understatement. He'd be intimidating if he were normal-sized, but he's like Hagrid. He has his own gravitational pull. He uses it when he shakes my hand."

Anthony looks to Elena for a laugh. Denying it, she continues, "My mom left him – left us – three years ago. In the middle of the night, just packed up and walked out. Not a word, nothing. Haven't heard from her since."

Anthony's eyes widen and he wisely keeps his lips shut.

"I've heard she might be in Chicago, maybe. I used to try to look her up and ask my grandparents, but it's gotten to where I really don't care anymore. If she wanted to stay in touch, she could."

Elena's face is stone. Anthony begins, "I'm sorry, Elena, I didn't know,

I just thought your folks…"

"Don't be," she cuts him off gently. "I told you that to explain my dad. Ever since she left, he's grown more and more possessive of me. The curfews, the phone tracker, all my social media passwords. It's rough. I know it's because he loves me and I'm all he's got left, but it's exhausting."

Anthony takes her hand. "I'm so… I mean, if there's anything I can do, you know. Just ask."

Elena stops, grips his hand tightly, and looks him square in the eyes. "Just be straight with me. I like you. A lot. And most of the time, it seems like you feel the same. And then, out of the blue, you just scorn me, shut me off." Tears press against her lids.

"Well, I…" Anthony stammers.

She squeezes his hand. "No, don't respond yet. Just listen."

He obliges.

"We have a great time together, and I'm sure I'm not the only one who feels an emotional connection here. And every time we start to go there, and I think, *here's a guy who gets me, connects with me, and treats me like a human being,* you get all nervous, and I feel less like a special person to you, and more like a prop in your play."

Anthony stands silently as she blinks her eyes, a single tear trickling down her cheek.

"Okay, you can talk now," she says, laughing.

"Wow, Elena, I had no idea you felt like that. I just figured we were cool together, you know? I've never meant to hurt you. I just want to keep it simple."

She laughs again, letting go of his hand. "We're in high school, Anthony. Nothing about relationships in high school is simple. I want us to try for a bit – to be a couple. See how that works."

Anthony's mind whirs. He's talked himself into focusing solely on baseball for this senior year so long, that's the narrative that feeds his decision-making. And here is Elena, baring her soul, requesting some reciprocation.

"Okay," he finally says.

"Okay?" she asks. "What does that mean, *okay?*"

"Can we try without giving it a title? I'm not sure I can handle the pressure of the boyfriend-girlfriend thing. And I have to focus on baseball. I have to."

Elena takes a couple steps and sits on a nearby bench. Taking a deep breath, she looks at Anthony and replies, "It's a start. I'll teach you how to handle pressure."

He takes her hand, parks himself next to her, and there they sit, shoulder-to-shoulder, as daylight melts away.

CHAPTER 38

The state high school baseball tournament starts the following Tuesday, with Vineyard Mountain matched up against a solid Springfield High team. The Mountaineer boys practice on Saturday in the gym because of rain, and they have their second player-led practice on Sunday outdoors. State rules limit the number of official practices per week, but this team is committed, so not having a coach present certainly doesn't deter them.

And by game time Tuesday afternoon, they are high as a kite.

Kai pitches the entire game, and thanks to a pair of two-run homers, one he hit himself and the other from Scottie, they eliminate Springfield, 8-3. Anthony hits an RBI double, scores two runs, and has a walk in his four plate appearances, nothing special but a solid all-around game.

Most importantly, the win moves them into the round of 8, with a matchup against the same Milwaukie team that defeated them in the pre-season.

Wednesday's practice is split between game film and live batting practice, with Coach Schneider walking them through video analysis of their early-season loss and the left-handed Marquis pitching to all the regulars, preparing them for Milwaukie's star lefty pitcher, Garin Henderson.

As the higher seed, VMHS hosts the game at their own field. The crowd is boisterous, and the school district's grounds crew has brought in additional bleachers for the occasion, lining each foul line with two extra sections of seating. The grass is cropped short, the dugouts swept of all the accumulated seeds and chaw spits, old cups and Gatorade bottles. Even the foul lines look sharper, straighter.

And when Mr. Berg bellows into the PA system, "Welcome to Sunset Oaks Park," the crowd thunders its approval.

Their work with Marquis in the cage pays off. After José makes quick work of the Mustangs in the first inning, Nick leads off with a walk and steals second. Anthony's single over the shortstop's head, one that certainly catches his father's attention, makes it 1-0. Two pitches later, Anthony has stolen second and third base, and Kai's double scores him easily. Scottie's groundout moves Kai to third, and Reggie's sacrifice fly to right field is deep enough to make it 3-0.

They don't know it at the time, but that will be enough. VMHS tacks on a couple late runs to make the final 5-1. The only loss of the season has now been avenged. All present demons are vanquished. The 26-1 Mountaineers are in the final four.

CHAPTER 39

After the game, Coach Shepard is approached en route to the parking lot by a stranger. "Coach Shepard," calls the man, mid-30s, in modern wireless frame glasses, with his hair fashioned in a slight faux-hawk. The man jogs slightly to catch up, a bag slung over his shoulder and a tablet cradled carefully under his arm.

Coach Shepard stops, waiting. Outstretching his hand as he nears, the man introduces himself. "Roberto Lopez," he says. "Scouting this tourney for the New York Mets. How are you?"

"I'm great, thanks, who are you here scouting today? Why didn't I know before the game?" Coach Shepard is a little defensive about being left out of the loop. They shake hands, and Lopez smiles kindly.

"My apologies, Coach, but I wasn't here for any of your kids. At least, not at first," Lopez assures him. "We've had our eye on the Milwaukie pitcher, Henderson. You guys really gave it to him today."

Grunting, Coach Shepard asks, "How can I help you, Mr. Lopez?"

"Well, I'm interested in knowing a little more about your team. You've had fantastic success, obviously that pitcher José Vazquez was amazing today, and we all know Kai Baker's a prize. How about your catcher, Robinson? And the second baseman, the Sumner kid? What can you tell me about those guys?"

Coach Shepard spends about half an hour talking with Lopez about his ballplayers, from which two messages became abundantly clear. First, Lopez is a modern, statistics-driven, analytics-savvy scout, and he needs numbers to complete his understanding of these kids. So he'll have to talk with Gus Schneider, Shepard's assistant coach, who is literate in that language. Second, Lopez has been assigned to scout the entire Oregon state tournament in preparation for next month's draft, so he'll be up in Salem for the final three games next week. They'll get in touch up there. Exchanging cards, they drive off. Coach Shepard's final sendoff is looking more and more spectacular every day.

CHAPTER 40

Over the weekend, Coach Schneider meets with Coach Shepard at a local coffee shop with a pleasant seating area. They position themselves at a broad table in a couple of leather chairs, Gus opening his laptop and plugging in a flash drive while Dwayne orders their drinks, a black coffee, house blend for him, and a nonfat, half-decaf, wet cappuccino, with chocolate powder, for his assistant. If their beverages are any indication, Dwayne thinks solemnly, it is definitely time to retire.

Returning to the table, Dwayne sets down the drinks and glances at Gus's machine. He has all sorts of windows open, with video screens, spreadsheets, and a program or two Dwayne doesn't recognize.

"I like this Lopez guy," Gus starts. "Thanks for giving me his number.

We talked for probably an hour or so last night. Went over some analytics and whatnot, having a look at our guys. I had it up on a virtual platform, so we could watch video and the program spat out numbers in real-time. Pretty cool stuff. And his perspective – man, he sees kids all across the northwest every day and compares their stats with players all across the country, from current players and with a warehouse of six or seven years back, so he knows his business."

Dwayne sips his coffee warily. "We're 26-1 and I haven't looked at a stat yet. What can you geeks offer me?" he laughs.

"Geeks rule the world, coach. Let's take Anthony, for example. How would you describe his running game?"

Dwayne thinks for a second, then shares his thoughts. "Speed is the name of his game. He's fast, aggressive, takes the extra base, steals at will, always has the green light. Why? Does your geek program disagree?"

"Not necessarily," Gus says. "Check this out. Watch this video of Anthony stealing second in last Thursday's game against the lefty from Milwaukie, Henderson. What do you notice?" He clicks on a window and a video pops up, various timers and boxes occupying the corners of the screen.

Dwayne watches intently. "I remember that. Great jump, went on the kid's first move to home."

"Really?" asks Gus, as if he knows something Dwayne doesn't. And he does. "Watch again, and watch the timer in the top-right corner." He halts the video and replays it, pausing after Anthony has taken a step toward second base. "What's that number up there?"

"Negative 0.21. What's that indicating?"

"That's his jump. You called it a great jump."

"It's negative 0.21, it sounds like a great jump to me," Dwayne replies, his ruffled forehead indicating his confusion.

"Great because the pitcher pitched, yes. The negative number indicates that he started running zero-point-two-one seconds *before* the pitcher made his first move to home plate. In a sense, he guessed. He was lucky."

"But he's fast, too, so he would have stolen it anyway, right?"

"He reached a top speed of 20.1 miles per hour, which is pretty darn fast, yes. It took him a couple steps to get there, and the throw made it close."

Dwayne looks at Gus. "What are you saying, Coach Geek?"

Gus picks up his specialty beverage and takes a sip, smiling. "I went back and watched all his stolen bases this year with this program, and Lopez watched 'em with me. He stole 23 bases this year, a school record. And in those steals, his *average* jump was negative 0.14 seconds."

"He guesses all the time, then," Dwayne nods, beginning to understand.

"And he was thrown out twice. Both times by a really good catcher, yes, and also with a split time of *positive* 0.15."

"What does this mean, though? For him? For us? For Lopez?"

"Only this," says Gus, sitting back and frowning. "If our opponents have access to these data, they'll never throw a pitch if Anthony's on base. He's so impatient; he'll eventually run anyway. All the pitcher has to do is step off the mound and throw him out. Or maybe Anthony notices a tell the pitchers have – a slight nod of the head, a clench of the jaw, something that tells him the pitcher's ready to throw home. The better pitchers we face, the less they'll have that tell. And he'll end up guessing."

"And that's not all," Gus continues. "How often do you suppose he went from first to third on a base hit to the outfield this year?"

Dwayne thinks for a second. "Probably a lot."

"Would you believe 100% of the time? Every single time he was on first base and a batter got a hit to the outfield, he went to third. Doesn't matter if the hit was to right, center, or left. He runs. With sub-par outfielders, which this program proved we have in our league, that's fine. With good ones with cannons for arms, he'll be in trouble. The long and short of it is this: He's a potential liability on the bases, especially next week in the state finals."

"Wait. But he's our best baserunner. What are you telling me?" Dwayne looks concerned.

"Best as far as success rates, yet. Best as far as brains? No way. He's going to have to learn to run smart, not just balls-out every time."

"Man, that's crazy," says Dwayne, slurping his coffee. "What other fancy stuff do you have there on that program?"

"I thought you'd never ask," says Gus, proudly. "Have you heard of exit velocity? Route efficiency? Launch angle? Spin rate? How about raw speed times, such as first to third? Secondary lead? First-step speed on defense? Arm speed for position players? Pivot times? Breakdowns against specific pitches, in particular areas of the strike zone?"

"Good lord, I'd better call my wife," Dwayne says, pulling out his cell. "Looks like we'll be here a while."

CHAPTER 41

The state finals are scheduled for Thursday and Friday afternoons the following week at Keizer Stadium in Salem, home of the San Francisco Giants' Class A team, the Salem-Keizer Volcanoes. With a seating capacity of over 4,000, lights, sunken dugouts, and clubhouses under the bleachers on both sides, it has the look and feel of a legitimate baseball stadium. As the Mountaineer players file out of their bus, they excitedly soak it all in. The deep fences plastered with ads for local businesses, the manicured grass, the rows of fir trees and a couple massive bigleaf maples, full and lush, creating a nice backdrop behind the fence, the giant scoreboard in left-center field, the red seats behind the plate…for many of those boys, it is the closest they have ever been to playing on a big-league field, and most likely, it is as close as they will ever get.

Coach Shepard sits the team in the right-field grass, keeping to his tried-and-true pre-game routine. He barks at his players about trusting their training, trusting each other, and remembering to keep their heads straight. When he marches back toward the dugout, Scottie has a turn, emphasizing all the work they've put into getting themselves ready for this game, this moment. Reggie even offers a few poignant words, surprisingly devoid of slapstick humor. He hadn't even played "Juke Box Hero" on the bus on the ride up. It is all business. They have work to do tonight.

Vineyard Mountain, as the third-seeded team in the tourney, has the first Thursday game, and they are matched up with difficult West Linn High School, a perennial powerhouse out of Portland, who has picked up the #2 seed. They battle back and forth for several innings, Kai pitching well despite a couple of surprising defensive lapses behind him, and it is 2-2 after four innings.

That's when lightning strikes.

As usual, Nick, Anthony, and Kai launch the assault, each hitting consecutive singles to load the bases. After Scottie and Reggie both pop out to the infield, José, playing left field, gets a hold of one and crushes it off the scoreboard for a grand slam, giving VMHS a 6-2 lead. The dugout is ecstatic, all meeting José at home plate for a momentary celebration of helmet-smacking and high-fives. Not until Stephen follows with a homer of his own do they realize the damage isn't done.

By the time the smoke clears, the Mountaineer boys have gone through three West Linn pitchers, accumulated 9 hits and scoring 10 runs in that dynamic fifth inning.

In the bottom of the fifth, Bryan Pendleton, West Linn's gifted, athletic center-fielder, cruises into second base with his third hit of the game, this one a double. Anthony, standing near the bag, playfully slaps his opponent's leg with his glove, and says, "Nice hitting, Pendleton." He recognizes the West Linn star's name from the high school athletic association's stats page.

"You're Sumner, right?" Pendleton asks.

Anthony nods, perhaps standing a little straighter, surprised and pleased that this phenom knows his name. "Heard you were all-league," Pendleton says, eyes turning toward his third-base coach.

"They haven't announced that yet this year, I'm hoping so, yeah. You too?"

Pendleton looks back at the second baseman. "What are you doing next year? Playing in college, looking forward to the draft, what?"

"Not sure yet," Anthony murmurs. "Gonna take it day by day."

"You sound like a stiff," Pendleton chides. "That's not what I've heard about you. You're supposed to be cocky, ruthless. A real pain in the ass. You sound like a wuss."

Anthony scowls at Pendleton. Kai has the ball and is back on the mound, so he retreats to his fielding position. After the next pitch, he wanders a little closer to second base.

"What the hell's your problem?" he glowers at the runner.

"That's better," Pendleton crows. "What are you doing to get over the top?" he says over his shoulder.

Anthony isn't sure how to answer that question, so he ignores it. Kai throws another pitch and the batter fouls it off. Anthony pretends to back up the umpire's throw to his pitcher, so he can once again stand near Pendleton at second.

"You juicing, kid?" asks the star, a glint in his eye. "You're hitting well, yeah? No homers, though."

"No," Anthony says defiantly, a quick flash of his visit to Dr. McGregor blinding his eyes. Perhaps a bit too quickly he adds, "I've got three homers, anyway."

Pendleton raises his eyebrows, "Oooh wee, listen to you. Three homers in a little-league field with the wind blowing out, and no 'roids? You're in the minority, then. Look at this, man," he flexes his forearm, muscles and veins bulging. "I'm hitting the ball 10 miles an hour harder this year than last. Scouts project me getting drafted in the first five rounds. And all that shrinking-ball talk, that's b.s. Think this game is that easy? Can't leave it to chance."

Anthony scurries back to his defensive position just in time for Kai's next pitch, a strike. Back within speaking range, Anthony challenges his opponent. "That ain't right," he says.

"Yeah, well, I'll be getting paid," states Pendleton, resuming his lead off second. "Good luck, Cowboy," he laughs.

Anthony slowly backed up. "It's Rooster," he says to himself. "Punk." As Kai strikes out the batter to end the inning, Anthony jogs back to the dugout. He catches a glimpse of Pendleton, still standing near second base, waiting for a teammate to bring his hat and glove. Pendleton looks over and raises his arms, flexing mightily, pointing at Anthony.

Was he right, Anthony thinks, *about being in the minority? How many kids are juicing?* Does he stand a chance without an extra advantage? Was Dr. McGregor wrong to shut him down? With those questions filling his head, he tosses his glove on the dugout steps and sits down.

A moment later, he stands and leads the chanting support of José, who is leading off the next inning. *Who cares what some chump from Portland says? I have better things to worry about.*

Coach Shepard takes advantage of the lead to get Johnny and Marquis each an inning of work on the hill. Each gives up a run, but the final, 12-4, advances VMHS to the state championship game the next day.

The celebration in the clubhouse below is short-lived, as the teams from the second game come in to take over. That meets with the approval of the Mountaineers, however, as they adjourn to the bleachers to revel with their parents, friends, and classmates who have made the 45-minute trek up Interstate 5 to support them.

Together, they agree to stay late and watch the next game, to conduct a little impromptu scouting session on their opponents for the state championship contest. Coach Shepard talks the athletic director, Mr.

Sanders, into paying for the bus driver to wait a couple extra hours, too. Turns out she is a baseball fan and loves ballpark kettle corn, so it isn't a hard sell.

Anthony spots Elena and Simon, who are evidently much closer than he thought and who have driven together, and waves them over. After quick hugs and congratulations, they march into the stands to find Anthony's parents. Numerous high fives, fist-bumps, and photos follow before everyone scooches over, spreading blankets on the bleacher seats, and they settle in for the second half of the double-header.

The evening is cool and pleasant, and when the lights come on in the stadium, the moths emerge and cluster around the bright white heat. The Hillsboro team beats Glencoe, 4-3, to set the matchup for Friday night's championship game, to be played at 7:30 under those same lights.

It is almost midnight by the time the bus rolls back into the Vineyard Mountain parking lot, and the boys filter out, excited about their win, anxious about the next day's opponent, and giddy to be just one win away from achieving their goal. Anthony shares a quick pep-talk about getting a good night's sleep and dreaming of making the play, whatever the play is, whatever the big moment is, *insisting* that the ball is hit to you and *rising* to the occasion. After a final "KATN," all but two scatter to their cars to head home – the underclassmen Dave Jorgensen and Marlon Mavis – who are assigned the responsibility of carrying the team's gear into the shed beside the field. Such is the price for being the team's youngest players.

Back at home, Anthony lies in bed, unable to get the replay of his conversation with Bryan Pendleton out of his head. *I'm doing great,* he convinces himself. *Hit almost .400 again, school record in steals, and we're playing for the state championship tomorrow. Screw him. I don't need to cheat to win. Mind, body, and spirit. I got this.*

Tossing and turning, he grabs his phone and texts Elena, just to tell her thanks again for coming to the game. Surprisingly, she texts back immediately. For an hour, they trade messages, jokes, and flirtations. He finally falls asleep with his phone in his hand.

CHAPTER 42

Friday brings with it a brilliant, sunny day in western Oregon. As he crosses the quad courtyard at lunchtime, Anthony's gaze is drawn to the salmonberry and Oregon grape plants growing in the grassy areas between the concrete paths and the creek running through campus. There, industriously hopping from one flower to the next, collecting and depositing nectar and pollen along their circuitous path, are dozens of thick, fuzzy bumblebees. Anthony resists the urge to lean over the nearby railing to pet them, instead opting to stop and watch. *Amazing*, he thinks, *how those wings can move so fast, and work so hard, to help those oddly shaped flying blimps hover and dart so easily.* He'd once read that bumblebees are immune to the laws of nature, and that physicists can't even explain their ability to fly. After a minute or so, with warmth in his heart, he moves along. The bumblebees continue their jobs without him.

In stark contrast to the Mother Nature's energetic displays outside, the bus ride to Keizer Stadium the next afternoon is rather subdued. Game faces take over, as each Vineyard Mountain player sits in his own seat, listening to his own headphones, putting the final touches on his own mental preparation for what will be the biggest baseball game of their young lives. Besides the rumble of the diesel motor and the zooming of the cars passing it by, the bus is silent. Even Coach Shepard and Coach

Schneider are staring out their respective windows, thinking strategy and steeling themselves for battle.

During warm-ups, as the crowd begins to fill the stadium seats, the bright lights ease the transition to dusk as the sun prepares to set behind the third-base dugout, and the Mountaineer players slowly begin to pick up their volume and intensity. Adam stands next to José as he fires his warm-up pitches on the bullpen mound, filling his head with confidence-boosting commentary, most of it phrased in rhyme, hat turned backwards as usual. Adam won't be starting that day, as Kai is manning left field and Coach Shepard has slotted Marlon in right, but his role as head cheerleader and resident rapper isn't to be diminished.

Anthony prowls the edge of the infield, running sprints and checking for possible inconsistencies in the field. Amazingly, he finds no bumps, no lips on the grass, no oversized rocks in the dirt, that might cause a funny hop on a grounder. *Boy, if I could have played all my games on a field like this, imagine how amazing my defense could have been!* He resumes his sprints, excited about another game in this magnificent ballpark. Up in the crowd, he spies his parents sitting next to Nick's parents, and a couple of rows above, Dr. McGregor and his wife. A quick cringe. *Glad they're not sitting with my folks.* Continuing his scan, he notes a couple teachers, and below them a cluster of his classmates, Elena and Simon and dozens of others, some holding signs, some waving Vineyard Mountain flags. Only his heartbeat thumps in his ears.

Hillsboro, the state's top-ranked team, supports the coaches' polls by playing flawless baseball over the first three innings. They set the high-powered Mountaineers offense down in order the first time through, thanks to solid defense and crafty pitching from their starter.

José gives up a run on a double and a single in the third, and it is 1-0 Hillsboro heading into the top of the 4th inning. Coach Shepard brings the team together and bellows his inspirational message, even forcing his boys to repeat their chant of "KATN!" three times before he releases them to hit.

The slug of adrenaline works. Nick leads off by tripling down the right-field line, putting the tying run just 90 feet away. Anthony steps to the plate, for the first time conscious that at this tourney, none of the players has walk-up music. He misses Mr. Berg's voice and the Johnny Cash selection. Thinking of it, though, raises goosebumps on his arms.

He gives an eye to Coach Shepard's signs at third base, scans the fielders and their positioning, and is hardly aware of Nick, dancing around at third base, trying to distract the pitcher. Digging in, Anthony watches two pitches: a fastball low for ball one, then a curve that drops in for a strike. Guessing the pitcher will throw another curve, Anthony waits for it, and gets it.

Thwack!

Deep into right field it sails, away from the setting sun and toward the rising moon, and Anthony raises his arms in exultation. The right fielder ranges back, deeper and deeper, and leaps. To Anthony's dismay, the ball lands squarely in his glove as the fielder crashes into the thick plywood wall, banging against the Les Schwab Tires sign. It is deep enough that Nick scores easily on the sacrifice fly, but Anthony's arms drop with a mix of chagrin and disappointment.

As he trots back to the dugout and receives high-fives for tying the game, Anthony imagines West Linn's Bryan Pendleton sitting in the front row, deriding him for having "warning-track power" and saying that he'll never make it if that's all the pop he has. "This ain't the short-porch at your elementary school, Cowboy," he imagines Bryan saying, picturing his mock disappointment, his uber-confident presence and massive biceps. "This is a real field. You'd better do something different."

Anthony looks into the first couple of rows of seats. Pendleton isn't there, of course. He's gone home with the rest of his team, season over. Instead, Vineyard Mountain's maroon and gold ocean dominates the backdrop, banners and signs taped onto the bleachers and waving in the arms of classmates, and clapping hands are all the feedback he receives. He tosses his helmet in the bin and stands to cheer on Kai, who is now in the batter's box.

Nine outs later, it is still 1-1, entering the top of the 7th, and final, inning. Despite a couple of rallies in the fifth and sixth, VMHS hasn't scored, and thankfully José is on top of his game. Adam sits next to him in the dugout between innings, chatting incessantly while José massages his shoulder and stares blankly into the field.

Despite José's hitting prowess throughout the season, Coach Shepard has decided to use the designated hitter that night, so José can focus solely on his pitching duties. This is in large part to Coach Schneider's recommendation, based on the advanced metrics, that José may have batted over .400 this year with seven home runs, but on days that he pitches, he averages barely .200 and hit just one out of the park. In his stead, Coach Shepard selects the left-handed hitting Marquis Delacruz for the DH, as Marquis has murdered right-handed pitching all season. Batting ninth, the move pays off, as Marquis begins the 7th inning by roping a double to right-center. A wild pitch ushers him safely into third.

Nick is next, and he works a walk. With the first-and-third in effect, Nick slyly steals second base without a throw, and Anthony eventually walks as well, loading the bases with no outs for the team's star, the Texas transfer Kai.

On a 1-1 pitch, Kai drills a line drive into the gap in left-center. Anthony sees it the whole way and takes off like a bandit. Marquis and Nick score easily, and as Anthony comes flying toward third, alarm bells ring in Coach Shepard's head. Thinking of the advanced metrics Coach Schneider has shared, and watching Hillsboro's centerfielder wheel and throw back toward the infield, he raises two arms and screams, "Hold it here, Rooster!"

Engines firing, dirt flying, Anthony churns right through Coach Shepard's *stop* sign. Nobody is going to throw him out, *not in a state championship game.* Full speed ahead, he cruises by. Then, much to Anthony's surprise, as he barrels toward home plate, the catcher receives the relay and tags him out without a slide. In one motion, the catcher then pivots and throws to third, where he nabs Kai trying to advance as well.

Two runs are in and it is 3-1 Mountaineers, but just like that, the rally is over. Anthony gives a dumbfounded look at the field. Bases empty, Kai walking back to the dugout, West Linn's players pumping their fists. And Coach Shepard, hands on his hips, glaring at his reckless second baseman. He doesn't need to say a word, and Anthony is glad he doesn't.

Scottie lines out to the shortstop, ending the inning, and the team gathers by the first-base coach's box, donning their hats and gloves for one last foray into the field, their last defensive appearance in high school baseball. Their crowd is cheering wildly in anticipation, thundering the metal stands with hundreds of stomping feet.

Anthony is caught looking up at the audience by Scottie, who slaps his chest, screaming, "Right here, Rooster! We need everyone, right now, all in. Nothing else matters but getting three outs!" He then slaps the chests of every player in uniform. "Make the play. Keep the ball in front of you. Infielders, you're a wall. Nothing gets by. Outfielders, nothing to the fence. Start deep, move in. José," he says, eyeing his pitcher. "Finish these punks off. On three. One, two three:"

"KATN!" comes the call, and the crowd erupts again. Coaches Shepard and Schneider haven't joined the huddle. They don't need to. This team polices itself, prepares itself, and fires itself up. They are either ready, or they aren't.

Out at second base, Anthony tries to direct his thoughts to the pitcher, the batter, the moment. He can't help but take it all in. The field, the buzzing lights, the raucous crowd, his parents in the stands. *What would Grampa Sumner say if he were here tonight?* He wonders if his parents have put him on video call at all during the game, even though it's late on the east coast.

He looks down at the smooth dirt around his feet. He carves a "6" with his spikes, then smooths it over again. He still can't believe he'd been thrown out at home. *Coach is pissed. At least we have the lead. And an insurance run to boot.* He looks up again: José is done with his warm-up pitches, so he darts to second to take Reggie's throw, which, as usual, is right on target. He flips to Dave at shortstop, who throws it around the horn before it gets back to José. With his back to home plate, standing behind the mound, José motions to each of his infielders with his glove. They each respond in kind, nodding and understanding the importance of the moment. Then he taps the pitching rubber with his right foot.

The first batter hits a lazy fly ball to center that Nick catches easily. One out. The thundering stands grow louder, but quiet noticeably when the next batter hits a double down the left-field line. By this point, José has thrown well over 100 pitches, beyond his typical limit. Coach Shepard makes no move to warm anyone up, or even to come out to talk to him, so it is José's game to win or lose. The state championship, more to the point, is in José's hands.

Even with a two-run lead, Anthony's stomach churns.

With a runner on second, the middle infielders jockey a bit, even though that run doesn't mean anything. Perhaps all that extra attention distracts José, too, as he walks the next batter. That is enough to bring Coach Shepard to the mound. All the infielders join the huddle.

"How's the arm, José?"

"Good, good. I got this, Coach."

Coach Shepard looks him in the eye, saying nothing. Then, with a quick glance around the squad, he says simply, "Let's get out of this right now," claps his hands, and walks back to the dugout.

Three pitches later, the batter hits a high chopper that bounds over José's head, destined for center field. Dave ranges far to his left, reaching beyond hope, and snares the ball behind second base. In a quick motion, he backhands a flip to Anthony, covering second base, for the force out. Not pacified with one out, Anthony whirls and gives his repaired shoulder one final test, hurling that sphere with everything he has to first base. Big Stephen catches it a half step before the batter reaches, completing the double-play and securing the win.

Vineyard Mountain is the state champion.

All sorts of pandemonium descend upon the pitcher's mound. Deliriously, players bolt out of the dugout, fielders sprint from their positions, and fans stream onto the field from the bleachers. In one massive pile, teenagers leap on top of one another and shout with glee. The coaches shake each other's hands, Coach Shepard with a hint of a tear in his eye, knowing his career has just ended at the pinnacle. *What better way to go out than on top?*

For the first time all season, the two teams don't line up and shake each other's hands. The Hillsboro players retreat to their own dugout in sorrow, either dejectedly watching the celebration or emotionally turning away from it. Eventually, most of the VMHS kids run over to shake hands or high-five with whatever opposing players and coaches remain, but their focus is quickly re-centered on the celebration.

Anthony hugs everyone he can get his arms around. This even includes one of the umpires who comes out to congratulate the team. It is a half-hour before the craziness decreases enough for the presentation of the trophy, which sets off another uproarious celebration, with all the players copying Adam's reverse-hat look and trying to mimic Reggie's incomparable gyrations.

Kai receives an additional honor for being MVP of the tournament, thanks to his two wins as pitcher, nine RBIs, and his .600 batting average, including the first-round homer. He humbly offers his trophy to Coach Shepard, who politely declines but appreciates the gesture. This is quite a team, quite a season, quite an accomplishment. Quite a career.

CHAPTER 43

Back on campus, the school year somehow manages to continue along, despite the baseball players' best efforts to halt time. Prom is coming up, graduation plans are in full force, and senior projects and final exams fill the docket. Anthony isn't too interested in any of that lot, thank you very much. Despite the significant development in his relationship with Elena, they have agreed to eschew the event and begin anti-prom date plans. Graduation is an inevitability, simply a formality to put a bow on the last 13 years of his life, and his academic requirements are just a pain in the butt. He'd rather live and relive the glory of the state championship.

Mrs. Andrews senses Anthony's agitation and sits him down after class one day. "How are you feeling these days, Mr. Baseball Star?"

Anthony reclines in a front-row seat, looking ever so comfortable. "I'm great. Couldn't ask for more, except maybe school finishing up a couple weeks early. Anything you can do about that?" He winks.

"Quit winking."

Anthony flushes. "Sorry."

Mrs. Andrews continues as if the exchange had never happened. "So you're graduating next month. Have you decided on a college yet? What are your plans?"

Anthony sits up a bit, feeling a little less comfortable and a little more self-conscious now. "Um, I haven't picked a college yet. Nick's going to UC-Davis, and he'd sure like it if I went to college with him – we're a good combo, you know, but there have been scouts watching me, and I might be able to go straight to the pros," he says.

"Really."

"Yeah, and I don't know, maybe one of the big Pac-12 schools will offer me something. We'll see."

"Kinda late in the year for that, isn't it?" Mrs. Andrews asks, and she would know. Her college basketball team photo sits prominently on her desk, a neon light flashing in Anthony's eye, reminding him of her history and ability to speak authoritatively on this subject.

"It's never too late," Anthony says, though in reality he doesn't know the timelines for scholarships and signing and official visits and all that business.

"I see," she smiles. "Any word from those colleges on your questionnaires and videos? I know you and Coach Shepard filled those out a while ago."

"Not sure," Anthony responds.

"Okay. You might want to check into that. And what's your game-plan for these next few weeks?"

"Well, I'm going to graduate, then American Legion season starts, and I'll be playing baseball all summer. What do you mean?"

Mrs. Andrews smiles again, this time picking up a notepad to write him a tardy pass. "Just wondering what intentional steps you're going to take to get noticed, to make contact, to put yourself in a position to reach your goals, that's all. Let me know if you want to talk about it more. Right now you have Mr. Francois, right? Stats class?"

"Right," says Anthony, somewhat lost in thought. He doesn't really have a game plan, he is taking it day by day, no matter how ridiculous that had sounded to Bryan Pendleton. The way he plays caught their attention, and Coach Shepard has told him the scouts are watching. Certainly he is pushing his star second-baseman to those guys. *It is going to happen. Mrs. Andrews can play these head games with me if she wants, but I have the facts in my corner. My numbers speak for themselves.* Taking his pass, he shuffles off to Statistics and Probability.

CHAPTER 44

In a flurry that surprises even him, the week after the state tourney provides ample opportunity for Anthony to thump his own chest a bit more.

On Tuesday afternoon, the day after his somewhat dampening chat with Mrs. Andrews, the town holds a mini parade for the state champs. With a police escort, parents and classmates line up their vehicles and cruise from the school campus and head downtown, with the ballplayers riding in the back of Stephen's father's pickup truck, a noisy, lifted Ford with a flatbed trailer they all cram into. There isn't a huge turnout, but it's a fun experience nonetheless. At Central Park, Mr. Berg has rigged up a PA system, and he introduces each player by name, number, and with a walk-up song of his own selection. Anthony walks out to another Johnny Cash number, this time "Ring of Fire." He doesn't understand the symbolism, so he struts anyway.

CHAPTER 45

On Wednesday, Coach Shepard calls. "Just got off a conference call with a bunch of the state baseball coaches, debriefing the season and talking about rule changes and all that business," he says. "Then we all voted for season awards."

Anthony swallows hard in anticipation. "And?"

"Congratulations, son, you made the all-state list as a second-baseman."

Anthony yelps in delight. "Yeah! Thanks coach! That's awesome. Anyone else?"

"Yup, Kai was a first-team pitcher, and José joined you on the second-team too. Scottie and Reggie were both third-teamers. Not bad, eh?"

"Wait," stops Anthony, making sure he heard right. "I was second-team? Who was first-team at second base?"

Coach Shepard senses the disappointment. "A kid out of Portland. Real power, already signed at UCLA for next year. Not to worry, Rooster, they recognized your season. Nice job."

"What about Nick?"

"Nick had a great season and was instrumental in our state championship. Earned an honorable mention all-state nod. Love that kid, love all you kids. Now, I gotta call the others. Have a good night!"

Anthony can't decide if he is excited or disturbed by the news. He decides he ought to be thrilled, so he acts that way when his parents ask what Coach Shepard said.

"Congratulations!" his father yells, slapping him on the back. "That's great news!"

"Really great," repeats his mother. "We're so proud of you. You've really worked hard this year, and it's certainly paid off." She looks at her husband.

"That's right," he follows. "Whatever you put your mind to, you can be successful. What a great lesson for life. And I'm so glad you boys won it all. What a season!"

After a quick phone call to his grandparents back east, the family celebrates at a local ice cream shop that night, a tradition they had begun years ago. The first such occasion had been when Jenna acquired the lead role in an elementary school musical, *The Wizard of Oz*, as the story goes. She probably was an amazing Dorothy, even though he didn't really remember. He hadn't been more than 7 years old. Silly or not, heaping spoonfuls of *moose tracks*, he feels like a kid again.

CHAPTER 46

Thursday night, Coach Shepard stops by the Sumner house with more good news. He hands Anthony's mom a packet. "They've named Anthony to the State team for the annual State-Metro all-star tourney this weekend," he says. "All the info you need is in there. It's basically an all-star game for the best seniors in the state. The place will be crawling with scouts."

Anthony appears at the door and grabs the oversized envelope.

"Please excuse my son," Amanda says, smiling at Coach Shepard. "He's forgotten his manners this year. Please come in."

Waving to the living room, Amanda offers their guest a drink. Declining politely, Coach Shepard steps inside. "Thank you, I can't stay long enough to even sit down. I just wanted to get these to you personally."

In his zeal, Anthony shreds open the packet. "How come I've never heard of this before?" he asks, looking through the rosters, bios, maps, and other papers.

"Well," says Coach Shepard. "You and Kai are the first players from VMHS to be invited to play in it in the past 12 years. I'm not surprised you've never heard of it. It's also going to be at Keizer Stadium, as you can see. I'll be there, but I won't be coaching."

"Oh, man," Anthony moans. "Then whose signals am I gonna ignore?"

"Hey," smiles the coach. "You gotta trust me, youngblood. I got you a state championship, right?"

"I think it was the other way around," laughs Anthony.

"There's also a nice team photo of our state championship squad," Coach Shepard says, motioning back to the packet. "I had one printed for everyone. Check it out."

Anthony slides out the glossy 8x10, eyes casting about the smiling faces. This particular shot was taken right after the final game, and the players are dirty, uniforms in disarray, full of joy and smiles. Reggie, true to form, is even squishing his face together with his hands, giving him a distorted, fishy appearance. On the bottom, Coach Shepard has inscribed it, undoubtedly personalized for each player. For him, it reads, "Anthony, thieving is an art. Stay out of jail, and you'll end up in a museum. Thanks for the crown. Love, Coach Shepard."

They embrace.

SUMMER

CHAPTER 47

Summertime weather comes early this year, and with it comes the parade of colors. Rhododendrons bloom their bright pinks and purples, daffodils add a brilliant yellow, and the apple, pear, and cherry trees hold onto their gorgeous blooms long enough to usher in the summer months. Why, even the holly trees and their bright red clumps of berries add to the palette of colors that wash the countryside. Bumblebees are everywhere, ensuring the proliferation of the local flora by engaging in the yeoman's work of lugging pollen from plant to plant.

For Anthony, summer doesn't start quite as hot as the weather. His parents drive him and Kai up to Salem for the State-Metro tourney's first day on Saturday morning, and once there, Anthony immediately has a sense that he is just one fish in an ever-expanding pond. His eyes dart among the all-star players from around the state warming up, stretching, and playing long-toss. He is in awe and jealous that they all seem so big, so strong, and their throws and strides appear effortless, natural, and impeccable.

That is just nerves, he surmises, for once their infield-outfield drills begin, he is right back in his element, offering encouraging words to his new teammates, taking grounders with flash and flair, and assuming the *de facto* role of leader. Batting practice is another thing altogether, as this team is stacked with power. Anthony is one of only two players who *doesn't* hit a home run during their BP session, despite his best Yaz and Rice imitations at the plate. Still, his confidence runs high as the games begin, Coach Shepard and his parents in the stands.

In game one, he doesn't start, but comes in to play defense in the fifth inning. He only gets one play, a routine grounder, and handles it smoothly. His lone at-bat comes an inning later, when he bats righty and hits a high fly ball to the West Linn center fielder Bryan Pendleton, against that same Milwaukie pitcher, Garin Henderson. He isn't sure, but he thinks he hears Pendleton snap, "Sit down!" after the centerfielder makes the catch. He flexes at Anthony from center field, trying to add insult to injury. *Yeah, well,* thinks Anthony. *We were state champs, so who's sitting now?*

The second game has Anthony penned in the leadoff spot, a rather unusual shift for him, as he's always batted behind his best buddy Nick. In fact, for as long as he could remember, they have been the 1-2 combination, and it is always that order: Nick, then Anthony. As far back as the middle-school summer leagues, they'd argue about the importance of the order, Nick claiming the leadoff guy was critical to get things started, and Anthony declaring that the #2 batter determined how the offense would go. With no winner in that impossible discussion, the boys had settled into their spots quite comfortably.

Regardless, he is the first batter up. After slapping a single the other way, a hard grounder between short and third, he settles into his lead at first base. The third-base coach goes through a series of meaningless signs, and Anthony assumes that means he can run at will. So, after two pickoff attempts and two pitches to the next batter, he steals second base easily. That batter eventually pops out to first base, and the third batter strikes out, bringing up Anthony's VMHS teammate, Kai.

With the dangerous hitter at the plate and two outs, the pitcher pays Anthony little heed. Noticing his disinterest, Anthony takes a walking lead off second and accelerates toward third. The catcher's throw is too late to catch Anthony, diving into the base. *That's right. Can't stop these wheels.*

As he stands and dusts off the front of his uniform, he senses the third base coach walking up behind him. "That was a terrible steal," the coach bellows. "What the hell were you thinking?"

Anthony, shocked, turns around. "What do you mean? I was safe, wasn't I?"

The coach spits on the ground next to him, shifting a wad of chaw around in his mouth. Flecks of wet tobacco dot the corners of his lips. He licks them back into his mouth. "You were lucky is what you were. Two outs, you're already in scoring position, big hitter up? Running then is not just risky, it's stupid. You've got a lot to learn, kid."

The coach backs up, and Anthony takes a step or two off the base. His heart is pounding now, not sure if it is the thrill of stealing two bases in an all-star game or the dressing-down this coach just gave him for it, in plain sight no less. *Why don't they appreciate the result? If there is a passed ball, or if the catcher overthrows the pitcher after a pitch, I can score from third, not from second. I have this under control – I'm a base-stealing machine.* He tries to calm his nerves as the opposing pitcher throws to Kai.

It all ends for naught, anyway, as Kai flies out to the warning track in left field to end the inning.

In his final two at-bats, Anthony grounds out to first and walks, but ends up stranded at first. Whether he just doesn't want to run or feels like he'll be assassinated by that jerk coach if he gets thrown out, he's not sure. The end result is him playing it safe. He is replaced in the fifth inning, just like he'd replaced the starter in the first game.

Back on the bench, he is feeling less like a leader, and more like an underappreciated star. Kai seems to be getting along gloriously with many of his new teammates, several of whom were in-league rivals just a couple of weeks prior. Laughing and cavorting with the enemy, even in the same dugout for this exhibition, feels traitorous to Anthony, so he steers clear. They've won one and lost one here on the first day, but the final scores are really meaningless. The tourney is a showcase for the players, their coaches, a bunch of parents, and a handful of scouts who have made the trip from wherever scouts come from to watch baseball games.

On the drive home that night, Anthony's parents offer their compliments. "Nice playing out there today, son. How did you think it went?" his father asks.

"Fine, I guess. A hit, a walk, two steals, no errors. Not bad for a skinny kid from VMHS, right?"

His mother and father exchange looks. "Not bad is right," Drew replies. "Two more games tomorrow. You ready?"

"Oh, yeah, of course I'm ready. Born for this, Dad."

Kai has taken a ride home with Coach Shepard, so Anthony distracts himself with his phone. After tomorrow's games, he has a week until prom weekend and another week before the American Legion season starts, which is the same weekend as the Major League Baseball first-year players draft. *This could either be a fabulous start to summer, or a bust,* he thinks. *Let's go with fabulous.*

In the rearview mirror, his father watches Anthony insert his headphones. He puts his hand on his wife's hand, and they all ride the rest of the way home in silence.

CHAPTER 48

On the second day of the State-Metro series, the New York Mets scout, Roberto Lopez, sits himself down next to Coach Shepard in the stands behind home plate. "Hey Coach," he greets him warmly with a handshake. "Roberto Lopez, New York Mets, remember me? Mind if I join you?"

Coach Shepard waves to the empty seats on either side of him. "There's no competition for you, so sure. Absolutely. How are you?"

"Great!" exclaims the scout, sitting down and clicking on his tablet. "Let's talk about Kai."

"Actually," responds Coach Shepard, knowing that Kai has already been offered and accepted a full-ride scholarship to play baseball at Cal in the fall, "let's talk about Anthony. After our last chat, I wasn't sure if you were convinced that he's the real deal. Then Schneider told me about all the analysis you young techie fellas did with your fancy metrics, and it didn't sound so good. But the kid's something special. Maybe I can help you understand that today."

Lopez shrugs. "Okay, can't hurt. What are his greatest strengths?" He begins tapping on his screen and clicking on various apps. Coach Shepard is certain these were the same analytics programs that Coach Schneider showed him a while back.

"For starters, Anthony was second-team all-state second baseman. First-team all-league. Batted almost .400 and had a 24-game hitting streak. Set a school record in stolen bases. And he's a leader."

Lopez stops typing and looks at Coach Shepard. "With all due respect, Coach. All that tells me nothing. I need to know what he's really like as a player, how he projects in the future."

"Yes, I'm starting to realize the change in baseball culture and how you geeks are taking over," Coach Shepard laughs. "Believe me, I'm just as happy to be retiring now, before I'm shoved violently out."

"When you put me in touch with Coach Schneider a couple of weeks ago, and I thank you for that, we looked through Anthony's video and created a profile, like we do with any player we're interested in pursuing," Lopez begins. "Here's Anthony's profile."

He holds the tablet so Coach Shepard can see it, but Coach Shepard just looks at the scout instead. "Best if you just explain it to me, in layman's terms, if you don't mind," he says.

"Sure thing, Coach. Position players like Anthony are rated on a scale, 20 to 80, for each of the five tools: ability to hit, hit for power, run, field, and throw. On those five, he scored 50, 40, 70, 60, and 40."

"Is that good? Great? What does that mean?"

"All the above, actually. Anything over 50 is positive. Below that is a deal-breaker. He's a decent hitter, but really no power. The 40 is a projection based on the fact that right now, he's not fully mature physically. In the next couple of years, he'll probably put on several pounds of muscle, and still that won't put him in home-run hitter category."

"You said a 70, too. That's good. Was that for his speed?" Coach Shepard asks, keeping his eye on the field.

"Yes, he's fast as lightning, though he has negative splits on his stolen-base attempts."

"Right, Gus and I talked about that one. Means he takes off before the pitcher's first move, yeah?"

"Yes, and in a track meet, that'd be a false start. He's had so many of those he'd have been DQ'd by now."

"I understand that piece. But let's go back to the hitting. There are plenty of major leaguers who can hit for average, steal bases, and don't have to hit home runs to be successful. Is the power really a deal-breaker?"

"In his case, the lack of power indicates he'll be overwhelmed by high-velocity, major-league pitching. As it was, this year he only batted .125, 1-for-8, against pitches over 90 miles per hour. And that's a way-below-average major-league fastball speed. And, not to kick the dog while he's down, but his defense worries us. Even at second base, his arm speed on competitive throws – those that he's really got to give it oomph to get the runner – barely hits 70 miles per hour. Most major-league infielders can hit 90 routinely."

"He's still recovering from a shoulder injury. That's why he was at second base this season instead of shortstop. I'm sure that'll improve," Coach Shepard states, a little edge to his voice.

"I'm sure it will. That's a big gap to make up, but it's possible, sure."

"I see," says Coach Shepard. Then, he makes his best pitch: "Baseball is a results-oriented game, right? And Anthony Sumner gets results. At every level he's ever played, he's been excellent. Superior, even. You can't deny the stats. Isn't there a place for results in all these fancy metrics?"

"Absolutely. The place for results is once you get into *The Show*. Up until then, from our perspective, in high school, college, and the minors, the focus is squarely on the skills. We look at potential, projections, and ceiling. That's it. The numbers you're talking about are just a byproduct, just the opening line of a novel that's being written."

"Weird metaphor. I can't wrap my head around a .400 average meaning nothing."

"Don't get me wrong, Coach. The kid's got good makeup. He's been successful, his team was state champs, heck that's *your* team that was state champs. To you, at this level, in that context, those numbers mean a lot. But honestly," he looks up from his tablet and squares Coach Shepard in the eye. "Your local league isn't exactly known for its amazing competition. Half the pitchers you faced wouldn't even sniff a varsity roster in southern California, Arizona, Florida, heck just about anywhere else. Yes, against these kids, Sumner has added quite a bit to his baseball résumé this year. I don't know what the other 29 big league teams are thinking, but I can tell you the Mets aren't interested. Now, can we talk about Kai?"

On the field, Anthony stretches his neck and gazes into the stands. His parents are eating hot dogs. Well, his dad is eating a hot dog, and it looked like his mom had a hard-boiled egg or something. She waves, but he pretends not to be looking up there. Behind home plate, he spies Coach Shepard, chatting with the fellow with the faux-hawk. *That's the guy Coach pointed out as the Mets scout at the state tourney! I knew it,* Anthony tells himself. *The scouts can't resist me. The Rooster crows! They're probably talking about how slick those steals were yesterday.* He sneaks a peek into his State team's dugout and spies the chaw-spitting, underappreciative coach, standing with one foot on the top step of the dugout, squinting. *Small fry,* Anthony snarls, maybe aloud.

He smiles, pounds his fist in his glove, whispers, "Bring it" between clenched teeth, and prepares for battle. *This is going to be a fabulous summer after all.*

CHAPTER 49

Anthony goes on and on in the car on the way home, excited as he's ever been, talking about the players he met on the other teams, how cool they were, the compliments he received and the contacts he'd made, how much people wanted to talk to him and ask him about how he played and the strategy, the games within the games, and the scouts in the stands talking with Coach Shepard, *probably wondering if they could draft Kai and me together*, and then recounting all the highlight-reel plays he's made over the two days. It's almost as if he wants to give his parents two days' worth of chattering to make up for the headphone-induced silence the day before.

Sunday had been far more eventful for Anthony, since the other second baseman on the State team had a family obligation back home and had left early, allowing Anthony two full games to showcase his skills. He hit two triples, one a line drive down the left field line that curled into the corner, the other a grounder over first base that the first baseman dove for and deflected into the other corner. Both were hit left handed, and both left him no opportunity to steal bases.

However, he'd also walked and reached by an error, once stealing second and once stealing third after moving to second when the pitcher threw the ball away trying to pick him off. That *certainly* got their attention, he declares. Defensively, he had a part in three double-plays and dove to catch a foul pop-up after a long run. In all, it was a very successful tourney. Plus, the guys were friendlier today, even the in-league fellows from the Salem schools that he'd tormented – *haunted* – this spring. Connecting with them hadn't been the act of treason he imagined it would be.

He doesn't mention the running battle of looks and words – spoken and unspoken – he has with West Linn's cheating sonofagun Bryan Pendleton. Some things are better left unsaid, especially after the debacle in Dr. McGregor's exam room. He wonders again, but never asks, if his parents know of that.

Drew and Amanda Sumner drop their son off at his buddy Nick's house when they get back to town, politely declining Nick's mother's invitation to stay for supper, and instead drive to Walnut Park to walk and talk.

"Well, this is all very exciting," Drew starts. "All-star tourney, scouts, great stats. Wow. What if we have a pro ballplayer on our hands? Do I get credit for any of this?"

Amanda links her arm in his. "You'd get all the credit, of course. Can we temper our enthusiasm a little bit, though?"

"What do you mean? You heard what he said!"

"Right, that's from our 18-year-old, baseball-is-the-only-thing-that-matters-in-the-entire-universe, caveman-brained son. You think he's seeing things rationally?"

Drew stops for a moment, then keeps walking. Their arms are still hooked. "Yeah, I know. But it's still exciting. I mean, I never had scouts watching me. And I certainly never had what, three hits, two triples, and two steals in an all-star game doubleheader in front of them!"

"And this isn't about you, right Drew?"

Ignoring that, he continues. "How many scouts do you think were there?"

Amanda won't bite. "Let's try to keep even-keeled. Remember what Jay and Sandy suggested. Focus on our goals and our beliefs. What do we value? Kindness, education, being successful, productive. Working hard, being nice. Happiness."

"He'll be happy in the pros," Drew answers dreamily.

"Let's just not let ourselves get so wrapped up in this that we can't see our way out, okay?" Amanda asks, squeezing her husband's arm gently. "I have a feeling he's already dived into the deep end. One family member in this fog is enough. We've got to be there for him, supporting all his efforts, not just baseball."

"Right," says Drew, walking on. "But still, a pro baseball player's salary..."

"Stop it," chides his wife, and they talk of other things.

CHAPTER 50

Prom Saturday arrives, and as Anthony's buddies and classmates are busy fussing with their tuxes and figuring out the confounding corsage-boutonniere coordination, he's on the phone with Elena.

"You up for our anti-prom date?"

"Sure. You?"

"Yes, you can't imagine how happy I am to avoid all the garbage that goes with prom. It's just an excuse to get dressed up, spend a lot of money, go party somewhere, and get drunk or high or something, then have careless sex."

Elena has Anthony on speaker. Scrolling through her feed of her friends getting their hair done, modeling their dresses, and showing off the exquisite features of their nails, gives her pause. They're excited to make memories, to experience one of the final social events of their high school lives. It can't possibly be all negative like he thinks. Maybe next year, when she's a senior, she'll go. For now, Anthony's clearly not up to it, so it's date night.

"Yeah, okay, but it might not be that bad."

"Are you kidding? Nothing about that sounds appealing. Mind-body-spirit."

With a wistful sigh, she closes the app. "What time are you picking me up on your white horse?"

"You mean the blue bomber? How's 5:30 sound?"

In agreed-upon informal attire, the two don tee-shirts and shorts, stop by their favorite local sub shop to pick up sandwiches, and make a picnic near the pitcher's mound of the high school baseball field, sitting on an old army blanket that Anthony keeps stashed behind the driver's seat in the pickup. They place their drinks, hers a sparkly water and his an Arnold Palmer, on the pitching rubber's flat surface. Anthony swears he can hear the oak galls popping from the mighty trees behind home plate between bites, though the two rarely have a moment of silence between them.

Chattering animatedly, they discuss what their friends are up to that evening, relaying the plans and outfits and locations of after-parties. Anthony contends none of it could possibly be more perfect, or more paradoxically elegant, than their ballpark picnic. Elena replies with a look. "Very romantic, indeed."

Their conversation flitters from topic to topic, shifting from friends to families, dances to designated hitters, and places they'd like to visit someday. Anthony teaches Elena a handful of his favorite movie quotes, and she returns the favor by explaining the lyrics to a couple songs he'd never heard. Even after their sandwiches are long gone and the sun disappears behind the backdrop of Sunset Oaks Park, they talk.

In the cool breeze of the fading dusk, Elena shuffles closer to Anthony, so her back rests against his chest. She asks if he is as cold as she is.

"I don't think so," he replies, and she waits for him to back off, nudge her away, or stand up and imitate one of those revered 1970s Red Sox batters. He has an incredible ability to avoid intimacy, even though he clearly needs it. Instead, he wraps an arm around her.

The warmth is immediate and deep, more emotionally than physically even, as Elena melts backwards into his embrace. They've hugged before, but this is different. This feels real. She closes her eyes and memorizes every detail of the moment, keen on recreating it at any point in her future life when she needs reminding of it.

For five minutes, maybe ten, maybe longer, they sit in silence, Anthony leaning on one arm and holding Elena with the other. Her head is now resting firmly in the crook of his elbow. He watches her pulse gently beating on her neck, illuminated only by the sliver of a moonbeam and the faraway school parking lot lights. She is so at peace, so beautiful.

He kisses her then, once on the neck, then again. And when she turns to look at him, he kisses her fully.

CHAPTER 51

The next week is a blur. With no baseball practices to demand his time after school, Anthony meets Nick at Cottonwood Park to hit every day, just the two of them. They still have a Legion season to prepare for, and the first practice is the coming Saturday. Anthony's shoulder injury has begun to fade into the background of his attention, allowing muscle memory to take over. He still can't throw as hard as he wants yet, but he doesn't really need to during their private practice sessions.

Anthony enjoys his time with Nick. It is easy. They get along so well, so comfortably, and just do stuff together. Baseball is their favorite, of course, and it is easy to see why. They simply pitch to each other, hit the balls all over the place, run and pick them up, and repeat the process. It is predictable. Gratifying. Easy. Fun. The only stressful part of the whole experience is when one or the other of the boys fouls one over the backstop or drills a deep home run and they can't locate the ball.

They have invented a modified version of Home Run Derby in which balls that soar over the fence are obviously home runs, hitting the fence on the fly is a triple, bouncing one over the fence is a double, and a hit that one-hops the fence is a single. They keep track of their scores each round, but the final tally influences nothing, forgotten in the joy of being outside, hitting baseballs with a best friend, and reveling in summer weather without a care in the world.

And each evening that week, after dropping Nick off at home with the bucket of balls, Anthony drives by Elena's house to pick her up. Even without the formal title, they enjoy each other's company and end up spending so much time together there really is no point in denying the reality of their relationship. They either go tree-hunting in the National Forest, walk peacefully around the shops downtown, or play the life-size chess board set up in Central Park. It is the week before graduation for Anthony, and all his final exams are complete. He is as light and carefree as a willow puff. He even looks forward to shaking hands – and bracing himself each time – with Elena's gigantic father when he is home.

That Friday night is the graduation ceremony, and Anthony's sister, Jenna, flies home for the weekend to be there for him. When he and his mom meet her at the airport the night before, it is a shock to see her. She is wearing running tights and her college sweatshirt, hair pulled back in a neat ponytail. College is having an effect, all right. She is turning into their mother.

"Well, little brother, I didn't think I'd ever see the day."

"I guess I had a good role model," Anthony wraps his arms around his sister and smacks her on the back of her head. "Thanks for showing me the path."

Playfully shoving him away, she sizes him up. "All dressed up and nowhere to go. What's next?"

"Do they have professional baseball in Spain? Maybe we could be roommates."

"Gross. I've lived with you before. *Gracias, pero no.*"

Half the excitement of graduation is the ceremony itself, and the other half is the seniors' all-night party that follows. It is a school-sanctioned event, planned by the student council and to be chaperoned by school staff and parent volunteers, though there is no guarantee it will stay under control. Anthony has mixed emotions, partly because it is seniors only, meaning Elena won't be allowed to attend.

As she is helping with his cap and gown, arranging photos with his family members in his father's rose garden in the back yard, she pouts her lip at the prospect of him spending the night with "all those senior girls."

"Right," he says. "Hey. Maybe you can sign up to be a chaperone."

"Not sure they'd approve, seeing as I'd only be chaperoning one person."

"Then you'll just have to trust me," he says, throwing his arms around her.

His mom springs into action to snap a photo with her phone. "That was cute," she says, smiling and admiring the photo on her screen.

"Okay, everyone, let's get ready to move out," Anthony's dad calls. "Elena, I assume you're going to ride with Anthony over to the school? If not, you can hop in with us."

Elena looks up at Anthony. "I think I'll take 'em up on that. I'd like to chat with your sister a bit, get some dirt on you from your childhood, you know."

"Fine," he kisses her on the forehead. "See you there."

Jenna takes Elena by the arm as they head off. "And there's plenty of dirt. Mud, even. C'mon."

As much as he doesn't think the graduation ceremony will be that big of a deal, because of either the inevitability of it all or the perception he's tended that he doesn't really enjoy school that much, well, Anthony is wrong.

From the moment he arrives at school and sees the hundreds of chairs lined up in the quad courtyard, the red carpet laid perfectly down the center aisle, and the podium up front, he knows this is special. School administrators, counselors, and a few student council members are busily tending to the audio-visual setup, testing the mics, and double-checking the arrangement of the diplomas, all neatly organized, in alphabetical order, Anthony surmises, in a series of wooden boxes on a couple neatly clothed tables. Someone has stretched miniature lights above the quad in a crisscross pattern, giving the illusion of intimacy, stars, and fanciness. Anthony wonders what will happen when the kids throw their caps in the air and shatter all the light bulbs. *Ah, never mind that.*

His classmates are gathering in the cafeteria as friends, family, and loved ones file into seats. Slowly, the courtyard fills with a festive blend of folks in their Sunday best, littler kids adorned with flowers and older ones sampling new outfits, along with plenty of phones, cameras, and tissues. The cafeteria, meanwhile, is a hotbed of emotional disasters waiting to happen.

There is a lot of hugging, crying, and pretending not to cry. Even classmates Anthony hardly knows are walking up to him, offering an embrace, and telling him congratulations. He returns the sentiment, and even as he tries to remain stoic throughout it all, the knots of nostalgia begin to churn in his belly.

It starts with firsts. The first time he met Nick, seven years ago, flashes into his mind. He'd been sitting in his sixth-grade math class, a little in awe of being a *middle schooler,* when he'd felt a tap on his shoulder. "When you're finished, could I borrow your calculator, please?" Turns out the kid in the green polo shirt would end up being his best friend, someone he'd spend innumerable hours with, growing up, playing sports, coming to this high school, and becoming a dynamite pair on the ballfield. And now he's going to California, effectively ending the championship run of the 1-2 combo. Anthony laughs as the memory of their first fistfight comes into focus, a rather innocuous event in the parking lot of a local convenience store, when two kids from another school challenged Nick's driving ability and Anthony had stepped to them. A couple punches and a busted gallon of milk later, the boys were hightailing it back to Nick's house, laughing all the way.

Then it is the constants. The friendships he maintained through all four years, many of which go back much further than that. The people he can always trust, the names and faces he always remembers – they are the same ones he'll never forget. And that pledge, not coincidentally, is offered more times than not. He intentionally seeks out his 12 senior baseball teammates, taking a special, private moment with each one, hands on each other's shoulders and foreheads nearly touching, the way Coach Shepard might have done.

Spotting Simon, for once not right next to Nick, Anthony gives him a massive hug. "Love you, bro," he whispers in his ear.

"Love you too, man."

"Am I interrupting something serious?" Nick laughs as he walks up.

"Nope, he's all yours," Simon wipes his eye with the back of his hand, kisses Nick on the cheek, and waves the boys together as he walks off.

"Dude, we did it," Anthony starts.

"Yeah, not yet. Don't count your chickens, my friend. There's still an hour to go."

"I'm gonna miss you next year, man. Seriously, we've been the 1-2 combination for what, seven years? That's a long time. How's the world gonna handle us being apart?"

Nick looks solemn. "What are you gonna do next year, anyway? One of these days you've gotta make a decision, right?"

"It'll work out, whatever it is."

"You're my best friend, Anthony." Now Nick is looking him dead-on. "I wouldn't trade the last seven years for anything."

"I know, me too," Anthony stammers a bit. He notices the red in Nick's eyes. "It's been a good run."

Nick hugs him then, and not another word is uttered.

By the time the school counselors are lining the graduates in alphabetical order, pairing them to march two-by-two to their seats, he is fighting back his own tears.

As the ceremony begins, Anthony takes a couple of deep breaths and his emotions settle back to normal. The guest speakers, including the principal and a recent college graduate who attended VMHS four years prior, do their best to motivate and inspire the students, but their impact is slight, if at all. Anthony finds it interesting how much energy is spent on inspiring the *now former* students of the school.

"Where were these speeches four years ago?" Anthony wonders aloud to his neighbor, Nathan Strong. "Or even nine months ago, when our senior year started? That would have been handy."

"Right. Now it just seems tardy."

The valedictorians offer their two cents, reminding the *young adults* to embrace the *fourth R* as they enter the *real world* beyond the schoolhouse: *Responsibility.* It is a captivating speech, partly because of the message, partly because the two academic honorees deliver it together, playing off each other and including quite a few hilarious anecdotes from the past four years. Soon the processional begins. Parents cry, cameras click, and the graduates pose, all the while simultaneously ecstatic and fearful for their futures. After he crosses the stage and collects his diploma, Anthony scans the crowd for Mrs. Andrews, who must be there, but he can't find her in the sea of faces.

Back in his seat, he nudges Nathan again. "What do you think is gonna happen to those lights?"

Nathan looks up and shrugs.

At the conclusion of the ceremony, the principal gestures to the crisscross lights, as if on cue, and says, "Rather than toss your caps, which some of you have so elegantly decorated, we invite you to trade caps with a classmate, hand it to a loved one, or hold it to your heart. You've graduated high school. Congratulations!"

And then, it is over.

Rather, it is just beginning.

Screaming, crying, cheering, arms in the air, arms to their sides. Like pollen dislodged from a windblown branch, all the graduates move in their own directions, scattering chaotically, eyes seeking their own targets. In the throng of people, dominated by maroon and gold robes, Anthony spies his sister and their parents. All they have time for are quick hugs, "Congratulations," and a couple kisses on the cheek. Elena sneaks in for one of each as well, and in the blink of an eye, Anthony and his classmates are whisked away to the Events Center for the all-night party.

CHAPTER 52

The Events Center downtown lives for this sort of thing. Equipped with all sorts of banquet halls and a gaming wing, they have themed the night, "Your Future Is Now," and decorated each room with robots, gizmos, and gadgets – many of them replicas from old sci-fi movies that predicted, rather poorly, what the future would look like.

Like kids in a candy store, Anthony and Nick race to play laser tag. Then bowling. Then a couple of makeshift arcade games. After a trip to the special pantry for snacks, they watch a movie in the giant theater. Along the way, the hugs and tearful memories of the joys committed to memory become a staple, and many of their classmates tote their yearbooks around for signatures and the all-important inscriptions. Anthony hadn't purchased a yearbook, didn't think it important at the time, and he feels rather out of place when he can't reciprocate when handed a classmate's book. He signs patiently, though, trying to ensure each note has a special meaning for the friend to whom he writes. For some, it is more challenging than others, but he thinks of Coach Shepard's ability to say just the right thing to each individual, and he musters the words. *That's a role model*, he thinks, *and that's what I'm going to be.*

When the excitement is wearing down, sometime around 3:00 a.m., Anthony perches on a bench overlooking the bowling lanes. Nobody is playing – they shut those down at midnight. As he leans back, he feels a presence nearby. Looking up, he sees Mrs. Andrews.

"Yo, Mrs. A, how are you?" he asks, sitting up.

"*Yo, Mrs. A?* What's happened to you since you graduated?" Mrs. Andrews sits down at a seat across a greasy bowling-alley nacho-snacking table from him.

"Sorry, ma'am. Nothing. Just happy to be done, I guess."

"Is it too late at night to ask you if you've got a game plan for your future?"

Anthony isn't surprised to hear this. "Well, not much has changed since the last time we spoke. Except now I have a high school diploma."

"When's the draft?"

Anthony stills for a moment. "Holy smokes! It's tomorrow! I'd forgotten all about it! It's also the first day of Legion practice. Better get some sleep." In a playfully exaggerated move, he drops to the bench and tucks his hands under his head. He peeks up at Mrs. Andrews to see her response.

"If you don't want to talk to me, that's fine. You'll have to face your future either way. I figured you'd probably want to be prepared for it, to be in charge of it, rather than have it run you."

Anthony leans up on one arm. "I know, you've always given me good advice, and I haven't always taken it. But I'm going to be fine, you'll see. In fact, I'm doing great. This Rooster is the king of the farm!" He winks, then he lies back down. "Better get some shuteye, Mrs. Andrews. Keep chaperoning these kids, you never know what they've tried to sneak in here tonight."

"I told you," says Mrs. Andrews. "Quit winking."

"Sorry, hard habit to break."

"One last thing," Mrs. Andrews leans forward. "Do you know why I've always insisted that you call me *ma'am*?"

"No, why?"

"Simple respect. You show me that respect, and that'll translate into you showing an umpire respect, showing a young woman like Elena respect, and eventually you'll show yourself that same respect."

Anthony lets her words rest on the bench next to him.

"Stay out of trouble, young man," she says, turning to leave.

"Yes, ma'am."

As his government teacher walks away, Anthony sits back up. Reaching into his bag, he grabs his phone. 13 texts from Elena, all rather innocent, just-checking-in messages, mostly accompanied by hearts and various smiley-faces. It is 3:07. He texts her back that he is fine, he appreciates her coming to his graduation, and hopes she sleeps well.

It shouldn't have surprised him at this point that she texts back immediately.

Their silent conversation continues until after 5:00.

CHAPTER 53

Anthony is jarred awake by loud bells, ringing and throbbing in his ears. Some joker has pulled the fire alarm. Bouncing up from the uncomfortable bowling-alley bench, he throws on his backpack, his head a clatter of flashing strobe lights, clanging bells, and lack of sleep. He moves to the grand hallway, joins his classmates in a rather sleepwalky exit, and meanders into the Events Center parking lot.

For a while, the recent graduates huddle together under blankets and jackets and the warm shrouds of each other's hugs, some giggling, some yawning, and some just shivering. To early-morning passers-by it must have looked like a battalion of teenage zombies. One by one, they drag themselves to their vehicles, heading home to get some much-neglected rest. The overnight party's planning committee had scheduled a colossal pancake breakfast as a send-off, but the fire alarm, finally shut off and restored by Center officials, has short-sheeted those plans. The only students that go back inside are those who are retrieving belongings or those on the student council for cleanup duty.

Anthony's first thoughts, as he warms up the rusty pickup and waves farewells to friends through fogged-up windows, are of baseball. Today is the first day of American Legion practice, and it is the first day of the Major League Baseball draft. He needs some sleep. Checking the truck's clock, he sees it is just 6:37. Practice is at 10:00. He groggily makes his way home.

American Legion baseball is a national summer program for youths up to age 18. Organized by local American Legion posts, it has grown into a network of over 4,000 teams, with a long and illustrious list of big-league players who cut their teeth in Legion ball. Anthony knows the Legion alumni who went on to play in the Majors by heart: Harold

Reynolds, who had starred for the Corvallis Post 11 program back in the day, plus Barry Bonds, Bryce Harper, Albert Pujols, and of course a host of Red Sox stars like Williams, Yaz, Rice, Jackie Bradley Jr. He is proud to join that lineage.

Each team is comprised of kids from various local schools, condensing the talent and creating a more competitive experience, in effect becoming a collection of all-star teams. Post 11 brings together players from the greater Corvallis area and all points west, through Philomath and Toledo to the coastal town of Newport. The summer before, Anthony and many of his teammates had played and done rather well, just missing a berth to the state tournament after winning 24 games. As opposed to the normal high school schedule, which has the schools playing twice a week so as to balance sports with scholastic demands, the Legion schedule runs 6 or 7 games per week, with Sunday being the only day of rest. *It was good to recruit from other schools,* Anthony thinks. *We'll need the pitching.*

There are still traces of summer dewdrops on the grass at Oregon State University's Coleman Field at 10:00 when the boys gather behind home plate. Since the regular Legion field is under construction, OSU has graciously offered to let them hold their practices and games in the college park, and Anthony is impressed. Just like at Keizer Stadium, the grass is perfectly manicured, the infield sharp, and the stands permanent, colorful, and official. As Anthony gazes about, he half expects to see his dad standing watch. *Of course he's not here, it's Saturday. He doesn't teach on Saturdays.* The stands and walkways beyond them are empty.

There are 40 or so out for the team, and Anthony recalls from the year before that the coaches will cut down to 24 by the end of the first week or two. Some kids will only play in one or two games, and some won't play at all before being sent packing. As an all-state second baseman, Anthony isn't worried, even though he is exhausted this morning. That extra two hours of sleep may or may not have helped.

Groggy or not, the boys start by running a couple laps of the field, stretching a bit, and going immediately into more running drills. The coaching staff, consisting of the grizzled veteran, Coach Chuck Garrity and his henchmen, including VMHS's Coach Schneider and Ryan Payzant, a former Legion ballplayer with the program record for hits in a season, must have known the night before had been the all-night senior party. Anthony can't see it, but he imagines their sinister looks as the sophomores and juniors outpace the veteran seniors in baseline sprints, backpedaling drills, and pole races.

Slipping Anthony's mind, at least until Coach Payzant mentions it, is one giant, concurrent event: the Major League Baseball draft. Consisting of 40 rounds, and including supplemental picks in between rounds, the first-year players draft is *the* baseball draft. High school seniors, college kids, and unsigned prospects keep fingers crossed, prayers launched, and hopes alive throughout the weekend. All eyes are on the online tracker, and those with legitimate prospects keep their phones charged and within reach.

Unbeknownst to Anthony, the draft's first two rounds had actually taken place the night before, and when the team takes an extended water break, several players check their phones for the online updates. No familiar names have gone in the first two rounds, and round three is almost complete. Coach Payzant agrees to man the tracker on his phone during the upcoming drills, though he actually hands his phone to his wife, Jill, who, expecting their first child at some point in the next month, accompanies Coach Payzant to the ballpark.

Anthony runs over to Jill and hands her his phone, too, saying, "If I get an unknown number, or if it's my parents or Coach Shepard, please answer it for me, k?" Jill graciously agrees. *Today might be the day.*

That first practice lasts three hours, but it might as well have been twenty-four, what with Coach Garrity barking orders and sending kids hither and yon, and Anthony stealing glances toward the bleachers to check on Jill with his phone. Nothing. Eventually, they take an infield-outfield practice and spend a tremendous amount of time talking strategy, since most of the players on the field know what they are doing, skill-wise at least. In addition to the VMHS-heavy roster, the Post 11 tryout mix includes several fine ballplayers from some of the nearby schools' attendance zones. From the looks of it, Anthony suspects the summer season is going to be as glorious as the state-championship run he and his teammates have just experienced.

Evidently, Anthony's phone never rings because Jill just sits there in the bleachers with it, sometimes walking up and down the aisle steps, but never straying too far from her spot behind the screen, and not once waving excitedly to get his attention. As practice concludes, Anthony thanks her and clutches his phone as he runs to the rusty pickup, hoping he'll make it home before the call, so he can celebrate with his parents.

CHAPTER 54

Drew and Amanda Sumner busy themselves with chores around the house, vacuuming and picking up and rearranging and organizing, completely unaware of Anthony's rising stress level. It is almost 6:00 p.m., and he's been glued to the TV in the basement, his laptop open next to him on the sofa, phone in hand, ever since he got back from baseball practice.

The hosts of the MLB network explain that rounds 3-10 are occurring today, and the final 30 rounds will be picked, in rapid succession, on Sunday afternoon. So far, the only names Anthony recognizes are Al Sherman and Grant Chadwick, both pitchers from the State-Metro tourney, and Bryan Pendleton, West Linn's 'roid-aided center-fielder, who goes to the Cleveland Indians in the 7th round. Anthony secretly hopes they drug-test him right away and nullify any signing bonus. He is surprised to not have seen Kai's name yet, so he constantly scrolls up and down the picks just to be sure.

Not until after the day's picks are complete does he text Elena back, who has texted and called several times during the afternoon. She calls immediately following his message.

"So?" she asks, expectantly.

"Nothing today, which doesn't surprise me. I mean, Kai hasn't gone yet, and I'm sure they'll pick him first. He hit .565 this year and was the league MVP. That's hard to top."

"I'm sure they'll wise up and grab you tomorrow. That actually sounds like a good idea," she adds, coyly.

Anthony forces a laugh. "I'm just going to stay home tonight. Sounds like my mom and dad are making dinner. Plus, I didn't get any sleep last night, thanks to you."

"Ha! Your own fault for going to that party. You could have hung out with me instead, you know."

"I know. Sure would have been nice if you were a senior too."

"Tell me about it. You, Nick, Simon? All leaving me at the same time?"

"Hey! How about tomorrow you come over and watch the draft with me? I could use the company, and I'd love to have you here to celebrate."

"Sure, what time?"

"Starts at 10:00. It could last all day, so bring some water. Gotta stay hydrated!" he teases.

"Okay, get your beauty rest then."

After dinner, he drags himself to his bedroom, catches a glimpse in the mirror, and recoils. *Definitely need my beauty rest.* He falls asleep, fully clothed, before 8:00.

CHAPTER 55

The next morning, the crackling of the griddle wakes him up; the sweet smell of bacon calling to him from the kitchen. As he drags himself into the bright sunlight, his mother's cheery smile greets him.

"I know we don't normally have this filthy swine," she laughs. "But today's a special day, so we're having bacon and my famous cranberry pancakes." Clearly, she has already gone running and, probably, for a bike ride. Anthony checks the clock. 9:30. *And I'm sure she's been swimming, too. What a nut,* he thinks blearily, as he kisses his mother's cheek on his way to the table.

"Bacon is nature's candy," he says over his shoulder.

Amanda smiles. She loves him dearly, and she also worries about him immensely. As she watches her son take his seat, the same spot at the table he's used for the last 15 years, as hard as she tries, she can't see the professional athlete in him. He is slight, strong but not too muscular, and certainly doesn't stand out in a crowd as a physical specimen. She wonders if scouts care about appearances like that, and thinks of the all-star tourney a couple weeks ago. He played well, hit well, and made no mistakes. And if they want someone who's truly dedicated to baseball, he'd be their guy. She crosses herself and hopes his phone will ring today. If not…

Her gaze turns back to breakfast, and she calls through the kitchen window to her husband, who is outside watering the rose bushes. They positively shine in the morning sunlight. Perhaps that is a sign.

By 10:00, Anthony is entrenched in his makeshift command center, now with two laptops, a phone, and the TV quietly chattering in the background. Elena, perched next to Anthony on the sofa, had arrived a few minutes earlier, and after devouring a piece of nature's candy was now attending to a cranberry pancake. His parents, as they had done the previous day, occupy themselves with various household tasks. As the day wears on, this includes washing the cars, running several loads of laundry, brushing Peaches, cleaning and refreshing the cat box, organizing the kitchen pantry, scrubbing the grout on the shower tiles, brushing Peaches again… and checking on Anthony carefully, mostly via drive-by trips through the downstairs living room. Elena makes eye contact and mouths "not yet" each time, but Anthony's focus only darts from screen to screen.

Around 3:00, they come rushing downstairs to an audible scream, and Anthony is standing, arms raised triumphantly. "What is it, son?" asks Drew, catching his of breath from the sprint downstairs. Or perhaps he's exhausted from brushing the darned cat so many times.

"They just picked Kai. 29th round, Chicago Cubs. I don't know what kind of signing bonus the 29th round is. I gotta text him. Maybe he won't go to Cal after all."

"How exciting for him!" responds Amanda, glancing at her husband. He is gathering his composure, at once thrilled and disappointed that the news isn't closer to home.

"Yeah," Anthony replies automatically, furiously texting a congratulatory note to his Texan friend. Once sent, he turns back to the screens. "Now it's game time," he says, once again scrolling up and down the lists. The folks on the MLB channel post Kai's name on the screen with a quick graphic showing his photo and a couple of his league stats, but it is gone before he knows it, and they move on to the next player selected.

Elena shifts in her seat, glad to be a part of the scene while keeping a safe distance from Anthony's command center setup. Amanda and Drew retreat upstairs.

"We'd better brace ourselves," Amanda says to her husband, once they are out of earshot.

"C'mon, there are 11 more rounds. He's got to be in the top, what, 1200 players in the country, don't you think?"

"Who are you trying to convince?"

"Well…"

"Remember the odds," Amanda replies. "One out of 2,000. And this draft picks from college players, too. Kids who have proven themselves against better competition, older, bigger, more physically mature. Have you seen our son? We just need to be ready with our response to his disappointment. Just in case."

"Right, I know. I'm just so excited for him. Even to think it's a possibility, that's pretty cool," he says, gazing out at his rose garden. "But you're right. So what's our game plan?"

Amanda thinks for a minute. "Well, if he's drafted, we go to ice cream, right?"

"Yeah, obviously. And if not?"

"Then bracing ourselves is even more important. First, we have to empathize with him. Tell him we're sorry, that we know he must be hurting. Let him vent if he has to. And you," she says. "You have to be okay with him swearing and having one of his limbic-system tantrums."

"Right, since his frontal lobe hasn't fully developed yet, I get that. I'm not sure mine has, either, so it might be a challenge for me to stay cool."

"The cooler we are, the cooler he'll be."

"When do we tell him to get a job?"

"Not funny," she says. "I think we tell him we love him and we're here for him, no matter what. If he wants to talk, we'll listen. Let it play out."

Drew sighs. "He'll be a nightmare around here. At least I've got you. Have I told you how grateful I am that you're so calm, so under control, so reasonable?"

"You know how to sweet talk a girl, don't you?" Amanda chuckles. "Compliment her prefrontal cortex. Mmm. Sexy."

At 6:00 that evening, the draft comes to its uneventful conclusion. Neither Anthony's name, nor his phone, has been called. Elena doesn't move, waiting for Anthony's lead. Upstairs, his parents continue to move around, unaware of the scenario, putting dinner preparations together. Peaches meows, and Anthony scratches her head.

Closing his laptops, clicking the remote to deaden the TV, and putting his tablet on the coffee table, he turns to Elena, and to her surprise, smiles gently. "Well, that's that," he says. "Let's go get something to eat."

Her expression gives her away, so he holds out his hand. "I'm okay, really. C'mon, let's go."

She takes his hand, and they walk upstairs, Anthony grabbing his wallet and keys by the front door. "We're out, folks!" he calls to his parents.

"We've got dinner for you two," says his mother, smiling above her worry. "Hope you can stay, Elena."

"That's sweet, mom, and I'm sure it's delicious, but we're going out. Gotta celebrate."

"What are we celebrating, son?" asks Drew, unaware of any cheering that he might have missed from downstairs. "Is it the draft? What's the good word?"

Anthony opens the front door and motions Elena out before him. "Not picked," he says. "So I don't have to ride on filthy buses on dusty roads to stay in flea-bag hotels to play in empty, grimy minor league ballparks all summer. I get to stay here – not quite as many fleas!"

Laughing aloud, he waves over his shoulder to his folks. "Back by midnight. Have a good dinner. It's date-night for you two!"

The door shuts behind him.

"Not what I expected, as far as his response," says Drew, looking back at Amanda, still at the stove in the kitchen.

"That's what worries me."

In the pickup, over the clicking and the rusty parts scraping against each other, Anthony explains his mindset to Elena. "There are a lot of good major league players who didn't get drafted out of high school. Some don't really get noticed until college. A lot of the players drafted today were college players, guys that really had great seasons in major divisions."

Elena just nods, and Anthony continues. "And just because you get drafted, doesn't mean you make it. Some of the first-round guys will never step foot on a major league field. Isn't that crazy? It's a crap-shoot, Elena. They win some; they lose some. I figure, I have four years of college eligibility, right? I'm bound to have a great season or two, or three, or four, then it'll be my turn. I might even get to play in the Olympics. That'll be cool. I'm in no rush. I'm actually glad I didn't get picked in the later rounds. There's not much money there, I bet. I'd rather wait and go high."

He takes a breath. "How about that sub place we like so much?"

Elena nods. All she heard was, *I'll be leaving. And you're staying for another year of high school.* Despite the unofficial nature of their relationship, she is already planning on missing him.

CHAPTER 56

The American Legion season starts on a down note for the Post 11 team, as Kai agrees to a moderate $45,000 signing bonus – moderate in the big scheme of the MLB draft, huge in terms of an 18-year-old kid used to making $7.50 an hour at the local sporting goods store – and reports to a host family (avoiding at least one of those flea-bag hotels) to join the Cubs' Class-A ballclub over in South Bend, Indiana. And just like that, he is packed up and gone. Then, in the season's opening game, José gives up a 7th-inning, game-losing home run, and his emotional reaction is to punch the ground in front of the pitcher's mound. The doctor says his hand is broken, ending his season.

The American Legion code of sportsmanship echoes in Anthony's mind:

I will…keep the rules, keep faith with my teammates, keep my temper, keep myself fit, keep a stout heart in defeat, keep my pride under in victory, keep a sound soul, a clean mind, and a healthy body.

Because of these personnel losses, the team stumbles out of the gate, losing five games the first week.

With the pitching staff depleted, the Post 11 team's opponents score early and often. Their offense is able to keep them in most of the games, but they still can only hover around .500 all year. This is distressing for many of the VMHS players in particular, who had grown accustomed to winning during the school season.

Nick and Anthony, still a dynamic 1-2 combination at the top of the batting order, are inflicting damage on a nightly basis. Both are hitting, stealing, and scoring runs, thanks to the offensive output from Reggie and Scottie, moved up in the order to replace Kai and José. After that, though, the lineup fizzles. Even the powerful first baseman, Stephen, is having trouble keeping up with the upgraded pitching they face.

Anthony's days are spent rather lazily, playing video games in the basement, going for daily walks with Elena, and getting in some extra hitting with Nick. Since his shoulder has serviceably recovered from his preseason injury, he opts out of swimming and instead sleeps in. The boys report to the ballpark around 3:00, sometimes earlier for road games. It is a carefree, easy life.

And then Anthony's graduation money runs out.

One afternoon, asking his father for money for food after that night's game, Anthony gets the response he dreads. "Nope, this well's run dry, son. Time for you to get a job." As soon as he says it, Drew Sumner braces himself for an argument.

"Yeah? What kind of job?"

Glad to engage in this chat, Drew and Anthony exchange ideas, with Drew eventually telling his son he'll check around the university campus to see if any of his colleagues have part-time, morning-only positions that will work around Anthony's baseball schedule. Anthony seems rather excited at the prospect, and when his dad comes home the next day with the good news, Anthony embraces his modified routine whole-heartedly.

It isn't glorious work, but it gets him some spending cash. Anthony's responsibilities in the maintenance department at OSU include donning work gloves and a helmet, entering the construction zone at the school library, and systematically removing books from shelves and stacking them on carts, careful to maintain their order, then disassembling the old book shelves and tossing them into dumpsters. He proceeds methodically, and after a week believes he's become an expert shelf-wrecker, learning to separate the metal connection pieces with a quick flick of his wrists. He is sure he is the fastest of the nine-person crew. The library is eight stories tall, though, and all the shelves are to be replaced. He'll have to pace himself if he is going to fit in and survive the summer.

CHAPTER 57

One late summer afternoon, the Sumners invite Jay and Sandy Young over for happy hour and hors d'oeuvres. Anthony is out somewhere with Nick, Simon, and Elena, as the baseball team has a rare rest day. When the Youngs arrive, Drew immediately takes them out to the garden to show off.

"I've collected over two dozen different varieties of roses," Drew explains, proudly. He leads his guests immediately to the closest row of bushes, each adorned with a handful of long-stemmed flowers of various hues. "This one," he gently pulls a tri-colored flower a bit closer, the white-yellow buttercream center framed by a brilliant pink outer edge on each petal, "is called Double Delight. It's a hybrid tea rose, smells delightful. Take a whiff."

Jay and Sandy each fill their nostrils with the flower's sweet aroma. They both nod and smile.

"And here," Drew continues, "we have a couple variations of English roses. See how their petals are really densely packed in there?"

Amanda calls from the kitchen window, interrupting the tour. "If you're done with your nature walk, I have us all set up in here."

"Thank you for sharing," Sandy says to Drew. "It's obvious you care very deeply for your rose garden."

Begrudgingly, Drew turns and follows their guests into the kitchen.

At the kitchen table, the Youngs and Sumners enjoy chips and guacamole, bean dip, and a Willamette Valley sauvignon blanc.

"So how's the baseball saga progressing?" Jay jumps right in.

Drew looks at his wife, who nods for him to take the first stab at the explanation. "Okay. Brief synopsis: Anthony didn't get drafted, and we figured that would ruin him, but instead he's been in a fantastic mood. Almost euphoric. In fact, I've never seen him so continuously upbeat. He's playing great baseball in Legion, he has a job, and he has money to go hang with his friends. He hasn't gotten into any trouble, so life is good."

Sandy sips her wine, then asks, "Is that how you really see it?"

Amanda's "Not one bit" is quicker and more emphatic than her husband's, "Well," so she gets the air time. "I think he's masking something. Over-compensating for his grief."

"Wait a minute," says Drew. "He doesn't really have anything to grieve about, does he?"

"He was pretty set on getting drafted," Amanda responds. "And we never heard one word from any of the colleges he sent video to. We don't know what he's doing in the fall, and that's right around the corner. He's had a lot to shoulder all this time, emotionally."

"And how has he responded, emotionally?" prods Jay, gently. He takes a scoop of guac.

"He's been acting happy, for the most part. Like Drew said, upbeat."

Sandy sets her glass down and asks, "Isn't that just about what you said you wanted, a couple of months ago when we had dinner? You said your goals for him were to be happy, successful, and productive, right? I think you just described all those things. So why the uncertainty?"

Amanda takes this. "I know our son, and I know how much he wanted – and still wants – to be a pro baseball player. That's his identity. Even though *we* see him as a well-rounded, intelligent, amazing young man, I'm not sure he sees anything beyond the batter's box."

"That's true," agrees Drew. "For a while now, he's defined himself as a baseball player first, and everything else a distant second."

"Interesting," answers Jay.

"What do you think?" asks Drew.

Jay finishes another chip loaded with guacamole before responding. "Unfortunately, as we discussed before, the percentage of kids whose baseball careers end before they make it to the big leagues is well over 99 percent. Those stats are undeniable, so the odds are stacked against him, right? Now he's got to be in the top couple of percent, seeing as he was an all-state player, so his continued career is not out of the question. But you're not asking about the odds, you're asking about his mental state, his self-image, and his confidence in life outside the baseball arena, yes?"

Anthony's parents nod.

"Well," Jay goes on. "It's typical for kids to disassociate themselves with their feelings, especially in times of loss, grief, or perceived trauma. And if it's not baseball that brings loss, it's life itself. You know, death of a loved one, divorce, fired from a treasured job, all sorts of things can and do happen to us through the ordinary course of events. It's important that he's prepared to handle that *before* it happens, so he's equipped *when* it happens. Does that make sense?"

They nod again. This time, Drew asks a question: "Okay, so what about setting him up for success? Amanda and I have noticed that he tends to just take life one day at a time, expecting good things to happen to him, and more or less they do. Life gets harder, right? I mean, that's been our experience. Nothing gets easier, that's for sure."

Jay gestures in agreement. "In all areas of life, we ought to have a plan. That doesn't mean everything needs to be scripted or mapped out, but if there's something we truly want to accomplish, or achieve, we can't leave it to chance. If it's important to us, the best way to get it is to have a clear picture of that goal, then build a specific, progressive plan to achieve it. Are you concerned about Anthony's work ethic as he goes off to college?"

Drew and Amanda look at each other, both shrugging. "There's no question he works hard at baseball. He and Nick are always getting extra hitting in," Amanda ventures. "He wasn't much for school work, even though his grades were okay and his test scores are pretty good. He has a job at OSU now, and that's work. I don't know. I guess I'm worried."

"What are you worried about?" asks Sandy.

"I'm worried that those college coaches never called, and he never bothered to contact them. Maybe it was his high school coaches here that should have guided that, but Anthony never took any proactive steps to connect, to let them know how he was doing, to talk about the teams, anything. I'm afraid he's taking too much for granted."

Drew nods some more. "Yeah, that's about right. He figures he'll get by on his performance alone. I think that's his M.O. And he's done well, but still no scholarships."

"It sounds like you already know how to help Anthony," says Jay. "Which doesn't surprise me, since you're caring, loving parents."

"Guide him in creating an action plan, take the bull by the horns, and be proactive," Drew summarizes, dragging a chip through the bean dip.

"A plan, yes," adds Sandy. "And a *contingency* plan, just in case the first one doesn't materialize. We've discussed the importance of a Plan B before, and in Anthony's case that seems like a pretty prudent idea."

A knock at the front door interrupts the chat, and a half-second later Reggie comes barreling through the front door. "Hi Mr. and Mrs. Sumner!" he calls, as Scottie follows and gently closes the door behind them. "And hello, strangers, I'm Reggie," he says, extending a hand and an enormously mischievous grin in greeting.

Jay and Sandy Young shake his hand, and Scottie's, while the boys hug Anthony's parents.

"And how are you spending your off day?" asks Drew.

"Making the rounds, trying to get all the guys to sign this card for Coach Shepard. As you know, he retired," says Scottie. "And he's moving back to Oklahoma next week. So we are gonna buy him an actual crown and have it engraved. You folks want to contribute? Want to sign the card, too?"

Scottie puts the card and pen on the table, and Reggie, presumptively, opens his palm to accept a cash donation.

"Sure, we'd be happy to further the cause," says Amanda, out of her seat and heading for her purse. "Honey, why don't you sign the card for both of us. And Reggie, dear, have some bean dip."

"No, thanks," Reggie exclaims. "I don't like that stuff. But thanks anyway!"

CHAPTER 58

After debriefing with Amanda, Drew Sumner agrees to put some of the Youngs' advice into action. Talking to his son is never a difficult thing to do…unless it is a serious topic. Superficial chats about sports and school and whether the truck needs an oil change are no problem, but when it comes to talks about drugs and the birds and the bees and drinking, it gets a little dicier. Fortunately, Anthony has naturally steered away from those risky behaviors. His compass always seems to point toward baseball.

Drew's father taught him a valuable lesson about parenthood early on. "If you want to talk about something serious, busy yourself while you do it. It's easier to get into the muck of our minds when we've got a different muck on our hands," Grampa Sumner had said.

So when Anthony drags himself into the kitchen a couple days hence, Drew has concocted a project.

"Good morning, sunshine," he laughs, as his son staggers toward the cupboard.

"Mmm."

Drew steels himself. "Hey, will you help me with something real quick? I need to get behind the fridge, I think we have an issue with the water line back there."

"It has wheels, Dad. Just pull it."

"I know, I need to keep the electrical cords away from the water line and the filtration system. I don't need to explain to you how bad it would turn out if we got those mixed up, do I?"

"Okay, sure. Then can I eat?"

"Of course, thanks."

Together, they wheel the refrigerator away from its cave of cabinets. Drew wedges himself in the nook and begins to examine the water line. "Hand me that quarter-inch crescent wrench, will you?" he asks.

As they busy themselves with the chore at hand, Drew launches into it. "You've had quite a roller-coaster of a year, haven't you?"

"What do you mean?" Anthony responds, trying to hook the fridge's power cord in the freezer door, so he won't have to hold it any more.

"Well, your shoulder, the baseball season, the draft, and getting ready for college. That's a lot."

"Yeah, I guess. Not really sure what I'm gonna do for college, though."

"Have you heard from any college baseball coaches?"

"Nothing yet. Just a couple emails that they got my profile and highlight vids. I've been accepted at a couple schools, but I don't want to pick until I know I can play ball there."

Flashes of the conversation with Jay and Sandy pop into Drew's mind. "I wonder if we should take the bull by the horns, call Coach Shepard, you know? And hey, I need that screwdriver," he says, pointing with his head.

Anthony hands him the tool, and his father continues. "Maybe he could put us in touch with the coaches at the colleges you've been accepted into."

"Good idea. You'd do that?"

"We would do that. Together. Maybe after you eat something and splash some water on your face."

Anthony laughs. "That'd be great. And I'm still starving. Almost done back there?"

"Yup," Drew grunts. "You know, you have a lot to look forward to. You have a lot of promise. How are you doing with all this?"

Anthony fidgets with the cord again. "Dad, I'm fine. Are you worried that you're going to miss me, is that it?"

"No, no. I mean, yes, of course. I just want to make sure you're doing okay."

They work in silence for a few minutes, just the clinking of tools and the rumbling of Anthony's empty stomach echoing in the kitchen.

"You know, your mom isn't the first woman I proposed to."

"Wait, what?" Anthony stops fidgeting.

"Just after college, I'd been dating Katherine something-or-other, you don't need to know her last name and go looking her up online. Anyway, I was madly in love, and I felt like she was too, so I asked her to marry me."

"Clearly she was smart enough to avoid that one somehow. What happened?"

"Well, she said *no*, plain and simple. Said we weren't ready, in fact she broke up with me, right then and there."

"You misjudged that one, huh?"

"Just hand me the wrench again, smart aleck. The reality was she was right, and even though I was devastated, it turned out to be one of the best things that ever happened to me."

"Of course it did. I know the rest. You met mom, had a child, then had a really awesome child, and lived happily ever after."

"Exactly. And this is almost finished, hang on." Drew, at this point, is tightening and loosening the same bolt over and over. "The point is, every time a door closes, another one opens. You may not always see it, but it's there. Just keep your eyes open."

He looks over his shoulder at his son, who is silent, perhaps even reflective, leaning against the fridge. "And no matter what doors you go through, your mom and I will always love you, we'll always be there for you, and we'll always be cheering for you. Got it?"

Anthony meets his father's eyes. "Roger that. I'll miss you too."

Drew smiles and shakes his head. "It's kinda filthy back here, and I don't really fit. Will you clean this up before you push the fridge back? I'll put away the tools. After you eat, we'll call Coach Shepard."

On his way out to the garage, toolbox in hand, Drew watches his son wet a rag in the sink and kneel down, wiping some back-of-the-fridge grime off the floor. He smiles to himself. In a matter of weeks, his son will be heading off to college somewhere. He'll need more than a magic wrench, but it is a start.

CHAPTER 59

"Do you really even need all that stuff now that you're retired?"

Dwayne Shepard heaves the last of the banker's boxes on top of the fourth and final stack next to the front door. The pile of receipts, lineup cards, bank statements, newspaper clippings, and who knows what else groans and teeters a bit, fighting gravity. *Leaning like the tower of Pisa. And that's a darn good question. When am I ever gonna look at all these files again?*

"I don't know, hon. Maybe. You never know when this *Cloud* will disappear and only the people with paper lives will take over."

"What if you scanned 'em and just kept 'em digitally? Or better yet, throw 'em in the fireplace! Retirement should be a fresh start. We could just leave all this...*stuff* behind." Tonya Shepard waves her arm at the stacks, rolling her eyes playfully.

Dwayne wipes his brow with his sleeve, exhaling emphatically. Wrapping the other arm around his wife's waist, he spins her around. "It will be a fresh start. No more baseball, no more paperwork, no more distractions, just you and me."

As if on cue, his phone rings. "Uh huh," Tonya mutters, as Dwayne unwraps her and grabs the phone off the table.

"Sumner!" he exclaims, and taps the phone. "Hey Rooster, how's it going, big fella?"

"Great, Coach, thanks. My dad's here, too."

Coach Shepard watches his wife balance the stacks of boxes and disappear down the hallway.

"Good morning, Coach. You must be about ready to head out of town. Congratulations on the retirement."

"Thank you, Mr. Sumner. It's a blessing and a curse. I believe I've earned it, but I'm sure gonna miss it. I'll miss working with kids like your son, that's for sure."

"Well, that's why we're calling, Coach. Anthony says he hasn't heard a word from any college coaches yet, and he's got to make his plan for the fall. Have you communicated with anyone about him? Is there any interest? Should we be calling the schools directly?"

"Oh, there's been interest, all right. Coach Schneider is in charge of the emails and all that online stuff. Let me connect with him and make a couple calls this afternoon." Coach Shepard reflects on his conversations with Lopez, the scout for the Mets and all his advanced metrics. He parks himself on the sofa and starts digging through a pile of stuff on the coffee table. "I need a pad of paper. Okay, Anthony, where have you been accepted? We'll start there."

"Arizona State, UC-San Diego, San Diego State, UC-Davis, and USC."

"Oh, that's right, schools with sunshine." A quick gaze out the window, imagining his return to the Oklahoma heat. "Okay, you two. I'm on it. Can't believe it's already mid-summer. And man, Anthony, I'm sorry I haven't made it to any of your Legion games. You tearing it up or what?"

"It's going okay. It's tough without Kai and José, but I'm having fun. Wish you were out there!"

"Me too. I've got your back, though, don't you worry."

___

"Thank you, Coach," Drew says. "When are you headed out of town?"

"This weekend, actually. Getting the truck tomorrow and hitting the road first thing Saturday morning. Oklahoma, here we come!" He looks at the piles of boxes again and sighs.

"Travel safe, Coach, and thanks again for everything! I'll let you know where I end up."

"You got it, Rooster. You've got a lot of baseball left in you. Maybe we'll see you in Omaha, it's only about a seven-hour drive, and I'll need to find stuff to do with all this time on my hands." Coach Shepard envisions a trip to the College World Series. It's always been on his bucket list. Perhaps now...

"Yes, sir. See you there!"

"Go get 'em, Rooster!"

After clicking off the call, Dwayne heads down the hallway, leaving his phone and boxes behind.

CHAPTER 60

Two nights later, Anthony sits in the dugout following a tough game against a surprisingly pesky team from Mountlake Terrace, Washington. Corvallis is just a pit stop on their way to a tournament in California, yet they brought their A-game. The whole affair had been scrappy, lots of tense situations, a couple hit batters, and more than a little chirping between dugouts, though in the end it finished peacefully. And now he sits, alone on the bench, one pants-leg rolled up, exposing a ripped-open scab above his knee. Pouring water from the dugout cooler over it, Anthony scrubs dirt out of the wound.

Elena's face appears around the corner above the dugout steps. "Hey, Anthony, everything okay? It's not like you to be the last one out."

"Yeah, I know. Just gotta clean this mess up."

"What happened?"

"Nothing, just an occupational hazard from diving into third base. This won't heal until I retire."

"Well, hurry up. There's a man out here that wants to talk to you. And if you have any energy left over, I'd love to go eat something."

"Who's out there?"

"I think it's a coach, talking to your parents."

Anthony decides the knee can wait, rolls his pants leg down, stuffs his gear into his bag, and leaps out of the dugout. "Where?"

Elena points, and Anthony bounds up the steps of the bleachers, where his parents are among the last fans still seated, chatting with a familiar face.

Phillip Cleary, the head coach at neighboring Willamette University in Salem, notices Anthony's arrival first. "Nice game, Sumner!" he calls.

"Thank you, sir," responds Anthony, channeling Mrs. A's advice. He knows Coach Cleary from summer camps he's attended in years past, before he was of age to play Legion ball. He's always felt a kinship with Coach Cleary, perhaps because he wears a Boston cap, perhaps because of his giant figure and gregarious nature, or perhaps because he is, through and through, a baseball man. He calls everybody by their last names, just like in the box scores.

"Been talking to your folks," says Coach Cleary. "And I got a call from Shepard the other day. He says you haven't landed on a spot for college ball next year yet. Gotta say I'm surprised, and honestly quite a bit excited, to hear that. I don't know what your plans are for next year, but if you're interested, a guaranteed starting spot at second base, I got it for you at Willamette. I think I've already talked Vazquez into coming here, if he promises not to break his hand again," he laughs.

"Wow, thanks, Coach."

"That's exciting, isn't it?" Anthony's father shares a knowing look with his son.

"Yup, lots to think about," Anthony replies.

"Well, don't think too long. Before you know it, the summer will be over. Just say the word, Sumner, and we'll wrap it up. You'd look good in our maroon and gold uniforms!" Coach Cleary hands Anthony a card.

To Anthony's parents, he adds, "Nice talking with you folks." And with a playful slug to Anthony's good shoulder, he steps down the bleachers and heads toward the parking lot.

"Thanks, Coach!" Anthony calls, smiling at Elena and turning back to his parents.

Standing to gather their blankets, Amanda is the first to speak. "Well, that's promising, right?"

Drew responds, "He's got this one in the bag! Nice work, son. What do you think?"

Anthony shrugs. "I love Coach Cleary, he's definitely a great coach, and I've always learned a lot from him. But…"

"But what? A guaranteed spot in the starting lineup? Right here in Oregon? We can drive to all your games! What's the 'but' for?"

"It'd be cool, but I think a bigger program would get me better exposure. Willamette's D-III, right? No scholarships, no big games, nothing on TV. I'd be wasted there."

Amanda and Drew share a look. Elena purses her lips. Anthony continues, "And if Coach Shepard called Coach Cleary, he probably called other coaches, too. I'm gonna wait. The flood gates are about to open!"

The next night, following a particularly satisfying 8-4 victory over their rivals in Salem – some of the same coaches and players Anthony had *haunted* in the high school season – Anthony and Nick find themselves in the ballpark's deserted lot, perched on the tailgate of Anthony's rusty pickup with Elena and Simon. It is a scene that has been repeated night after night that summer, the boys still wearing their uniforms, grimy, sweaty, and animated as they replay the evening's highlights. The excited chatter halts abruptly when Anthony's phone rings. A California prefix. It is almost 10:00.

"Hello?"

"Anthony, it's Charlie Jefferson, head baseball coach down here at UC-Davis. I heard you've been accepted here and you're looking for a team to join this fall," he says, not beating around the bush.

Anthony hushes his companions and hops off the tailgate. "Yes, sir," he responds. "How are you, Coach?"

"I'm great, thank you. Your high school coach, Shepard, gave me a call today. Also gave me your number. Hope you don't mind me calling so late, my schedule's wall-to-wall. This is my cell. If you're up for it, I'm going to email you a couple things we'd need ASAP. I see you already filled out our recruiting profile. Looks like you've done well up there in Oregon."

"Yes, sir, and sure thing," answers Anthony, as his heart bounces in his chest. "And my buddy Nick's coming, too. I'll get you his email too," he adds, nodding to Nick, who is listening intently from the pickup.

"Nick Greene? Already got his," answers the coach. "Well, it's late, and I just wanted to welcome you to the team. Oh, and hey. I don't know if you knew this, but the school record for stolen bases here is 29. If what your Coach Shepard says is true, that should be well within your reach."

It is too dark to tell, even in the parking lot lights, but Anthony probably blushes a bit. "Yes, sir," is all he can manage.

When he hangs up, he puts his arms out and wraps his best friend in a bear hug. "Yeah, buddy!" he exclaims. "We're playing ball in Cali, for sure!"

"What do you mean?" Nick asks.

"That was Coach Jefferson. UC-Davis. He invited *us* to play there! Wants me to break the school record for stolen bases."

"Just like that? Is that your decision?" Elena asks, hopping off the tailgate.

"You bet! I've already been accepted, Nick's going there, and they have a good baseball program. D-I. I can walk-on and eventually earn a scholarship, I bet. It's in California, so we can play year-round, and if

I end up wanting to transfer to one of the bigger schools, it should be pretty easy."

"Are you sure that's what you want?"

"Well, I want to go straight to Fenway Park," he grins. "In the meantime, Davis should cut it."

"This isn't something you just leap into. Didn't you say yesterday that the flood gates are about to open? This is a big decision. Why don't you take some time on this?"

"I've taken plenty of time," Anthony responds. "The big schools missed their chance. All the major league teams did, too. I'll find a way to make 'em regret not picking me in the draft. I can haunt 'em. Plus, Nick and I have always talked about us going to school together anyway, and I think that'd be awesome. He'll need a roommate to keep him in line," he adds.

"Well, congratulations, then! Shall we celebrate?" Simon starts a group hug, and Elena isn't far behind.

"I've just gotta call my folks, maybe they'll meet us for ice cream," Anthony says. Nick is already on the phone with his parents.

As he dials his phone, Anthony wanders through the gates and leans against the fence down the right-field foul line. The groundskeepers haven't turned off the stadium lights yet, though the place is deserted. After telling his parents the good news, he surveys the ballpark, the home of so many wonderful memories, a collage of uniforms and green grass, the pop of baseballs landing in mitts, the smell of the concession-stand barbeque, the aching joy of the game, filling his head and heart. As he turns away, the lights go dark, and it is silent again.

In the parking lot, his friends await. After a few more hugs and wolf-howls into the night sky, they pile into their respective vehicles and head off for ice cream. He has all but forgotten he isn't one of the top 1200 amateur ballplayers in the country.

CHAPTER 61

There will be no dream ending to the American Legion baseball season for the Post 11 team that year. Injuries decimate the lineup, with Kyle, their best remaining pitcher, tearing his rotator cuff and Scottie having to undergo sports hernia surgery, knocking the active roster to 19.

Behind the clutch hitting of Nick, Anthony, and Reggie, they make it to the second round of the league playoffs, but their path ends there, finishing a 25-24 season, thanks to a two-game sweep at the hands of their Salem counterparts, many of whom had watched the VMHS squad run roughshod through their high school teams just a couple months prior. The voracity of their celebration is not lost on the Post 11 team, whose departing seniors implore the younger members of the squad to remember that feeling, that hollow, angry sensation of watching the enemy prance and gyrate, to fuel their passion for next season. There isn't much else they can do.

In the end, the local paper runs a summary article and prints the players' statistics after the final game. Anthony and Nick pore over the stat page, extrapolating their 49-game season into the major-league equivalent, 162 games.

"Let's see, over a full major league season, assuming neither of us got hurt, I'd have gathered 188 hits, and you'd have, um, 52 times 3.306,

172. That's a lot of hits! The 1-2 combination is in full effect!" Anthony exclaims, starting down the line.

"Your .328 average was great, fantastic, not to mention pretty good," laughs Nick.

"I'd take .310 any day of the week and twice on Sundays."

"Ah, man, it says I'd have only gotten 99 walks. If I knew that going into the last game, I'd have fouled more pitches off to get to triple-digits," Nick notes, typing furiously on his phone's calculator app.

"Check this out. Over a full season, my 47 steals would have set all sorts of records: 155!" Anthony sits back, impressed with his own accomplishments.

"It *did* set all sorts of records. 47 was a Legion record. That's amazing anyway, man. Congratulations!"

They fist-bump and continue this drill until all the stats are properly exaggerated.

"So," says Anthony, getting up from the kitchen table and pouring a glass of water. "What kind of numbers will we put up in college? How different will it be?"

Nick gestures that he'd like a glass of water, too, so Anthony fills a second. "Probably something like these, but who knows? Maybe we'll do even better. All I know is that whatever teams are in their league better watch out; the 1-2 combo is coming to California!"

CHAPTER 62

The following night, Anthony extends an invitation to his teammates – it is open to all, actually – to chill in the Sumners' back yard for a fire pit. The long summer nights have begun to shorten, and when the shadows finish creeping across the yard, shrouding the rose bushes in darkness, the glowing fire takes over, casting flickering figures that dance on the nearby western hemlocks' droopy branches.

Eleven of the friends gather by the fire. Simon and Nick park side-by-side on an old snowboard Anthony's dad had fashioned into a bench. Reggie, Scottie, and their two dates, Amy and Janae, have positioned themselves in Adirondack chairs. Then there is Adam, noisy as always and wearing his hat backwards, and Johnny and big Stephen, splitting space on a wooden park bench.

The night is alive with stories, laughter, memories, and heartfelt pronouncements. The friends know their time together, as wonderful as it has been and as long as it has lasted, is coming to an end. Despite their most earnest commitments to stay in touch, to visit each other as often as possible, and to get together during vacations at home, they know deep down that very few of those promises can be held. Life is going to happen, young adults will go their separate ways, priorities will shift, and things will change.

Anthony sits next to Elena, the lone junior of the crew, and watches her in the twinkling firelight. Her eyes sparkle, her smile a glowing ember. As their friends leave, one by one or two by two, it is soon just the pair of them, staring at the fire.

The unspoken words and emotions dominate their minds. Over the course of the summer they've become cautiously inseparable. Their interactions are lighthearted and carefree, concealing the challenges lurking beneath the surface. They offer each other attention and affection, though both know it – they, their relationship, this summer – has an expiration date that's rapidly approaching.

He is preparing to go to college, in another state, gearing up to live another life. She has a final year of high school still to go, and her future is yet to be determined. To each other, they have agreed to keep their relationship simple, emotionally safe, as it were. They've used the words, "Neither of us needs a formal title. That whole boyfriend-girlfriend thing just makes this complicated and leads to heartache later," or language to that effect, more times than either wants to admit. To themselves, they acknowledge the emotional toll will be higher.

Reaching around to a small wooden stand behind him, Anthony grabs two skewers. "I can't believe nobody wanted s'mores! You?"

Elena nods, her thoughts far away.

"Hey," he says, stabbing the skewers into the ground. "First off, you and I will always be close. That's a given, no matter where I go to college or what you end up doing next year. Right?"

He touches her chin, guiding her eyes to face his. She smiles.

"And," he continues. "You know I'll be checking on you to make sure you're doing okay. High school can be rough, believe me. Even though I made it look so darn easy!" He laughs, rolling his eyes at himself.

Picking a marshmallow out of the bag on the table beside him, he spears it with one of the skewers and holds it over the fire, rotating it slowly clockwise, then counter-clockwise. It seems to mesmerize both of them, as neither speaks for several minutes.

"I think it's ready," Elena says, when the mallow bursts into flame, a brilliant explosion of yellow against an otherwise simmering red-orange fire pit.

"Oh, crap," says Anthony, lurching forward to blow out the blaze. "Ah, well, that's how I like 'em," he laughs, and gently eases the burnt mallow onto a graham cracker square, gently placing a peanut-butter cup on next and squishing it together with another square of graham cracker. "Most people just use chocolate, but this is something extra-special."

He takes the first bite, easing the treat away from his mouth as the melting mallow slowly breaks off.

"Delicious," he says, and he can feel the marshmallow on his lip. Elena spies it, wipes it with her finger, and licks it off.

Her eyes haven't left his. He sees the tears before she feels them. Scooting her off her seat and onto his right leg, he holds her tight, feeling her tremble, silent, subtle.

The fire crackles on.

FALL

CHAPTER 63

Labor Day comes and goes, and with it depart the sunny, summer days, replaced by the cool, crisp air of the impending autumn. The leaves of the Oregon trees begin their colorful transformation, cautiously at first, then bursting across the landscape as the full splendor of fall consumes them. The Pacific dogwood, in particular, paints the countryside with its wild array of brilliant reds. The bigleaf maple offers a dynamic contrast with its bright, eye-popping yellows, lighting up even the grayest, drizzly days.

Their colorful mosaic is brought back to earth by the drab brown of the massive oak trees behind the backstop at Sunset Oaks Park, where Anthony finds himself one rainy afternoon. He stands in the bleachers, under the canopy provided by the scoring booth's protruding roof, and replays the memories. He thinks of gobbling up ground balls and flipping them on target to first, diving headlong into second base, stretching to grab the stolen base before feeling the tag, blasting the sphere over the fence and into the next county, seeing the scoreboard reflecting yet another Moutaineers win. The celebrations shared with a great group of guys and a coach who ended on a high note. It was an amazing career, an amazing experience, playing high school baseball here. As he stands and looks at the field, watching the leaves fall gently around him, listening to the rain tumbling onto the roof above him, he gazes also at the school that lies beyond. He imagines Elena, among the thousand-plus kids making their way to and from their classes, playing the school game.

And then he thinks of college. California. His baseball dream. His future. It is all just waiting for him.

As are his parents. "You good, son?" hollers his father from the car, parked fifty yards behind him. "Ready to go? It's a long drive to Davis if we're going to make it today."

With one last look, from foul pole to foul pole, he hops down the steps and runs to the car, dodging leaves and raindrops along the way.

Nature's landscape changes dramatically over the course of the next eight hours. In Davis, nestled just to the west of Sacramento in what's considered northern California, it doesn't look like summer has even thought about leaving yet.

The mighty sequoias and ponderosa pine trees stand proudly over the main streets, with palm trees and their fronds blowing in the late afternoon breeze. Flowers are still blooming, the sun is still shining, and the grass is still green. *I doubt the grass in California ever isn't green*, thinks Anthony, as they park by the freshman dorms.

Nick isn't scheduled to arrive until the next day, which means Anthony has first dibs on the room's bed, desk, and dresser. They both requested each other as roommates, so the housing form he received via email was just a confirmation and an address. He grabs their key-cards downstairs and shuffles up to the second story, room 208, with his parents right behind. The room has a nice little view of the courtyard below, blocked in part by a couple of thick white firs which send their long needles and cylindrical cones toward the windows to offer some privacy.

"Looks nice enough," his mom says, examining the cleanliness of the mattress and the closet. "You going to be okay here?"

"Of course, this is great. I just can't wait for Nick to get here!"

"Looks like this bed is longer than an average twin. We'll have to get new sheets for you. And you have your own pillow, right? What else will you need?"

"Mom," says Anthony, standing in the middle of his new dorm room. "I'm good. I'm sure they have extra-long sheets at the school bookstore or student union. They deal with this every year, right? And I have a credit card and money in my account. I'll get what I need, and what I can't get here, I'll order with your Amazon password," he winks.

"Not so fast, junior," laughs his father. "Once you decided to go out of state, I switched the password. You'd better find a kitchen, so you can start washing dishes!"

"Sounds like you're inviting me out to dinner. I heard there's a great Mexican place called Dos Coyotes here. I accept. I'll get all unpacked later, after you say good-bye and go cry yourselves to sleep at your hotel, now that your favorite child is all grown up and off to college." He ushers his parents toward the door.

"Sure, that sounds nice, too," Drew says, eyeing his wife.

"Yes, okay," she agrees. "I suppose we can trust that we raised you well enough to get your own sheets, and toothpaste. Do you have toothpaste? We'll be right downtown at our hotel tonight, so if you need anything, we can take care of it first thing tomorrow before we hit the road."

"C'mon, let's go," Anthony takes his mom's arm and shuts the door to his new room behind them.

Halfway through his Border Burrito, Anthony's phone buzzes. Grampa Sumner. Swallowing a massive bite of carnitas, black beans, rice, and guacamole, he answers his phone. Immediately, Grampa Sumner launches into some energetic cheer, punctuated by an emphatic "hoo-rah" or two. Anthony giggles sheepishly at his phone, looks around nervously at the other patrons to see if he's making a scene, and tries to assess when he can speak. Finally, he gets his chance, giving Grampa the highlights, waiting for him to relay them to Gramma Sumner, and thanking him for calling.

"You know, he thinks the world of you," Amanda says.

Anthony digs back into his meal. "I know, he's awesome. He loves baseball."

"He loves you."

"Yeah, I'll keep in touch with him, no worries."

Grampa and Gramma Sumner had ramped up their grandparenting responsibilities many years ago after Amanda's parents, Anthony's maternal grandparents, passed away within a year of each other. Anthony and Jenna were both under age five, and his memories of them were strictly from photographs and stories told during lap-time as a kid. Weekly phone calls from New Hampshire had become a staple, and Grampa Sumner had developed a particular fondness of Anthony's trajectory as a ballplayer. And now he was going to college to continue his baseball career! *Luck has nothing to do with it, right Anthony? Not with your skill set.*

The rest of dinner proceeds rather quietly by comparison.

Once back from dinner, the teary good-byes are left in the parking lot. Anthony doesn't need his mom hovering around the dorm room any longer, cleaning and rearranging all the furniture. He wanders upstairs, proud to be on his own, and gives the space a once-over. This is not his bedroom at home. He glances over at Nick's side of the room, and it hits him. He is alone. For the first time in his life, he is truly alone.

Tossing a suitcase onto the dresser, Anthony opens it and spies an unfamiliar brown paper bag, folded over itself and containing a small, rectangular object. Carefully opening it, he finds a small frame, and behind the glass is a poem, hand-written in calligraphy:

Hold on to your dreams

Don't ever give in.

If you keep trying,

You're going to win.

Hold on to your dreams,

Though sometimes it's hard.

Just hold your head up

And reach for the stars.

Hold on to your dreams

Though they seem far away.

Those dreams will come true,

Somehow – someway.

Taped to the back of the poem is a small scrap of paper, on which is simply written, *To Anthony, Love always, Elena. P.S. Dream on!*

He immediately snaps a picture of the framed poem, sends it to Elena, and begins a text. Staring at his phone, he changes his mind.

Her voice answering, "Hello, Mr. California," releases all the anxiety out of his body. She says "Hello?" at least three more times before he finally speaks.

"I just needed to hear your voice, and thank you for the poem. I love it!" His belongings remain unpacked as they talk for hours.

CHAPTER 64

College life in California is exhilarating and excruciating for the two Oregon boys in room 208. Between orientation sessions, interminable lines at the bookstore for textbooks, the exorbitant prices they charge for said textbooks, and the multiple bike trips they take around campus to figure out where their classes are, there is always something new and the to-do lists never end.

The dorms host social events every day, the dining commons is always packed, and soon the faces begin to appear a little more familiar. Names are easier to remember for Nick, but no matter how hard Anthony tries, it appears names aren't his forte. They concoct a plan, agreeing that if Anthony scratches his eyebrow, that means he doesn't remember this person's name, and Nick will weave it into their conversation naturally. The scene plays out repeatedly.

New friend: "Hey guys, how are the Oregonians? Have your webbed feet acclimated to the sunshine yet?" They fist-bump or high-five.

Anthony, scratching his eyebrow: "Hey man, what's up? Yeah, we're good. The gills are closing up!"

Nick, noticing keenly: "What's up, Tyler? It's Tyler from Escondido, right? What's the food like today?"

And on it goes, until Anthony at least has a grasp of their closest neighbors and the classmates they run into frequently. Two of their fellow dorm-mates, a taller, lanky kid named Chris Amano and a muscular, athletic fellow named Daryl McClendon, are both also out for the baseball team. Daryl, built like a barrel, has an easy name to remember. It rhymes. Chris pitches, and Daryl plays right field, which means they aren't competition for roster spots, so Nick and Anthony have no issues befriending them. Plus, they seem like nice guys.

On the first day of practice, the four of them – Nick, Anthony, Chris, and Daryl – ride their bikes through campus and across the giant parking lot next to the Pavilion until they reach the baseball stadium. Cut a little below street-level, it is a snug little ballpark with recently refurbished dugouts, stadium seats, and bleacher seats down both foul lines. There are no seats beyond the outfield fences.

After noting the dignity of the field, which they've stopped to admire a couple of times before during their bike trips around campus, the next thing that catches their eye is the horde of people gathered on the field. Stretching, playing catch, standing and talking, there have to be over a hundred young men in spikes, practice gear, and ball caps, filling the field. Like the gulls on an Oregon beach, they hop around in pairs, or solo, sizing each other up and preparing to put their best foot forward.

"Holy smokes," is all Anthony can say. "Is everyone here trying out for the team?"

That question is soon answered, as they lean their bikes up inside the perimeter fence and join the masses on the playing surface.

"Gentlemen!" comes the call, as four coaches stride from the home-team's first-base dugout onto the field. "Gather 'round, please!"

The gulls bop eagerly to the area between the dugout and first base, jockeying for position and seeking the precious few clams or other morsels that might be available for this meal. The Oregonians and their new friends follow suit.

The coaches introduce themselves. The first is Charlie Jefferson, the head coach whose voice is etched into Anthony's memory from the late-night call not too long ago, followed by his three top assistants. The players will meet the trainers, team psychologist, media squad, and athletic director in due time. For now, Coach Jefferson holds court with an air of military experience, a no-nonsense command of his audience that leaves little to interpretation.

"As you might know," he announces. "The baseball season doesn't start until the spring. We use fall ball to determine our roster and to keep the rust from gathering. We have a roster of 25 here, 25 Aggies who will suit up for every game. Undoubtedly, we'll have a couple of redshirts for injuries and various other reasons. As you might also know, there are 15 returning lettermen on this team, and that crew holds all our, how many is it?" he turns and looks at one of the assistant coaches. Getting his answer, Coach Jefferson turns back to his hopeful players.

"Somehow they've got all our 11.7 scholarships this year. Unless one of them is injured or screws up mightily," he casts a glance at a few familiar faces, who shift uncomfortably, causing a gentle breeze of laughter from those in the know. He continues, "They'll all be back, leaving 10 spots.

Throughout the fall, we'll keep five extras, just as a precaution. That's 15 open spots, no scholarships, no guarantee of playing time. As you have likely gathered," his arm sweeps across the sea of bodies, "there are a few more than 15 of you here, competing for those 15 spots. Over the next two weeks, we'll have a look at each of you, many times. We have your baseball résumés in the office, and that's where they'll stay. Out here, you prove yourselves worthy of becoming an Aggie. Good luck, gentlemen, and go Ags!"

With that, the coaching crew starts reading off names, assigning them to specific practice-jersey colors: blue, gold, white, black, and silver. Anthony runs to the box of blue jerseys and nominates himself as the volunteer jersey-distributor, partly to show initiative and partly to ensure that he receives #6, which he keeps for himself when he finds it in the box. Players all over the field strip off the shirts they wore in favor of the new threads, muscles bulging and ripped, and Anthony opts instead to just put the blue jersey on over his old tee shirt. College baseball has begun.

CHAPTER 65

The first couple of practices are rather pedestrian. Used to lively interactions with teammates, barking orders, and serving as a leader, involved in almost every play, Anthony has to settle for being part of a massive crowd of middle infielders, all taking turns during infield-outfield practice, grounders, and footwork drills. At first it is exciting, knowing each time a ground ball is hit to him, who knows how many coaches will be watching him capture it and fire a perfect throw to a fellow baseman. He imagines the coaching staff turning to each other, nodding at the Oregonian's precision and smooth efforts with the glove. Returning to the end of the line and waiting for his next opportunity, however, quickly becomes agonizing.

With over a dozen players competing for the second-baseman job, there is a considerable span between plays. A lot of time to daydream, to look around the field, so clean and crisp there isn't a hint of clover, and suddenly Anthony misses seeing bumblebees in the field. This isn't home; it is a big, foreign, crazy place. And who knows how the coaches will trim the list from 100 to 15? As he stands, awaiting his chance to turn a double-play, he thinks how he's been led to believe he has a guaranteed spot on this team. He hadn't realized he'd have to fight for it. At least not like this.

When his turn comes, the coach hits a fungo to whatever shortstop is at the front of the line. Anthony sprints to cover second, but the shortstop's throw is wide, and Anthony has to contort to make the catch. As he lands, he goes to pivot to complete the double-play with a throw to first, and his right ankle slides awkwardly off the side of the bag. He feels a sharp pain and collapses to the ground.

"Dammit!" he exclaims, knowing at once he's sprained his ankle.

Refusing to stay down, he hops up on his left leg and tosses the ball over to the first baseman, determined to finish the play. *The coaches would notice that*, he figures. He spies a trainer, already walking over with an icepack, and he hobbles off the field to meet her by the dugout. There he sits for the better part of the next half-hour, nursing his injured wheel. As he sits, he thinks, *none of the coaches said anything when I got hurt. No one has asked how I'm doing. I wonder if they even noticed. Coach Shepard would have come over and grabbed my head and looked me in the eye. "You okay, Rooster?" He would have asked. "That footwork around second base can be nasty, especially if there's a runner bearing down on you. You got this, Rooster!*

I know it." That's what a real coach says.

30 minutes later, he is back in line, limping but upright, his wounded ankle taped and throbbing, anonymously taking ground balls and throwing them around the infield.

CHAPTER 66

On Saturday, baseball practice takes a twist. Instead of tireless drills and a lot of standing around in the sun, the team hosts a youth baseball camp. Kids of all ages, from tykes of 3 or 4 to hopeful future Major Leaguers of 16 and 17, descend upon the Aggie field for a day full of games, activities, challenges, and contests. Over 300 youth from around northern California attend, many of whose parents sit in the stands with their cameras out the whole day.

Of the 100 or so players vying for a roster spot, only about 60 show up, and Anthony brings his A game. He volunteers to take some of the younger kids, and spends the next five hours with two fellow blue-shirted Aggies and a squad of a dozen kids under age 7. Down into the leftfield corner they go, where they play a series of games that build fundamentals, emphasize the joy of baseball, and keep the kids occupied and moving.

Anthony assumes the role of head coach, as he notices his two partners, Jimmy and Jeff, are less than thrilled about being with the young 'uns. Fortunately, teaching is in Anthony's bloodline, and coaching is a close relative to teaching, so he is able to do the heavy lifting. Though his mobility is limited by his bum ankle, his attitude and energy are off the charts. Together, they play "500," swing off a tee, hit wiffle balls into a fence, and practice throwing at a rolling tire.

When Anthony takes the tire and wedges it onto his coach-mate Jeff's body, pinning his arms against his sides, the youngsters screech joyfully, and on Anthony's command, they fire wiffle balls at the tire – and its imprisoned human. Playfully, Jeff wails and head-butts some of the more errant throws, much to the kids' delight.

By the time the day ends, Anthony is exhausted, but he feels like a hero. The kids all hug him, several parents hug him, and one of the Aggie coaches thanks him for his exceptional work. Jimmy and Jeff agree that they each owe him dinner. He appreciates that comment, especially when he proposes Dos Coyotes and they agree.

On the bike ride home at the end of the day, Nick, Chris, and Daryl all share their stories, laugh, and agree to meet for a foosball tournament after showers. Later, the foursome deals cards in the dorm commons until 2:00 a.m.

CHAPTER 67

Sunday afternoon comes, and Charlie Jefferson assembles his coaching staff around the big conference table in the clubhouse beneath the stadium seats. They've ordered pizza, and someone brings a case of beer, since you know, it is Sunday and therefore not a real workday. When Coach Jefferson's eyes burn a hole in the box, it remains unopened for the duration of their session.

The topic of their work session? How to select the top 15 players from the robust collection of student-athletes that have descended upon them so far this fall. Jefferson has pre-written all 127 names on the white boards that surrounded the room, and their job for today is to share their scores, their ranks, and the coaches' impressions of each player, by position, to add to the massive chart. The assistants dare not groan, at least not audibly, at the magnitude of this task.

When Anthony Sumner's name comes up, Coach Jefferson immediately smiles. "This is the kid with the wheels, yes?" he asks. "One of the boys from Oregon. How's he doing?"

Coach Simpson, a former minor-league infielder himself, gives the overview. "He's a second baseman. Claims to want to play shortstop, but he hasn't got the arm. #6 in blue, just to remind everyone. Makes all the routine plays, and kind of adds his own flash to everything. First guy to dive at a ball, even if maybe he doesn't need to dive at it, if you know what I mean. Turns two just fine, but the arm strength is a little concern. Hurt his ankle the other day, but it hasn't kept him out of practices. Skinny as a rail. How's he hitting, Jake?"

Simpson, Jefferson, and the rest of the coaches turn to Jake Stephens, another former minor-leaguer who is the team's batting coach. "Switch-hitter, line-drive hitter, maybe gap power, makes good contact. We haven't seen any live pitching yet, so we don't know how he handles heat or benders, but his cage work is good."

"Attitude?" asks Coach Jefferson. The assistants look at each other. Coach Simpson speaks up. "I've probably spent the most time with him. When it's his turn, he's all about it. Fired up, intense, cocky, even. Other times I've found him drifting off, wandering around the field, almost disinterested."

"He was amazing at the camp yesterday. Had the little guys, and they're tough, believe me," offers Coach Stephens, rubbing his head. "I think he's a gamer."

"Sounds like he's on the bubble. I like that; he's gonna have to fight," says Coach Jefferson, writing some numbers next to Anthony's name on the white-board. "Let's keep an eye on him. We could use a utility infielder, pinch-runner type, and you never know how the season unfolds. A kid with wheels like his could be a game-changer. And Thomas," he adds, turning his intense eyes on the strength and conditioning coach. "See if you can connect with the kid, create a weight training regimen that'll put some meat on his bones and up his arm strength a bit. Sounds like this kid's got potential."

They turn to the next name on the list.

CHAPTER 68

Classes have started, and the Oregon boys are getting accustomed to their new routines. They registered only for morning classes, except one English class Anthony schedules for Tuesday and Thursday evenings at 7:00, so the afternoons will be clear for baseball practices. Rising and shining proves to be a challenge, though, since there is so much action later in the days.

Because they are on their own, away from their parents' watchful eyes, there also is no curfew. One of the dorm's common areas has a little grill, The Junction, that stays open until midnight, serving grilled cheese, nachos, fries, and burgers. They also have foosball, billiards, and table tennis, so Nick and Anthony spend quite a few late nights challenging each other and eating not-so-healthy options. "What would your mom say?" Nick often asks him, laughing. They keep owl-like hours, and neither complains.

The second week begins much like the first. Anthony tries to talk the hitting coach, Stephens, into letting him take 10 swings right-handed *in addition to* the 10 cuts he gets lefty, and Stephens simply replies, "You get 10 cuts, and you can choose how to use 'em. Maybe take five from each side. And make 'em good." With an extra snarl on his lip, Anthony swings out of his shoes. He has no idea what scores the coach writes down after his round, and he doesn't know if it really matters.

After practice one day, Coach Thomas, the strength and conditioning coach, approaches him. "Hey Sumner, got a minute?"

Anthony springs at the opportunity and joins a squad of a half-dozen players that Coach Thomas waves over. Together, they walk across a dangerously busy bike path and into the Activities & Recreation Center, entering a giant weight room. For the next half-hour or so, the boys learn an array of weightlifting and fitness exercises designed for baseball-specific purposes. Excitedly, Anthony tries each and every one of them, imagining how hard he could hit a baseball with a few added pounds of muscle.

Leaving the ARC a bit later, he can't help but wonder why he hadn't gotten into strength training more seriously when he was in high school. Pushups had been the extent of it, and while that had worked for the great Ted Williams, it probably wasn't enough for this skinny kid from Oregon. Anthony's mind flashes to the swim workouts he half-heartedly did, the physical therapy he tended to avoid, and the exercises he so often eschewed, opting instead to toss a football, shoot hoops in the driveway, or corral Nick for some tennis or Home Run Derby.

At that moment, he pledges to hit the weights three days a week, between or after classes, whenever he can fit it in.

School itself is going well, even though Anthony is thoroughly lost in his coding course. Fortunately, their outfielder pal Daryl, unbeknownst to them, has a dizzying array of hidden skills in his arsenal, including computer programming. Anthony is sure to sit next to him and lets Daryl guide him through the steps and the foreign language of coding.

When the homework is done, and sometimes in lieu of homework, the three boys discover a new thrill: pickup basketball.

Every evening, at the Pavilion recreation center, the gym opens into four full-court basketball games. You win, and your team stays on the court. You lose, you get back in line. Nick and Anthony, the self-proclaimed 1-2 combination, find that speaking their own silent language and understanding each other's patterns and preferences translate into tremendous success. They also have a keen eye for picking up teammates, such as Daryl, who are solid ballplayers and won't complain if Nick and Anthony take the lion's share of their team's shots.

Often, en route to the ARC to lift, Anthony spies the pickup games happening on the courts next door, calls Nick and Daryl, and diverts his attention to *running wood* instead of *pumping iron*.

After the games, the boys race to catch dinner before the dining commons closes, usually still sweaty but feeling like warriors. Beating the locked doors usually leads to a wild array of personalized high-fives and fist-bumps. A win is a win, and the three of them are collecting as many as they can.

Nick's relationship with Simon, meanwhile, is still going strong. As planned, he is playing golf for Sacramento State, just 20 minutes east of Davis, and though they don't see each other in person very often, Nick spends many hours talking with him on the phone, cooing and making himself obnoxious across their dorm room. Frequently, Anthony just leaves the room during these calls, opting instead to wander the campus and check out his surroundings.

Examining the diversity of trees gracing the university's grounds, Anthony's thoughts often go to Elena. To Central Park back in Corvallis, to their walks and their talks and her playful rib-poking. He wonders how she is doing, what adventures her final year in high school is offering, and who she hangs out with. She'd appreciate these trees. He misses her friendship, her company, and the special way she made him feel. They text and video call on occasion, but he can sense their relationship slipping away.

He picks up a decidedly large, two-inch acorn and softly tosses it against the trunk of a nearby pine tree. It hits dead center. Smiling, Anthony continues this target-practice, memories flooding his head, emotions bounding this way and that, like the ricocheting acorns, until he feels it is time to return to his room.

CHAPTER 69

On Tuesday night of week two, alone on one of his strolls through campus, he gathers his courage and calls Elena, conjuring up the strength to go where they had agreed was forbidden. After a little small talk and discussions of her plans for Homecoming week and his description of the depressingly crowded and slow-paced baseball scene, he reaches deep. "So, what if we were to take a shot at, you know, *us?*" he offers gingerly.

"You mean, try a long-distance relationship?"

"Yeah, a real one. With a title and a definition. We'd be an official couple."

"Now? When you just got to college? Are you serious?"

"Yeah. I miss you, Elena. I miss us. I miss spending time with you and feeling like I've got somebody who really gets me, who cares for me. What do you say?" His heart thumps in his chest, awaiting her response.

"Where was this for the past few months?" she demands, the frustration in her voice audible. "When we were physically together? When you were still here?"

It is quiet on the line. It seems like eternity. In retrospect, it is probably only about five seconds. Then she continues, "Anthony, I miss you too. And when we agreed to go our separate ways, that's what we did. Now you're lonely, and I get that. You're in a new place. You have to get settled there, and you will, and you'll make great new friends. Your adventure is just beginning."

She sighs audibly.

"You can't just come calling whenever you're lonely and hope to rekindle something you never really tried to kindle in the first place. That's not fair to me. It's not fair to you."

Anthony is struck silent. "Yeah, I didn't know then." That statement hangs in the air, a wispy cloud awaiting a breeze to take it away.

"You're coming home for winter break, right?" she asks.

Good heavens, thinks Anthony. *I can hardly think about this week, let alone months ahead.* "Yeah, I guess."

"I'll see you then. In the meantime, I gotta go. You good?"

"Sure," he says, dejectedly kicking a busted, browned palm frond that had fallen onto the sidewalk.

"Okay, talk to you soon. Bye!" She tries to finish upbeat, but when the phone goes silent, she put her head in her hands, legs hanging off the edge of her bed, crying for Anthony for the last time.

Several hundred miles south, on a walking path on the UC-Davis campus, the lonely freshman stares straight ahead, leaning absent-mindedly against a palm tree. A gentle rain begins to fall, typing indiscernible messages delicately on the ground all around him. He stands there for an hour, heedless, the rainclouds reluctantly moving along to find a new target to drench.

CHAPTER 70

Later that night, Chris and Daryl stop by their room, challenging the boys to a foosball game at The Junction. Anthony is in no mood to be social, so he declines, claiming to have homework to battle with. Alone in the room, he sits placidly on his bed, contemplating this new college life.

His ringing phone jars him from his melancholy. Dad.

Putting on his brave face, he answers, "Hey Dad! How's it going in Oregon? Miss me yet?"

"Of course we do. Mom's here, too," replies his father. They were on speakerphone, probably in the kitchen.

"Hi, son, glad we caught you. Figured you probably stay up late, lots of homework, right?" Anthony can sense her sarcasm through the phone, and he laughs.

"Something like that," he says. "So what's up?"

Anthony's dad speaks first. "We hadn't heard from you in a while, wanted to check in. Plus, we couldn't help but notice all the charges on the credit card. *Our* credit card. That's why we got *you* a credit card, right?"

Busted. "Yeah, but all the things I charge to your card are school-related expenses. My card is for fun. And you wouldn't believe how fast money disappears around here. I don't know if it's college, or California, or what. Crazy!"

His mom takes that one. "We understand, Anthony. Both of us have been to college, remember? And your dad is still there. I'm still waiting for him to graduate," she laughs.

"Here's the deal," his mom says next. "We'll send you a little money each month, and we're paying the dining bill each month, and we'll pay your books and registration fees – all of that is covered in your college account for now. But everything else is on you. If you need more cash, you need to find yourself a job."

"Man, I don't have time for a job," Anthony exclaims. *15 credits, 18 hours of baseball a week, plus the homework is probably going to pile up any day now*, he thinks.

"How's baseball?" his father asks, eager to avoid an argument and wanting an update.

"Boring. Luckily they'll cut the riff-raff soon, and then it'll just be 30 of us or so. I think we play fall-ball scrimmages against other local schools in a couple weeks. I'll get you a schedule when they give it to us."

"Are you eating well?" asks his mom.

"Dorm food. I'll gain the freshman 15, that's for sure. But it'll be muscle. I'm doing 200 pushups a day, Ted Williams style. And we have access to an amazing weight room."

"Good for you," she responds. "Just let me know if you want me to send you some quinoa or set you up with the hummus-of-the-month club."

"Thanks, guys. Gotta go. Homework is calling. Don't want you to pay for a kid who flunks out of college!"

"Okay, love you son! Take care!"

"Love you too. Thanks for calling!"

Anthony resumes his pose, staring out the window.

CHAPTER 71

Moments after he hangs up with his folks, Anthony grabs his laptop, opens it, and stares at it absently. He doesn't really have homework to do, and for this he is grateful. Still, he lets the login screen sit, unattended, his mind elsewhere. The screen goes blank.

Homework. Home seems so far away, so distant. His past was a different life, lived by a kid in a different time. His future is a giant question mark.

He looks at his phone again as the memories and faces parade in front of his glossy eyes. Without even recognizing it, he unlocks the phone and begins a text.

Hi Mrs. Andrews, it's Anthony. He pushes *send*.

Staring at his phone, he is jolted back by a near-immediate buzz.

A return text from his former teacher in Oregon: *Hi Anthony. How's college life?*

Good ol' Mrs. A. He replies with a smiley-face emoji and a thumbs-up.

And, as usual, she cuts right to the chase: *How's baseball?*

He copies his response from before: smiley-face emoji and a thumbs-up.

Really? That's great!

Anthony stares at the message for a while, not responding. Should he tell her that baseball here is killing him, it is boring as heck, and he is getting homesick?

Before he can act, her next text comes in: *Are you being strategic, following a plan? Or are you winging it?*

Ever the smart aleck, he replies with emojis again, this time a bird and a crying-laughing face.

She responds with an emoji too, this one an angry face. *Do you want to talk about your goals, your plans? I'm happy to give you feedback on your strategic action steps. Any time.*

Anthony looks casually over to his desk. Somewhere in one of the drawers, he had put the manila envelope she gave him with the forms. That really isn't his cup of tea. Plus, what could he do differently, anyway?

His simple, noncommittal response: *Thanks.*

Immediately back: *I'll go through it with you right now if you want. I'm up grading papers anyway. If you're ready to commit, let me know.*

Through the window, and between the tree branches, Anthony spies Nick, Daryl, and Chris walking across the courtyard, laughing with a couple of girls, who peel off to another dorm building. He'd better end this. *Can't right now, maybe another time. I appreciate your support. Don't stay up too late grading papers!*

I know this is important to you. Don't leave it to chance. Be in charge. I believe in you.

Anthony smiles, realizing how much he values his former teacher's encouragement and willingness to help. She is – and always has been – the only teacher that truly gets him. As he hears Nick reach the door of their dorm room, he sends a final response: *Seriously. It means a lot. Thx.*

With a burst of testosterone, the boys pile in the room. Anthony starts shuffling the deck of cards on his desk.

CHAPTER 72

Daryl and Chris always meet the Oregon duo by the dining commons for the daily ride to the baseball field. By Friday afternoon of the second week, the weight of their course loads, homework, sleep deprivation, and dorm food looks like it has run the foursome over with a truck.

"Is anyone else having fun with this?" asks Anthony, over his shoulder. He likes to assume the lead spot in their riding formation.

"What, college?" asks Chris.

"I think he means baseball, man," yells Daryl, over the wind in their ears. No one has a helmet.

"Yeah, baseball. How much fun is this so far? I'm getting 10 ground balls a day, pretty much on my own to run my sprints, and I get 10 hacks in the cage with some coach scoring each swing who never really seems to be paying attention. We haven't played scrimmages, we haven't had any live BP, heck I haven't even gotten to show them my wheels. Is this really how they do it in college?"

"It's about the same for the outfielders," Nick says, looking at Daryl for agreement. He nods.

"Talk about being fish getting lost in a big pond," Chris laughs. "Actually, it's more like fish in a barrel, it's so crowded on that field!"

"Don't you all love baseball, though?" Anthony calls back.

"Oh, yeah!" is the chorus.

"Then, wait, guys." Anthony slows his bike to a halt, as do his three buddies. "What are we spending three hours in the barrel for, then? Let's go play baseball this afternoon instead!"

The other three exchange puzzled looks. "We are going to play baseball, Anthony," Nick is the first to say.

"Right. Stand around in the heat, field 10 balls, hit 10 more. I don't know what it's like for you pitchers, but it's brutal for the position players. I think I'm actually getting *worse* at baseball by being at these practices. Let's go find a field and hit, just the four of us. In two hours, we can each get 100 swings in. Plus, we can field each other's hitting and work on the stuff we need to work on. You can throw us some live BP at the end, Chris, to get your work in too!"

Chris nods. "Sounds like a great idea. They'll never miss us – they probably don't really know who's there anyway."

Daryl says, "I'm in. Where do we get the balls?"

Nick has an answer ready. "I've got a bucket in our dorm. My folks gave me five dozen new ones. Pearls. Just for days like this."

They turn their bikes around, truly excited to play baseball for the first time since they got to town.

On an empty field with a scant backstop and tiny basepaths, one obviously used only for intramural softball games, the boys set up their batting practice session. And it is a blast. Nick and Anthony hit first, as is custom, while Daryl and Chris field.

"Finally, some BP worth something!" Anthony exclaims through a mouthful of gummy worms, as they re-bucket the beautiful pearly baseballs after his round. "You're up, Daryl. Let's see what you've got!"

Anthony pitches to the muscular lefty, and Nick gets an exhausting workout chasing Daryl's moonshot fly balls all over the outfield. *Wow,* mutters Anthony under his breath. *This kid can hit!*

As the afternoon wears on, the enthusiasm of the boys only grows more intense, more excited. It is as if new life had been breathed into their baseball souls, and they are taking full advantage of it. Laughing and sprinting after each ball, it is a scene straight out of a Norman Rockwell painting: boys playing a boy's game in the sunshine. No uniforms, no umpires, no crowd. Just the thwack of bat hitting ball, the thump of ball hitting glove, and the supportive calls of friendship from around the field.

Chris, as promised, paces off 60 feet, 6 inches and tries to throw some live pitches to his buddies, but the softball field's flat surface doesn't agree with that plan. Plus, the boys hit foul balls that fly over the tiny backstop and bound across the adjacent street, and that is risky, so that adventure is halted in a hurry. Instead, Nick crouches in a catcher's position and catches some hard throws, just so Chris can get a pitching workout in.

By 4:15, their baseball fix is complete. Hopping back on their bikes, they ride past the baseball field, watching the gulls, still mostly standing around, the meat market of hopeful baseball players. "See you tomorrow, suckers!" Anthony calls, only loud enough for his friends to hear. "Now we're rolling!" Laughing and excited, they tease Nick for the awkward way he holds the bucket of baseballs on his handlebars, back to the dorms a good hour before normal.

CHAPTER 73

Anthony and Nick run into a couple of the other baseball prospects down at the Pavilion basketball courts that evening. Nick recognizes Ian, an outfielder who is a tremendous all-around athlete and joins their team. Despite Anthony's eyebrow scratching, Nick never repeats his name aloud.

During the course of the games, which are pretty light because it's Friday night during pledge week, so many of the wanna-be athletes were somewhere on Greek row, Ian asks if the boys are nervous about the cut list going up tomorrow.

Judging by the shocked looks on their faces, Ian follows with, "Didn't you hear that announcement today?"

Nick explains that they hadn't been at practice today, and what they'd been doing instead. Ian laughs. "Sounds like a good idea. Today was pretty slow. They said they'd start intra-squad scrimmages on Monday, and they canceled practice for tomorrow, since it's supposed to keep raining. But they said they'd cut from 125 down to 50."

Anthony and Nick exchange raised eyebrows. "Good," Anthony says, confidently. "Get rid of the fringes. That extra day of hitting helped. We'll be ready to kick some butt next week!"

CHAPTER 74

On Saturday morning, Anthony and Nick sleep in until 11:45, which gives them just enough time to race across the courtyard, heads down against the relentless rain, to the dining commons in time to eat the weekend brunch, a giant buffet spread that takes the place of the regular restaurant-style offerings during the week, before the doors shut at noon. Daryl and Chris meet them there, all a little bleary from their late night playing cards. Even their high-five routines lack the customary luster.

Outside, raindrops pepper the cafeteria's windows, blurring the nearby dorms, palm trees, and shrubbery. Eventually, the topic of baseball comes up.

"Want to ride over and check the list?" asks Nick. "Ian said it'd be up by noon."

Anthony is shoving heaps of blueberry pancakes into his mouth, making quite a scene. They aren't as good as his mom's, but for dorm food they fit the bill. He nods, cheeks bulging, points to his plate, and holds up a couple of fingers.

Daryl is done eating, and eager to see the list, he stands and waves his arms theatrically. "I don't have two minutes to wait for all this mess."

Chris and Nick follow, and Anthony's last bite is larger than the previous. "Okay," he says, syrup spilling out the side of his mouth. "Let's ride." They clear their own plates, laughing and heading to the doors.

"Man, I hope Ian's name isn't on the list, he seems like a good guy," Nick says.

"And a good basketball player, too. We've got a good starting five here, as long as the baseball coaches will let us keep running wood," Daryl echoes.

"Want to hit the courts after we check the lists?" Chris asks.

"Heck yeah, can't wait!" Anthony exclaims as they exit the dining commons and are immediately pelted by rain.

Biking in the rain is a brutal affair, as they quickly realize. Not only do the raindrops sting their faces and arms, hitting harder the faster they ride, but the rear tires send up a splattering of water and mud that splashes up their backsides, a phenomenon known as "the streak."

Once at the ballfield, the four boys enter the gate and huddle under the overhang by the clubhouse door, a brief respite from the relentless autumn rain. Taped unceremoniously to the door are two pieces of paper. One has a heading, *The Aggie 50: Practice starts Monday, 2:00 sharp.*

The other reads simply, *The following players need not continue to come to practice. Thank you for your interest in Aggie baseball.* All of a sudden, a knot forms in Anthony's chest, as all four scramble to find their names.

Dread takes over as the *Aggie 50* list shrinks away from him, smaller and smaller, as he progresses to the bottom. His name isn't there. He reads it again to verify, each name tinier than the name before it. His eyes blur as he shifts his focus to the *Need Not* sheet. The names are listed alphabetically, by last name, printed off a spreadsheet. And there, screaming at him from the fluttering page: *Sumner, Anthony.*

In shock, he blinks and sets himself. Like viewing the world through the wrong end of binoculars, he becomes aware of an odd, hollow feeling. The lists distancing themselves from him, everything caving in from all sides. His eyes flicker back and forth at the lists again. The *Aggie 50.* Nothing. The *Need Not.* There he is, still there, still waving at himself from the paper. *Sumner, Anthony.*

Anthony has no idea what hit him until he has stumbled backwards several steps, staggering into the falling rain. The sky is dark, ominous, foreboding, angry. All at once, his eyes pop, and he sees Nick standing in front of him, the same expression on his face. Daryl and Chris are off to the other side, hands on the papers, double and triple-checking the accuracy.

Nick looks back at Anthony. "What the…" he starts, blankly.

Anthony howls. Raindrops pummel his forehead as he stands, unblinkingly, a haze suffocating him. He bellows again, incomprehensibly. His shock, now anger, brings him back to reality. He steps back under the eave, scrutinizing the list. On the *Need Not* side, he finds Nick, Chris, and Daryl's names, too. "All of us? That's insane!" He yells again, flailing at the list affixed to the door, ripping it in half, the tape on either side preventing any of it from falling to the ground, now both sides taunting and cackling in the breeze.

Without another word, he grabs his bike and rides off alone, into the pelting rain.

CHAPTER 75

Coach Jefferson convened his assistants in the "war room," surrounded by the names of their players, numbers of various colors, and stars, arrows, and parenthetical notes on the white-boards surrounding the conference table. It was Friday night, and their sole job was to trim the list to 50.

One by one they went down the list, crossing off names of players who didn't have the skill, the potential, or the heart to cut a college baseball roster. They also erased names of players who had quit or had left school entirely. Coach Stephens typed furiously on his laptop, trying to keep up with the conversation, wondering why Coach Jefferson hadn't agreed to just use the spreadsheet and project it on a screen. That would have made his job ten times easier.

When they came to Anthony's name, Coach Jefferson asked for an update.

"Coach?" ventured the infielders' coach, Simpson. "Sumner didn't show up today."

"Why, is he sick?"

"Don't know. No word."

"What the hell?" thundered Coach Jefferson. "You sure he wasn't there?"

"Wasn't in the cages, either," added Coach Stephens.

"Makes me feel a little better, 'cause I was looking all over for him," said Coach Thomas, the strength and conditioning coach. "The kid's skinny and thought he'd turned sideways all afternoon…"

The head coach's look shot down any attempt at cracking jokes.

"I made it clear, if you're going to miss a practice, because of homework, illness, family issue, anything, you let us know, right? Didn't I make that clear?"

"Yes, sir."

"They all have my personal cell, right?"

"Yes, sir."

"Did any of you hear from Sumner about today?" He scowled around the table at his coaching staff. Everyone nodded.

"Damn shame," muttered the head coach, putting a line right through Anthony's name.

WINTER

CHAPTER 76

How far Anthony rides his bike that Saturday afternoon is a mystery never to be solved. Whether he stops along the way to cry, throw rocks, curse the heavens above, break limbs off trees, or just hunker down under the broad canopy of a giant walnut tree could likely be confirmed by casual observers, though forgotten entirely by Anthony himself.

By the time he steps back into his dorm room, dusk is taking over, and he is drenched, dripping water all over the floor. Nick sits on his bed, looking bleak, talking in low tones on his cell. The lights are off in their room, and the darkness shrouds them.

Far away in the distance, Anthony hears Nick's voice. "Anthony's back, can I call you later? Okay, thanks. Love you too." Then: "Hey, man, how ya doing?"

Anthony simply stands, a step or two inside the doorway, a puddle growing beneath him. The only sound is water dripping off his fingertips, his nose, his soggy shirt, his shorts.

"You all right, man? I know, it sucks."

Neither boy has moved. Anthony's eyes are somewhere, anywhere, nowhere.

"Dude, you're soaked," Nick says next, trying to get some sort of reaction from his buddy. "Grab a towel, will you? Or why don't you go take a shower?"

Only then does Anthony realize he is shivering. "Yeah," is all he can muster, and he grabs his towel off the back of the door. A second later, he is back out the door, sleepwalking toward the showers in the communal dorm bathroom down the hall, towel in hand, and the door ajar behind him.

Nick hops up, grabs his towel to dry the floor, pokes his head out into the hallway, and watches his friend trudge away. Back in the room, he dials Simon back. "Yeah, sorry about that. Anthony's in a zone. He is *not* okay."

There is no foosball, no billiards, not even a game of cards that night, despite Nick's best efforts to raise his friend out of his funk. Instead, Anthony goes straight to bed after his hour-long shower, during which he'd stood, palms against the tiles, letting the warm water cascade over his head. It washes nothing away, however. When he steps out, the filth of his failure still mires him. All he's said to his roommate that night is a simple, direct, "Good night, man," an indication of his unwillingness to talk about it and his resignation for the evening. It isn't even 8:00 yet.

CHAPTER 77

The next day is Sunday, and when Nick tries to rouse Anthony for brunch, he gets no response. Whether his buddy is sleeping or depressed or a combination of both, he doesn't know. The end result is a trip to the dining commons by himself. Happily, he runs into Daryl in the courtyard, and they walk together to eat.

"Chris went home, man," Daryl informs him as they enter the commons.

"What do you mean, home?"

"To his folks' house in Redwood City. Said he ain't staying if he ain't playing."

"What, he left like he left, left?"

"I guess so. He was pretty shook up. Just got in the car and drove off, didn't even pack a bag. Texted me later and said he was home, told me I could sell all his stuff, I don't know. He was tripping."

"So what'd you do?" Nick asks as he loads up his tray.

"I started an eBay account, man, right? He left some nice stuff in there!"

Laughing half-heartedly, the boys collect their meals and have a seat. By this time, most of the tables are empty and the custodial staff is hard at work, cleaning up and resetting for dinner.

"After Chris left, I had the rest of the night to myself. I mean, I was pretty pissed off, so it's probably a good thing there was no one around, but later I made a list of pros and cons for this." He takes a bite of his omelet.

"And what'd you come up with?"

"Well, weird as it may sound, the pros kicked the cons to the curb."

"How do you figure?" Nick tinkers with his bowl of granola.

"Brother, I just bought at least 18 hours of my life back every week. Not that I'm going to use it for homework, but I could if I wanted to. That's 18 hours that we can go play basketball, and how fortuitous that all four of us get that gift!"

"Fortuitous?"

Daryl shrugged his shoulders a couple times in a silent laugh. "Are you questioning my vocabulary or my point of view?"

"Um…"

"Don't matter. Anyway, if it's not basketball, it can be foosball, cards, we can get jobs, have a social life. I can teach you skinny Oregon boys how to lift weights and put some meat on those wings. Shoot, man, thanks to those nincompoops cutting us, we're back in the game. With a little work, I can get some money, pick up that fake ID I've been thinking about, you know."

Nick sizes him up. "You look like a 25-year-old man. You don't need a fake ID. Though maybe I'll go with you. Sounds like fun."

"That's right! We get the full college experience now!"

How industrious and clinical, Nick thinks. *I should have thought of that. Imagine how Anthony would have responded if I'd have brought up a pros and cons list! Or if I bring up the fake ID idea.*

Nick laughs out loud. He hasn't thought about the upsides yet. He has focused on the loss, the pain, and the disappointment. And he knows his best friend is devastated.

"How are you doing with all this?"

"It sucks," Nick says, pushing his bowl away from him. "I mean, I didn't come here to play baseball, but I sure thought I could. I thought *we* could."

"Same."

"I guess I figured the way I'd stop playing baseball is when a season ends, you know? A natural break. Not like this. Not getting cut."

"I take it Anthony's a wreck, huh? It's not like him to miss the pancake pile."

Nick nods. "Yeah, when I left him, he was still buried under the covers back in the dorms. I've been trying to think of a way to cheer him up. Wanna help?"

"Sure," Daryl laughs, clapping his giant hands together. "I'm a prolific brainstormer! Perhaps Anthony would like a tattoo. What's that expression he's always using?"

"Which one, 'blink twice'?"

"That's the one. What does that mean, anyway?"

"I think it's something you say when you see something amazing. Like a bald eagle catching a fish, or a bunch of shooting stars all at once. You know, you have to blink twice to make sure it was real, that your eyes aren't deceiving you."

"We could tattoo those on his eyelids I guess," Daryl laughs. "What else you got?"

Nick finds Daryl's upbeat mood soothing, and the two of them spend a good hour laughing and creating preposterous scenarios and implausible ideas. Nick can't help but wish Reggie were there with his obnoxious practical jokes and his irreverent attitude. Anthony would laugh at that dude no matter what.

In the end, they agree to something familiar and make plans to go play pickup basketball later, and Nick returns to his dorm room. Anthony is still there, but at least he is sitting up.

Nick starts the conversation. "Man, you okay? You've slept all day."

"Mmhmmm."

"This sucks, huh? Just like that."

"At least you've got Simon," Anthony says.

"What do you mean?"

"Someone to talk to. Someone who cares. Someone who gets you. At least Simon's there for you, right?"

Nick feels the weight in the room. "Well, have you talked to Elena?"

"She told me to take a leap," Anthony says softly.

"Really?"

"Basically."

"I'm sorry, man. You've got me, though. I'm here."

Anthony looks up, his expression blank. "Dude, you're my best friend."

"Yeah. And you're my best friend, too."

"But we don't talk. Not really. You know this. We are men of action. We do stuff together. Play ball. Play cards. Ride around. We're not the talking type."

Nick thinks hard about this. "Well spoken, Sire." Usually, quoting – or even misquoting – The Princess Bride makes them both laugh. "I guess you're right. But if you ever want to talk, I'm here for you."

"I know, and I appreciate it. I also…" he trails off. "Anyway, are we playing hoops today or what?"

Nick laughs out loud, surprised and overjoyed at the question. "Yeah, buddy! I thought you'd never ask."

CHAPTER 78

The days turn to weeks, and the weeks pile into winter. Anthony creates a way to deal with his grief, Nick notices. He bursts completely out of his shell. After the disastrous rainy afternoon that his dream came crashing down upon him, the proud and cocky and brash and confident part of Anthony had exploded itself back to the surface.

One ordinary Tuesday afternoon, the sort of early winter day that might otherwise be swallowed into the abyss of the calendar, Nick, Anthony, and Daryl find themselves walking along one of the dozens of bike paths that meander through campus. As they head toward the student union building, Anthony chirps "hello" and waves a greeting at everyone they encounter.

"You guys ever notice how many people don't acknowledge other humans unless we say 'hi' first?"

"Nope," Daryl has one eye on his phone, texting.

"Watch," Anthony says. Two bikes approach and roll past the threesome without a word. Anthony raises his eyebrows at his pals. They shrug.

"Ready for this?" As a stream of four new riders nears, Anthony raises his arm and calls, "Hello, friends! Great day for a ride, eh?" He's received by a chorus of greetings, cheers, and smiles. Anthony turns and bows triumphantly.

Daryl's eyes roll and he does his silent shoulder-shrug. "Yes, you can manipulate the independent variable, well done."

Anthony frowns at Daryl. "It's more than that, buddy. It's about connections. People need to know they're not alone, that we're all in this together."

Nick watches silently, agreeing with his roommate at a much deeper level than is probably intended.

"So let's do this!" Anthony springs off the path, hurdles a fire hydrant, and plants his hand against the bark of a massive sequoia. "I'm not leaving this tree until a hundred people say hello! Do you hear me, folks? I'm stuck to this gnarly, thick, and wow, surprisingly spongy-feeling beast of a tree! I can only be set free by the loving smiles and generous well-wishes of my fellow travelers!"

"Seriously?" Nick asks. "I've got stuff to pick up at the union."

"Then you can help. You're a numbers guy, count 'em as they say hi."

As riders and pedestrians cruise past, Anthony calls to them, Nick maintains a tally, and Daryl launches video on his camera to post the proceedings. Anthony fills the spaces between passers-by with a high-volume monologue, doing his best to replicate stand-up routines he's watched, cracking his own jokes, and infusing some physical humor to the mix. Shortly, a small crowd has gathered, intrigued by the boisterous, laughing, over-the-top friendly fellow stuck to the tree.

"That couldn't have been my goat, the farmer said, 'cause my goat's tied to a post over there!"

Laughter rumbles through the audience.

A young woman ambles up next to Nick and Daryl. They recognize her as Kim, the starting point-guard on the women's basketball team. They've played ball together at the Pavilion on occasion. She gestures to Anthony, "What's this all about?"

Daryl shakes his head, camera still rolling. "Dude, he does stuff like this sometimes. He's out of his gourd."

Anthony crosses one leg over the other, pretending to sit in an imaginary chair. He wobbles, yelling, "What is this, wicker? This won't hold me! I'm going down. Watch out below!"

"Is there something wrong with him?"

Nick wonders the same thing. This isn't the Anthony he's known for seven years.

A clump of riders approaches, and Anthony calls, "Hello, bikers, top o' the mornin' to ya!"

With a handful of waves in return, Nick's tally indicates success. "That's 100, man. Can we go now?"

Anthony rises dramatically from his invisible chair. "Mission accomplished. However, there's still a lingering lesson to be learned. Does anyone here know the proper response to that Irish expression?"

Nick and Kim look at each other, baffled, as Anthony joins them on the path. Daryl has quieted his phone for the time being.

"I say, 'Top of the mornin' to ya,' you say, 'And the rest of the day to you, laddie.' You're welcome. Have a great day, and thank you for watching the show!"

The crowd disperses, and Anthony greets Kim with a formal handshake. "How'd you like that? 100 people said hi, everyone laughed. It's a good way to bring light into their day, right?"

"Very funny," she responds. "And how's baseball going?"

Anthony's quick to reply. "We've taken the year off from baseball. There's too much fun to have here, and the three of us agreed not to waste it on collegiate sports. No offense, I'm sure you love it. It's just not for us."

"You need a new hobby. And our basketball team needs a manager. Interested?"

"Tell me more."

As Nick watches his buddy, his roommate, his best friend walk away, now arm-in-arm with Kim, he finds his curiosity growing. *Anthony always answers that question for us. He's never asked how I'm doing with the whole dead-baseball-dream thing. And I know it's killing him inside, yet he tells this story, does all these outlandish stand-up bits, and gets really loud and really distant. He's gonna crash, and it's gonna be ugly. If he won't talk to me about it, he won't talk to anyone.*

Daryl looks up from his phone. "C'mon, Nick, let's go before we lose the dude."

Ah, well, he's right. We do stuff together; we don't talk about it. He is like a human bumblebee, visiting all these flowers and building connections, even though according to the laws of physics and his own psyche, he shouldn't be able to fly at all.

CHAPTER 79

Back home in Oregon, word spreads that Anthony and Nick have not made the baseball team at UC-Davis. Not wanting to rock the boat, Elena gives him a couple of weeks to recover, sending friendly texts and noticing that he hasn't answered any of her questions about how baseball is going. He has to know that she knows, but he acts like he doesn't.

Finally, she calls him.

"Hey," he says simply as he picks up.

"Hey. How's it going? I don't hear from you much these days, Mr. California." She tries to keep a light, friendly tone.

"Yeah, it's pretty busy in college. You'll find out next year. It's nothing like high school, so much better, so many more cool people." His voice is devoid of affect.

"That's good. How are your classes going? Have you figured out that coding class yet?"

"Not really, but I'll get through it."

"Is your roommate a pain in the butt, or what?" She tries another angle.

"He's cool. Maybe you know him, he went to your high school."

"Listen, Anthony, we haven't talked much in the last month or so."

"Thanks to you," he responds quickly, snarkily.

She tries to ignore that barb. "I just want to know how you're doing. I miss talking to you."

"Yeah."

Finally, she goes all-in. "I know you're not playing baseball."

Silence.

"Tell me about it. What happened?"

More silence.

"I want you to know I'm here for you if you want to talk."

For the better part of a month, Anthony has suppressed whatever beasts lurked beneath the surface. He has played, he has danced, he has joked, and he has deflected. With Elena, the façade not only crumbles, it shakes and falls violently to the earth.

"You're here for me? You're *there* for me, or rather you're just *there*."

Elena isn't sure if she is glad or afraid that he finally lets down his guard.

"Nobody's *here* for me," he says, now sternly, angrily, teeth clenching into his phone. "Nobody understands a damn thing about me here. Or there. Not you, not anyone."

"I..." Elena starts, but she is cut off.

"If I hear one more person ask me how baseball is going, or why I'm not playing baseball, and am I sure I want to take a year off from baseball, I'm going to tear their *freakin'* lungs out," he says, enunciating every word and punctuating the euphemistic f-word with unbridled intensity. "All I want to do is run away. Run. And I hate running. You know?"

"Yes."

"No. No you don't. Because you weren't *here* for me, and you weren't *there* for me. I am *totally* alone here. What do you think happens to a baseball player whose career ends at age 18? Whose career is over before it even starts? That was my identity, my dream, my life, my everything. Now I have *nothing*. Are you listening to this?" His voice is really starting to rise now. "I have absolutely *nothing!*"

"Anthony, I…" Elena's voice trembles.

"No you don't," he says, chopping off whatever she's begun. "Now, if you'll excuse me, I have to go to the rest of my jacked-up life." Hanging up before she can respond, he tosses the phone across the room, screams something even more profane at the top of his lungs, and punches the wall adjacent to their dorm-room door.

A fist-sized hole in the drywall is the only proof that his conversation with Elena ever happened.

CHAPTER 80

Nick's parents had been the ones to share the unfortunate news that the boys hadn't cracked the *Aggie 50* list with Anthony's parents. They meet up for coffee and bagels one Saturday soon after to discuss their approaches to parenting through this tumultuous time.

Nick's folks report that their son seems okay with it all and that he is moving on. Their friend Daryl shared some helpful advice with him to help him keep it all in perspective, *and if you remember, Mom and Dad, playing baseball here at college wasn't the most important thing to me anyway. I'm fine. Anthony's a different story, though.*

In their calls and texts, Anthony has either seemed distant and uncommunicative or hyper and distracted. He refuses to have a serious conversation about baseball, often directly saying, "Hey, I just don't want to talk about it, okay?" For a while, Drew and Amanda allow that to go on.

After meeting with the Greenes, they agree together that there's got to be more they can do. Amanda is more eager for outside help than Drew, probably because she has seen this day as one that, in all likelihood, was *bound* to happen at some point, so they ought to be ready for it. Drew has kept his head in the sand as long as possible, wishing against hope that the dream will win out.

Jay and Sandy Young are happy to accept the Sumners' invitation to a home-cooked dinner. They shake the early-winter cold off their coats as they enter the house, delighted by the warmth and happy to socialize. In the living room, the four sit and chat about life and school and the weather, sipping wine and sharing a couple bowls of edamame and strips of bell peppers. Amanda tends to the dinner preparations during their small-talk happy-hour.

As she dishes up the meal, Amanda launches into an overall summary of their current plight with Anthony. He's been cut from the team; he won't talk about it, is staying excessively busy, and probably has some pent-up frustrations to work through. Amanda summarizes by stating she and her husband believe he is grieving, which is something the four of them discussed this summer. And what's more, he doesn't have an emotional outlet, so he's suppressing his true feelings and overcompensating with his old cocky, louder-than-life ways.

Jay and Sandy exchange an impressed look. "Amanda, not only does the dinner look fabulous, but I think your attunement skills are right-on.

From what you've said and from what we've known of this saga throughout the last couple of months, I'd agree that it sounds like Anthony is grieving. Would you pass the pepper, please?"

Drew hands the salt and pepper, together, across the table. "They're named Abbott and Costello," he says, gesturing at the salt and pepper figurines, which don't look anything like the famous comedy duo.

"Yes, of course," responds Jay, laughing.

The clinking of silverware takes over for a few minutes as everyone digs in.

"Delicious, Amanda," Sandy offers. "We're so glad you invited us over. And we're hopeful that whatever we can offer is helpful."

"Thank you," Amanda says. "I feel like we're always asking your professional advice. One of these days you might have to start charging us for this."

"Oh, I'm keeping a log of billable hours, not to worry," Jay laughs, and his smile puts the Sumners at ease. "So tell us exactly what the question that's got you unsettled is. Perhaps you can start, Drew, if you're comfortable with that."

"Of course," Drew says, holding his fork above his plate. "If Amanda's right and he's grieving, how do we help him through this? Especially from 500 miles away."

"And how do we help him see and embrace a Plan B? That's always been the struggle for him, for us, is to see life *after* baseball as something wonderful, magical, worthwhile," Amanda adds.

Drew's shoulders slump a little as he nods, and Amanda continues. "We're worried about him. Not worried that he won't be successful someday, more worried because we want him to be able to be in touch with his feelings better, to truly embrace the optimism that brings all the possibilities of life to the forefront."

"We get that," says Sandy. "You've said before you want him to be happy, productive, and successful, isn't that right? It's a challenge to do that when you're in psychological turmoil. And being far away physically is far different than becoming distanced emotionally."

"Indeed," Jay responds. He then proceeds to explain the stages of grief, the natural evolution of one's feelings, and how to help Anthony process his way through it.

"There's denial," he starts. "The shock and numbness might result in him acting like it was no big deal, that it's not a loss at all."

Amanda and Drew nod at each other, having heard that from their son over the phone.

"And anger, of course. Anger is often simply a veneer covering pain, and it can be directed at anyone or anything. Anger," he emphasizes, "is not the opposite of love; indifference is. Anger demonstrates the deep meaning of the relationship – in this case, between Anthony and baseball."

"Well, that's for sure," Drew sighs as he sits back in his chair. "The kid's definitely showing that! Nick told his folks, who told us, that he punched a hole in the wall of his dorm." Then, forcing a smile, he adds, "There goes the security deposit."

Jay continues. "Bargaining is another normal step. He may play out scenarios that open himself to blame. You know, 'if only' this or 'what if' that. This step shows that he's beginning to understand and cope with his reality."

"What about depression? Should we expect that?" Amanda asks, envisioning her son locking himself in his room, in the basement, in his truck, away from the world, dark and gloomy. Her eyes well up.

"Absolutely, depression is part of the process. We often associate depression with grief. Grieving is sad, and depression is used synonymously with sadness, perhaps a little too much, but certainly they're related. And expected. And natural."

"When can we expect him to, you know, get over it and move on? I mean, he can't stay depressed and grieving forever, right?" Drew looks cautiously at his wife as he asks this question. She bites her lip in anticipation of the response.

"Well," Jay raises his eyebrows. "It's important to note that the stages I've mentioned, as well as acceptance, which is what you're asking about, Drew, don't necessarily progress in that order. We may see signs of multiple stages simultaneously, or we'll see them presented in a different progression. Since we're all unique, and our circumstances are unique, the way we process grief and come to grips with our lives – our new realities – is likewise unique."

"So you have no idea, is that what you're saying?" Drew rests his hand on his wife's.

Sandy takes this one. "I think the key is this: As you can understand what he's going through, empathizing with him, you can help him feel and think and be clear on who he is as a human being, who you are as a family, and who you know he can be. There doesn't need to be a timetable.

With that support and love from you, he'll work his way through this – *you'll* work your way through this, *together.*"

After dinner, Drew delights their guests with some homemade tiramisu and a cup of Italian-ground decaf, a nice wrap-up for their evening together. Bundling up against the awaiting rain and wind, Jay and Sandy Young hug their friends goodnight.

"If there's anything, anything at all, please give us a holler," Sandy says.

"Any time," Jay adds. "And thanks again for a lovely dinner."

Drew answers with a gentle wave, "It was our pleasure."

"Thank you," Amanda adds. "Seriously, we appreciate it."

The Youngs turn and head out, the wind whistling through the door behind them.

CHAPTER 81

After the explosive phone call with Elena and the unfortunate hole in the dorm wall that is now hidden behind a taped-up newspaper article about an impending stock market crash or something else the boys don't really pay attention to, Anthony reverts back to behaviors that offer him some semblance of control over his life.

He goes to class, he chats incessantly with strangers, he plays hoops with his buddies, he talks trash on the court, he does the minimal amount of homework to remain caught up, and he stays up late with Nick, Daryl, and whichever other friends they can corral from the dorms when they want to play foosball or pool or have some other sort of competition. True to his word, Daryl's roommate Chris had completely abandoned ship, walked out of college and never returned, and the university had yet to fill the empty half of Daryl's dorm room. So for the most part, it's now just the three of them, doing whatever they choose to do.

Despite many offers, the three young men never stray too far away from this routine. Invitations to off-campus parties that promise alcohol in red solo cups, pills of any nature, and anything involving a lighter are strictly, and not always diplomatically, declined. Anthony's volume will rise; he'll offer the introduction to some thesis about valuing the mind, body, and spirit, and end up turning the tables, extending an invitation to join the guys for a couple hands of Egyptian Rocular or a trip to the foosball tables at the Junction, challenging them that it will be more fun than getting drunk and waking up with a terrible headache and severe remorse.

One Thursday evening, which seems particularly busy around the pool tables, Anthony's phone lights up with an Oklahoma number. Who does he know in Oklahoma? One person. Answering immediately, he runs outside.

"Hello?"

"Rooster, it's Coach Shepard. How's life treating you, young man?"

Anthony is glad to hear his voice. "Not too shabby, Coach. How's retirement?"

"Can't complain. Actually, I can. My wife has me working on this house 24/7. She's relentless. I wish I had a lineup card to fill out and some BP to throw."

Anthony returns a laugh, shivering. Should have grabbed his coat before he came outside; the wind is tossing the fallen leaves all over this end of the courtyard. He shields the phone with his other hand while he talks.

"I hear ya. It's all homework and classes here," he grimaces, acknowledging the exaggeration as he says it. He is looking at another three, maybe four hours of games in the Junction.

"Look, son, I just wanted to check in with you," Coach Shepard's voice has dropped an octave or two. "Word's come my way that you and Greene didn't make the team at Davis. I was sorry to hear that."

"Yeah," chirps Anthony, turned against the breeze and putting on his cocky voice. "We decided it wasn't in the cards. Wanted to experience college this first year. We'll see what next year holds."

He waits.

"Is that the official line?"

Anthony's shoulders shrink. Of all the people he doesn't want to disappoint, to let down, to see him as a failure, just a loud mouth and a quiet bat, it is Coach Shepard. Somehow, he figured if his coach has moved to Oklahoma, he'd never hear about the *Need Not* list.

"Yeah," is his less cocky response.

"Want to talk about it? Tell me what happened? Maybe I can help."

"Nah, Coach, it's okay," he offers with bravado. "They don't know what they're missing. Nick and I are weighing our options. If we decide to go out for the team again next year, it'll be a different story, trust me. They won't be able to stop this freight train."

Shivering, now wanting the conversation to end.

"That's the spirit, kid. You gotta *haunt* those guys. Whoever they chose ahead of you better watch their backs, yeah?" Coach Shepard is in full third-base coach mode, and Anthony thinks he hears his wife say something in the background.

Coach Shepard says something muffled, then is back.

"Keep this number, Rooster, got it? Call me any time. Trust me, I could use the distractions!"

"Thanks, Coach, I will."

"And seriously, youngblood, stay positive. I know you, and I know how you operate. Be sure you've got someone to talk to. Trust me on this – this is a damn hard path to travel alone."

Anthony wants to open up, to talk to his former coach. The memories come flooding back, the games, the victories, the practices, the drills, the one-on-one, eye-to-eye talks, the championship, the celebrations. But he can't. He won't. It is excruciating. And it isn't the wind causing his eyes to water.

"Roger that, Coach. Thanks for calling!" His final attempt at projecting confidence, that he is okay.

He hangs up before his coach can reply.

Sitting down on a bench outside the Junction's main doors, Anthony shivers. Or trembles. Or both. The wind whips, sending the branches of the white firs and western junipers planted nearby to wave and dance, like fans in the bleachers of a baseball game, cheering and encouraging and rooting their star player, dejected and downtrodden, head slunk between his shoulders, alone in the dugout.

CHAPTER 82

With winter break approaching, so is the end of the first academic term, and the long, late nights at the Junction are replaced, at least in part, by studying sessions and a little cramming for final exams. Daryl seems to have a pretty good handle on his courses, but Nick and Anthony each battle a particular academic demon. For Nick, it is an astronomy class, and as amazing as he is at remembering people's names, he can't for the life of him recognize constellations or remember the characteristics of the different types of stars that fill our solar system. Anthony's Achilles' heel is the coding class, and even with Daryl's patient help, every line he writes feels like his first exposure to the science. He resigns himself to coming up with a plan to sit right behind Daryl for the final.

Daryl laughs at this strategy, saying, "I'll alter the screen dimensions so my programming lines will show in a giant font."

As much as they chuckle over that idea, Anthony hopes Daryl holds up his end of that bargain.

Somehow, they make it through finals week, which includes a pretty competitive 3-on-3 basketball tournament, which Anthony, Nick, and Daryl play in together. They come in third place, which isn't too shabby, though it doesn't get their picture on the Wall of Fame on the Pavilion's interior hallways. Every once in a while, the boys will survey the hundreds of framed team photos, looking for their inner-tube water polo champions' picture. It hasn't been hung up yet, but they kept searching.

Because neither of the Oregonians has brought a car to college, Nick's father drives down to pick them up for the winter holidays. They'll be out of school for almost a month, and since neither has a job, they might as well lounge around at home, having someone else cook their meals and pay their bills for a while.

The drive home is rather uneventful, both boys taking a couple turns behind the wheel, careful to stay exactly at the speed limit, as Nick's dad is pretty particular about the rules. No one speaks of baseball, just classes, their intramural exploits, and their frequent shenanigans at the Junction. Every two hours, on the nose, they pull into a rest stop and switch seats. "Let's keep the driver fresh," Nick's dad asserts.

When he's dropped off at his house, Anthony is immediately glad to be there. *Hard to believe it has just been three months!* With long, frequent hugs from his mom, and a hearty bro-hug from his dad, Anthony finally gets inside and settles into their warm home.

"Jenna will be home early next week," says his mother, immediately busy with some baking project in the kitchen. "She'll just be here for a couple days, so be nice."

"I'm always nice to Jenna," answers Anthony, poking through the various envelopes and notepads on the counter, looking for nothing in particular, just acclimating to being home again.

"Have you talked to her much?"

"Not recently."

"She's halfway through her senior year, you know. Probably going to teach overseas next year. Looking at an American School outside Barcelona, though I think she wants to catch on with a local school, you know, she likes to dive in deep."

His sister is a go-getter, that's for sure.

"No, haven't spoken with her at all, really," answers Anthony, immediately depressed by that reality. Jenna had been gone to college for most of his high school years, but she's always been a good big sister. They never fight, and she hasn't come home for the holidays that often, always busy with work and volunteer projects and that sort of thing. The last time he saw her had been graduation weekend.

Anthony's dad wanders through the kitchen. "Smells good, hon, whatcha making?"

"Banana bread, no nuts," she replies sticking a toothpick into a loaf, then closing the oven door again and re-setting the timer. "I know how much you hate nuts."

Turning to Anthony, Drew asks, "So what's your plan for the break?"

"Nothing."

"Ah, I see. All worn out from college, looking to catch up on sleep, probably. Maybe you'd like to help me clean out the garage, pick up the yard, split some firewood, rotate the tires on the cars?" he smiles, tussling Anthony's short hair.

"No plans, and that's how I like it. Don't try to sucker me with chores, Dad. I just got home. I believe there's a 24-hour moratorium on that."

CHAPTER 83

The next morning – well, truth be told he doesn't wake up until after noon – Anthony arises with a purpose. Ignoring whatever messages and alerts might have been on his phone, he throws on some clothes and marches downstairs. The kitchen is empty, though a half-loaf of banana bread sits on a plate in the center of the table.

"Be back in a little bit," he calls out, grabbing his truck keys off the hook.

"Well, good morning, sleepyhead," calls his mother from another room. "Where are you headed?"

He can tell from her breathing and the rhythmic whirling that she is logging miles on her bike trainer downstairs. Increasing his volume to be sure she can hear, he calls back, "Out. Gonna go for a drive, that's all. Make sure you guys haven't ruined my truck."

The rusty pickup starts right away, but it takes a while for the heater to kick in. Sitting in the cab, he notices the absence of the metronome's incessant clicking. *Did my folks take it to the shop to get fixed?* Smiling, he looks out the defrosting windows. It is cold, drab, a gray winter day, neither raining nor snowing nor sunny. The ground is wet and he has shreds of needles, leaves, and dirt on the bottom of his shoes. They squeak on the gas pedal as he revs the engine. And there it is: the clicking resumes. He is officially home.

Driving blandly, Anthony finds himself circling his old high school, driving so slowly around the bend behind Sunset Oaks Park that a fellow driver honks, politely, and passes him. He hardly notices. He takes in the scoreboard, dark and lonely, the right field fence, and watches his game-winning grand slam from a life gone by sail and soar into eternity. The infield grass looks a little shaggy and is littered with busted branches and scattered leaves from the nearby oaks. A couple empty beer bottles are strewn about, too, at which Anthony frowns.

His smile returns as he pictures Reggie, chewing multiple pieces of bubble gum and sticking the massive bubbles on an unsuspecting teammate's hat. Probably Adam's, who was so busy yelling, "Rock and fire, kid, c'mon you got this punk," that he'd wear the gummed-up hat for two innings before finally realizing it and cussing at Reggie. Anthony wonders what those two are up to now. Reggie is supposedly at some college in southern California, but he hasn't heard if he is playing baseball. Adam? Who knows? Over the past few months, he's kind of let his old high school friendships disintegrate.

His phone buzzes in his pocket. He looks at the screen. Grampa Sumner. Anthony sighs, thinking of the joy and optimism and excitement that his grandfather exudes. He's been so hopeful and sure that Anthony will make it to *The Show*. He smiles dolefully as he recalls all the wiffle balls his Grampa pitched to him during their annual summer-break trip back east. Even in the sweltering, mosquito-filled New Hampshire afternoons, he'd been upbeat, encouraging, complimentary.

Not right now, Anthony thinks. If that call with Coach Shepard had been tough, explaining himself to Grampa Sumner would be disastrous. He presses *decline* and tosses the phone onto the passenger seat.

He drives on, passing the stores and restaurants and parks he used to frequent with Nick, Simon, Elena, and the guys. He rolls past some of their houses, too, never stopping, not even really looking that closely, just to see what feelings pop up. Exhaling deeply, he realizes he is glad – glad that no one is home, out in the front yard, raking leaves, noticing his car, waving him over, inviting him in for hot apple cider and a chance to catch up, forcing him to re-live his shame. Glad to be alone.

He parks in the lot across Madison Avenue from the southwest corner of Central Park, the same spot where he'd parked so many dozens of times before, racing to gallantly open the creaking door for Elena, then jogging across the street to walk the paths of the park. Those had been brighter days, full of promise, lively, vibrant. He felt like he could conquer the world.

Today, trudging across the street and onto the paths by the gazebo, he feels thoroughly defeated. The trees lining the path are strangely unfamiliar. Stepping closer, he reads the label. *European White Birch.* *Betula pendula.* Slowly, recognition takes hold. The peeling white bark, the droopy branches. Only now, the leaves are gone. The branches hang limp, lifeless, naked to the winter.

The crabapple next door is even more depressing. Brown leaves clutter the ground beneath it, a sloppy mess of chewed up, moldy little apples among them. Outcasts left behind, a few of its serrated leaves, wrinkly and curled against the cold, brown and long dead, cling to the reddish-brown limbs, breaking off into all sorts of directions, confused, desperate, seeking sunlight that won't offer renewed life for several months.

Even the evergreens offer Anthony little consolation. In the center of the park, the old Colorado Blue Spruce, some eighty feet tall and usually projecting an image so broad and powerful, tipped in the spring with soft, almost rubbery needles, stands lifeless, patient, solemn as Anthony walks by. Across the grassed park, Anthony spies the chess board, vacant of its pieces, as a groundskeeper has certainly lugged them to a storage unit somewhere, if only to keep them from molding and harboring slugs over the winter.

That's what winter is, a pile of mold and slugs, Anthony thinks, eyes sweeping the park again. He knows, deep down, that the barren branches, the brittle leaves under his feet, and browned needles are just signs of dormancy. The park isn't dead, it is sleeping.

His understanding of forestry, no matter how rudimentary, doesn't improve his mood.

CHAPTER 84

Back in his truck, he blasts the heat. Living in California for the past few months has already altered his sense of what cold is, and he hasn't brought the right coat for the Oregon chill. He checks his phone, noting the declined call from Grampa Sumner and flicking past old text strings from Nick, his folks, Daryl, and a couple other college friends. One name leaps out at him: Mrs. Andrews. Couldn't hurt, he figures. Despite his original desire to be alone, Mrs. Andrews is always good for him, even if she will undoubtedly press him about baseball and goals and whatnot. Maybe that's what he needs.

He clicks her contact and sends a text: *I'm in town and could use a friendly face. Coffee or hot cocoa?* He adds the winking emoji, just for old times' sake.

The heat fills the cab quicker this time, since the truck hasn't sat too long in the cold during his walk. He stares at his phone, waiting, not really expecting an immediate response. Within two minutes, his phone buzzes: *Campus java? 15 minutes?*

On my way now, he types, and shifts his truck into gear.

Somehow, Mrs. Andrews has beaten him to the coffee shop, even though his drive is less than five minutes. Stepping in from the cold, he sees her wide smile, and they hug somewhat awkwardly before he joins her at the table she's selected, nudged up against the brick wall toward the back of the dining area. "Hi Anthony, it's good to see you," she says. "I haven't ordered yet, what can I get you, something warm? My treat."

"How about hot cocoa? Lots of marshmallows, please. I won't argue with you; you're the boss," Anthony says, smiling.

Mrs. Andrews strides to the counter to place their order, then sits down while the staff goes about fixing their drinks. "So, how does it feel to be back? Are you at home, or are you visiting a place away from college?"

"I'm home, I guess."

"When do you head back?" she asks, eyes never leaving his.

"Gosh, are you already trying to get me out of here?" he laughs, avoiding eye contact by looking around the coffee shop. She waits. "I have a couple weeks. I guess I could go back as soon as I want, the dorms will be open, but I'd just as soon eat my mom's cooking for a while. It's healthier than college food." He pats his stomach, pretending to have gained weight.

"Good," she says, smiling. "That'll give you time to connect with your old pals. Talk about life. Catch up and chill. How were your classes this semester, tougher than high school?"

For the next half-hour, former teacher and former student sit and talk, she with her vanilla latte, and he with his cocoa, little by little loosening up his knotted self, letting down his guard, relaxing. She tells him stories from school and gives him updates on his old teammates, juniors Dave Jorgensen and Marlon Mavis, who lugged all the gear off the bus prior to the state championship game a lifetime ago. She also mentions Elena, whom she knows he'll be interested to hear about, who is in her government class fifth period, right after lunch.

Elena. He hasn't spoken with her in a while, and their last chat hadn't gone smoothly, to say the least.

"Does she have a boyfriend?"

"Would it matter if she did?"

Silence. Anthony's eyes go out the window.

"Tell me about your new friends in California," she goes on, changing the subject seamlessly.

Anthony gives an overview of Daryl the barrel, and how he's assimilated quite nicely to the 1-2 combination's routines and competitive challenges. He is an athlete, too, smart and funny and totally relaxed about life. He describes the Junction in great detail, including the greasy food and greasier foosball handles. He finds himself smiling as he talks, something Mrs. Andrews subtly points out.

"Sounds like a lot of fun, that college," she says, sitting back and folding her hands. "I never really got to experience the college life like that. I was in the gym 24/7, working out or shooting or getting taped up or watching video. I'm kind of jealous."

"What? You had it all. Playing in front of crowds, doing what you loved. I've seen the photos in your classroom. Don't give me that."

"Make no mistake, I loved every minute of it. It was a different experience. All those things you mentioned, that wasn't my college life. Not at all. That's neither good nor bad. I just sometimes wonder what I missed."

They sit quietly for a minute, Anthony stirring his empty mug.

"So do you miss baseball?" she asks. She has to go there, it is inevitable.

"Of course," he says, still staring at his mug, the dried remnants of chocolate staining the inside.

"Want to tell me what happened? How it ended?"

Anthony sighs. He hasn't talked about this with anyone yet. Not Nick, not his folks, not Coach Shepard, and certainly not Elena. But Mrs. Andrews, she is so calm, so understanding. She's been there, she knows what is going on with him, even if he doesn't.

"We didn't make the team," he says simply. "They cut us." Short and sweet, it is out there. No more *taking the year off* or *gonna live the college life instead* talk. Finally, some honesty.

It isn't lost on Mrs. Andrews. "That must have been rough."

"Yeah," he mutters, eyes focused on his spoon. He can feel hers on him.

"Do you know why? Were the other players better than you? What's the story?"

Anthony taps the spoon against the inside of the mug, then leaves it alone. "There were over a hundred guys out for the team. They were everywhere. At least 10 guys in line at second base. The coach – the head coach, Jefferson – had told me he wanted me to break the school's stolen-base record, but the tryout was like a meat market."

Mrs. Andrews smiles, not happily but kindly. "Did you feel like a big fish that had swam out of your little pond and found yourself in a bigger lake, surrounded by even bigger fish?"

"Huh. We talked about that metaphor," he says, remembering how Chris had described the tryouts. "I guess so. But I don't think the other guys were as good as me. In fact, I know I was better. I never got the chance to show it, that's all."

"Why not?"

"The tryouts were useless. Too much standing around," Anthony says, his ire picking up a bit. "The coaching staff screwed up. They missed me. Overlooked me. Left me out there, taking 10 grounders a day and casting me out to pasture." He is sort of proud of the agricultural reference.

"And what did the coaches say when they cut you?"

"What did they say? Nothing. They just posted our names on a list on the clubhouse door." Anthony cringes at the memory, but he has to share it, has to get it out.

"Ugh. What did the coach say when you went to talk to him? Did he explain it?"

"What? I didn't go talk to him. He's an asshole. Lied to me about wanting me to play there. Bait and switch. A used car salesman. I'd probably kick his ass," Anthony rumbles.

Mrs. Andrews, for the first time in this conversation, looks surprised. Her eyebrows leap up.

"Sorry about the language, ma'am. I'd kick his butt."

"Wait. You never talked to the coach? Even after you were on the cut list? Have you talked to him at all since then? Any of the coaches?" She sits forward now, more intense, looking closely at Anthony's expression.

"No. I've got nothing to say to them."

"Don't you think you'd like an explanation? Maybe a little feedback, some words of encouragement, their perception of you as a ballplayer, a potential teammate? They might give you some pointers on what to work on during the off-season, just in case you want to try out again next year. Is that in your plans?"

"I don't need to hear from them. I know what they'd say. 'We had some tough choices to make, and we made them. Gotta do what's in the best interest of the team and the program. Sorry it didn't work out for you, kid. You'll be a helluva intramural softball player I bet. Maybe we'll come watch your games and realize what a terrible mistake we made.'" His Coach Jefferson voice needs some work, but Mrs. Andrews couldn't tell the difference.

"I see." She sits back in her chair.

A few moments of silence pass. She looks out the window; he looks down at the table.

"So what are your goals now?" she asks. Of course she would ask that. Every conversation with her turns to goals, action plans, and life strategy.

"I'm a college kid now. Like you said, I have the chance to live it up, to experience all that college has to offer. Make friends, stay up late, do crazy stuff like playing pool. What's better than that?" his volume is raising, a sure sign of his insecurities creeping in, the cockiness taking over again.

"And then what? Have you thought about a major?"

Cripes, a major, he thinks. That is the furthest thing from his mind. He's applied and been accepted in the School of Letters and Sciences as a potential Statistics major. "Not sure."

"You know," Mrs. Andrews leans forward again, cradling her empty mug in her hands. "You've got a lot going for you. You have an outgoing personality, you're sharp, and people are drawn to you. You've had fantastic experiences with baseball, being part of a team, working together toward a common goal. That'll serve you well. You ought to think about what that means for your future. What you could do with your life. And if you have other interests, other skills, other things that you enjoy doing, I'd recommend that you keep track of them. Write them down, talk to your professors in college, and see how they might connect to your life goals."

Then, moving even closer to the table, she lowers her voice. "The world is a giant place. It's full of possibility, and you can be whatever you want to be, do whatever you want to do. So think about this, Anthony: What do you want from life?"

Scooting her chair back, Mrs. Andrews grabs their mugs to clear the table. As she steps to place them in the nearby bin, Anthony shakes his head. "Do you want me to answer that, or what?"

Turning back to her former student, his bravado in check, eyes questioning, she replies, "I told you to think about it. So think about it. We can talk again later. Maybe I can help you craft your plan."

Then, wrapping her scarf around her neck and snapping her jacket, she gives him a quick hug, leaning over to where he is still seated. "Enjoy your visit," she says. "Let me know when you're ready to chat again." Leaving Anthony in the coffee shop behind her, she steps out into the cold.

CHAPTER 85

Over the next two weeks, Anthony's head begins to swirl more than the leaves that escape the neighborhood rakes. Besides venturing to hang out with Nick and his family, he spends the majority of his time sleeping, reading books he's already read, and flipping mindlessly through the channels in search of something to distract himself. The word Amanda and Drew use to describe their son to Jay Young is "glum."

"Keep talking to him," Jay suggests one evening at the middle school staff's holiday party. "Remember he's grieving, and he has to follow his own path."

Drew counts on his fingers as he mentally recalls the five steps Jay outlined at dinner a while back. "Yup, we've seen several of them already, that's for sure."

Jay adds, "Ask him questions and see if he'll open up. Remember to empathize, to understand his emotions and to help him name them. Even *glum.*"

Drew and Amanda stir their eggnog and process Jay's advice, not wanting to turn a festive faculty gathering into another pro bono counseling session. Drew looks at his wife and says, "And remind him that we love him, unconditionally." They nod at Jay, who nods back, and everyone returns to the staff party.

The next day, as Anthony takes roost on the sofa downstairs, feet propped on pillows on the coffee table and the remote control in his hand, his parents sit on the chairs adjacent to their son. "Whatcha watching?" his father asks.

"Nothing," comes the glum response they predicted.

"Want to shut it down for a minute and we can talk?"

Anthony sighs and clicks the power button, eyes still fixed on the black screen. "What's up? I'm on vacation."

Amanda leans forward a bit, and thinking of Jay's advice, tries a line of questioning. "We love you, and we're worried about you. How are you doing? Is there anything we can help you with?"

"Nah, I'm fine," Anthony answers, eyes flashing to his mom and then down to the remote. "Just tired from school."

"And how is school?" This time it is Drew asking. "Everything going okay? I mean, with your classes? Friends? And how are you doing without baseball?"

Anthony sighs even more audibly at this. "It's fine."

Drew continues, "Remember the talk we had a while back, before you went to college? About doors closing and opening?"

"You mean slamming and locking?"

Amanda's shoulders drop. These questions aren't getting them anywhere. Glum, as it turns out, may have been an understatement. Nevertheless, she persists. "How are you doing emotionally? Do you want to talk about it?"

Flashes of memories flicker through Anthony's head. Mrs. Andrews and their chat at the coffee shop. Coach Shepard urging him to have someone to talk to. Nick agreeing that they *do* stuff together. Elena wrapped in his arms on the pitcher's mound on prom night. The state championship. The *Need Not* list.

Anthony rolls his eyes and leans back in the sofa even farther, if that were possible. "Irritation comes to mind, but only because of this talk. Are you my counselors?" he growls.

"Son, that's no way to talk to your mother," Drew interjects. "We're trying to connect with you here. Being a snotty smart-aleck isn't helping any."

"Well, neither is this," Anthony says, tossing the remote aside and standing up. "I'm going to get something to eat. You guys can watch whatever you want."

"Hold on, young man," Drew also stands up. "This college conversation isn't over."

"What do you want to know?" Anthony turns, lip quivering a little. "Yes, I passed all my classes. Yes, I'm going to stay in college and get an education – your tuition payments aren't being wasted. Yes, I'm going to do something productive with my life. No, I don't know what that is. And no, I don't want to talk about it anymore." Careful to avoid his mother's legs, he steps past them and bounds up the stairs to the kitchen.

Amanda looks at Drew, sadness in her eyes. Drew eases himself onto her chair and sits down, throwing an arm around her shoulders. "That didn't go well," he says, clearly frustrated.

"I'm pretty sure it's part of the process," Amanda whispers. "Not that that makes it any better. I just wish he'd open up to us."

"In due time," her husband reassures her. "I don't think I helped by getting frustrated. He can just be so damn irritating."

Amanda nestles deeper into Drew's arm, breathing deeply. "We'll get through to him, together."

They remain downstairs until the clattering in the kitchen subsides and Anthony has grabbed his keys, fired up the rusty old pickup, and driven off.

SPRING

CHAPTER 86

The latter part of his freshman year is somewhat of a blur for Anthony, as he's set a precedent the previous few months of staying rather busy, socially, athletically, and academically. To combat the winter blahs, he registered for an even heavier academic load, 18 credits, none of which have anything to do with computer programming, coding, or similar dastardly topics.

His moods change more frequently than the California weather, even with its unpredictability during the spring months. He is at times surly, cranky, and short-fused, even with Nick and Daryl and their newfound friends, and at others joyous, upbeat, and a one-man stand-up comedy tour. And his friends never quite know which Anthony to expect on any given evening: the one who sits and quietly keeps to himself or the one in front of the crowd, reveling in the attention and single-handedly generating enthusiasm for whatever pedestrian endeavor stands before them.

Grampa Sumner's call has been declined a second time, and twice Anthony preps to call him back, yet he hasn't gathered his nerve. That is a demon he isn't yet ready to face.

To compound his issues, it turns out nachos cost money, as do movies, bowling, and gas, which he freely contributes whenever the urge strikes them to head to San Francisco for the day, seeking authentic Ghirardelli chocolate, or Sacramento for a dinner excursion, sitting in the train car at the Old Spaghetti Factory. So, clearly, he needs a job.

In searching for part-time employment, he stumbles across some postings for youth league basketball coaches. He ends up taking on a team of 4th and 5th graders from one of the local elementary schools, a mix of 10- and 11-year-old boys and girls, some of whom have never played organized basketball before. His course schedule allows him to run practices twice a week in the school's gym, and every Saturday morning for six weeks, he drags himself out of bed at the ungodly hour of 8:30, so he can arrive at the gym before their 9:00 games begin. Having more fun than he thought he might, he even shows up that early when his team is scheduled for the 10:00 tipoff, just so he can scout the other squads for future weeks.

The kids offer him something he hadn't realized he lacked: Pure, unadulterated, unfiltered joy. Coaching the finer art of the cross-over dribble is one thing; coaching it to a 5th grade girl and watching her perform it in a game, her defender's feet tangling up, leading to a wide-open layup, is heaven. His players listen to him, follow his simple directions, and play hard. He makes sure the drills in practice are fun, something they can replicate at home, and deepen their repertoire of basketball skills. The parents seem to appreciate his energy, too, his always positive, encouraging, deeply caring approach to each of the kids. Now he understands why Coach Shepard stuck with it for so long. And, continuing the legacy, he finds himself taking his players' heads in his hands, forcing eye contact, and giving each a tailored pep-talk before each game, sometimes at halftime, or during time-outs, or even after a random whistle.

He considers teaching them Coach Shepard's post-huddle chant, "KATN," and, eyeing the parents in the stands who have entrusted him with their impressionable children, thinks better of it.

Arriving back at the dorm room after the games, he throws open the blinds and chirps a sing-song good-morning to his drowsy roommate, who sputters along to brunch right before the dining commons closes.

Some traditions had a hard time fading away, and who is Anthony to fight this one?

With the spring comes either rain or sunshine, sometimes both in rapid succession, and when it is the latter, the Oregon boys are prepared with their bucket of pearls for a round of spontaneous batting practice. Daryl will sometimes join them, but more often than not it is just the two roommates, the best friends, the former teammates, who so enjoy just *doing* stuff together. They have found a couple parks that are big enough for their sessions, one a local high school field that requires them to hop a fence and then explain themselves to a school district security guard. That is a one-time affair, and they stick with public parks from then on.

The air is often thick with pollen, and when it rains, the throaty, thick powder turns the puddles and gutters into a foamy, yellowy mess, painting the entire town with sloppy brushstrokes. Flowers are blooming all about; manzanita hedges and their thick clusters of pink flowers dominating the walkways, occasional bursts of sharp lavender penstemons soaking up the spring showers, and even the majestic California sycamore gets into the act by producing its own tiny green flowers among its massive, leathery leaves. Together their artistry welcomes the new, life-bearing season. With such glory offered in a 360-degree panoramic on a daily basis, who even has cause to remember the heartache of months ago?

CHAPTER 87

One ordinary evening, midway through the spring semester, a Wednesday like any other, Anthony, Nick, and Daryl head into the Pavilion, intent on playing some pickup basketball games. Unfortunately, a high school volleyball tournament has taken over the gym floor, so their plans are foiled. On the way out the door, Anthony's attention is diverted by Kim, the point guard from the basketball team, who is behind the equipment counter folding towels. Telling his friends he'll meet them back at the dorms, he leans on the counter and says hello.

"Hi Anthony. You know," she says, waving at the pile of towels. "If we had a new manager, I wouldn't have to be doing this."

"I hear ya. I hope you find the right person."

"What are you guys doing here tonight? Playing ball?"

"Nah, there's a volleyball tourney. We're headed back. Interested in some foosball later?"

Kim explains that she's got mandatory tutoring on Wednesdays, and she's way behind in a couple of her classes, so he bids her farewell and walks off. The dusk sky is aglow with all the shades between yellow and red, and he stands there, just outside the Pavilion doors, taking it all in. The beauty, the effortlessness of it, the view he's so often ignored.

His trance is pierced by a strangely familiar voice. "Where've you been, Sumner?"

Blinking and following the voice, Anthony sees a figure marching toward him. Having very intentionally avoided the baseball field for the past six months, he'd never crossed paths with Coach Jefferson.

He swallows hard. "What do you mean, Coach?"

"Haven't seen you out there lately. Thought you were going to be our wheels guy."

"You cut me, Coach."

"We lost track of you, son. Hope you're doing well."

Without breaking stride, Coach Jefferson opens the Pavilion doors and steps in, the reflection of the sunset flashing brilliantly on the glass and the nearby windows.

Anthony isn't sure how to take that interaction. Was that sarcasm? Dismissal? Honesty? He doesn't know. Coach Jefferson doesn't seem to be one who will say anything but exactly what he is thinking. And if that is true… Anthony can't bear the thought.

Right where he is, he sits down. Running the events of last October through his head, overlaying this conversation in that context, his shoulders grow heavier. His head droops. A billowing cloud buries the sunset as all the remaining energy in Anthony's body drains onto the sidewalk and disappears into the shadows and cracks.

Several minutes lapse. Anthony remains motionless, the bloated cloud now nestling itself between his ears, around his eyes, under his nose. Footsteps pass him by, the doors open and close, leaves rustle past, bicycles whir unnoticed down the path.

Blinking now.

Rubbing his eyes and looking up, Anthony emerges from his stupor.

Reaching into his gym bag, he extracts his phone. Opening a text line with Mrs. Andrews, he sends: *I think it was me.*

He doesn't have to wait too long for a response, as his phone rings almost immediately.

"So what happened?" she asks.

In painful detail, Anthony rips down the wall that guards his shame. He explains his fateful decision to skip practice and go hitting on a different field during tryouts. He shares everything, right up to the conversation he's just had with the college baseball coach.

"So what does that mean, your original text to me: *I think it was me?*"

"I've been telling myself, and anyone who would listen, that cutting me was the coaches' fault, that they'd missed their next All-American infielder. It wasn't their fault; it was mine. I skipped practice. I stood around during practices. I wasn't thrilled with how it was going, and I let it affect me. My decisions, my attitude."

He takes a deep breath, and with her patient silence on the other end of the line, keeps going. "I'd had such a great time playing baseball up there. We won the state championship, for heaven's sake! I was all-league, all-state, all-world, as far as I was concerned. You remember, all cocky and trash-talking."

She hums in agreement. He goes on. "Getting down here was a drag. Too many guys, not enough action. The coaches never made me feel special, hell I wasn't even sure they knew who I was. You asked if I ever felt like a tiny fish in a big lake, yes, that's exactly how I felt. Unappreciated. Lost. One of the crowd. Just a number."

Another deep breath. *She is a good listener*, Anthony thinks. "For someone as confident as I was, okay super-cocky, that was hard to take. And it was even harder to take that they cut me, so I've made up a story that makes me sound better ever since."

"Is there anything you could have done differently to change the outcome?"

Anthony thinks. "Well, yeah. Right off the bat. Gone to all the practices. Not skipped and gone hitting with my buddies. That was dumb. Probably cost them too. I bet they hate me. I'm such an idiot."

"I can understand why you'd feel responsible, sure. Remember, we all make our own decisions. What else could you have done differently?"

"Well, I've actually thought about it a lot. Remember when you asked me what the coaches had said when I asked them about being cut? Well, I'd never talked to 'em. Any of 'em. Until tonight, and that was five seconds. I should have gone into the office and demanded an explanation!"

"That would be pretty ballsy," she replies, laughing a little.

"Well, think about it. If Coach Jefferson, that's the head coach, just told me that they lost track of me, that was probably related to skipping practice. If I told 'em I was committed and why I'd gone hitting, they might have changed their mind. Right?"

"Sure. And what about before that," she continues. "During the tryout-practices themselves? You didn't think they knew who you were, that you were just a number."

"Well, it shouldn't have been too hard for me to let them get to know me. I could have talked to them, met with them after practices. Asked for extra BP. Begged 'em to hit me more ground balls after practice. Made 'em call me by name: 'Rooster, turn two on this one!'"

She laughs, an understanding gesture from the other side of a phone line. Kind, patient, caring. He has called the right person.

"And Mrs. Andrews," he says, softly now. "I never took advantage of your help. You always wanted me to set goals, to have a plan, to write it down, to stick with it. I'm sorry I didn't listen."

"You don't need to apologize to me, Anthony."

"Actually," he says. "I'm sorta apologizing to myself. I'm sorry I didn't listen," he laughs. "You offered me guidance and all that, and I brushed it off. I figured everything would work out for me, that the scouts would come calling, that I'd make the team…" His voice trails off.

"Now that I think about it, I let all sorts of stuff go by. I never followed up with any of the college programs. I never talked directly to major-league scouts, and I ran away from the college coaches. Shit! This really was all me."

Quietly, she lets him ruminate. "Sorry about the language," he whispers.

"That shit doesn't bother me," Mrs. Andrews laughs, louder now. "I teach high school. I'm just glad you're finally being honest with someone, and I'm especially glad it's yourself."

"I thought I was being honest with you," Anthony grins, as if she could hear it.

"I'm just the conduit," she says. "And hey, Anthony."

"Yes?"

"You've got a bright future, young man. Like I told you before, you can do anything you want to do. I'd suggest you go write down the lessons you've learned here – not to give to anyone, just to synthesize your thinking. Even if you burn it afterwards. Writing can work wonders."

"Roger that," he says, thinking about his foolish decisions. "Man, I was stupid."

"Not stupid, Anthony. You just didn't know. You didn't get it. There's nothing wrong with not knowing something, or not knowing exactly what to do, how to handle yourself. That's part of growing up, learning, and for you, becoming a man. The best thing you can do is move forward, make the most of your reality, which is pretty special, by the way, and set new goals, create a new action plan."

"And write it down, yup. You can bet I will this time. Thank you, ma'am."

"Any time. Have a good night, Anthony. Go be amazing."

He hangs up, irritation and pride jostling earnestly for space in his mind.

CHAPTER 88

Anthony's course load consists of an English class, U.S. History, Spanish (so he could converse with his sister), Sociology, Beginning Business, and Genetics. It's the sociology class, in particular, that captures his fancy. His professor is a sociological experiment in and of himself, a bearded, dreadlocked fellow with bright, sparkly eyes, and an infectiously joyous attitude.

While he lectures in several of his classes don't really add much to Anthony's universe, Mr. Sorensen's ability to generate discussions about perceptions, bias, the natural and unnatural groupings of humans, and our ultimate interdependence upon one another, is truly captivating. He finds himself looking forward to Tuesdays and Thursdays from 10:30 until noon.

Anthony has found that, for the most part, he and his college classmates tend to keep it pretty close to the chest in their classes, trained by their factory-model high school experiences to venture forth only with the correct answer, and generally, only when asked directly. In Mr. Sorensen's class, hypothesizing, sharing ideas, debating, and plain old thinking out loud are normalized behaviors, welcomed, invited, and celebrated. Anthony chimes in and questions his classmates more in that class than in all his others combined.

In fact, after having his groundbreaking conversation with Mrs. Andrews less than 24 hours earlier, he takes it upon himself to visit his professor's office hours directly following class.

"Mr. Sumner, how nice of you to join me," cheers Mr. Sorensen from behind his stand-up desk. "I was wondering when I'd finally have a chance to go up against you, one-on-one. I hear you're quite a basketball player."

"Uh, yes, sir. How are you, sir?" he asks.

"Oh, my. Please, don't call me sir. I prefer, 'Mr. Hans Sorensen the Great Professor of Sociology and Life Itself.' It rolls off the tongue so much easier, don't you think? Tea?" he asks, laughing at himself.

"Sure."

"Don't tell anyone I have this, especially the fire marshal," Mr. Sorensen chuckles, readying a pot of tea on a portable heater, which he lights with a long-armed match. His dreadlocks are everywhere, almost down to his waist. "And to what do I owe this honor?"

"Just want to check in, see how you think I'm doing in class. Maybe there's something I could do to bring my grade up, make sure I'm learning all the stuff I need to learn, you know. Extra homework, more reading. Talk more in class, whatever you think."

Mr. Sorensen looks at the pot of water, making sure it is stable, then turns back to his student. He is younger than most college professors, probably just in his early 30s. His bright eyes are wise, regardless of his age. "Two things all societies, and all people, need: water and fire. Have you got all the water and fire you need?"

Anthony scowls at the beads in Mr. Sorensen's hair. "I don't know what that means."

Mr. Sorensen turns around. "What do you want from life?"

Anthony grunts, thinking of Mrs. Andrews. "You're not the first person to ask me that."

"So it is."

A moment of silence follows.

"And what are you prepared to offer life?"

"What?"

"The universe demands some sort of quid-pro-quo, you must have learned in your years on the planet, no? A need for balance. There's give, and there's take. You must give in order to take. Or perhaps you've already given, and it's your turn to take. But I don't suppose that's your story, is it, Mr. Sumner?"

The tea pot is screeching, and Mr. Sorensen pours two mugs. He doesn't ask about milk or sugar or even what flavor Anthony wants. He sets one in front of Anthony on a long-legged table that stands in the middle of the room, and Anthony notices there isn't a chair in the room.

"Nope, no chairs," calls Mr. Sorensen, slurping his tea. "I can't sit down on the job, no way. Too much to do, not interested in my muscles atrophying. So do you have answers to my questions, or do you need time to process, to think about it?"

What do you want from life? And what are you prepared to offer life? Goodness, that's a lot for a last-minute visit to office hours. "I think I'll think about it."

"Great! I was hoping so. In the meantime, you look like a decent fellow, and I've heard you're good with kids."

Anthony just stares.

"There's a group of social activists, the type interested in equity and productive change, you know," he says with a smile. "Including me and my wife, that'd be *Mrs.* Sorensen." He nods at a framed picture in the bookshelf behind him. "We've been volunteering at a local women's shelter in Sacramento for the last couple of months. Not surprisingly, there are many kids there that could use some guidance. Fine, upstanding young man like you would be a terrific mentor. You wouldn't be with us at the shelter; you'd meet the kid – one kid at a time, pal, only bite off what you can chew – anyway, you'd meet him at his school. No curriculum, no religion, no pressure. Just being a good, consistent, positive role model. Did you hear me say 'consistent,' Mr. Sumner?"

He sips his tea. Anthony nods.

"Every time he expects to see you, you'll be there. End of story. Do you have a car?"

"No, sir."

"Stop it with the 'sir.' I keep turning around to see if my father is here." He snorts.

"Can you get a car, so you can demonstrate your reliability and provide a consistently positive influence upon a needy and deserving young person?"

Anthony sips his tea, thinking of his rusty pickup truck. He can take the train home this weekend and drive it back. Maybe Nick will come with him. Road trip! Eight hours with music turned up loud. "Sure, that shouldn't be a problem."

"Good, it's settled then. I'm looking forward to working with you," Mr. Sorensen smiles. "And I want you to remember a couple things. Lesson number 12: When it's time to rise up, rise up. Know what that means?"

Anthony's mind instantly takes him back to his high school baseball field, the hits, the wins, the defensive plays, the state championship. "Yeah, I'm pretty sure I do," he says, smiling.

"Oh, I bet you think you do," Mr. Sorensen takes another sip of tea. "These lessons aren't just about sports, young man." *How did he know that's what he was thinking about? And why did he start with lesson number 12?*

"Now, why don't you tell me about basketball. You're down there just about every night. It must be love," he sings.

They talk for at least two hours longer, and none of it is related to his grade in the Sociology class.

CHAPTER 89

It turns out that Nick has already planned to head down to Santa Barbara to watch Simon's golf tournament that weekend, so on Friday afternoon, Anthony takes the plunge and hops the Amtrak solo. He snags a seat by the window and sleeps a surprising amount of the 16-hour ride to the Albany station, where his sister Jenna meets him with his truck. She is home for her spring break, and the 20-minute drive home gives them a much-needed opportunity to reconnect, in a wide-ranging conversation that blends English and Spanish together, peppered with healthy laughter.

"I'm sorry about baseball," she says when the small talk evaporates.

Anthony didn't expect that. "Thank you. It sucks."

"I'll bet. You were always very good at that. You got a lot of attention for it, too."

"Yeah."

"I never really got much attention growing up, which I kinda appreciated. I flew under the radar. You know," she says, glancing sideways at him, "I sorta grew up in your shadow, even though you were younger."

"What? That's crazy. You were good at everything you did. Everyone knew that."

"Yet folks were always focused on you and baseball. Honestly, it's been a pain the ass. You were a pain in the ass little brother. I mean, I just wonder if you ever realized it." Anthony immediately thinks of Grampa Sumner, and how their family conversations almost always turn to focus on him and his ballfield exploits. He needs to make that phone call soon.

"Yeah, but look at you now. You're going to work overseas, travel the world. I'm just a college kid."

"Your future is a lot brighter than that, and you know it."

They drive in silence for a while before Jenna adds a simple, "I love you. And I'm proud of you. Always will be."

Anthony looks closely at his sister, driving, growing up, mature, confident. He still has a ways to go.

"Even though I'm a pain in the ass?"

She offers an exaggerated exhale through puffed-up cheeks. "Yes."

Anthony's gaze turns to the window, the trees and houses and gravel driveways and metal mailboxes sitting on wooden posts passing in a blur. *How does a younger brother get all the attention? I didn't mean to. I was just playing baseball.*

"You just did your stuff louder than I did, Anthony."

Another moment of silence ensues.

"I love you, too, sis."

Jenna extends their alone-time by stopping at the local donut house for a treat. Anthony relents and gobbles down an apple fritter, the first food he's eaten since he left Davis the afternoon before.

When they pull his truck into the driveway, Anthony spies a familiar shape on the roof. Bent over awkwardly, digging a gloved hand into the gutters, removing a glob of leaves and debris, and tossing it unceremoniously into the ferns below, crouches his father. Anthony watches the pattern unfold a couple of times before stepping out of the truck.

"What are you doing up there, Dad? Spring cleaning, huh? Is it slippery up there?"

Without looking down, Drew responds, "I'm happy to trade you places, buddy. Your young legs and back would probably withstand a tumble better than mine."

"I'd never want to deprive you of something that gives you so much joy."

Jenna rolls her eyes and heads inside, wrapping herself tightly in her coat.

Shutting the pickup's door, Anthony follows the sound of raking to the side of the house. All bundled up, his mother ushers clippings and trimmings into small piles throughout the yard. Anthony snatches the rake from his mom's hands and answered her quizzical look with a giant hug.

She smiles through the cold. "Well, hello. And what was that for?"

"Nothing. I'll finish this. Want them in those big ol' plastic bags?"

"Sure thing," Amanda responds, eyes fixed on her son. "I probably ought to go hold the ladder or stand beneath your father with a trampoline, just in case."

"Or a pile of mattresses."

He immediately begins raking. *Man, it is cold,* even with the sun wrestling the puffy clouds for access to their property, and the metal handle of the rake reminds his fingers they are alive, at least for now.

"I could start some apple cider," Amanda calls over her shoulder. "There are fresh cranberry muffins that need to be eaten, too."

"I'm all in for that," Anthony says, pausing to blow warm air into his hands.

To her husband, Amanda says, "When he's finished bagging that stuff, come inside, will you? We need to have a snack, it's cold, and," she arches an eyebrow over her shoulder at Anthony. "I think he's ready to talk."

"Good timing," Drew says, holding up a handful of goop, a mixture of pine cones and needles and a drippy gray glue. "This is really making me hungry!"

Anthony arrives at the kitchen table after tossing three bags of dead branches, dried-up leaves, and assorted other yard clutter into the bed of his pickup, racing inside, and holding his hands under the running faucet, first with cold water, then progressively warmer so as not to shock his system. Soon his hands have feeling again, and they are ready to spare the plate of muffins a bit of its load. Only when his mouth is full does he realize his mom and dad are staring at him from the other side of the kitchen island. Jenna must have gone upstairs.

Amanda pours a mug of steaming hot apple cider, careful to avoid the cinnamon sticks and mulling ball, and smiles as she places it in front of Anthony at the breakfast bar. A favorite winter treat, the extended cold keeps it on the menu for a few extra months.

Cheeks bulging, he sheepishly accepts the mug with a nod.

Amanda steps back, leaning casually against the island, and looks at her husband. On cue, Drew clears his throat and asks, "So Anthony.

How's college life?"

Anthony swallows his bite of muffin and looks up. "Did you talk to Mrs. Andrews?"

"No," answers Drew, making a mental note to call Mrs. Andrews.

Amanda picks up from there. "We haven't really talked to you in a while, that's all. You know, *really* talked. And you've been at college for almost an entire year so far. You've taken finals. You're home for the weekend, and we miss seeing you, miss knowing what you're up to, how you're feeling. The last time you were home, it didn't go so well."

"Yeah, sorry about that," Anthony picks at crumbs on the counter. "I may have hit a rough patch."

"And we haven't seen your report card, either, ahem," Drew says, pretending to clear his throat again and laughing, perhaps too vigorously. "We believe you've been in college, care to comment on this story for the press?" he asks again, holding a muffin like a microphone in front of his son.

Anthony gives a quick karate-chop with one hand, dislodging the muffin, and catching it with his other hand, takes an enormous bite. "Reflexes like a saber-tooth tiger, which evidently had a soft spot for cranberry muffins, thank you very much, mother."

While they talk, Drew and Amanda heed Jay and Sandy Young's advice on communicating effectively, openly, and inviting dialogue. While Anthony is sharing stories of college life and, inevitably, answering questions about what happened during baseball tryouts several months prior, they listen.

"Truly, deeply, and with a sense of wonder, listen," Jay had said. "Many people use another person's 'turn' as an opportunity to prepare for what they're going to say next. Instead, soak in what he has to say and embrace the real place where it's coming from."

This they try, which prompts many uncomfortable moments of silence. Moments, both Drew and Amanda would agree later, that in the past they'd have filled with comments or statements – or, in Drew's case, an ill-advised attempt at humor – just because gaps need to be filled, even if they derailed the conversations inadvertently. And, to their surprise, Anthony fills many of these quiet moments with continuations of his story, honest reflections, often uncovering additional layers that unveil his emotions and perspectives.

They reassure him, thanking him for opening up to them. "I'm so glad you shared that with us," his mom says, wiping muffin crumbs off the breakfast bar with a paper towel. His dad is drying their mugs for the umpteenth time while they talk. Jay agrees with Grampa Sumner's age-old advice that doing things together beats sitting and talking, most of the time, so he is trying to occupy himself somehow. Anthony is fiddling with his keys but otherwise maintains pretty consistent engagement.

After explaining the abridged version of how he and his pals had been cut, then the informative and all-too-brief encounter with Coach Jefferson outside the gym, he looks out the window and says, "That's why I'm so ticked off."

Amanda runs a wet rag over the stove top, and, noticing Drew is fully immersed in the mug-drying, thinks of Jay's advice on the four steps of effective communication: Listen, reassure, validate, and then – and only then – respond. This is a prime moment for step three, and she calmly takes advantage of it.

"I understand why you'd be angry about that," she says, softly, and subtly raises an eyebrow at her husband.

Drew continues, "I'm pretty sure anyone in your shoes would be irritated, son. That makes a lot of sense. You've been through quite a lot over the past couple of months. Heck, the past year and a half has been a whirlwind of ups and downs. Lots of doors opening and closing."

Anthony nods, eyes dry and squinting, thoughts cascading in front of him. Memories and emotions clang clumsily, splitting apart and reattaching randomly, a veritable blender of thoughts – the shoulder, Dr. McGregor, Elena, the state championship, his buddies splitting up, moving away from home, heck he's even had a birthday somewhere in there that should have been joyous, but he is having difficulty identifying the emotion with the event, due to the intensity of a couple of those instances. He blinks and shakes his head.

"Yeah, but I think I've kinda been a jerk to be around," he states flatly. His thoughts turn to Elena. Jerk is an understatement.

"Now that you mention it..." Drew starts.

Amanda cuts him off. "Not at all, Anthony. You've been human. You've been going through a lot and dealing with it the way you're prepared to at your age. Every teenager I've ever known has acted like you at one point or another, even your sister," she adds, nodding toward the stairs. "There's nothing wrong with working through things in your own time. Now that we know more about your past year, we can be more helpful, if you want."

"So I'm not a big ol' jerk after all?" Anthony grins.

"Well..." Drew starts again.

"Of course not. You're wonderful, you've obviously been hurting, and we haven't always known how to be there for you."

Drew sets down the mug he is drying, finally satisfied that it is ready for reshelving. "We love you, son. We just want you to be happy. And, of course we want you to be a productive member of society, earning money to pay for our retirement and paying your fair share of taxes. Oh, and it'd be great if you left the world a little bit better than you found it. That's all we want as parents."

Anthony may or may not acknowledge with an eyebrow twitch. Amanda may or may not roll her eyes. She takes his hands as she leans onto the breakfast bar, face-to-face with her only son. "We will always be there for you, no matter what you're doing, no matter where you are. Please know that you can talk to us about anything, and if we don't understand," she nods back over her shoulder at Drew, who nods in agreement. "You might just have to explain it to us a little better. We're quick learners, and when it comes to you, we have all the time in the world."

Anthony stands up and hugs his mom over the counter. As he does, he clasps hands with his father. "Thank you, guys," he whispers.

When he pries himself loose of his mother's grip, Anthony takes her shoulders in his hands and says, "Okay, well, I don't have all the time in the world. I have to gas up, drop all your yard muck at the dump, and get that truck down to California, so I can go to work. Gotta be productive, right dad?"

"Jenna!" he calls. "I'm off!"

His sister appears on cue and gives him a lengthy embrace. "Be safe, brother."

"See you in Spain," he laughs. And, grabbing his keys, he announces, "Love you," and bounds out the door.

Before he pulls out of the driveway, he calls Grampa Sumner.

CHAPTER 90

On his way to the gas station, Anthony makes a quick pit stop. Or at least that's what he thought he was going to do. It is Saturday, so he has no reasonable expectation to find her at home, but he drives by Elena's house anyway, and when he sees her little car in the driveway, he pulls in behind it, his heart thumping in a churning mix of excitement and trepidation.

As she so often does, Elena opens the door before he reaches it. Her eyes, clear and blue and as perfect as he remembers, meet his. He stops a couple feet short of the doorway, unsure of exactly how to greet her. He played this out in his mind a dozen times on the drive over, but the reality provides a sensation he couldn't have planned for.

She steps out, slowly, and lets the door close behind her, never taking her eyes off his. He looks at her gently, apologetically, thinking of their last interaction months ago, full of anger, fear, and hurt. She steps toward him, softly, her hair moving ever so slightly in the afternoon breeze. And then at once they connect, understanding one another, embracing one another, holding tight to their feelings, once strong and powerful and now a warm memory, a gentle, kind, and forgiving embrace, silent, motionless.

Neither knows how many minutes they hold that position, communicating with each other the understanding of lives divergent, of apologies unspoken, of a caring eternal. By the time they break apart, gently, he holds her at arm's length and looks into her eyes, whispering simply, "I'm sorry."

"So am I."

Another long embrace is broken when Elena playfully pokes Anthony in the ribs, jarring him right out of the moment. "C'mon in, are you cold?" she asks, reaching for the door behind her.

"Um, sure. Is your dad home? I still don't think he likes me."

"Oh, I'm quite sure he doesn't like you," Elena says, smiling mischievously. "But he's also upstairs watching TV, and we can stay in the kitchen and talk. Hungry?"

Anthony follows Elena inside, where, without asking, she pours two bowls of Frosted Mini-Wheats, fills them with milk, and hands Anthony a spoon. "You look like you could use some meat on your bones, and since we don't have any meat in the house, good ol' cereal will have to do. You haven't developed an allergy to cereal since you went to college, have you?"

Whatever hesitancy Anthony had prior to this pit stop fades away with the first mouthful. For the next three hours, which includes a hearty – perhaps too hearty – handshake from her father, he and Elena sit in the kitchen and discuss their lives. They compare high school with college, laugh about this and that, and when it comes time to tackle their relationship, topics range from their past, star-crossed romance to their current situation, living lives that are naturally separating from each other.

As Anthony sits across the table from her, thinking of the hundreds of miles between their schools, he knows this is it.

Their hug is a hug good-bye.

CHAPTER 91

Anthony realizes he doesn't really know where to park his truck when he returns to campus, since he hasn't had a vehicle there all year. Finding an open spot in a permit-only lot, he makes a mental note to get himself a permit. It's 2:00 a.m., and for some reason, the light is on in their dorm room. Anthony finds Nick awake, sitting on his bed playing Solitaire.

"Brother, what are you doing here? I thought you went to the golf tournament."

"I did. Turns out it was a one-day tourney, so we all drove back this evening."

"How'd he do?"

"74. Came in fourth. Not too shabby. There were some serious golfers there."

Anthony tosses his keys on his desk, then looks back at his buddy. His best friend. The first half of the self-proclaimed 1-2 combination. Another former baseball player.

"Want to shuffle 'em up? Egyptian Rocular, best of 7?"

As Nick preps the deck and sets 'em out, three down, three up, and three in the hand, Anthony settles at the foot of his bed. *It's easier to get into the muck of our minds when we've got a different muck on our hands,* his dad once said. "You know, they didn't cut us because we weren't good enough."

Emotions and playing cards are dealt, exchanged, and discarded until they both fall asleep.

With his vehicle on campus with him, Anthony's popularity grows immediately, especially with the many dorm-dwellers who are without. A pickup truck, in particular, is a hot commodity. Anyone needing to move some furniture, boxes, or even a keg, seems ready to fraternize with the rusty pickup's owner. Anthony sees right through it and quickly implements a rental plan and a pricing guide. This slows the requests immediately.

The whole reason he has the truck is to transport himself to and from Bella Ridge Elementary School in West Sacramento, the school at which Mr. Sorensen sets him up to mentor a boy, fourth-grader named Galen, whose mother brought him into the shelter where the Sorensens work, escaping an abusive husband.

At first, the boy is a tough nut to crack. The school counselor suggests a couple of strategies, and none of them works. Anthony approaches his teacher, Mrs. Miller, during lunch one day, asking if he can just volunteer in the classroom for a bit, *you know, help out with whatever you need, perhaps build his trust. Even if I'm not working with Galen,* he proposes. *Just being around might be a good start.*

Amazingly, it works.

Anthony makes the trek to West Sacramento twice a week, on Thursdays before Sociology class and on Friday afternoons. It is on

Fridays that he most enjoys the mentorship opportunity, and not because of Galen, though the two of them are getting along famously. There is another reason.

Indeed, Mrs. Miller has a pre-service student teacher, assigned through the Education department at Sacramento State, who spends every Friday in her room. And when Anthony first sets eyes on Suzy, he isn't quite sure what comes over him. Even Mrs. Miller laughs when she introduces the two college kids to each other, as Anthony fumbles and nervously misspeaks.

Her eyes are dark, hauntingly so, with a mesmerizing quality that he can't avoid. She keeps her hair cropped short, blonder on top and pushed behind her ears, with the most perfect, flawless skin he has ever seen. That neck, he thinks immediately, trying to catch himself before his eyes stray any farther. She has an air of confidence about her, her own cockiness, self-assured yet welcoming and empowering. When she smiles at him, he melts.

Over the course of the next few weeks, he looks forward to Fridays and his opportunity to talk with Suzy, and of course to mentor Galen, who assumes the role of matchmaker during a classroom activity when he announces, "Look, they're dancing!" Anthony and Suzy certainly aren't dancing, but Anthony's blush gives away his feelings.

After school that day, as they walk to their respective cars, Suzy takes the first step. "Would you like to go dancing, you know, for real? I know a place that teaches a whole slew of dances, and then they host some kind of ball once a month. Interested?"

Simpering, Anthony replies, "All I know is the Macarena."

She laughs, holding out her hand. He takes it. She spins once, gracefully, and ends up wrapped in his arm. Looking up playfully, she says, "Just let me lead for a while, k?"

Anthony nods, then watches her walk to her car, a little maroon Mini Cooper. "See you Friday, and wear your dancing shoes!" As she drives off, she waves out of the sunroof.

Anthony beams. Leaning against his truck, he looks up at the sky, back at the ground, then surveys the parking lot. Between the hedges lining the edge of the parking space, brilliant yellow daffodils explode from their bulbs, blooming as a collection of earthbound sun rays for passers-by to embrace, offering a loving fragrance to the breeze. And there, flitting in and out of the flowers, working its scientifically impossible magic, is a bumblebee.

ABOUT THE AUTHOR

This is Pete Hall's first novel, though it's not his first story. As a kid, he wrote "Three Bears: Panda, Reddy-Teddy, and Buttercup." Only his brother Dave enjoyed that one. In his teenage years, he penned a short-story called "Green Eyes" that he kept in a private journal. In college, his thriller, "A Table for One," had exactly zero readers. The absence of an audience didn't stop him. For Pete, writing has always been a passion, and in his career as a teacher and school principal, he channeled that passion into publishing 10 books, dozens of articles, and countless blog posts designed to support educators across the globe. And now, as a husband, dad, mentor, speaker, life coach, and regular guy, he strives to provide support, encouragement, motivation, tools, and opportunity for his fellow travelers to get the most out of life – and to offer the world their gifts.

Visit www.ChasingTheShow.com to connect with Pete and to access discussion guides, video clips, blog posts, and links to additional resources. You can scan the QR code below to go there immediately:

You can follow Pete on Twitter at @EducationHall. You can also check out the professional work he's doing by visiting www.EducationHall.com (educational stuff), www.StriveSS.com (the home of his universal leadership firm, Strive Success Solutions), and www.FosteringResilientLearners.org (where you can learn about childhood trauma and building resilience). Be on the lookout for his next book, "Always strive to be a better you: How ordinary people can live extraordinary lives." Pete asks you this: What are your gifts, and what are you prepared to offer the world?